SUFFER NO KINGS

SUFFER NO KINGS

OTHERWORLDLY ANARCHIST

BOOK THREE

Dreamer's Riot

This is a work of fiction. Names, characters, places, and incidents are either products of the author's imagination or used fictitiously. Any resemblance to actual events, locales, or persons, living, dead, or undead, is entirely coincidental.

Cover design by Kongsi

ISBN: 978-1-0394-8585-3

Published in 2025 by Podium Publishing
www.podiumentertainment.com

Podium

SUFFER NO KINGS

PROLOGUE

Skaya

I spit a handful of seeds on the ground while waiting for my ailur friend, Miro. He seems to be running late, if he is coming at all this time. Neither of us can necessarily make it to all our shifts, but we try. Since he's from the Republic and I patrol for the Council, our schedules don't line up perfectly. Neither of us can afford a whisper sphere either, so there is no way to warn the other when we won't make it. We aren't really supposed to meet up like this anyway, so there isn't much we can do to improve communication.

But who can blame us, really? Chewing sunflower seeds can only keep a girl awake for so long, after all. I was always told being a Guardian of Stone was an important and prestigious job. Everyone was. Most people still believe it, and I admittedly get a lot of discounts if I wear my uniform or lapel in town, so I can't complain too much. Still, there isn't quite so much "glory" as the papers and posters report. In reality, the job is just a whole lot of hurry up and wait. At least until your superior officer leaves. Then it's either finding a partner to take turns on watch while the other naps, or meeting up with someone to talk shit with. This holds especially true for guardians on the night shift like me.

Very few people choose a Republic guardian to spend their time with, partially because we have to meet up at the border and partially because of some bullshit tribalism. But we've had an alliance for decades now, so I say it's time to let it lie. It's also rare for a volu and an ailur to befriend each other. It's not racism or anything, but our cultures do tend to clash a bit. People just like friends with similar interests, tastes, and experiences. Or so my father always tells me, but he also always extends his talons a bit when passing an ailur in public, so . . .

Nevertheless, Miro and I don't care about all that. We've always been birds of a feather, or bird and cat of a feather, if you prefer. Both of us grew up, egged on by our patriotic parents, planning to be heroes for our respective countries. Both of us chose the stone to escape unwanted marriages, if for different reasons, and both of us were severely disappointed in the reality of the guardians. The most daring thing I have done since joining was give a fake address to the swarm of sergeants who accosted me the second I was assigned to their flight.

"Sorry about that, Skaya, commander wanted a post brief," Miro apologizes, and I nearly jump out of my skin.

"Shit, you've gotta stop doing that!" I protest before hitting his arm with a half-playful punch.

"I'm just keeping you alert—it's important work we do, can't have you dozing off," he lies, and I scoff. I look up at the massive obsidian stone. It's floating miles away but would be visible from farther than this. Even as a black stone at night, its size makes it hard to miss. It creates something of a void in the darkness, where ambient light disappears. In contrast, the night around it actually looks brighter. I spit a few seeds at the barrier it maintains and they bounce off harmlessly.

"Would you look at that, no signs of a breach. That makes"—I mock counting on my fingers—"nine, maybe ten thousand years? Yeah, I think we're all right."

Miro laughs and sits down on a tree stump near the trunk I'm leaning against.

"How do you do that?" he asks, and I tilt my head, inviting elaboration. "Get all that velocity when spitting from a beak? The science doesn't check out."

I scoff. "Oh, I don't know, the same way you stand upright with that extra fuckin' joint in your legs, I guess."

He chuckles. "Fair enough, although my mother may disagree with your positive appraisal of my posture."

"Yeah, I don't think it's your posture that your mother doesn't consider straight enough," I lament, and he nods sadly before pulling a flask out and taking a drink. I look at him in envy. "I can't believe you are allowed to drink on duty. I'm not even allowed to bring a book. Sometimes I think the Republic has it right."

"They just know the same thing you and I do," he says. "The stones are staying as cold as they always have. If whatever 'prophet' who said otherwise was allowed to be drunk on the job, why should the guardians remain sober?"

I can't refute the logic; everyone knows it's true.

"Yeah, the Council knows that, but they go the other direction with it. If nothing is ever going to happen, well, there is no problem with running their guardians ragged. Who needs well-rested guardians when they'll never have to fight anyone? Much better to hold up our supposed 'discipline' like some kind of trophy," I complain.

"Well, that's what comes of putting a council of ancient loons in control of your country," he teases.

I roll my eyes. "The Republic is ruled by sages too. You just occasionally pretend to choose which one and stop talking to your friends when they pick the wrong one. I say fuck all the sages," I retort.

"I'll drink to that." He winks before taking another drink. I groan in envy as the alcohol improves his shift in a way I will never understand. "Speaking of crazy old sages, one of ours is pushing for reform. He actually thinks the stones are going to fall in our lifetimes. Claims we need to recruit more guardians or we'll be facing invasion in a matter of years."

I give him a blank stare. Then I look at the cold stone in the sky again. "So . . . it's an election year, huh?" I guess.

"Hit the nail on the head!" He laughs. "Yeah, he's an idiot hoping to scare us into voting for him with some mythical doomsday. As if that has ever worked. I don't know why human sages always try shit like that. No one else has ever claimed to see the future like they do; it's like they all get the same playbook at birth."

I shrug. "Aren't you forgetting someone?"

He closes his eyes and curses. "That's right. Sorry, this may be my second flask."

"It's fine, I'm just saying. Assholes are gonna be assholes whether they have a beak, tail, or bald face," I say, and he relaxes. The reminder of the creep who drove me to choose the stone makes me shudder despite the warm night.

"Do you think my mother would believe me if I said a Nexus sage prophesied I was destined to have a boyfriend?" he jokes, referencing the moron volu who tried a similar line to recruit me as his eleventh concubine.

"She'd probably have shipped you here whether the Guardians wanted you or not, just to keep you away from the sages after that," I say.

"No joke, if anything could shake her faith in the sages, that would be it," he sighs, and I sniff. They have all the power in the world but no Nexus sage would ever go anywhere near a stone. It's the only thing in the world they are afraid of. So I chose the post that would keep me away from the one who wanted to use religion to own me. Miro came here for a similar, if far more complicated, reason.

"Well, that's one thing that fucking stone actually does, so cheers to that," I say.

He wrinkles his nose and scoffs, "I suppose with all the taxes spent on guarding them, it's good they do something." We have both grown to resent the useless, cold stones and their barriers. You can only be treated like shit for so long while working fourteen-hour shifts before everything associated with your job leaves a bad taste in your mouth. "Although, if they ever came down, the fucking sages would probably shit their pants. Might be even better without them."

I consider his suggestion for a moment and shrug. "Fair enough," I agree. "I suppose it's not the stones themselves those creeps actually fear. Do you think if I take a drink from your flask, my negligence will cause it to fall from the sky?"

He offers it to me. "Only one way to find out."

I look at it for a moment, then decide to just go for it. With the hours they work us, I'll be sober again before guardmount breaks anyway. I take it and throw back a deep swig of the smooth liquor. As I hand it out to him, he holds up one finger and we both look around in mock vigilance for a moment. The stone remains cold and colorless, floating as it has for millennia.

"Well, fuck. No demon queen, no chimera pet, and no army of chaos. I guess drinking on duty isn't so dangerous after all," I sigh.

Miro takes back his flask. "I guess not. Maybe if I vote for fuckface the human sage, then it will fall?"

I laugh. "Well, electing a new sage is about as likely to cause major changes as that drink just now was, but feel free to give it a shot."

He sighs as well. "Yeah. Guess we'll just have to rely on this supposed demon queen to bring it down herself. Honestly, it might be a relief."

"Honestly, I agree," I say, sitting down next to him. "We could use some mythical demon to knock some sense into these fucking sages. Almost makes you want to believe."

"Fuck *almost*; if I thought for a second she was real, I'd help her get past the stone myself," Miro spits, and I can't blame him.

"You know what? You're right," I say. "Here's to the stone falling and the army of chaos making the sages work for their fucking luxuries. To Demon Queen Lillith!"

Miro raises his flask in a mock toast.

CHAPTER ONE

Carrying the Burden

glance over at Sara as I pull the cart through the woods. These woods aren't so . . . radiant, so to speak, but mundane ones surrounding one of the communities she and I helped build. The redwood trees are familiar and consistent, and the smell of pine reminds me of camping as a girl. As Sara catches my look, she blushes and rapidly looks in the other direction. I was surprised by her confidence when she made the first move on me as we sat on the beach a few weeks ago, but apparently, I have two things to thank for that. It seems she overheard me telling Mom about my feelings, which helped her sort through a few of her own. More important, however, was my own vulnerability.

Sarafyna's status as the hunter of the Radiant Woods has always promised a confident woman somewhere under all her nerves. That and the way she behaves when she sits in front of her hat block. I hadn't seen her so forward in an emotional context yet, but my weakness opened a gap for her strength, I suppose. Whatever the case, the night after our double date with the king and the priest, she was a whole new Sarafyna. That passionate fire burned between us, danced with us, and cloaked us in a warmth we desperately needed. And it lasted . . . just long enough to get me to my front door.

After an awkward moment in the doorjamb, her mind and lifetime in an archaic culture caught up to her heart and she blushed furiously before excusing herself and rushing back to her own family. I don't mind. I hardly expect a woman to discover her sexuality and jump headfirst into it in the space of a few hours. If we hadn't known each other as long as we have, even the move she did make likely would have taken longer.

All this amounts to a new flavor of shyness around me. I smile at her and she pulls the brim of her hat down to hide her blush.

It's been a few weeks since she first kissed me, and I'm not worried that she regrets it. We have, in fact, repeated the event quite a few times since. She definitely has a harder time manifesting confidence at the same time as me, however. That's all right. It's nice to have her in my life, visiting me every day and being around me just because she likes my company. She has been a light through a canopy of rotting leaves. A large part of me is sick with guilt. It feels like spitting in Leo's face to be happy while he is so miserable. So wounded.

I've tried to visit him a few times since we both got here, but he turns me away every time. He'll talk to Sara but . . . barely. I try to remember what Sara reminded me of the night I saw him for the first time since the attack. It's not about me. His trauma isn't mine and I can't own it for him. That's true, but that doesn't mean it's not my problem. He needs support but . . . seemingly not from me. I'm not sure what it is, but he doesn't want to be anywhere near me. It's all I can do not to make a thousand guesses about a thousand of my failures as I struggle to sleep each night. But until he opens up, I won't know.

That said, soon we will have someone in a far better position to connect with him. Someone Sara may be able to help. After today's delivery, we are finally bringing Leo's mentor to him. It's taken some work to get to her, as a few things went wrong with my plan. Rather than the disorder and infighting I was expecting, the nobility is stronger than ever. Godfrey must have been working behind the scenes from my very first move. My stupid story about bandits on the road was too poorly researched. I should have asked Autumn and August for more details; if I'd trusted them earlier, maybe it would have taken Godfrey longer to catch on.

In any case, he rallied the nobility far too quickly. To make matters worse, he'd apparently been keeping a close eye on anything I bought from very early on. Almost all my safe houses in the capital have been destroyed and the bit of Radiant Woods inside buried. I can hardly trust the ones that are still open either, in case they have been left that way intentionally. All this to say . . . fuck. By which I mean, it has taken a great deal of effort to reestablish a safe route back into the city, and more to find Lady Charlotte. But everyone deserves safety, and Leo needs his mentor. We will bring her to him soon.

We just need to get through this delivery, a herculean task I'd much rather avoid. Because we are delivering supplies to the "Kingdom of Endings," as they call it. The community most determined not to end the monarchy but to supplant it. They aren't the only community stubbornly hanging on to such ideas, but they are one of the worst. I let everyone choose where they want to go when I get them out of Potestia, and the Kingdom of Endings largely attracted some of the wealthier families. Very few former slaves choose to live there, so it consists mostly of previously upper-middle-class workers who got caught in the new wave of labor-replenishing laws.

This will go one of two ways, broadly speaking. Either they are going to start trying to limit who can leave their community and forcing people to bow to them, ultimately earning my ire and everything that entails, or they won't and I have nothing to worry about. Of course, a tiny monarchy without any actual authority will collapse in maybe ten minutes, but they remain part of a wider support network. The people will be all right in either case. Right now, however, they insist I am their monarch. This is just a huge headache for me more than anything. It is, at least, a manageable headache. Something to focus on so I don't spiral while thinking about my friend.

"Hey, Sara," I call, and she jumps, squeaking a little in surprise. "I don't suppose I can introduce you as my fiancée?"

Her face transcends red as she starts spluttering in response.

"F-fiancée??" she stutters. "Annie, that's a bit . . . I'm just . . . I don't know if I . . ."

"Oh, relax." I laugh. "I'm not asking you to marry me. I just want to avoid meeting whoever they try to spring on me this time. If they know I'm courting you, maybe they won't ride me so hard about marrying random generic man number forty-two."

She reveals a small self-satisfied smile when I say I'm courting her, but still protests.

"Uh, but don't they want to marry you because they are so attached to how Potestia does things? Wouldn't courting a woman just . . . upset them more?"

"Yes, yes it would." I groan. "That's kinda why I want to do it, truth be told. Sometimes grumpy, stubborn, power-hungry people deserve to feel appalled and powerless to do anything about it, you know?"

"Do you really think that's a good idea?" she asks with an amused side-eye.

"I think it's a fucking great idea, to be honest," I say, and she chuckles before looking at me a little shyly and pressing two fingers together nervously.

"I mean, I don't exactly mind if you introduce me as your f— your fian— your partner," she stammers, "but you know it's only going to make this visit harder."

I don't like it, but she is right. At least she was adorable while shattering my dreams.

"Fiiine, but if they try to hook me up with the eyebrow guy again, I'm sending him your way," I threaten, and her face pales.

"Annie, don't you think I spent more than my fair share of time tangled up in time- and space-defying bushes?"

I choke a little on the laugh that rushes to meet the joke. "All right, all right! I won't subject you to further misery," I promise.

By this time, the little town is in view and I release a deep, beleaguered sigh as I see a man in makeshift armor standing at a wooden gate with a spear. Who are they even guarding against? There is no one out here and they live on an island. As I pull the large cart close enough to make out the man's face, I see him regarding me with horror. I'm fairly certain there is nothing on my face, so I have to assume he is surprised by how much weight I am pulling. I return his shock with a look of confusion. Most of the people living in these communities have either seen me in combat or are close to someone who has. It shouldn't be that shocking that I lift, so to speak.

The truth of his contorted expression sours my mood as soon as it comes to light. "How dare you allow the queen to act as a . . . a beast of burden!" He reprimands Sara, spittle flying from his quivering lip as he lectures one of the women responsible for his continued freedom. Sara and I share a brief look, then shrug together.

"I don't know what queen you are talking about, but I'm happy to stop being her 'beast of burden.' I have walked for miles and my feet are hurting. Care to take over?" I ask.

He begins to deflate a little as he looks at the overloaded cart behind me, but he sets his jaw in determination.

"Do I have your leave to abandon my post and aid you in this, Your Majesty?" he asks. I look at him as if confused for a moment, then over at Sara. I let go of the handle of the cart so I can point at her and she shakes her head.

"I think he's talking to you, Lily," she clarifies, and I point at myself, then tilt my head as if asking the man for confirmation. His face begins to turn a little red.

"Yes, Your Majesty, I am of course referring to you. I would be happy to carry your burden for you, with your permission to leave my post," he repeats.

I cross my arms and lean back against the cart. "I think this guy might be losing it, talking to people who aren't here. Come on, Sara, we have a delivery to make," I say before grabbing the handle again. The guard grits his teeth and grips his little spear in frustration.

"Lady Lillith, please allow me to leave my post so I can carry the supplies for you," he insists in an artificially calm voice.

"It's just Lillith, but thanks. As far as I'm concerned, you can go wherever your little heart desires, bud. If you want to give me a break, I'm happy for the help." I release the handle again and step aside to allow him to take my place. He eyes the large cart nervously, starts toward it, then pauses to lean his spear against the wall before approaching again, this time with free hands. I just watch him patiently as he grabs the handle and begins to pull. I have to hold back a laugh as his boots slide through the dirt and the cart stubbornly maintains its position.

He grunts loudly and pauses, rubbing his hands together, then takes a deep breath and throws himself into the handle again. Again, it fails to move. Even on wheels, it is far too heavy for him to move at all.

"I have a friend who can help you out if that's too heavy?" Sara offers innocently, and I cover up my laugh with one hand. Her delivery is the picture of the polite femininity he might expect but the implication is clear. Although it's a less . . . direct approach to mockery, I still wonder if I am rubbing off on her or if the snark was always buried in there somewhere. Either way, the poor man is growling and sweating in a renewed effort by the time I stop him.

"All right, sport, that's enough. We have an appointment I can't miss later and I don't have time to watch this forever. In the future, if you see me pulling a cart, assume it is because I want to be pulling a cart and leave my girlfriend alone, please," I request. The desperate man tries to push a few more times before finally giving up. He looks like he is going to snap at me, but to my immense irritation, he bites his tongue. Not to avoid being an asshole, but because he still thinks I am in charge of him. The clearly embarrassed guard rushes to bring up a new subject to distract from his failure.

"Uh, the, uh, stewards have requested you bring the supplies to the palace today so they can distribute them appropriately," he says, and I narrow my eyes. Then I look across the community. I can see every building from the entrance.

"Palace? I don't see anything like that. It's a pretty small town, guy," I say.

He looks sheepishly to the side. "The, uh, two-story house on the east end."

I give him a blank stare. "Right, I'm going to distribute supplies from the center of town as usual. If your 'stewards' have questions, they can find me there."

Pulling the cart forward, I mutter to myself, "Those jackwagons better not mean what I think they do by 'distribute appropriately.' Palace, my ass."

Sara curtsies to the man. "Thanks for the help," she says as he looks away. She then catches up to me. "So, what's a *girlfriend?*"

I smirk a little as we make our way to the center of the small, new town.

CHAPTER TWO

The Stewards

I'm sorry, I just don't understand what you mean. You sound insane," Sara argues, confusion coloring her face as we pass out different supplies from the center of the small town. Unlike the cities of Potestia, resources aren't conveniently, and suspiciously, found in abundance just outside the town walls. I've always thought it was strange that everything a city could possibly need was so readily available, with no need for any kind of trade. These communities are a little more like one might expect, with different flora, fauna, and minerals only existing in localized areas. Every community has its own regional resources and specialties.

Without Sara, these communities wouldn't exist. No one else can even leave the Radiant Woods once they enter—not on their own. Not only can she leave, but she can move through them in an instant and take people with her: me, traders, escaped slaves, apprentice priests. Everyone I have ever saved from Potestia, I saved because of her. I don't know what I would have done without her, but I know building this much would have been impossible this early. We've set up thriving towns full of free people all over the planet—anywhere the disjointed Radiant Woods grow near an empty but inhabitable landscape. All thanks to my girlfriend. She carries this new society on her back. As incredibly attractive as that is, it can't be permanent.

Sara gives us a huge advantage in the short-term, as we can share these resources extremely quickly. This means, unlike on Earth, we can expand in a lot of places at once without travel-based infrastructure. This eliminates a huge number of problems any society might have in supporting itself, but . . . it's not sustainable. Currently, travel, trade, and communication all rest on Sarafyna's shoulders. Without her, it all collapses. And these idiots want to call me queen? I'm just the punchy girl; if I die, these people survive. If something happens to Sara . . . well, she is far more important than I am. Of course, many societies give authority to the punchy people and blue-collar wages to the important ones, but it still feels less than self-aware.

In any case, this means we can't plan long-term. I'm not sure how long someone like her will live, but you can't build a society around one person and hope for the best. Even if she manages to share her abilities like the Collector, or Radiant Woods, maybe, it's still far from the society I hope to build. We need people to be able to move around freely without a specific person controlling their travel. I don't want acceptable forms of trade to be only ones Sara or I agree to. I want trade to be so easy that anyone can do it. Fortunately, magic exists. With knowledge being spread and advancement encouraged, I'm hoping to discover a workaround in the coming years. This reminds me that I'd like to visit Clarrise once we've retrieved Leo's mentor and I've gotten a better sense of the state of Visenar.

For the time being, however, we have to rely on Sara. This is another problem. Sara wants to help me fight. She knows the fighting isn't done and she is perhaps the only person I can trust on all fronts to watch my back. I want her to stay in safety for her own sake and because she is too important. We've had a few discussions about this that weren't quite heated but the angels didn't descend from the heavens to praise our harmony and cooperation either.

Fortunately, this is not what we are currently arguing about. Not here with all these people coming to collect the steel, clay, and ingredients we brought. No, the only entity nearby that might understand my and Sara's current argument is the Radiant Woods.

"I understand I haven't seen the story, but it's nonsense. If he isn't a girl and he isn't a Gilmore, how can this 'Kirk' be the best Gilmore girl?" she asks again.

"I don't know, Sara," I sigh. "All I can tell you is, he indisputably is. Maybe someday we'll find a way to show you and you'll understand."

We get a few odd looks as we continue the now-forty-five-minute discussion, but we never get the chance to finish because two extremely irritated women march toward us like mothers preparing to use our middle names.

"Your Highness, what is the meaning of this?" the shorter woman demands, crossing her arms and tapping one foot. "I had thought it was made clear we would be deciding on the distribution of goods from the palace from now on?"

I give her an appraising look before crossing my own arms.

"So, you are one of these 'stewards,' I take it? Well, if by 'made clear' you mean the goofy ass with the pointy stick told me where you wanted it, yeah, I'm aware. I just don't really give a shit," I retort, "and I'd prefer you didn't call me Highness. Unless we can find a spot where some fucking weed grows, the term has nothing to do with me." I see Sara begin to raise a question so I answer it, diverting my attention from the severe women for a moment. "Weed is kinda like green mist but better for cramps. I'll tell you about it later."

"How are we supposed to get anything done if we just throw supplies around randomly?" the second woman protests, throwing her arms up in exasperation. I'm about to tell her to screw off but realize, in a way, she is right. I have a tendency to assume the community that wants to start up a new monarchy is just doing stupid shit, but perhaps I was a little rash. I probably should have gone to the supposed "palace" just to see what they meant first. I'm just . . . not good at this part. This is what happens when people rely on the punchy girl too much.

So I sigh. "You're right, uh . . ."

"Rebecca," she answers.

"You're right, Rebecca. Organization is good. A few people helping distribute things and organizing labor is why most people are doing well outside of Potestia.

You are obviously the organizers here; it was wrong to just ignore that. I apologize. Please, explain to me what your plan is for distribution. I'll try to be more amiable in the future," I allow.

The two women straighten up a bit. They share a quick look, and the first woman clears her throat before speaking.

"These resources are limited on the island and therefore carry inherent value. To establish a proper societal order, we first need to draw a line between the new nobility and the lower—"

I interrupt her with feigned puking noises.

"No. Absolutely the fuck not," I respond. "These were shared freely by other communities, we are not using them to establish a fucking caste system!" I was right that I shouldn't have come straight here. I need to let organizers organize. But I was also right that the people suck.

"You told us it was up to us how to build this city! Well, we have chosen a kingdom and a queen," she insists, setting her jaw. We stare at each other, both completely certain the other is contradicting themselves. A million responses climb up my throat and stumble over each other, leaving me quiet for a moment. Finally, I rub my temples with one hand.

"What was your name?" I ask.

"April."

"All right, April." I look at the crowd around us. "You are right, in a way. You are all welcome to choose a leader, in whatever manner you think is right. Maybe you have people volunteering to play the role of 'commoner' so you can have your nobles. I doubt it, but maybe you do. But the society you grew up in maintained that system in ways that I will end if I catch so much as a whiff of them. So I'll bring these supplies to your 'palace' next time, but keep that in mind. I'm really only good at one thing here, and you put it in the name of your 'kingdom.'"

April looks down her nose at me. "I'm from Satusmor, you know. I've seen firsthand how your way of doing things ends, you self-righteous bitch," she scoffs.

I guess she took my request not to call me Highness to heart. Suddenly, Sara steps between us, carrying a storm in her eyes.

"Excuse me?" Her body language is more combative than I have ever seen. I haven't seen this side of her much and can't help but be a little charmed at how defensive of me she is. "What kind of stupid—"

I hold a hand up. "Woah, there, Sara, I think we know how a fight between the two of you would go. Be easy on her. Imagining a new world is hard before you've seen it," I say placatingly, and Sara gives me a sharp look before realizing what she is doing. Her brain catches up with her body, then her face turns bright red, and like the flip of a switch, she is back to her regular self.

"I, uh . . . I'm . . . I have to . . ." She trails off before stepping backward a bit awkwardly. This is just as charming as the outburst in a different way, and as she hides her face in her hair, I smile, the bite of the woman's remark completely fading.

"You're not stupid, April. My girlfriend here is a little defensive of me." April *isn't* stupid. Sara heard the story of Satusmor as just that. A story. She was on the outside, with all the context and framing she needed to understand what happened. Anyone who learned about it that way and considered it evidence that we need a king or queen or any authority would indeed have to be stupid. But that's not April. She only had her lived experiences. All she saw was the resulting violence.

I tried to help people share resources, knowledge, and services. Sharing knowledge and resources, on its own, is obviously not a moral failing destined for disaster. It was the power that was denied to the monarchy and the church that was the problem. My early attempts failed because I tried them inside the monarchy. The system in place was still an authority-based one, and that authority was the point of failure. Outside of that system, with the church and their fucking confessions, and the guards hunting people for their knowledge, my system is just . . . sharing. Does it need organization? Yes. Is Satusmor evidence we need a queen, king, or any other authority? I guess in the same way bloody gums are evidence flossing is bad.

But, when someone has only ever seen one way to live, it's hard to sell them on a new one. So yeah, Satusmor is clear evidence of the flaws in the system this woman wants, and with all the context, it's moronic to use it as the opposite. But she doesn't even believe the church has been brainwashing people. I can't argue sense into her. All I can do is give everyone options and prevent coercion, and the "Kingdom of Endings" will collapse all on its own. It just isn't how I usually do things and it's hard to default to it.

"Look, this isn't worth arguing about," I say. "I'm just warning you: if people are coerced, I will give them other options. So if this is what you want, think of a way to do it without coercing people. And for Christ's sake, choose someone else as your fucking monarch. I'm not taking the job."

April huffs and Rebecca answers for her. "We have chosen our queen."

I roll my eyes. "Then, as queen, I dissolve the monarchy," I quip.

They share an awkward look.

"Only the king can dissolve the monarchy, Your Majesty," April answers tersely.

I narrow my eyes. Maybe Sara had the right idea, because slapping them is looking pretty tempting.

"So you insist I am a queen, but I can't choose not to be queen, only a king can do that? Can I do anything?" I question, genuinely curious.

"Potestia was never ruled by a queen," April answers, "so the stewards will govern until a king assumes the throne."

I give her a blank stare. We are all quiet for a moment, and I hear Sara innocently whistling from somewhere behind the cart. I look up and down at the two of them.

"Are you two not women?" I ask. At their offended looks, I discern that they do, in fact, consider themselves women.

"We are women, but we are simple stewards moving things along until you marry, at which point the king will take control," Rebecca explains. Fuck it, whatever, I don't care. "Speaking of which, there is a gentleman we'd like to introduce you to. My son Jin has invited you for a preliminary meeting. If you'd be so kind as to visit the palace tonight, he—"

I walk off in the middle of her sentence and pull the embarrassed Sara back out, hold her face in my hands, and kiss her. Rebecca stops explaining her invitation and both women gape at me. In fact, everyone gapes at me.

"You're not getting a king by picking someone to put in my bed, all right?" I announce while Sara looks around, dazed. "And if one queen can't do anything, neither can two. Now, if you don't mind loading this cart up with various delicious citrus fruits, we'd like to get back home. We have more important shit to do in Visenar tonight, and as you can see, a blind date with your son is unlikely to get anyone anywhere." I turn back to Sara and we walk to the front of the cart.

"Lily, that was . . ." Sara trails off, and I lean against the cart.

"Well, I couldn't help it. They were being annoying and you were being cute. Both situations called for a common action. That was a very impressive two seconds of confidence, you should lean into that more," I suggest.

Sara covers her eyes with both hands in embarrassment.

"I don't know what got into me. That was so embarrassing," she complains, and I smile. Her presence really does make all this more bearable. If only I could bring her tonight. I have a feeling my trip is going to be far more dangerous with Godfrey in charge of the knights.

CHAPTER THREE

The Quiet Capital

What's wrong?" Sara asks as we rest inside her old cave. None of our "safe" houses in Visenar can be considered safe anymore, even if Sara can reach them, so she brought me here instead. It's the only place near the city that we visited regularly that Godfrey wouldn't have known about.

I take a deep drink from the waterskin on my waist and sigh. "I'm just . . . struggling, I guess," I answer half-heartedly. "Back on Earth, this part was never my job. Organizing, I mean. I can't help but feel like I am just . . . entirely inadequate. Back in that sad little 'kingdom,' I could feel the limits of my abilities. Worse, I could feel the temptation to overstep. Even now, part of me wants to just roll up my sleeves and mold them into something more . . . palatable. But . . ."

"But that would just be the same as what they are already doing," Sara finishes for me, and I nod. She looks down in thought for a moment. The quiet has begun to settle on my shoulders by the time she speaks again. "I know even less about this than you do, Annie. I've only known two lives before you, and neither treated me well. So I don't know how you can do better, but for what it's worth, I think you are doing great. I'm not the only one whose life is better now. Maybe it's all right to take your hands off all the way."

"I want to. I really do. That's the end goal, after all. I just . . . worry. It's a lot of change for a lot of people in only a few years. And it's all on your shoulders right now. It's unstable and a place like the Kingdom of Endings could push the whole thing over. So I want to stand out of the way of the people holding these communities together, but I worry. What if I do, and these 'stewards' start stepping on the bodies of people I tried to help? What if I ignore them entirely and in a hundred years we have a new Potestia? My ideas can work perfectly, on the first try, in nine out of ten places, but if that last one is a group of conquerors, they are all in danger.

"It's just . . . It's all a house of cards right now. And I am not a person with a gentle touch. I just don't want to destroy everything, Sara. I'm scared I'm going to leave this place worse off than I found it," I admit.

She looks at me like a warm fire on a cold night.

"Annie, you are amazing, all right?" she says. "You are carrying too much. You told me yourself: you don't know if you are right about the best way to build a new world. Neither do I. That's okay. But you have given a lot of brilliant people the opportunity to come up with their own ideas. Don't torment yourself that not every town looks like you imagined it. You are going to go mad, letting people build their own futures and marking it as a failure every time that looks different than you think it should. Maybe, instead of second-guessing yourself whenever someone else makes a decision you don't care for, you can start thinking about your own future? About *our* future?"

She's right, of course. This whole plan wasn't structured around realizing the exact world I always wanted, but around giving people the option to imagine their own. And it's working. But it's not easy, having the power to direct people in the direction I want and refraining, especially when I hate the direction they choose so much. I can share my ideas, but letting people ignore them is grating. I suppose that's normal, but . . . I sigh. She is right. I need to make up my mind and commit to my own damn plan.

I take another drink of water before standing up. It's time to go. "Thanks, Sara," I reply with a half smile. "It's a lot harder than I thought it would be, that's all. I should probably get going."

"Are you sure you'll be all right on your own?" she asks, and I pause. The lie I want to respond with rests eagerly on my lips, but I don't free it. Instead, I take a deep breath. I'm in a relationship with this woman now, and there is no room for comfortable dishonesty.

"No. I don't know what else Godfrey has done to prepare for me. He's far more competent than his brother. I have no idea what is waiting for me in that city. But I have to find out. I may not be all right without you, but I know everyone else won't be. Everyone I love, every good thing I have ever done, still needs you, Sara. So I'd like to go alone," I answer. I can see the lines of worry drawing themselves on her face, but she gives me a tight nod. "I'll keep you updated with my whisper sphere. I'll see you soon, Sara."

Just before I leave the cave, she speaks again. "Come back safe, Annie. I need you," she whispers. I look back at her and offer a full-mouthed smile before turning and walking into the night.

I have to use heat mana to warm myself as I put on my radar goggles and walk through the quiet. A deep anxiety tries to strangle me with every step. My own footfalls ring in my ears as the large city wall grows nearer.

Something doesn't feel right. I'm not sure this city ever feels right, actually, but tonight feels like a poorly mounted painting. The tilt bothers me in a way I can't quite describe. I push through anyway. It's not safe to leave Lady Renatus on her own, and Leo needs her. It was no secret Leo and I were friends, and while pretty much everyone who cared is dead, I don't want to risk leaving her in the city any longer than I have to. I can't shake the feeling of wrongness, however, and have gooseflesh by the time I reach the tunnel I have been working on for the last few weeks.

I descend into the dark to make my way under the wall. My plan is to eventually have a full network of tunnels under the city where we can grow more patches of Radiant Woods to travel between. For now, however, it only leads to one spot. A room on the first floor of the tavern I rented while living here. I used my radar goggles to wait until its occupant checked out before emerging and booking it for myself. Now it is my only way into the city. I emerge in the quiet room and sigh. It's so . . . quiet.

I hear the door creak in the quiet hall as I emerge from the room. It sounds like a scream in the dead air. I feel self-conscious as I enter the more public dining area and find it empty. Now I know something is wrong. It's night, but it's not that late, and I've never seen this room empty. My hackles rise as I immediately worry I've walked into a trap, but as I reach for my mana, I feel the familiar flow like water in a hose. Even more, I feel the weight of the grief mana that has grown so familiar over the years. When I lived in Visenar, I used safe houses where Sara had grown plants connecting to the Radiant Woods. At the time, these served as a great way for us to travel quickly and help people escape the city. They are mostly buried now, since Godfrey had tracked many of my safe houses, apparently. But I can still feel the grief they carry. I would know if I were in a mana-dispersal circle targeting me specifically.

This means that whatever is happening, it's not about me. I walk, heel to toe, through the dark tavern and sniff the air. It smells like fire. I lower the radar lenses on my goggles and look around. It seems the tavern isn't empty, exactly, but the huddled figures in each room tell a story of fear. People aren't missing, they are hiding. This realization tastes sour and I tense. But I have a job to do, so I keep moving. Every half-rotted floorboard announces my presence, and I grit my teeth as I reach the front and open the door.

The smell of fire climbs my nostrils and pricks at me. The night air remains mostly dark, however, lacking the orange glow I expected to accompany the scent. Whatever is burning, it's not nearby. I take a deep breath and take a step outside. Still, nothing happens and I grow more confident as I walk through the city. I make it nearly three hundred yards, past the familiar brothel and the run-down restaurants, before I feel it. My radar goggles blink out and the colors I have grown used to are replaced with simple glass. At the same time, a massive weight slides off my shoulders like rain, running down my body and pooling beneath my feet. The grief mana is gone. I am inside a dispersal circle.

The muscles in my body tense and adrenaline floods me, my vision sharpening and my mind racing. I think it's exactly what I feared and I'm being ambushed again. My eyes dart from dark alley to dark alley, straining to catch any sign of movement to react to. I take a step backward and my mana returns, nearly drowning me with the force of its arrival. I gasp and look around. That doesn't make sense. If it were an ambush, they would wait until I was near the center before completing the circle. It's too easy to flee otherwise. I kneel down but can't find any sign of the circle on the ground. I can't find where it is drawn.

I look around again and realize something isn't quite right. I didn't notice through the lights of the radar, but there is a subtle difference in the city right where the circle starts. The lighting is different. Warmer. I look behind me at the streetlights and realize what it is. I didn't notice before, since where I have been living everyone uses light mana and enchantments. But when I lived in Visenar, the poorer quarters only used oil lamps. But every light I have passed has instead housed an enchanted stone. Except inside the circle.

This tells me two things. This circle isn't targeted. Well, it probably does target me, since standard mana remains active inside, but it's not one circle where they knew I would be. This circle has been here a while. A safe place to fight me. And it's probably not the only one. Godfrey must have these all over the city. It's not a terrible idea, as it limits my movements. If I avoid these circles, Godfrey can patrol a smaller portion of the city. Considering recent manpower shortages, that could be a huge boon for him.

It also tells me the city is beginning to rely more on magic to combat its labor shortage. If even the poor quarter is using magic to light itself, Godfrey must be leaning on it. That's a good thing for the residents but could be a headache for me. On the other hand, it's probably one of the reasons the entire city isn't surrounded by a single dispersal circle. I sigh again. This trip is already more stressful than I'd hoped and I haven't even seen anyone yet. After a moment of indecision, I step into the circle again. I lose most of my combat power and my early warning system, but I decide Godfrey is less likely to have these areas actively patrolled. I still have my strength and speed, and being less predictable is worth more than my spells right now.

I feel naked as I creep toward the noble quarter. I don't like feeling so vulnerable. Godfrey isn't going to be as easy to throw around as his little brother was, and I don't have help, nor am I in the Radiant Woods. But I can't give up. As the run-down homes give way to mansions and estates with extravagant gardens, I thank the stars my heart doesn't beat. If it did, it would surely give my position away with the noise. The night sky begins to glow orange and I realize I am getting closer to the source of the fire smell.

Finally, I arrive at the Renatus estate. It is directly in the middle of one of the many dispersal circles I have passed through to get here, which isn't encouraging.

I also haven't encountered a single other person the entire time. Whatever is happening, it has people worried. I examine the large home from a distance for a while but don't see or hear anyone. Hesitantly, I circle around to the back of the building and climb up the trellis. Still, there isn't a sound. I slowly push open a window on the second floor and climb inside. I'm careful to remain quiet as I enter the dark room. I miss my radar spell more than ever as I finally see movement.

A man, dressed entirely in navy blue, emerges from the darkness. He has a mask on, but his body language is amused. My breath catches. I fucking knew it. Someone is waiting for me.

CHAPTER FOUR

Guards and Wards

My shoulders slump in exasperation. I knew it was possible Godfrey would connect me to the Renatus house, especially with how closely he had apparently been watching me. The dispersal circle surrounding it was unlikely to be a coincidence either, but it didn't change anything. I had to try anyway. Still, it's irritating to find someone waiting for me. It's been weeks and there is clearly something more important going on right now. Surely Godfrey can't have every place I might go staked out all the time like this? Not considering how many guards and knights have died over the last few years.

"I don't suppose you'd be happy to just let me walk by?" I venture. The man doesn't speak, but he crosses his arms and his mana flares. As my worry grows, so does his aura, and I groan audibly. This man is either anxious enough to manifest worry mana, or he is a bard. "Seriously, do we have to do this right now? I still have a couple of aching joints from kicking your king's ass. I swear I won't tell anyone if you just take a nap. It's not like I have Godfrey's phone number," I suggest, but he starts to form a spell. It looks like fire mana. I'm about to jump out of the way when I realize there is something off about the spell.

Instead of dodging, I surround myself in a wide sphere of unaspected, colorless mana. As the fire and heat of his spell collide with the wavering air of my magic, they dissipate. It was an amateur fire spell made of pure mana. This is the worst way to cast any kind of spell because mana can dissipate itself. It also takes a lot to cast it. Summoning some kind of fuel for it and only using mana for the ignition is typically far more effective and efficient, and I wouldn't have been able to stop it so easily. I narrow my eyes and try to measure my opponent's aura. It seems to adjust with my curiosity. It doesn't intensify but its nature feels different. This man seems to be a bard, but . . . he's much weaker than the last one.

Weaker and less experienced. I notice his fists clench, and he starts summoning something with what looks like wood mana with its tannish brown tint and green undertones. Less experienced and less original. He has no particularly unique mana so far, and as his spell completes, I am a little taken aback by the result. He holds a simple wooden spear. I look around the room a bit. It's small, with little room for broad attacks. I love a good spear, but it's an odd choice for the environment. "Are you, uh . . . sure about that?" I ask, but he lunges at me instead of answering. I quickly dodge to the side and the spear gets caught in the curtain.

He holds a hand out to me while wrestling with his spear in the other. Since he telegraphed his attack, I have pure mana rushing to crush it before I even see the red fire energy. I expect to succeed before any fire forms, but it is unusually fast. Another look back at the man's aura and I realize why. My worry has shifted to open amusement, which has affected the intensity of the bard's magic. Even so, he remains weaker than me, even without an endoaspect on my side. If I could cast an actual spell, I'd already have him restrained. As I silently reprimand myself, I kick the legs out from under a nearby stool and grip one broken end in my right hand.

Just in time, I lift the makeshift shield and block a thrust from the newly freed spear. Two more jabs rapidly aim for my side, then face. I redirect the first with my free hand and block the second with the shield. The man actually seems fairly competent with the weapon now, and I begin to understand the choice to use it. Before I lower the stool from my face, a red glow behind it reveals another fire spell. The jab at my face effectively obscures my vision for long enough for him to cast it, but I am able to dissipate the mana before it reaches me just by overpowering it. My brave little stool isn't so lucky, however. The spell leaves it burning with a more natural flame.

It's the bard's turn to look amused, an impressive feat with a mask on. His body language broadcasts arrogance, and I roll my eyes in the brief pause and throw the burning stool at his head. He startles and tries to raise his spear to block it, but the idiot failed to protect his weapon from his own spell. The burning stool collides with the spear, which splinters, sparks flying in all directions. Both the stool and bits of spear hit him in the head and he speaks for the first time.

"Fuck," he grunts under his breath. He looks up at me like he wants to yell something he really shouldn't say in front of a lady as refined as myself, but I'm already throwing a small makeup mirror at him. Just after his eyes meet mine again, kindling a spark in my memory, the steel base collides with his nose, making a sickly *crack* sound. In the meantime, the reckless fire spell has set other things in the room ablaze. My opponent glares at me, one hand covering the blood staining his blue mask. The fire spreads and crackles as the heat bears down on us. I'm about to find something else to throw, but the bard makes a decision and throws himself out the same window I used to enter.

I have something of an arm on me, so even a quick throw without all my strength must have hit pretty hard. I consider pursuing but, looking at the burning room, I decide against it. He could be going for help and Lady Renatus could be sleeping in the burning building. I briefly worried she wouldn't be here at all, but the man's level of competence has me questioning things. There is no way Godfrey thought someone like that could do anything to me. If he did leave people guarding every spot I might visit, it would be more effective for them to go fetch help when they spotted me. This man seemed . . . eager to fight me.

It's true a bard's endoaspects make them dangerous, but his base mana seemed weaker than expected and he used it like a blindfolded child with a flamethrower.

The spear was the only thing he had any chance with, and he ran pretty easily. I'm not certain his presence had anything to do with me at all, and if it did, it's unlikely he was there on Godfrey's orders. That entire exchange left me more confused than anything. It was very strange.

But I don't have time to consider it further. The fire and the fleeing man put me on a tighter schedule and I have to do what I came here for. I kick the door to the room open and enter a quiet estate.

Dust covers the various artwork and furniture, and I begin to worry no one lives here, until the large double doors down the hall burst open and the woman herself emerges in a flowing nightgown, her wide eyes examining me with growing panic.

"Lady Renatus?" I ask to confirm, and she takes a step back.

"W-who are you?" she stutters.

"My name is Lillith of Endings," I say, holding my hands up. "I'm here to help."

Like the flip of a switch, she immediately straightens up and gives me a quick nod. She disappears into her room and emerges a moment later with a loaded bag and a shawl wrapped around her.

"Let's go, take me to Leo," she says, calm and determination settling on her face now that she understands the situation. It is a huge relief that Leo prepared her for my visit before everything happened. I see her struggling to carry the heavy bag, so I hurry to her side and take it, hefting the luggage over my shoulder. "Thank you, Lily," she says, and I allow myself a small smile at the corner of my mouth at the nickname. Leo must have told her enough about me that I already seem familiar.

"Lead the way," I say, and she strides through the neglected but rich halls and toward a split staircase, to the landing. I see she intends to exit through the main entrance and I stop her.

"Wait, has anyone been with you here? Keeping an eye on you or expecting me?" I inquire. She shakes her head. "What about servants or staff? We can't leave anyone behind," I add. It may be a bit difficult to get a full group through the city, but most people seem distracted tonight.

"No servants," she answers. "And no, it's only been me here since Leo disappeared. Is he . . . is he all right?"

I almost don't hear her question. There is no way someone knew to come here tonight specifically to intercept me. Only Sara knew I was coming for Lady Renatus tonight. So who was that? I have to gather more information in the future. It seems like I'll need to find out where these circles were drawn anyway, and how to interfere with them. For now, I just redirect her.

"All right, do you have a servant's exit at least? There was someone waiting for me when I got here. He could be back with help any second; I'd rather not leave through the front door," I say. She looks troubled that someone else has been in her home, but she wastes no time.

"Of course, this way," she agrees, and we go through a surprisingly clean kitchen, to a smaller door that leads out the side of the estate. I am cautious when opening the door, but the night is quiet outside. If the man I fought earlier is getting help, they aren't here yet. Which means it's time to leave. I clasp the older woman's hand in my free one, and we make our way into the quiet city. We are silent for much of the trip. The tavern housing my tunnel is near the wall, and I circle around a bit in case we are being followed. I find it unlikely the buffoon I fought can follow me with any stealth, but someone else could.

It's not until I have put a panel of wood over the hole in the room and used a spell to light our way that the woman finally speaks, nerves from the dark and damp environment causing her voice to waver only a little. "You . . . you never answered my question," she says, and I tense up, knowing what is coming. "Is Leo all right?"

I stop walking and take a deep breath before turning.

"Leo is . . . alive. He's alive, healthy, and safe. But . . ." She sees the worry in my eyes and her face falls, guessing where I am going. I finish anyway. "No. He's not all right. And I don't know what to do for him. I think maybe only you will." My breath catches and I can see on her face that I failed to fully suppress the anxiety in my voice. She looks at me with the determination of a mother with an injured child.

"Tell me everything," she demands. As we make our way back to Sara, I begin to tell her about Leo's last night on campus. I see the sorrow and violence dance back and forth through her eyes as I speak, and I'm comforted to find someone even more prepared to fight for Leo than I am. "Thank you," she finally says, almost inaudibly. I recognize the look in her eyes as she tries to process the story she just heard. I've seen it many times before, and as always, I cultivate a desperate hope that I'll never have to see it again.

Hide

Charlotte's Journal

As a child, I didn't hide. I was always lonely. Always uncomfortable. Always wrong. Everything I did was wrong. The clothes I liked. The colors. Even the way I preferred to sit drew the ire of my father. I liked the wrong games. The wrong friends. When I read the wrong books at twelve, my father locked me out of the house and banned me from reading at all. When I introduced myself as Charles of Renatus instead of Charles Renatus, he instead locked me in.

I never understood it. Each time I found something I loved, or even liked, it felt like a weight off my shoulders. Like finally bathing and scrubbing dirt away after a hard day's work. But my father would always drift in like a storm and put that pressure back. He would put it back and press harder. Over the years since his death, I've nearly forgotten his face. In my memories, he is the dark clouds preceding a storm. The wind and the rain and the hail. The barrier between me and the warmth of the sun I craved so badly.

I had to learn, each year a little more, where the balance was. Where I could bask in the sun and where I had to hide in the shade. I lived on that boundary, because it, however narrow, was the only place I could live at all. It was a razor-thin line I had to walk. Disdain and hate from my family on one side. Disdain and hate for myself on the other. So I learned. To dip my toes in the things I loved, and to pull my feet back when I felt the cold. As a child, I learned to hide.

CHAPTER FIVE

Safety

I feel nothing but anxiety as we make it home. Lady Renatus, or Charlotte as she has asked to be called, has been preoccupied with Sara the entire way home. This is perhaps unsurprising, as Sara and I can help her actually transition in a way this world has likely never seen, and Sara is the key actor there, while I am more likely to have some answers Charlotte is looking for, seeing as no one else even knows what hormones or chromosomes are. But I can't focus on the conversation. For weeks I've put a lot of stock in finding Charlotte and bringing her home. She is the only person I can think of who could help Leo.

We don't exactly have therapists to go to, and I'm certainly not qualified to fill the role. Leo has never mentioned his family either. So Charlotte is my best bet. But now that I've actually managed to get her to safety, I can't help but worry that it won't be enough. No one should have to go through what Leo went through. The way he is coping with it . . . it's not going to lead to anything good. I have been promising myself I had a way to help him; I just needed to get to his mentor. But now . . . It's hard to describe. I have now done what is possible for me to do and I'm back to being helpless to fix it. I am not a woman who enjoys being helpless to make things better.

As soon as we leave the beach and enter the settlement, I know where Leo is. It was hard at first, with the Radiant Woods so near. That massive, ancient grief can be all-encompassing, like a foghorn on a quiet night. But over the weeks of getting used to it, I started to notice the small things again. The loneliness and the nostalgia. The quiet grief everyone, in every world, feels. These aches and pains have become as familiar to me as my own. In a way, they always were. But I now have a sixth sense for them. Leo's is powerful and I can feel it from anywhere in the little town. It's . . . naked. Like a vulnerability he never wanted to expose and a shame he doesn't deserve. It carries with it a sense of wrongness and longing, each warring with a deep-seated fear.

I carry my own shame whenever I feel it, which has made me hyperaware of it. As such, it takes little effort to lead Charlotte directly to him. The woman with me does draw more than a few looks and murmurs from the residents. Attention she shouldn't have to be as numb to as she clearly is. A cold reminder that, however much progress we have made here, these are still people plucked out of an archaic, medieval world where those who don't fit the mold are quickly ushered out of sight. No wonder Leo is presenting himself as a woman here. I bite into my lip as I approach the door to his home. I hold one fist up to the door to knock, but it shakes. I have waited for fights to the death with calmer nerves than this.

Sara puts one hand on my shoulder and I look back at her. We lock eyes for a moment, then I set my jaw and knock. It's silent for a moment, but much to my chagrin, I can feel Leo's grief tighten as soon as my knuckles hit the wood. I don't know if he knows it's me or if he just hates the idea of seeing anyone right now. "One moment," his voice calls through the door. It takes several minutes for anything to happen, which confuses me. He let us know he was there and it's a small room; there should be little reason to delay so long. Then I feel it. His grief growing in intensity while settling into a familiar seat. It tastes like stagnant water. It's clear then what is happening. He's getting dressed for company. He must dress comfortably, for him, while he is alone.

This is confirmed as he opens the door in a simple sundress. As soon as our eyes meet, a mess of emotions splatters across his face like paint. The same old comfortable look of a friend, quickly colored by anxiety, disappointment, and finally irritation. Then he sees Charlotte next to me. His eyes widen before filling with tears. For Charlotte's part, I don't see her face right away, but I can feel a deep, throbbing grief emanating from her as soon as she sees the boy she has been looking after for so long. Wordlessly, the two embrace. For all the sorrow now coming from Charlotte, Leo's has, if only for a moment, dampened. It's been swallowed whole by relief and joy.

I know it won't last, but it's the first time anything has put so much as a dent in Leo's sadness. Finding Charlotte may not fix everything, but it sure as hell didn't hurt.

A moment later, Charlotte withdraws and looks at Leo's face. "Poor child," she whispers to him, "what have they done to you?" My chest hurts as I picture him, bloodied and broken the night I found him. It shouldn't—my heart is as still as ever—but somehow the familiar throbbing from my life as Annie still shows up.

"I'm sorry, Charlotte. I wanted to finish school. I really wanted to show everyone what we could do . . . That you weren't an idiot, or fool, or anything else. I tried, I did. I'm so sorry . . . I let you down." Leo begins to sob while Charlotte shakes her head.

"No, Leo. No. You didn't let me down. You were . . . you *are* so brilliant. I am more proud of you than anything I've ever accomplished. Don't put this on your shoulders. I'm the one who failed you . . . I . . ."

Suddenly, I feel like an intruder. As Leo glances at me and Sara tugs on my shirt, I realize there is no room for me in this reunion.

"S-sorry," I apologize before bowing my head slightly and turning to leave. The two need time, and privacy, to talk everything through. I take a few steps to leave, but as I do, I consider the looks Charlotte got on the way over. The proof that, even here, Leo can't feel comfortable as himself. I turn to see him closing the door to his home. "Leo, I—" I start, and he pauses, looking at me. "I'm sorry I was so slow before. I should have been there sooner. I should never have let them lay a finger on you. But I will keep you safe here. I will."

Leo lets out a deep breath through his nose and closes his eyes for a moment before looking at me with a small, sunken smile. "I know, Lily. I'm not angry you were slow. I'm not upset you didn't stop them sooner. You did everything you could with the information I let you have. I am so grateful you showed up for me when you did. You have a lifetime of my gratitude, really, that's not what I . . ." He has to take another deep breath as his voice starts to waver with the telltale signs of poorly fought-off tears. "I know you will keep me safe here. But . . . that's the thing. I don't want to feel safe because the great and magnanimous Lillith will save me. Not that I don't want you to keep me safe, but . . . I don't want to be the victim in your story. I don't want to feel safe because you are there. I just want to feel safe because I am safe. Because I have nothing to fear. Can you understand that?"

I open my mouth to respond, but . . . I don't have a good answer for him. So I shut my mouth and nod. He closes his door and I sigh. Sara rubs her hand against my shoulder. "Everything all right?" she asks.

"Yeah," I respond, "the world is just too big. Too much. Sometimes its wounds feel too deep." My entire body feels sore. It hasn't been the most exhausting day I've ever had, but I must have expended too much emotional energy. My vision is starting to blur if I don't consciously focus.

Sara doesn't respond. She just walks with me back to my own home. I can see in the concerned wrinkles around her eyes that she has noticed my fatigue. She leads me to my room, where she sits on a chaise and gestures me over. I curl up on the open spot and rest my head against her side for a moment, then slump over into her lap. She runs her hands through my hair. My hand hangs off the side and it's not long before Suzume appears from under the chair and rubs her whiskers along my wrist. As she rolls on her back and starts batting at my fingers, Sarafyna speaks. "It's all right, you know. To rest. To let other people take a little of the burden. I know what it's like, to live a life without rest or reprieve from worries. It changed more than my body. I don't want to see that happen to you."

Blackness edges at the corners of my eyes. She could be saying anything; the soft curve to her voice would have the same calming effect. Instead of answering her, I release my weight and let her support me entirely. We lie there for some time. I don't sleep, not yet. Just feeling her beneath my head is more restful than sleep could ever be. It must be at least half an hour before I speak again. "Leo is right, you know," I say. "He should be safe here, with or without me protecting him."

"I know," she answers, her fingers beginning to comb through my hair again.

"I need Leo to be all right. I can't build a new world where he still can't be himself. I need this to be a safe place," I lament, and she nods.

"I know. Give it time. Charlotte is going to let us help her—maybe Leo will finally do the same. But for all of it, you have to give it time. Hearts won't change overnight."

"It's fucking stupid that it takes time," I groan.

"Yes, it is," she agrees with a chuckle, her free hand joining the first in my hair, around the other side of my head.

"Are you . . . measuring my head?" I ask, and her hands pause. She's quiet for a moment as I roll over to look up at her face. She's blushing.

"I . . . didn't even realize I was . . ."

I close my eyes while a silent laugh escapes my throat. Even subconsciously, Sara is Sara. Just as I am getting ready to stand and say goodbye so I can sleep for the night, a light illuminates my nightstand on the other side of the room. Sara frowns. "You are too tired, Annie. You don't have to talk to him tonight."

I shake my head. "I do. Every conversation is an opportunity, in more ways than one," I respond, resigned to the extra hour this is going to take. I pull myself to my feet and Sara starts playing with her own hair.

"You need sleep. He can wait until tomorrow," she pleads, and I smile.

"I'm all right, I promise. Thank you for caring so much. But I have to. You can stay if you like," I offer. She simply shakes her head.

"No, Dad and Peter will be wondering if I'm safe. I should see them. Just . . . don't push yourself, all right?"

"I won't, I swear," I assure her, and she reluctantly nods before standing and leaving my room. Once she is gone, I wearily retrieve the whisper sphere before sitting at my writing desk. Suzume jumps into my lap and curls into a comforting ball. I center myself as I hold the sphere. Sara's old sphere, the one tied to my old one. The sphere that I was carrying when I was arrested. Finally, I answer, as I have several times a week since killing the king.

"Hello again, Godfrey," I say.

CHAPTER SIX

Brands of Violence

The glowing sphere resting on my writing desk conveys a weary sigh from Godfrey. "Hello, Lillith." He greets me as I scratch under Suzume's chin.

"You sound tired, bud," I reply to a chuckle from the older man.

"It's been . . . a day," he says. "Things are getting out of hand."

"I did hear something about a fire over in Visenar. Near your house too. How did that come about?" I poke.

"You heard, did you? With your vast network of spies, I'm sure. So, what did you think of my recent additions? Those magic lamps really brighten up the roads, don't they?" he asks.

I click my tongue. "Their coverage seems a bit spotty, to be honest."

"Yes, well." He laughs. "*Someone* cultivated bits of an ancient, unknowable deity forest all around the city, so we did need to make some tough choices."

"You literally worship the guy," I scoff. "How was I supposed to know he wasn't allowed in town?"

"You know, many priests were horrified at the disrespect you showed the Collector, using his woods that way," Godfrey muses.

I allow myself a half smile. "Oh, I'm sure they were. Rumor has it temple attendance has been a bit meager recently."

"The head priest did go missing—it didn't exactly inspire confidence in the church."

"Oh, he just got a little closer to God. The whole city did, in a way. What kind of church loses the faith of its followers when that happens?"

"Speaking of, I don't suppose you have my little brother kicking around somewhere out there?"

"How many times do you think you'll ask me that? Trust me, Godfrey, I'm the one knocking the crown off your head, not him," I promise.

"Won't that be fun? Still, something . . . came up. If you have him, bringing him back could help a lot of people," he says idly.

"I'm sure he's wandering around the Radiant Woods somewhere. Maybe you should head in after him. I'll meet you there and help you look," I offer, and he rewards me with a humorless laugh.

"I think I'll have to decline. Seriously, Lillith. If he's out there, I—"

I interrupt him with a yelp as Suzume bites my fingers. I glare down at her, then realize what she wants as I look out the window and see the sun has long past set. Godfrey pauses what he is saying before asking a friendlier question. "Forgot Suzume's treats again, huh?" he guesses.

"Ugh, yes," I answer. "I just need to remember where I hid them."

"Left drawer of your writing desk last time," he says, and I shake my head even though he can't see it.

"Nah, the genius little idiot figured out how to open the drawer. I got home one day to find the jar knocked over and empty. Hold on." It takes me a moment, but I find the jar of homemade treats on my bookshelf, hidden behind a collection of books I stole from Godfrey once upon a time. I put three on the ground for Suzume to lick up happily and I return the jar. Finally, I return to my desk. "Sorry about that. So, what happened, what do you need the old king for? Seems like you would be . . . less than pleased if he showed up again."

Godfrey grumbles something through the sphere that I can't make out. "Let's just say, someone else is looking for him, and it would prevent a lot of violence if we could deliver," he says. He sounds casual on the surface, but there is a slight hitch in his voice. Interesting. I put my hand to my face and rub my lip while thinking.

"I'm sorry, Godfrey. If it's your brother you need, I genuinely can't help you," I respond as empathetically as I can.

"So he's definitely dead, then. I thought as much based on your past responses," Godfrey says. "Can't exactly say I'm sorry to hear it, truth be told. It would have been convenient if he wasn't though."

Something falls to the floor next to me, startling me before I can respond. I glare at Suzume, who gives me a wide-eyed look of innocence as she sits next to the book she managed to remove from my shelf in her quest for more treats.

I narrow my eyes at her before returning to the conversation. "What's happening, Godfrey? Is this about that fire? Who wants the king, and more importantly, who is in danger?"

There is a moment of silence before Godfrey responds, failing to answer the question directly. "Lillith, I need my people back." There is a serious and commanding but also desperate edge to his voice.

I sigh, and we move toward the same argument we have had half a dozen times now. "Your people?"

"Yes, my people. The people born and raised in Potestia, who owe us their loyalty. The people we need in order to protect everyone you left behind," he snaps at me.

"Godfrey, no one owes Potestia loyalty. Especially not these people. You know that as well as I do," I counter.

"I know this country has failed a lot of people, Lillith. I know. But how am I supposed to make things better without laborers? How are we supposed to move forward if everyone isn't here to move forward together?" he asks. "This is their home. They should be allowed to contribute to its future."

In a way, he touches on the truth there. I can't just move everyone away from the shitty monarchy and hope things get better. It is their home, and people shouldn't have to leave their home for a better life. But they should be allowed to. "There are more people left in Potestia than I took away, Godfrey. If these ones were so important to moving forward, they shouldn't have been treated as the least valuable members of society for so long."

"I know that! I have always known that; that's why I have been working to point us in a better direction! But that takes work. It takes time, and above all, it takes people. Like it or not, this country has been running this way for a thousand years, and we can't kick the legs out from under it and hope for the best. It needs the support of its people until we can build something new. Fully trained and educated mages don't pop up out of nowhere. I'm not trying to keep people in slavery, but we need to rely on their labor. We can't start by removing the stone beneath our feet, however filthy it may be. We start by cleaning it up, then replace it when we have something else to stand on."

I roll my eyes at his lecture. "How old are you, Godfrey? How rich? How powerful? How long have you had the power to start 'cleaning it up'? How many people lived and died as slaves while you were waiting for the right time to give them a better life? A life not even half as comfortable as yours. You want me to tell you where people are so they can help you make it better? People who had to flee from your country just to live? People who were very likely born years after you first had the power to effect change? What happens now matters. I'm not going to let you drag them back to keep waiting on promises you didn't even start working toward until they were already gone," I spit back.

"The world isn't so easy as that. It doesn't matter how much power and wealth I technically have. There are too many people too attached to the world as it is. You know what I mean, I know you do. If I'd offered a helping hand, dozens of other people would have tried to stop me. They *did* stop me. They stole my mind and banished me to a bookshop in the countryside. I needed real power before I could change things, and I have that now!"

"Do you though? I fought with the last king. He was a joke. A moron. The very definition of aimless power. If he were the only one in your way, you would have held the throne decades ago. But he wasn't. Do you think I haven't been paying attention? The king, in order to hold power, needs the support of the other nobles. No powerful mage can rule this country alone. So what, your fancy gold hat changed things? Now the nobility won't resist when you take their comforts away from them? When their slaves come back to the city and you don't return them to their posts? They'll just shrug and say, *Well, if you say so, Your Majesty*? No. They'll find a new king. The only reason you can push changes now is because the nobles have no slaves to command and your ideas are offering them some of their comforts back."

"Maybe. Maybe, in the short term," he says, "what you have done has made reform possible. I can acknowledge that. But we need to build something we can stand on, not just for a few years or a few decades. We need to build a foundation that keeps people safe for the coming centuries. And sudden, radical, and overly violent change isn't going to do that. I don't know how you have all survived this long, but it can't last. Nothing bought through so much needless violence will, unless you plan to stay around killing slavers forever."

"What are you talking about? My method is a drop in the fucking bucket! My needless violence? You are the violent one. Yeah, I've killed a lot of slave owners," I say, my hands curling into fists. "I've killed rapists too, and thugs who steal food from children. I've killed a lot. But I could do that for ten lifetimes and fall short of the violence of your method of change. I couldn't dream of being so radical or fanatic. You can only say that because the things I do are *visible*. A single drop of guilty blood in the light will always look more extreme than eons of cruelty in the darkness. But leaving these people in slavery? Leaving everything as it is until it's easier to change comfortably? That's fucking extreme. That's real violence, and your brand? It's not only violent to the guilty. Calling what I did extreme is just defending slavery in a palatable way."

"Flowery words, as usual, but it won't change reality. It won't change what is necessary for long-term change. You are just being selfish. Casting yourself as a hero while you lead people to their deaths. Do you think pulling people out of their homes and banishing them to who knows where is less violent than fighting smart and giving them a chance in civilization? It's just instant gratification, Lillith." By this time, he is shouting. "And it's about you, not them. Now tell me where my people are so I can build this fucking kingdom into something worth believing in!"

The argument is getting heated, as it usually does, and we are getting to the point where I can usually get useful information out of him, but black begins to border my vision. "You don't know what they are building, Godfrey, you have no idea what we are putting together. Just . . . just seeing the slavers die and the people disappear isn't . . . isn't enough to make that call. If they wanted . . . to go . . . back . . ." I struggle to retort, "I would bring them . . . back." Something feels off. I feel more than tired, I feel sick. "In order to . . . build a better . . . world . . . people need . . . to . . . choose." I trail off, my voice growing weak as I collapse onto my desk.

Suzume meows at me with concern. "Lillith? Lillith, what is going on? Are you all right? Lillith!" I hear Godfrey calling but I can't respond. I can't even move. All I can do is listen. I start channeling mana through my body, trying to reinvigorate myself, but I don't feel the usual rush like a powerful river. My stomach churns and I put all my strength into reaching for my other whisper sphere, the one I use to contact Sarafyna. It's no use. I can't move. All I can do is listen to Godfrey and Suzume.

For the first time in years, I feel completely helpless.

CHAPTER SEVEN

Bedside Manner

The world is hazy as I regain my senses. It takes me a moment to make sense of the blurred image hovering over me, and I blink a few times before I make out black hair in a messy bun and red eyes, weighed down with concern. "Mom?" I ask through dry lips.

"Oh, thank the Collector, she's awake!" Mom calls while looking over her shoulder. I want to look in the same direction but I feel remarkably weak. *Where am I?* I feel the familiar comfort of my bed contrasting with an unfamiliar aching all throughout my body. *How did I get here? When? Why am I so stiff?* I can't even lift my head at the moment. It feels a bit like waking up in the emergency room after a doctor takes too many blood samples. Mom wraps her arms around me, not unlike she once did after I escaped from a certain noble's basement. "You scared me, Lily. Again. Are you all right? What happened to you? Did something happen while you were out?"

I groan weakly into her shoulder as she grips me, and she hurriedly releases me.

"I'm just peachy," I respond in an entirely unconvincing whisper while closing my eyes again. "I don't remember anything happening. Poi—" I start before pausing and looking up at my mother again. I promised not to sugarcoat things with her anymore, but the temptation is strong. ". . . Poison, maybe?" I guess, and the worry lines on her cheeks harden. "I'll be able to take a look in a minute. I just feel . . ." I trail off as I see light shining through the window. "Uh, how long have I been out?"

Mom opens her mouth to respond, but another voice answers first. "About a day and a half," Edward says as he walks in, Gilbert just behind him. "And Henry says he can't find any signs of poison in your blood, although he has been working pretty much constantly, testing it with all kinds of nonsense." I didn't even know Henry knew how to test blood for poison, although I have been a bit too . . . preoccupied to follow his advancements as an alchemist over the past few years. I look over at my other two brothers and wince at the tension in my neck.

"Hey, Ed, Gil," I say as nonchalantly as I can.

"Rise and shine, Lil," Gilbert says, a slight hitch in his voice revealing concern behind a wide smile. "Why'd you have to go and sleep so long? You worried us. A bit."

"How else would I stay so beautiful?" I ask, and he smiles with one corner of his mouth.

"Yikes, I'd hate to see what you look like with less sleep," Ed quips.

Mom waves a dismissive hand and says, "Hush, Ed," but I smile. There was a time when a similar joke would have irritated me, but with our improved relationship of the past years, all the bite in the words has vanished.

"It's fine," I reply. "I'd have a hard time seeing beauty past that nose of his too."

Ed fakes a gasp of offense and Mom stifles a chuckle, but the levity doesn't last long.

"Seriously, Lil, what happened?" Mom asks. "Sara found you passed out on your desk. Your drool had blood in it. And I haven't seen you sleep this long since you were just a girl . . . Are you all right?"

"Give me a moment, I'll take a look," I say before closing my eyes and trying to cycle mana through my body.

"Uh, take a look at what? Your eyes are closed; you look like you're going back to sleep," Gil says.

I wave one hand at him in a dismissive gesture.

"Not a literal look, you goon. Haven't you been practicing with your own mana lately?" I say without opening my eyes. Everyone is given access to a mana circle and support when they join this community, including my family, but Gilbert has failed to take any interest in learning how to use his. Too busy enjoying life, I suppose. The silence in response to my question is answer enough. "Right. Well, a mage who actually likes learning magic can feel the parts of their body that contain mana. I mean, a lazy mage can too, but with practice you become familiar enough to examine it. I'm trying to determine what's wrong."

"You haven't been sick since you first learned magic . . . Do you have any idea what it could be?" Mom asks.

At the same time, Ed interjects, "I have no idea what you're talking about. I practice with magic constantly, but I can't tell my toe from my dick."

"Can anyone?" I quip, and Ed clicks his tongue.

"With mana, I mean, shut up!" he protests, and I smile. Gil and Ed start to make similar jabs at each other but I tune them out while I run mana through my body like water. Physically, I feel like shit, but whatever stopped my mana from working properly last night is gone. I have full control and can easily examine myself. It takes almost no time at all to identify the problem. My blood runs cold and sweat starts to form on my forehead. I have to carefully police my expression.

"Fuck," I say without thinking.

"What? What's wrong?" Mom asks pleadingly as I open my eyes.

"I need Sara, now—where is she?" I ask instead of answering.

Ed and Gil share a concerned look.

"She's . . . gone," Gil reluctantly responds. "She was with you all night and most of the morning, but . . ."

"She had to help the other communities, right," I finish. Shit. I don't understand how this happened. I've been keeping an extremely close eye on myself for years. I've had to since I've been altering my own body for so long. Yesterday, this problem didn't exist. Or . . . two days ago? It doesn't matter. Before Visenar I was fine. Whatever happened, it was recent. Which means its progress is far too fast.

"What's the issue, Lily? Is it dangerous?" Mom asks again, and I grit my teeth.

"I don't know. Maybe. It depends on how much Sara can help me," I respond.

"But . . . didn't you say Sara's abilities don't work well on you? She couldn't help you with your . . . modifications, right?" Mom asks.

"She couldn't, but she has successfully helped me heal injuries before. However her power works, there is a good chance she can fix this. In the meantime . . . I can handle it a little on my own. Gil, Ed, get Henry. I need his help."

My brothers race each other out the door without question, leaving me alone with my mom.

"Lily, what is it? I don't think I've ever seen you this scared . . ." she asks one final time. I didn't realize I was wearing it on my face, but she's right. With how severe this is and how quickly it developed, I am terrified.

"I don't . . . I don't know how to describe it to you in a way that makes sense," I say after a few moments of quiet. "It's a disease that . . . well, my body is growing too much, on the inside. It can be extremely dangerous. Especially with how fast it appears to be growing, and especially where it's growing. But it's too soon to panic. Sara can probably get rid of it. I just have to keep it under control until then, and I can do that." I don't actually know if Sara can help. I don't know how this happened at all. But, if I redirect all the mana I was using to try to make new changes to my body to this, I can fight it off. Slowly.

What's strange is, Sarafyna and I examine and heal people all the time. Not once have I found anyone in this world with this problem. I'm sure it exists, but most of its causes don't. It seems to be even rarer here than it would have been on Earth at a similar time period. Then again, if cancer can manifest and grow this fast here, maybe no one else with it has survived long enough to meet me or Sara. That thought does not go to great lengths to calm my nerves as I try to use mana to eat away at the tumors. The largest one is near my spine, which explains my inability to move last night.

It's a miracle I woke up at all. As I carve away at it, trying to burn up the useless cells with pure mana, it's clear it should have killed me already. With the way I lost the ability to move, it must have been even larger at some point. Someone did something to make it shrink. Which is why I asked for Henry. It sounds like he took some blood; he may have given me something else as well. Sara may have managed to do something as well. I don't know how divine magic works, and she usually needs my help, but maybe she made a start. I'm taking a deep breath, focusing on my hand, gripped tightly in both of my mother's, when all three of my brothers burst through the door.

"Lily, what's wrong? Are you all right? What happened?" Henry interrogates me. The panic in his eyes cultivates mine, but I take another deep breath, keeping part of my mind focused on burning the tumors away.

"It's all right, but I need your help," I say. "Did you give me anything while I was asleep? Anything at all?"

"Uh, y-yes," Henry replies, still out of breath from running here, then he rummages through a bag at his belt and pulls out an orange potion. "It's just for fevers—you were running hot last night . . . Here." He goes to toss the potion to me, looks at my pallor, then walks close and places it in my hand.

"What is it; did it help?" Mom asks.

"I don't know." I furrow my brow. "Maybe. I'll have to examine it. In the meantime, I want to make a list of potions I want to try. Can you write these down, Henry?"

"I got it," Ed responds, rushing to my writing desk and pulling out a few supplies. He pauses when he sees a brown stain, but after a shudder looks up at me, ready to write. I list out a few things for him. There are plenty of chemicals and hormones Henry can manipulate that should help, although it's a bit of work explaining them all. Enough that we spend a few hours discussing it, everyone but Mom, who leaves to wait for Sara near the woods. I attack the tumor directly all the while. I'm really hoping that with my direct control and whatever Henry can come up with, I'll be able to keep this under control. Very hopeful, in fact. If all goes well, it shouldn't slow me down too much. Especially if Sarafyna can help.

What really worries me is how it happened. How did it progress this much in a single day? Because if it happens again . . . Well, I need to prevent that, which means I need to see it coming.

"How do you know all this stuff?" Gil asks, now sitting in the chair Mom had brought in to watch over me. "I've never heard anyone say anything like half of what you just . . . know. What you have somehow always known."

I shrug before taking a drink from the juice Gilbert brought me some time ago. "I must have sold my soul in another life," I joke. At that moment, Sara and Mom burst into the room in what is becoming a regular occurrence in my bedroom.

"Ann— Lily! You're awake!" Sara cries, clutching a badly abused hat she seems to have torn at on the way over.

"Can we have the room?" I ask. "I need to speak to Sara alone."

I can see the desire to protest on everyone's face, especially Mom's, but they comply. Ed moves for Henry and I idly realize this is the first time in years the two have spoken so warmly and comfortably. Mom lags behind, giving me a tight hug after the boys leave.

"Be okay, okay?" she whispers.

"I promise," I whisper back, and she reluctantly follows her sons. Then Sara rushes to my side and holds my hand. "It's going to be fine, Sara. I'm already feeling better. But we have a lot to talk about."

"I love you," Sara blurts out. I shake my head in surprise for a moment. "I'm sorry, I just realized last night, I've never actually said that, and I got scared you wouldn't wake up, and, well, I . . ."

"I love you too." I smile warmly at her. "And I will for a long time yet. But please, I need your help with this." I feel the familiar healing warmth of her divine magic before she even touches me, and it clashes with the cold fear in her eyes. But it's all right. As soon as she touches me and I start directing her abilities to the tumors, I know it's all right. I'll be able to get it under control. I just don't know what caused it in the first place. "I love you too," I repeat quietly. Then we get to work.

CHAPTER EIGHT

Motivation

Godfrey

I was prepared for Lillith. I have been prepared for Lillith for years, at least in Visenar. She is a known, if admittedly unpredictable, quantity. I wasn't prepared for her to somehow overpower my brother, but she's right. The man was a fool. He was an overflowing goblet of wine. All that power did nothing in his hands but make a mess for the maids to clean up. Still, a woman without a single mage in her ancestry managing to take him down? It's beyond impressive. We give grief mana to our bards, and not a single one can use it to such an effect.

This is partly why I have been so wary of her all these years, even if she was barely a woman when I first began setting countermeasures in place. It is also partially why, frustratingly, I can't shake my concern for her. I must be the greatest fool in Potestia. Here I am, setting all these traps to capture and fight her, knowing there is only one way that ends, especially since she is so stubbornly resistant to reason: she is going to have to die eventually. And yet, a single conversation where she seems to collapse, and my blood races through my veins like a man before his own execution. I don't know when I started caring about her so much, but it's a liability.

Of course, she isn't the problem at the moment. The attacks are getting worse, and I can't contact any of the other cities. I haven't spoken to my grandson in weeks and I have no idea what the state of my country is, outside Visenar. Because there is another threat. The pretender to the throne, "King" Darian. With him and my idiot nephew, Kallon, in town, I am only the third most powerful mage in the city. And Darian's power is truly terrifying. He's my little brother's bastard, which means he started with all Donatello's mana and must have spent decades in his own circle. If not for the goodwill I've fostered with the other nobles in the city, I'd be dead already. And that goodwill is fragile, what with my own former apprentice being one of the primary threats to their livelihood.

Thankfully, I have one bargaining chip, an unwilling gift from Lillith that is keeping them on my side for now. Without it, Darian's assault the other night would have ended my reign. She tried to hide it when she was in her cell, and did a decent job, but she's decades too young to get it past me. I saw that circle hidden among the other nonsense tattoos on her body. Lillith didn't find a way to leave and return to a magic circle. The brilliant little madwoman found a way to *bring her circle with her.* I couldn't make out every rune, but it was unmistakable. She has been connected to her magic circle since she was a child, and she still is. The power this could grant the next generation of nobles will change this world forever.

Of course, sharing some magic circles with the commoners is already going to do that, but that's not an easy sell for the other nobles. Or it wouldn't be, if I didn't have something even better to offer them. I just need to work out how she did it. From what I could read of the runes, it almost seemed like she designated "everything" as the circle's reference space. I'm not certain how she managed to convince mana, the fabric of the world, that she is always at the center of everything. But it does work—that much is evident from the power she has cultivated over the years—which means it will work for me. I can advance society for the poor and maintain the position of the monarchy at the same time, and I have Lillith to thank for it.

She would have some nonsense to say about this, I'm sure. She always does, and it always sounds convincing on some level or other. But she didn't spread her new circle around either. For all her flowery speeches, she held back her most powerful tool for herself. I don't think this is intentional. I think she, like anyone, is blind to the fact. Her ideas are all idealistic in a shallow way. But the very fact that she is as effective as she is, is evidence that, on some level, she knows I am right. Someone needs to hold the reins, and they need a firm grip on them. Her treatment of this miracle circle is a result of that inborn knowledge.

Of course, my allies are impatient to see results. With the recent attacks, I haven't been able to experiment as much as I'd like. I walk to the window of my new, extravagant study and look out the curved window that occupies most of the space on the wall. Again, burning red runs down the side of the shield of pure mana that surrounds the palace. These attacks, which have been coming for a week now, mark the edges of the invisible bubble I've encased the building in. Darian has relied primarily on his spells of molten rock. This alone would be manageable, despite the man's terrifying mana reserves, but Kallon seems to have formed some kind of temporary alliance with him to kill me.

They can't disperse the shield without dispersing their own spells, and I have enough allies to maintain it at all hours. But it's difficult to run the city with it up, and Darian has already burned down several noble estates while their owners help protect the palace. He claims he wants me to "turn over the king for justice." Another consequence of Lillith killing my brother is that many believe I was involved. Darian seems to subscribe to this theory. He also either believes I don't have the stomach to kill someone so close to me, or he is desperate to make it true. Perhaps he is right, as my still-aching concern for the girl implies.

But, of course, I can't give him my brother. Honestly, I would if I could; he wasn't a good man and there was no love lost between us. It would certainly be worth the freedom to do more than sneak a few enforcers in and out of the mana barrier. We'll have to go on the offensive soon, or things will get dangerous. But it'll be hard to push the less powerful nobles into such a risk without a proper incentive. And so I must focus on recreating Lillith's circle. The perfect incentive. Anyone inside this barrier is guaranteed to be a more powerful family in the coming years, and anyone outside will be left behind.

I return to my desk and ring a bell. It's only a moment before a well-dressed man opens the door and bows his head to me. "How can I help you, Your Majesty?" I restrain myself from sighing at Piper, my new aide. I cannot wait for Ansel to recover. I haven't been able to uncover what happened to the man, but even with the help of some of the best priests in the city, he has failed to regain consciousness. Piper is a competent bard as well, however, if one lacking the familiarity with my preferences that Ansel has.

"Is the subject ready?" I inquire.

"Yes, Your Majesty. He is excited to get started. Do you have a new design prepared?" Piper asks.

"I do," I say, pulling a sheet of paper from my desk. I eye the various dispersal runes spiraling toward the center of my latest attempt. I was skeptical of the use of these when I first saw her in her cell, but it was obvious why she included them once I thought about it. If she has truly managed to consider her own body the center of everything, her circle must gather a truly absurd amount of power. She must have predicted it would be too much, especially with a circle tattooed directly onto her body. I am tempted to remove some, but I ultimately decide to get it working first and increase its power later.

"Right this way, Your Majesty," Piper says as I collect my things. We leave my study together and walk through the palace. It still feels surreal to be home. To own this palace. While I did grow up here, my movements were limited. I spent much of my life as the crown prince, believing these halls would all belong to me when my father died. When I was already a man, however, he married a new wife. A woman with twice the mana my mother had, and the mother of my brother. He started with more mana than me and spent longer in the royal circle. And with that, my claim to the throne evaporated.

Now, of course, he is dead and I am king. A better king than he could ever dream of being. A king who actually looks toward the future, past the border created by the Radiant Woods, and past the comforts that keep us complacent.

We arrive in the bedroom I have converted into something of a clinic. A nervous man, absent his shirt, lies with his eyes closed on a simple bed as if for surgery. Both of the women attending to him, as well as the quiet man in the corner, stand and bow their heads as I enter.

"Welcome, Your Majesty. We are ready to try again," says Rowena, the taller of the doctors present. She gives the subject a potion to put him to sleep, and the man in the corner approaches quietly and takes the design from me. Without a word, he unfurls his needles and ink on a steel table near the volunteer and begins to work.

It takes hours, as always, to tattoo my new design. My heart tries to beat out of my chest as we wait. We have done this dozens of times, with dozens of designs, and not once has it done anything at all. Fortunately, there is no shortage of commoners willing to face the risks of an untested circle for the chance of becoming a powerful mage.

"If you don't mind my asking," Piper ventures, equally invested in the experiment, "what changes did you make this time?" The doctors give him a quizzical look at his casual tone, but it's something I insist on with my aides.

"Just an idle thought, truth be told," I answer as I nervously toy with the end of my beard. "Instead of designating the circle as the center of everything, I considered its mobile nature. It never made sense to me, that a single point could move and still be the center. So I gambled this time. Instead, I specified everywhere as the center of everything. That way, it's not the circle itself that is the center. Rather, the circle never leaves the center."

Piper's mouth turns down at the thought. "I'm sorry to say I don't exactly understand the logic, Your Majesty."

I shrug. "We'll know in a moment if it's worked."

As the artist wipes blood from the final black line on the volunteer's torso, my breath catches. It catches every time, and every time I feel nothing but disappointment when the center rune is completed and nothing happens.

For a moment, it seems this experiment will be no different. However, just as I am readying a curse, mana begins to rapidly gather, distorting the air above the volunteer like heat from a stone oven. And then, his eyes fly open and he begins to scream. It's a cry of pure, unadulterated agony. This does cause my breath to catch once more. However, I knew that having one's body essentially rebuilt as a mana space would be excruciating. But Lillith survived it as a child, so I'm certain this able-bodied man will as well.

But the scream doesn't end. Or rather, when he is out of breath and his voice fades, his mouth remains open and he tries to continue it. If it doesn't stop soon, he will suffocate. And it doesn't stop.

"Knock him out, he needs to breathe!" I order, and the nearest doctor pulls out another potion in a syringe, injecting it directly into him. At first, it seems to do nothing, but a moment later he finally collapses limply to the bed. Rowena cautiously approaches him as a bead of sweat runs down my brow. She puts two fingers to his neck, then covers her mouth in horror with her other hand.

"He's dead, Your Majesty," she announces.

CHAPTER NINE

Monuments of Progress

It's been a couple of days since I passed out, and I seem to have the issue under control. Well, I am active again, anyway. With Sara's help, my know-how, and a new potion from Henry, I have been able to shave away at the various tumors. Enough that they don't hold me back from my regular schedule, and I don't think they will be a liability in a fight. They do take constant attention, however. All the mana and focus I had been using to alter my body is now dedicated to preventing the tumors from growing. Even that wouldn't be enough without both Henry and Sarafyna, considering each growth is itself bursting with mana.

Of course, Sarafyna's divine magic continues to misbehave exclusively with me. Much like with her attempts to heal my scars or aid in altering my body, her magic is extremely slow and ineffective. Without learning how divine magic works, it is difficult to determine the source of this issue. And Henry's potions, close estimations of Earth chemicals and hormones, make me feel sick. But I am all right, provided whatever caused the initial tumors doesn't hit me again. I was working on claws too, now that I don't have to hide the changes. I suppose they'll have to wait.

I pull out one of Henry's potions and throw it back, then recline into my pillows again, doing my best to ignore the repulsive taste. It's only a few moments before the back of my mouth grows hot and the urge to vomit seizes me. I have to use the mana in my body to suppress the impulse and allow the potion to do its work. This is going to take some getting used to, but I can handle it. I'm more concerned about someone else being targeted than anything. I am surviving thanks to the abilities of two close confidants and my own expertise from another fucking reality. If this isn't an isolated incident, the next person to get hit is dead.

This presents something of a problem. I have too much to do. We need to take advantage of the time we have now to offer people in other cities a way out. The bits of Radiant Woods in every city have been keeping them relatively free of the church's control, and Godfrey should be distracted with, well, everything. I've made some trouble these last few years, and it seems like I'm not the only one. If I want to completely dismantle the monarchy, outreach in all the other cities is paramount. Especially while the capital is resolving its power struggle. Godfrey did take the throne faster than I expected, but that doesn't mean he is ready to stabilize the entire country just yet.

Every city is struggling with the same labor shortages and every commoner in them is looking down the barrel of slavery. I, and as many volunteers as I can get, need to act now. We must either evacuate as many people as possible or, even better, simply liberate the cities entirely. This depends largely on the state of each city and how the city lords have been handling their labor shortages. There are a few that, I believe, will happily take the city itself from the kingdom. It will be harder to suggest a new method of doing things to these places, but people will also not need to leave their homes to have a better life.

But I can't just ignore the capital either. Especially if that's where I got the cancer. That's what scares me the most. Sure, I'm scared that Godfrey, or Darian, or the Collector, or some noble whose brother I killed found a way to target me with a weapon I can't effectively fight. But I am *terrified* that they haven't. That it just happened because I went to Visenar. Because if it isn't targeted? The danger is *everywhere, to everyone.* It would explain why everyone was cowering in their homes and rooms. I like to believe the entire city isn't toxic, but . . . Godfrey sounded pretty concerned about *something.* If that wasn't just whatever fire was in the city . . .

I shudder at the thought. Suzume, sensing my discomfort, jumps on the bed and lies by my side. I idly scratch her chin as I worry. I can't ignore the capital, no. But I can't send someone else there, with the unknown danger, yet I am probably the worst person to go, since it seems to be a massive trap for me specifically. How the fuck did Godfrey even get so many circles up so quickly? Especially while dealing with whatever he is dealing with? Truth be told, the only person I can safely send would be Sarafyna. But, aside from my personal concerns about her, she is too important. Without her, everything falls apart. I need to at least research the dispersal circles. How they work, where they are, and how I can disable them.

I sigh. There is only one thing to do. I meant to visit Clarrise days ago, and it seems my reasons have only grown. I need to ease the burden on Sara as soon as possible and establish these communities in a sustainable way. We need long-distance communication, and Clarrise's town is my best bet.

I scratch Suzume a few more times, then groan as I climb out of bed. I truly feel like hell. But hey, I was a grad student. Who better to melt mountains of ice while exhausted beyond belief? I open my door, ready to head to Sara's house, only to find her standing before me. She has one fist in the air, prepared to knock, and a straw hat in the other.

"H-how are you feeling?" she asks with a nervous smile.

I cross my arms and lean against the doorframe.

"Sexy as shit, as usual; how about you?" I respond.

She bites back a chuckle. "First of all, Annie, you know what I meant. Are you okay?"

"Yeah, Sara. I'm okay. It's been a rough couple of days, but I'm pulling through. Thanks for all your help," I answer earnestly.

"I'm glad to hear it. I can try and help again, if you need?"

I don't think it would do any good at the moment, so I shake my head. "Not right now. We need to . . . Wait, what do you mean 'first of all'?"

She gives me a small, guilty smile. "Second, you have like twelve rat nests in your hair and your skin looks like an onion. I mean, you are beautiful, as always! But, yeah . . ." She trails off, offering me the hat she prepared for me. I smile as I cover my apparently dreadfully tangled hair with it. It matches the one she is wearing, both designed based on a goofy cartoon I drew for her maybe a week ago. "Why did you want a hat like this anyway?" she asks, examining the simple, round design.

"Because"—I interlock my fingers and crack my knuckles—"I wanna be king of the pirates. Now, come on, I want to visit Clarrise."

"Since when have you wanted to be the king of anything? And are you sure you're feeling up to it?" Sara prods me, a skeptical look weighing her eyes down. "It may be better to rest more?"

I give her an apologetic smile and shrug. "I'll sleep when I'm dead," I say, then hurry to placate her when she is immediately strangled by anxiety. "Which won't be for a long, long time, I promise! But the world can't wait for my best days. Come on, Sara, will you take me?"

She looks hesitant, but nods after a moment. "All right. But I reserve the right to take you to the nearest bed if it looks like you need it!" she insists.

I have to bite back the obvious joke that comment inspires, but she doesn't seem to notice.

"Thanks. I'll take it easy, I swear!" I hold one hand up and another over my heart and she rewards me with a quick nod.

My muscles throb as we walk down the beach but I don't let it show too much. We spend less than a second in the Radiant Woods before we emerge in a large valley, snow-capped mountains peering down on us from all directions. In the center are three massive buildings. From a distance, they almost look like skyscrapers from Earth. Sarafyna grips my hand as we walk quietly together and the reality of them becomes clearer.

Unlike the buildings of my past life, these have been erected with the earth mana of at least a dozen mages. Each is only occupied up to the tenth floor or so, but they were built with a much larger capacity in mind. Surrounding the outer walls, every floor has a wide terrace of farmland. Small orchards and fields create vertical agriculture all the way up to the highest occupied level in each building. This is an idea I idly mentioned to Clarrise, and she really ran with it. Instead of the travel- and trade-based cultures we are all used to, this town plans to sustain a potentially huge population in a limited space by growing up rather than out.

At each corner flows a magically created waterfall, channels in the wall helping direct the water to the various elevated farms as needed. It's already amazing and it's not half what it can be. Sara and I make our way to the second building and enter the ground floor. A boy runs by, maybe thirteen years old, leaving both me and Sara wide-eyed. Not because thirteen-year-old boys are unlikely to be found running in public, but because we both remember him. I carried him here myself, straight from a house of penance. A house of penance he had lived in because he was missing a leg.

Sara had, of course, volunteered to help people like him heal to the best of her abilities. But there are too many people to heal everyone perfectly and right away, especially since it requires both Sara and me to participate in the healing. Missing limbs are even harder since, although divine magic can increase a person's body mass to an extent, it can't completely grow new limbs without another source of organic matter. At least, Sarafyna's can't. The abilities of divine magic always seem inconsistent to me. In any case, we certainly didn't help this kid.

Now he seems to have a new prosthetic leg, built from stone and glowing with the mana that moves it. "Did they have those last time we were here?" Sara asks, and I shake my head.

"If they did, they didn't show us," I reply, impressed. I am always impressed when I come here. "But necessity is the mother of invention. In a way, this is one of the things that has made me so angry about Potestia for so long. Think how many hundreds of years ago people could have used this, if the ruling class didn't just shove their undesirables in . . ." I pause as Sara winces. "Well, you know what I mean. Mana is . . . amazing. It disgusts me that something that can do so much good has been looked at as nothing but a way to maintain power for so long."

"Yeah . . ." Sara agrees quietly. She is looking around as we board a large platform on the inside wall of the building. I grip one of its rails and start pushing pure mana into it. The mana follows channels in the railing to four different steel mechanisms on each corner. Force mana radiates from them, and we slowly elevate along rails in the wall. I keep channeling mana until we reach the sixth floor, where Clarrise lives. As I stop, the devices lock into the wall and the mana elevator halts.

It doesn't take us long to navigate the earthy but orderly halls of the open building and reach Clarrise's lab. She answers the door only a moment after we knock. Her smile is warm and welcoming, radiating genuine joy at our presence. This fades immediately as she looks up and down my body with concern.

"Lillith, you look terrible," she says in greeting.

CHAPTER TEN

Rest

Thanks, you're looking lovely yourself," I reply to a concerned Clarrise, who frowns at me.

"Sorry," she says, a little mortified, "I meant are you all right? If I had a student show up with such a pallor, I'd send them home immediately. Should you be here?"

"I'm all right. Just been getting a little too much sun lately; it's left me drained," I lie.

"None of that," she says with a stern look. "I know an exhausted woman when I see one. I know a sick woman when I see one too. I'm a teacher—do you think I can't tell when someone is working themselves too hard?"

I think back to my grad school professors and my own experience teaching, and genuinely don't know how to respond. In my experience, the answer is *depends*.

"I told her she needed to rest more, but you know how she is," Sara laments, and I give her a narrow-eyed look of betrayal.

"I'll sleep when I'm dead," I repeat. "Besides, I'm alive, awake, alert, and enthusiastic. In the flower of my youth, really."

Sara actually glares at me when I say this and I immediately feel guilty.

"This isn't a joke, Lillith. You'll kill yourself if you keep pushing like this," Clarrise scolds me, and I close my eyes for a minute. I guess it does look like that from the outside. But I just . . . I can't linger on this. I'm only halfway to anywhere worth going and I can't stop now.

"I know. I don't think it's a joke, but laughing moves me forward, and we have to move forward. Can we talk about this later, please?" I beg. Sara and Clarrise share a look, but Clarrise nods.

"Well. All right, but I reserve the right to bring it up again," she says. "Come on in, I'll make you some tea."

I sigh in relief before following her into her apartment. It's strange to me, the walls made entirely of magically formed earth. Plants from the terraces outside grow through the windows and I could pick fruit from the dining room table if I reached. The expected inconveniences of such a design are entirely mitigated by the building's nature. Effective combat magic takes massive amounts of mana because, without that, a much stronger opponent can crush any spells with brute force.

But practically applied magic? Heating in a stone building? Pest control? Generation of clean water? Most of this can be handled with magically enchanted items alone. Even brand-new mages are capable of maintaining a higher quality of living than most nobles in Potestia were tolerating. A thought I find endlessly frustrating. It's true the nobles are used to the comforts of free labor. It's also true most of the greatest minds in the country have probably always died as slaves or commoners with no magic. But even so, Potestia is an old, old country. Maintaining power, as motives go, is not an unfamiliar one to me.

But usually, those in power do like shiny new toys and luxuries. As I take in the neat, well-tended environment of Clarrise's room, it can't be denied. I feel like I am in an air-conditioned apartment on Earth. This community has been here for a relative speck on the timeline of Potestia, and it has, with relative ease, surpassed the comfort of the wealthiest noble's mansion. Nearly every community has, in fact. Although this one is certainly on the forefront. Because we have fucking magic! Why any country with access to literal magic would be locked into a medieval society for thousands of years is beyond me. It takes a fraction of the knowledge Earth had to achieve similar technological results, at least for the basics.

No one is designing a microchip in the next couple of years, but that doesn't matter. It's better than Earth, in fact. Mana is a completely clean, renewable energy source that is more efficient than electricity ever was. Hell, even if we need electricity, we can just generate some. It is just . . . asinine that people are freezing to death on the streets in a magical world. It infuriates me. And it fucking confuses me. The way resources are perfectly placed around cities yet merchants still sell them as luxuries, the lack of even simple progress for so long . . . everything. The country feels like a still photo of a movie set. Everything was perfectly placed and just . . . left that way.

"So, if not your health, to what do I owe the pleasure of your visit?" Clarrise asks, pulling me from my usual, frustrating thoughts as I sit down at her table. She walks to her kitchen and fills an enchanted kettle with an enchanted stone that creates water.

"The usual suspects," I answer while Sara sits next to me and examines me with concern. The poor woman clearly can't think of anything but my health at the moment, which is both endearing and a little distracting. "You seem to be good at making badass things here. I saw a magical prosthetic on the way up. I wanted to see if I could help with research into possible transportation methods. I want to take the burden off Sara as soon as possible."

"Ah, of course. Well . . . it's not terrible, truth be told. Your ideas for most vehicles have . . . varied in their plausibility, although we have been waiting for your help to test a couple safely. But they have the same problems they always have," she explains.

I sigh. The first problem is, of course, geography. We don't actually *know* where each community is on the globe. This, predictably, makes it difficult to arrange travel plans even if the trains I described are built correctly. And of course, they will be slower than magic-hell-forest teleportation even if we manage to implement them. Finally, they will take years to implement. By the time we have them, the reliance on Sara will be far less intense anyway, as most communities will be entirely self-sufficient.

"Right. I'm trying my best with the stars, but it's not really my area of expertise. I don't suppose the kid has made any progress, has he? What was his name, Victor?" Clarrise grimaces and Sara perks up.

"I can help if Victor is stuck. While I'm here," she suggests, as usual. Sarafyna is really the only person with any concept of what Victor, a former priests' apprentice, is trying to do. Because what we really need right now are teleportation gates of some kind. A way to travel instantly between communities without an eldritch horror looking over your shoulder. And without relying entirely on one extremely adorable *and* sexy hatter. "Why are you looking at me like that?" Sara asks with a blush as I admire her instead of answering right away.

"Oh, uh, right," I respond, blushing a bit myself. "I think that's what we'll have to do. Sorry to keep relying on you so much, Sara. I know you need rest as much as I do."

Sara shakes her head emphatically at this.

"No, I'm happy to. Genuinely. I can't even describe to you how happy I am to do all of this!" she insists. I give her a half-affectionate, half-feigned-skeptical look, then smile softly. I don't know why working her ass off makes her happy, but she is obviously being genuine.

"Well. Thank you, Sara. I don't know what we would do without you. If you're sure you are up to it, yeah, let's go see if you can help the kid out," I suggest.

Clarrise raises an eyebrow at me and Sara crosses her arms.

"Lily, you should stay and rest. We'll be all right without you," Sara suggests.

I scowl. This is going to get old quickly. "I have neither the time nor the luxury to be treated like porcelain. I know you are all worried about me, but I'm really all right. We have treatment handled and I am ready to get back into it. People need me to get back into it. Starting a fire only helps if it's a controlled burn, and—"

"Lily, I love you," Sara interrupts, "and I love your little speeches, but we don't need one right now. We are just asking you to rest while you can, all right? I'm not going to hold you back where you can help, but . . . what are you going to contribute here? Yeah, you are brilliant but . . . this isn't something you can provide much input on, at least not yet. Why do you need to overwork yourself now, in this moment?"

I want to retort, but I'm left without much of a comeback. She's right. There isn't much I can do right now. I don't understand what the Radiant Woods feels like to Sara, and I have no idea how divine magic works.

"I'll motivate you. I'll sing you a song while you think, to help you focus," I joke.

Sara's face immediately pales and she bites her lip. "Um, no, thank you . . . We'll, uh . . . we'd better get going, Clarrise. Lily, enjoy some time to yourself maybe."

Clarrise looks confused while Sara stands, and I scowl.

"Fine, I'll sing to myself, then." I pout.

Sara freezes, then leans in toward me. "Uh, Annie . . . you are joking, right?" she whispers. "People share walls in this building; Clarrise has neighbors . . . Wouldn't it be better to lie down for a bit?"

I narrow my eyes at her. I swear, you try to sing "Simple and Clean" around a girl one time and suddenly she discovers a new form of PTSD. It's not my fault. My hair is wavy instead of curly and black instead of brown, my eyes are red, and I'm shorter than ever. How was I supposed to know tone deafness was going to be the one thing I carried between realities?

"Yeah, yeah, I get it. Go ahead, I won't gift Clarrise's neighbors with my heavenly voice, I promise," I respond, and genuine, visible relief washes over my traitorous girlfriend.

"Right, well. Uh . . . Take care, Lily," she says more loudly. She leans forward for a quick kiss, then turns toward the door. Clarrise lags behind, gaping at us, and I realize I haven't actually told anyone in this community about our relationship yet. Sara immediately begins to blush and it dawns on me that we don't generally do that in front of anyone. The kiss in the middle of the other town must have knocked that wall down a little. I curl my lips in amusement and Sara coughs. "A-anyway, we should go, Clarrise. I want to get Lily back home and into bed as soon as possible."

I should resist. It would be kind to resist. But she is very cute when flustered. "Oh, do you?" I tease. Her face burns at the implication and Clarrise joins her.

"Uh—right, we . . . should . . . go . . ." the still-confused Clarrise agrees.

The two finally leave, and I laugh out loud. I needed that, just a little. Clarrise will be fine after processing for a moment; it's not like this is the first major change she has witnessed since, well, I killed her husband. With that, however, I'm left a bit lost. I'm not actually all that tired. I'm serious when I say I'm feeling better and fully combat ready. Sleeping all day is just going to make me anxious. Sara might not need my help, but . . . Well, I'd love to take a look at what other wonders they have put together since my last visit. I want to see how those prosthetics work.

I throw back another dose of the foul potion Henry made for me and head out myself, looking to find a meal and see what I can examine in the common area downstairs.

CHAPTER ELEVEN

Divine Inspiration

Sarafyna

The walk to Victor's lab is . . . awkward. I can feel my cheeks burning almost as constantly as I can feel Clarrise's eyes on me. I have been unraveling in a way, lately. Or maybe I'm doing the opposite. Maybe I have always been unraveled and am only now taking shape. It would perhaps be the more appropriate metaphor, considering how I met my, uh, girlfriend. I spent a long time in that hell. A long time hating myself, and a longer time losing myself. My mind had followed my body, melting into something hideous to behold, barely forming thoughts for a single task.

These last few years can't erase that. But Annie is always there. It's like she never took her hand off me after piecing me back together. She has been helping me find my way ever since. But I'm still . . . discovering things about myself. I'd never even heard of two women courting before I met her. I'd always failed to work up any interest in marriage before, but I thought I just wasn't interested in romance. At the same time, when I met an attractive woman, I have always immediately wanted her to like me, or wanted to be just like her. Until I heard Annie on the other side of that door, I thought I just . . . admired them. The realization of the reality hit me like a brick and I'm still working through it.

I love courting Annie, but I don't know how to act. I don't know how to move forward. It's all like shaping mud. I just can't get a hold of it, and it's confusing and frustrating when I try. Of course, my feelings for Annie aren't the only confusing things in my life. I have my dad back. I have a son now, in a way. I'm not exactly sure how that happened, but it did. It was just like when I heard Annie talking about me. The first time Pete called me *Mom*, I felt so happy I could barely respond. I'm really, really unprepared for the role, but my dad is there to help.

It's all amazing and it's all terrifying. I essentially grew up in hell. How am I supposed to give Peter what he needs? How am I supposed to talk to my father when our time apart comes up and his face goes dark? Forget working through my sexuality; I can't even figure out who Sarafyna is supposed to be. I want to blame the Radiant Woods, but recently, I have been doubting that. I think I have always struggled with this. Annie hasn't noticed yet, or if she has, she hasn't said anything, but my clothes are getting a little baggy. My body is changing again.

Not like it did in the Radiant Woods, but . . . I'm growing a bit slimmer, a little at a time. Not skinnier exactly, but less curvy. It's not enough that anyone but me would notice . . . yet. This startled me at first, like I was losing control of my divine magic. My divine magic, which has never worked like I want it to. But . . . I'm not sure that's true. I think it might work exactly as I want it to. Or exactly as some part of me wants it to. My scars come and go, or so my loved ones insist. They are usually there, and they are always there when I look in the mirror. That was my first clue.

I was always a pretty girl. Prettier than any of my neighbors. And I grew up to be the perfect woman, physically at least. With my mother's hair and a figure without flaw. More accurately, a figure without any of the flaws I spent my life worrying about. As a girl, I thought I was lucky. I would hear my neighbor complain of love handles and mine would fade. I would hear a boy talk about a woman's chest and mine would start to develop in the same way. I would see a woman I "admired" and, the next day, notice a beauty mark on my face in the same spot she had. Extraordinary luck, to skip every flaw and develop every desired trait.

Then I fell in love with Annie. A slim, if muscular, woman with a boyish build. And my body slowly started to grow slimmer. Not right when I met her. When I realized she was beautiful. When I realized I "admired" her like I had those women I grew up around. It's funny how my relationship with Annie opened my eyes to this. I didn't grow up to be "the perfect woman." I grew up to be *my* perfect woman. The woman I had, either through my own taste or others' criticisms, believed was perfect. Now I am enamored with an entirely different kind of woman and my body is complying.

It's my divine magic, understanding the thought *I want to be her* and acting. But that doesn't feel right either. Because going from an old ideal to Annie isn't what I need to do. I need to figure out who I am actually supposed to be. Or want to be. I don't want to shift to a new fantasy appearance for myself. I need to figure out what makes me comfortable. Until a week ago, that was my primary concern. But now Annie is sick, and my divine magic won't cure her. Like it won't cure my scars. Like *I* won't cure my scars. If everything I have been figuring out is true, does that mean I am, on some level, holding back my help from her? Have I always been?

Annie thinks she is putting too much on me. But she is putting too much on herself. I love feeling needed. I love having direction. And I hate the thought that, when she needs me most, part of me is holding back. So I am going to figure out how to create safe transportation for everyone. For her. And maybe, by working through that problem, I'll figure out how to actually control my supposedly divine magic. When I do, I will throttle this sickness that's tormenting my Annie. And maybe I'll throttle Annie a bit too, if she doesn't take it seriously until then. Yeah, she is feeling better. But I had to find her, passed out and helpless. I had to get her into her bed and find help. And I can feel the tumor's malignance when she guides my power to it.

It's more serious than she is letting on. I can feel it. I can see the little shadow of fear behind her smiling eyes. I can hear it in her flippant jokes. She may be back in fighting shape, as she insists, but she is terrified. Well, she can put the whole world on my shoulders if it'll take even a little weight off hers. I have lost a woman to sickness before, and she tried to spare me from her fear too. It's not going to happen again.

"Are you . . . all right?" Clarrise asks, and I startle. Somehow I spiraled all the way from *Oh no, I kissed a girl in public* to *the most important woman in my life is killing herself with responsibility again.*

"Yes, sorry. I just . . . have a lot on my mind," I assure her.

The kind but often severe face of the older woman softens.

"Worried about Lillith, huh?" she guesses.

I wince, definitely blushing again. "Obvious, huh?"

She gives me a gentle smile. "I don't know what's going on with her, and I don't know what kind of relationship you two have. But I know stubborn people well enough. You're lucky that yours is also a decent person. But, eventually, she is going to push too hard." Her smile shifts to a serious stare. "You'll want to confront her before that happens. Trust me, even well-intentioned stubbornness has to run into the word *stop* or it'll get away from the person. And it has to be stern. And the longer you wait, the harder it will be."

I don't respond, instead just looking forward and thinking about her words. I'll stop Annie before she pushes too hard. I have to. But first, I'll try to ensure that she doesn't have to.

With that, we make it to another earthy apartment, and Clarrise opens the door without knocking. This one lacks the various vines and foliage entering through the windows, favoring cleanliness for experimentation. Victor, the older boy I once helped free from the temple's basement, appears to be meditating. Clarrise holds a hand up to stop me from speaking, and we wait for a few minutes for him to open his eyes.

Finally, he does. His focused face shifts to one of curiosity, then relief. "Sarafyna! I was hoping you would visit soon! Where were we last time? You said everywhere feels like the same place? Can you elaborate on that more?" He immediately interrogates me in lieu of a greeting. I would be surprised if I hadn't visited him a few times by now. He seems to always pick up conversations from days or even weeks earlier as if they never ended.

"I can try, but . . . can I ask you a few of my own questions first?" I reply. We have been discussing the nature of divine magic and the way space feels to me inside the Radiant Woods. But today, I want him to be the one to describe it to me. He pouts a little but crosses his arms and nods.

"Sure, what did you want to ask?"

"I'll leave you two to it," Clarrise says as a way to excuse herself. She may be an academic, but she seems to like quantifiable numbers far more than talk of divine magic. I wave politely but my focus remains on Victor. I really want to get to the bottom of my divine magic.

"Right. So, you didn't have divine magic until the priests did their ritual, right?" I ask, confirming the difference between us.

"That's right. As far as I know, I couldn't do much at all before that, much less use divine magic," he answers easily.

"Are you sure? I've come to a realization recently. I think I've been using it a lot longer than I thought. My whole life maybe, or at least since my mom . . . Well, since I was a kid. Long before I even knew what it was. Are you sure you haven't as well?"

He shakes his head before I even finish. "Nope, I remember the moment I got it. It was like an alarm in my head. Or maybe a set of instructions? It felt like a pull that had never existed before," he responds, then leans forward in interest. "What have you been using it for, do you think? Are you sure you can use it subconsciously? No, of course you can. Lillith says you periodically remove your scars. How does that work, I wonder?"

"That's what I'm trying to figure out. Has your divine magic ever, I don't know . . . ignored you? Or done anything you didn't try to do but kind of . . . wanted to do? Or vice versa?" I prod, and he shrugs.

"I don't think mine works anything like yours, I'm afraid. I have no control over the Radiant Woods, for one. That could be a lack of exposure, but based on your descriptions, I don't think that's the case. For me, and for everyone but you who I've spoken to, divine magic sort of operates itself. There are a few things we can do really, really well, but we can't do much else. Most of these things are related to healing and altering perception. They all came with the package too; I knew how to do all of them as soon as I got my magic. The way you describe it . . . it sounds far more versatile, but also far more difficult to use," he explains.

I frown. "Are we sure that we are even using the same kind of magic?"

"Oh yes, I can feel it. You feel like the Radiant Woods," he says, then as I recoil he quickly corrects himself. "Not exactly, but . . . the energy is the same. To put it in simple, if crass, terms . . . you are like water and the woods are like piss. But your energy ebbs and flows the same way." So far Victor is the only divine mage who can actually perceive the feeling of divine magic, and that's fairly recent. He works with and studies it far more than any of the other former priests' apprentices. This news feels strange though.

"What do the others feel like? The ones who got divine magic the same way you did?"

He wrinkles his nose. "Like the Radiant Woods, truth be told. I think it's because we got our power from the woods, but you already had yours."

"So . . . perhaps my divine magic is mine, but yours belongs to the Radiant Woods?" I guess.

"It's a good theory," he agrees. "And it would explain why ours seems to follow a script yours doesn't. But there is no way to test it."

"That's true," I say. "I was just thinking . . . if my magic is unique, and yours is tied to the Radiant Woods, why am I the one who can control them? I can grow large plants and trees from the woods with only a single flower or a piece of bark. I can . . . absorb bits of the woods and increase my own divine magic. I can move through them freely and even fight them directly. Yet my magic feels clean and yours feels just like the woods? Why is that?"

Victor's eyes widen as he considers the implication. "Oh," he says quietly. "Why didn't I think of that?"

CHAPTER TWELVE

Relationships

What do you think you are doing, young lady?" a stern voice reprimands me.

I freeze, then put down the goggles I am tinkering with and turn to see a glaring Clarrise.

"You told Sara you would rest! You should have seen the look on her face as I walked her to the lab. And I find you here, working!"

I wince as a few onlookers at nearby tables give me sympathetic glances. I'm in something of a communal research center on the first floor. Clarrise has set up a number of stations stocked with paper, something not unlike fountain pens, and other tools for magic experimentation. This particular community thrives on sharing and supporting knowledge. This room is where a lot of it happens.

I had come here just to see if anyone was working on anything interesting. I had a friendly conversation with the kid whose extremely cool prosthetic had caught my attention earlier and . . . had a thought. "Hold on, I'm innocent, I swear!" I protest, and she glares at me.

"Okay. So you are courting a woman. It took me off guard, and she was right there, so I didn't say anything." I get varied looks when she says that, and one woman blushes at least as red as Sara does, but Clarrise doesn't notice. "But I've thought about it now. And you know what? Courting is courting. And it only works if both of you respect each other. It does not work if we make promises that we break as soon as the other person turns their back. I've seen where that leads, and it's nowhere good. So tell me, are you innocent, or did you lie to that poor girl and break a promise the second she left the room?"

The question hits me like a slap in the face.

I just came to take a look. I wasn't pushing myself. I had an idea that would help with my illness—I was actually helping to relieve her stress, not add to it. All these protests press against my lips but fail to escape. I didn't exactly lie, but I wasn't honest either. Or at least, I abandoned an honest interpretation of our conversation pretty quickly. "Well, shit," I say instead, and Clarrise crosses her arms.

"That sounds right. You promised to rest, now come with me and rest," she insists. I really want to finish what I'm doing, but I suppose I can talk to Sara first. It's not like she is going to actually hold me back here. I should have just waited, but I've never been much good at that. I nod and pick up the goggles, along with the circle I have been drawing for them. Clarrise raises an eyebrow at me. "Still bringing them with you?"

"She'll want to know what I'm working on. But I promise, for real this time, I won't touch them until I've spoken with Sara," I say. She looks at them in my hands and I roll my eyes. "You know what I mean. Come on, let's get back before she does, at least."

She gives me a derisive sniff but nods.

"What are they, anyway? It looked like you were drawing light runes, but don't you already have goggles enchanted with light magic?"

"No. Well, yes, but these are different. These are for my can—my sickness," I explain.

"You are planning to treat it with light goggles?" she guesses sarcastically while waiting for the real explanation.

"No, it's a bit late for that. But one of the most likely causes of this disease is various types of invisible light. These goggles will make those ones visible."

"And you will be able to find the source," she finishes. "That makes sense, I suppose, aside from your certainty that you have some as-yet-unheard-of light-based disease. Where do you get these ideas from? Some of the things you say are a little . . ."

"Out of this world?" I guess, to a shrug and a nod. "It's a long story. Well, depending. For all intents and purposes, it's a long story. But trust me. If we find somewhere with a lot of this light, we'll find what made me sick."

"And avoid anyone else getting it?" I nod. "Well. I see why you were in a hurry to build it. Still. It hurts, you know? When someone you love tells you one thing and does another. I've never met a kinder woman than Sarafyna, and if your relationship is as . . . unique as it appears, it will only hurt more. Take it from me."

I feel a little pang of regret.

"You're right, it does. I just . . . hate being treated as fragile, and I have a lot to do. Sara and I just need to have an actual discussion about ground rules. But don't worry, I'm taking your words to heart," I say. I shouldn't have needed to be told that, but I haven't been in a relationship in a really long time. In a way, it feels like my first. In a way, it is. Which makes it easy to make a few rookie mistakes. Unlike my life as Annie, where I was completely without fault in all my relationships, romantic and otherwise. Right. The point is, I understand what she means. I need to be upfront with Sara.

This doesn't mean I can slow down like Sara would like. But I understand this fucking cancer sort of ambushed us. It's not going to be an easy transition or a simple topic. It is, however, something we, for now, have under control. And Sarafyna didn't fall for me because of my quiet demeanor.

"And here I had heard you didn't have such a thing," Clarrise jabs, her stern exterior beginning to crack.

"Such a thing as what?" I ask, a little distracted.

"A heart," she quips.

"Completely untrue." I chuckle. "I have a heart. It just lacks a little work ethic, that's all." This earns a half smile as we finally make our way past the other tool-laden tables and focused workers. My still heart has been something of a hot topic around this particular community. It and my other enhancements. Clarrise, having said her piece, is mostly quiet as we ride the elevator back up to her floor. She does ask me about my cool hat, with somewhat less polite phrasing. Before long we are back in her home and I am, as promised, lying down on her bed while she examines the half-designed circle I brought with me.

"Isn't this usually how you alter a light's color?" she asks. "I'm failing to see how it's making you sick . . ."

"I'm resting, Clarrise," I intone without opening my eyes. I can, nevertheless, feel her unamused glare in my direction.

"I don't believe that for a second," Sara's voice interjects, and I'm on my feet in a moment.

"Sara, you're back, how did it go?" I ask happily.

"Welcome back, Sarafyna," Clarrise says without looking up from the paper on her table.

"What's she looking at?" Sara asks, and I grimace a bit.

"Oh, I was just trying to design some radiation-vision goggles. I mean, I guess my other goggles are already doing exactly that, but this time I'm looking for worse radiation. I want to see if what happened to me is happening to anyone else," I answer honestly. No point in lying; we are going to need to talk about it anyway. Sara's face looks . . . conflicted.

"Well, all right" is all she says. She doesn't seem pleased that I immediately started working on something when she left, but she is far from angry. I can feel a cold grief radiating from her, one that has been leaking out in intervals since I woke up and found the tumors. But her face has her telltale signs of guilt fighting for control.

"Uh . . . so, how did work with Victor go?" I ask. Her face immediately brightens and the ice of her sorrow begins to melt.

"I don't think the Radiant Woods are the Collector," she announces. She and I have more or less been referring to them as the same entity for years now, so this is surprising.

"I can see why that makes you so happy," I joke. "I certainly wouldn't want one god to feel lonely on the guillotine . . ."

"No, that's the thing, I don't think it's intelligent at all! Oh, I'm sorry, are we bothering you, Clarrise?" she asks.

"No, no," Clarrise says. "Please, talk heresy all you like, I'll be looking at this for a while. Do let me know if Lillith wants to share the source of these ideas though . . ."

"Anyway," I say, "you don't think the evil hell forest that mutates people and taunted you for a decade is intelligent. I mean, I can see your point, but . . ."

"Right. Thank you, Clarrise! Anyway, I was thinking about how my divine magic works. How can it control the Radiant Woods as well as it can? Why can I wrestle the woods away from itself, move through it with ease, and grow bits of it wherever I want?" Sara says.

"I don't really know, but divine magic kind of plays by its own rules. I take it you have a theory though?" I ask, and I start biting a thumbnail in thought.

"I don't think it's a god or anything like that. I think it's just a place. A place with a lot of divine magic cast on it. I think the Collector, or some other monster, lives there. But I don't think they own it. I think they use it the same way you and I do. As a tool," she explains.

"That makes sense. So that means . . ." I trail off, offering her the chance to say whatever it is she is so excited to tell me.

"It's hard to describe. Like explaining the feeling of mana to someone without it. But . . . with divine magic, a shift in perspective feels like a shift in power. Until now, I have thought of it in the way you described it. Using the enemy's weapons against them. And for Victor, that's exactly what it feels like. Because he was given his magic by whatever lives in the Radiant Woods. But the idea that it's not the enemy's weapon . . . the idea that it is no one's, or even mine in a way . . ." She pauses for a moment and I look at her in anticipation. "Well, I have been growing bits of the Radiant Woods because it's what I know. But . . . what if it doesn't have to be *the* Radiant Woods? What if I can just grow *a* radiant wood?"

My eyes widen. "Do you . . . think you can do that?" Clarrise is looking up at her as well, the conversation suddenly more interesting than my radiation circle.

"I mean, it didn't work when I tried it with Victor, but . . . I don't know. It was like with the whisper spheres. Even now I can't tell you how they work. Just that . . . once I could feel them being enchanted . . . once I knew they could work, they did. I might not need the Radiant Woods. If I'm right, it doesn't have to be woods at all. It can be anything," she says.

"But . . . the Radiant Woods are, to put it delicately, fucking massive. That's a lot of divine magic. And you said it doesn't belong to whatever god or king or fuckface lives in it. If his doesn't belong to him, why would yours belong to you?" I challenge her.

"See, I was afraid this would happen. It's so hard to quantify. I think, whatever the Radiant Woods are, it was already there," Sara says. "I think the Collector moved in and started using it, but it can be changed by anyone with divine magic. But . . . I don't know. I feel like it must have come from somewhere. I just feel it. And . . . I don't need an endless forest to torture thousands of victims. I just need . . . a medium-sized room . . ." I'm starting to see why she is so excited. I don't know how divine magic works, but if she feels this hopeful . . .

"Sara, you are fucking amazing," I say, bridging the gap and hugging her. "That would be amazing. Do you really think you can do it?"

"I don't know. It didn't work when I tried, but Victor seems hopeful. And it feels right somehow . . . Lillith, I want to stay here for a bit. I want to live here while we work on it." This statement sounds more like a question. "Well, I want us to live here while I work on it."

A smile creeps over my face.

"All right, that sounds like a good idea. There are certainly enough rooms. We'll have to talk to our families about moving everyone when we get back from Tumult tonight," I say in thought. "Clarrise, this is the third floor of building one, right? I don't suppose the twelfth unit is empty, is it?"

Before Clarrise can answer, Sara interjects. "Actually, I was thinking you and I could share— Wait, you still want to go into the city tonight? Lillith, you always end up fighting someone when that happens. Usually a lot of someones! Are you really in shape for an actual fight to the death right now?"

"No rest for the wicked," I reply a little guiltily. "The people in Potestia need a fighting chance. You and I are the only ones who can offer them one. We have to, especially with the state we left the country in." Her hopeful mood melts away and she sighs, rubbing her forehead with one worried hand.

"All right, fine. But we are bringing your brother with us this time," she insists, her tone inviting anything but argument.

Self-Awareness and Other Irritations

So, what do I need to do, exactly?" Ed asks as we walk down the beach, approaching the Radiant Woods.

"Just backup today," I answer. "I'm still a little under the weather, so we just want to have our bases covered if we need to fight again today." I take another drink of the vile concoction Henry made for me. The tumors haven't grown at all and remain manageable, but if I want them to consistently shrink, I have to keep up with every form of treatment.

"Sounds a bit like you aren't quite as confident in your recovery as you have been saying," Ed muses, and Sara nods along. The two dozen or so volunteers pulling carts alongside us look away in innocence as if they haven't been listening in.

"Even if I were in perfect health, we were going to need to divide the labor eventually. There are a lot of cities in Potestia and a lot of people who don't feel safe anymore. That's all this is, all right? Getting you ready to go on runs like this alone. Besides, don't pretend you haven't been dying to use all that magic you spent so long learning," I say, and Ed takes his own turn looking away innocently. He was one of the more stubborn mages, staying in his circle for months rather than weeks. Since he had fewer dispersal runes than mine, this makes him something of a formidable mage.

He hasn't had the continuously growing mana that I have, but in many ways, the circle I use for others is superior to my own. Magically, at least. Even after all this time, I have been unable to identify the cause of my physical enhancements. Nevertheless, Ed is surprisingly competent for a first-generation mage. Barring some kind of special circumstance, he would eat Hugh alive if they ever fought. All this together makes him an excellent choice for support. The cancer is just a good excuse to finally get him some experience.

"Actually, I wanted to talk about that," Ed says, rubbing the back of his neck nervously.

"Your eagerness to use cool magic? We can talk about that if you want," I say.

"No, not that," he groans. "I mean . . . dividing the labor. Look, you're sick. We don't know what caused it, but we know you are. And I figure, taking on some of the load for you could . . . I don't know. Make up for some choices I have made in the past," he begins.

I pause, turning to look at him. I notice a few volunteers look away in a sudden and unnatural way. Yeah, all right, pretend you're looking at the waves. Whatever, we aren't discussing anything too sensitive. I ignore them and focus on my brother. "I mean, I am happy to have you help. You know I'll take any volunteers I can get. But you don't have to do it for me . . . You and I are good, Ed. The bad blood has spilled. The hatchet is buried. You should come with me because you want to change things, not just for me . . ." My worry seeps into my voice. It's impossible to avoid, but I'd really rather no one risk their life just out of loyalty to me. I especially don't want anyone risking their life to make up for being a bit of a dick as a kid.

"No, not with you, it's not . . . Look. I have, in the past, been something of a coward. I want to make things better, and I want to do that by taking the load off you a bit."

I shrug. "Well, all right, then. Like I said, you were always going to eventually. I can't be the only person protecting people when we try to aid these cities. I can't even always be there, not if I am going to handle the capital as well," I say, a bit confused by his clear anxiety.

"Right. That's sort of the thing," he replies sheepishly. "You're really sick. You'd have to be, to drink that bottle of cruelty Henry devised . . . And based on what you said, Visenar is dangerous . . . for you. In a sense, you are the worst person to go back there. I think . . . I think I should be the one to handle the capital for now."

I freeze. I feel Sara approach, preparing to back my brother up. Apparently the volunteers aren't the only eavesdroppers. I pretend not to notice, responding to Ed before Sara can cut in. "Ed . . . you have a kid on the way. You have a family counting on you. Visenar is the most dangerous city in Potestia, and you have no combat experience. You can't seriously want to go there, where the most powerful mages in the country are fighting?"

Ed sets his jaw and crosses his arms. "They are counting on me for what, exactly?" he throws back. "Mariah loves me, yes. But she doesn't need me to survive. She can do everything I can, and at home, people don't exactly need a breadwinner like they do in Potestia. They don't need me, they just love me. And people love you too, Lily. For every danger in that city, it is more dangerous for you. Yeah, you are a badass, I get it. You are the monster hiding under the nobles' beds. But that's why the entire city has been rigged against you. Like it or not, someone else needs to do this for you."

"He's right, Lily," Sara cuts in. "If everything is as bad in Visenar as you claim, if it is actually filled with dispersal circles targeting you specifically, you may just be the weakest piece we can play."

"And if that's where I got the cancer? If the whole point is to draw out my friends and loved ones? What if the circles aren't targeted at just me?" I say.

Ed lets a sharp breath out his nose and Sara rubs her temples, then says, "Now you're just being stubborn. You saw a bard using magic, didn't you? You know those circles are for you. They can't target everyone but still use magic themselves. As for your other points, well, you aren't the only one who is allowed to take risks.

We could spend all day talking about what-ifs, but we have to find out somehow, and your brother is right. You shouldn't be the one to do it. And people love you too. Besides, you literally just started designing those goggles specifically to avoid anyone else getting sick."

I want to argue further but I already know they are right.

I don't even know why the idea bothers me so much. I have sent other people to take risks before. Sara went to the church on her own the first time, and she helped me fight two of the most dangerous people in the country. The most incompetent of the dangerous people in the country, but it was a risk all the same. Even now I am bringing people to a city whose rulers are hostile to them. I look at my brother, then my girlfriend. I see the concern in both their eyes, and it dawns on me.

They aren't asking if Ed can go risk his life in Visenar. They know I won't stop him. If both of them decide he is going to do that, well, he is going to. No, they are asking me not to risk myself. It's not just about the risk to either of them. It's about letting someone take on a risk so I will be safer. That's what bothers me. There is a certain arrogance in that idea I don't much like the look of. Because I might want to believe it is safer for me to go, but they are right. The city is currently built around repelling me. I haven't been anywhere so desperate to get rid of me specifically since Christmas at my dad's house during my first year of college.

Edward is a better choice to go and investigate the circles in the capital than I am. Even more frustrating than this realization is its failure to change how I feel about it. I still would rather go than send Ed, and it still feels like the smarter choice. Which means that arrogance is deep-seated enough to resist self-awareness. Not an attractive look on anyone, and the thought makes me wince.

"Ugh," I reply with irritation, "fine, I will stay away from the capital. But please, be careful. And wait to go until we can plan the safest way to do so, please."

"Yeah, sure," Ed agrees. "Thank you. For trusting me." His satisfied smile is almost enough to banish my irritation but not entirely. I don't much care for being wrong, knowing I am wrong, and still feeling right. I can handle one or the other, but the flavor combination of both curdles in my stomach. My bad mood persists as we enter the forest and then, after the briefest flash, find ourselves emerging underground. I keep it to myself, where sour moods born of stubbornness belong.

Before we head into the city, Sara and I examine everyone. We don't find it likely, and Sara has experimented a bit the last couple of days, but we want to make sure the woods aren't responsible for the cancer. They do have a history of changing people's bodies in undesirable ways, after all.

As expected, everyone else is cancer-free. In fact, after three trips through the woods today, my tumors haven't grown either. I'm not ready to write them off completely as a potential cause, but it's comforting to know we can still use the woods. That is sort of my motif, after all. Every weapon of the enemy, and all that.

As with every other city we visit, the tension in Tumult is palpable. Every city has seen changes over the last few years. The way different city lords have handled the lack of labor has varied, especially since the only answer to the problem the king ever offered was to demand slaves be sent to the capital. A message that rarely even made it to any cities, what with the limited communication between them.

One theme has remained consistent, however. The lower classes foot the bill. When there are not enough slaves to provide for nobles' needs, the other commoners are enlisted to fill the gap. Most cities like Visenar try to maintain the facade that slavery is a punishment for criminals and simply expand the definition of "criminal" as needed. In some places, this involves creating new laws to target commoners. Others reinterpret current laws or militantly enforce long-forgotten ones. Tumult isn't bothering with the lie. If they need a baker, they send the guards to find and enslave one. If they need a carpenter, they do the same. In a way, this city has one of the most honest lords in the country.

Honesty is a luxury afforded only to the most untouchable of rulers, however. Or the most arrogant. Lord Nathanial of Tumult is the arrogant kind. I could strike a match in this city and it would almost ignite. Almost. A thousand years of fear don't evaporate overnight. Magic solves many problems from my old world, such as clean energy, shelter, and transportation. But it also creates them. Nobles have generations of accumulated mana. They don't need any degree of separation from the common people to feel safe. With all that magic propping them up, they can do whatever they want without fear of effective revolt. They have less to fear from pushing the masses too far. At least, in the short term. Conversely, commoners are even more afraid to confront a noble than they would have been on Earth.

What they are less afraid of, however, is going to a safe and stable home when it is offered. It especially helps when their neighbors come back with the things they need. Food being chief among them, stories being next. Every day more people believe they can have something better, and every day the powers in place prove inaction will only make things worse. Of course, there is pushback as well. Many people want to hold on to the home they grew up in, and rightly so. Others blame the Mage of Mourning for how bad things have gotten, because, well, before me it was only this bad for other people. It's easy to ignore suffering when it is out of sight, out of mind, and most importantly, somebody else's problem.

It is, in a sense, my fault this misery has become more visible. But I'll gladly take the blame from anyone who is looking for someone to pin it on. I'm not exactly looking for friends who would be happy with comfort bought through enslaving someone else. As such, we receive a variety of receptions in town. Many are happy to see us and the supplies we bring, but others swear as we pass by. And of course, there are those who are the most comfortable, least affected, and most furious at the change. These do what they always do: try to contact the guards.

As we have people gathering to collect much-needed food, as all of theirs is being confiscated by the guards and nobility, a street gang not unlike the Manticorps surrounds us. Many expected such gangs to disappear as the need for slaves increased, since they are actual criminals, but this was never going to be the case. These gangs are now what they have always been, an extension of the city guard.

"Now, perhaps it's because I was never schooled properly, but this looks an awful lot like an illegal trade of noble property," a man in a dingy suit announces as I groan and rise to my feet. There is no way this is their real plan. It's hardly the first time we have visited, and they know we have powerful mages with us. I have to keep an eye out for something else while these idiots work through their aggression.

"You're up, Ed," I whisper.

CHAPTER FOURTEEN

Stained Glass

Edward

You're up, Ed," Lillith whispers, and my heart starts beating its way out of my chest. I shouldn't be so nervous. I have been practicing magic for years now, and these idiots don't even have mana. They are here to intimidate the people around me, not me. My little sister could have wiped the floor with them when she was thirteen. But I'm not my little sister. I'm the man who, after planning an escape from thugs just like these with Henry, pushed him over and ran away. Thugs who Lillith later killed herself.

I didn't have my mana yet and Lillith did. But Henry didn't. And Henry wouldn't have run. I did. I hated Lillith so much. Henry too. Both were my younger siblings, and both were so much better at everything than me. I tried to step on them and chase after my father instead. I guess, in running away and leaving scars on my family, I filled my father's shoes just fine. But I don't want to be him anymore. I want to be the reason none of these people have to run away. So I stand up and walk to the front of the crowd. I separate myself from the group and stop a half dozen paces from the man in the dingy suit.

"Hey" is all I say. I want to say something quippy. Something clever, like Lillith would say, but that's what comes out. The man's face splits with a wide grin.

"Are you in charge of this little crime ring? A bit young for thievery, aren't you? It breaks my heart to see it." The man practically drools. I instinctively look behind me for Lillith when he asks if I'm in charge, but . . . she is nowhere to be seen. A drop of sweat immediately runs down my head but I clear my throat.

"I'm not too clear on it either, but I don't think anyone is supposed to be in charge. Sorry to disappoint you," I say.

The gang leader crosses his arms and tilts his head. "Is that so?" he muses. "Well, I was going to make an example of the leader alone and let everyone else disperse. For the public order, you understand. But if there is no leader . . ." He pauses and somehow widens his grin even more. I can smell his breath from where I stand and fail to restrain my wince. "Well, I guess I'll have to make that example out of all of you."

I take a deep breath through my nose and clench my fists. I take a look over my shoulder and see Sarafyna is still there. I can do this.

"That's not going to happen," I respond with all the false confidence I can muster. "But I can give you this opportunity to go away and leave us alone, while you still can." With this, I cast my first spell. Floating shards of glass circle each other over one extended palm. My opponent smirks, and chuckles ripple through the men surrounding us.

"While we still can, huh? Is that it?" He laughs and winks at Sarafyna behind me. "We knew we would run into a couple of mages, kid. You think you're safe just because of a little glass? You aren't the only one with backup. Even in the unlikely event you have the spine to do something with that magic, a dozen knights are a whistle away. You really think your little spells can stand up to an actual mage?"

I start to panic a bit. Lillith disappeared and he's right. I've never fought another commoner, much less multiple trained mages. How did Lily get so good at this so fast?

Something doesn't quite fit, however, and I start to calm, the panic washing away with the confusion the threat inspires. "Uh, why didn't they come here in the first place, then?" I retort. If there are a dozen magic knights to spare on this, why not just . . . use them? What's the point in sending some gang after us? The other man's grin briefly falters as he considers the question himself, but it returns quickly—slightly less confident.

"Because they aren't needed to deal with a child like you. I think we've talked enough. Unfortunately, we'll have to . . . confiscate the stolen goods. Stay out of the way and you won't need to find out why they thought we would be enough for now," he threatens, taking a step forward. I tense up as he moves, but as I look back, Sarafyna nods at me. I have practiced and practiced my magic. I can hold back a few thugs.

I take a deep breath and yell, "Anyone who gets too close will die. Stay back!" With that, I summon wind from all directions and create a sparkling wall of constantly moving air. It arcs past the terrified people around us and a few thugs step back, but the leader sighs and crosses his arms. It looks like he sighs, anyway; this spell is a bit loud, and I can no longer hear him. He gestures to the man next to him, and the moment of truth arrives. The bulky henchman grabs a shorter man next to him by the collar. The two exchange a few words and it looks like the smaller man is protesting, but to no avail.

The larger man throws his weaker companion directly at me and into the wind wall to test how dangerous it is. The wind itself doesn't act as a barrier, however, as much as the sparkling light inside it. Or rather, the sparkling shards of glass swirling through it. Before the man reaches me, the glass tears into him as the wind throws his body around. It's seconds before he is unrecognizable as his blood sprays across me. I don't know what happens. My spell is down, I'm on my knees, and emptying my stomach onto the dirt road. What's left of the smaller gang member falls in front of me and my head spins. He is still recognizably human, but I'm not sure if that makes it better or worse. I can . . . smell him. The blood and shit.

"Well, would you look at that," the leader gloats. "An impressive spell, to be sure. We'd be in danger if you aimed that at all of us, but . . . it looks like your mana exceeds the abilities of your spine. You don't have the stomach to do that again, do you?" As he laughs, I curse to myself. Lillith was right. Again. She warned me, when I came up with this spell. She told me it wouldn't be as easy to use as I thought, even if I was able to cast it. But she has been doing this since she was a girl . . . How is it so easy for her? I thought she was just looking down on me again. She always has, but I've accepted that. As a kid, I wasn't the kind of brother you look up to.

But she was right. Again. I'm not like her. That was . . . horrible. That was the most horrible thing I have ever seen. The body's eye twitches as I gape at it. How am I supposed to protect these people? I can't do that again! I hadn't even done it the first time, not . . . not on purpose. But my stomach is still twisting from my role in the death. The leader whistles and my eyes widen as I remember his earlier words. A dozen knights are a whistle away. Fuck, I can't fight a dozen other mages! I don't even know how to fight these guys! I clench my fists around the bloodied dirt and close my eyes while I wait for the backup to arrive.

And I wait. And wait. The man hesitantly whistles again and I look up at him. Both of our expressions shift to confused and then blank as everyone realizes there is no backup. I don't know if he was lied to or if it has something to do with Lillith, but they are on their own. *Come on, Ed, you can do this. Your kid sister handled worse than this before you even learned to read properly.* I force myself to my feet. My legs may be trembling, but so are more than a few thugs. I wasn't the only one shaken by the violence of the death we all just witnessed. I can feel my breath shortening, but I summon all the confidence I can. I also start gathering wind mana again, leaving the glass out this time. I only have to defend the people here; I don't have to kill anyone else.

"You're right," I admit. "It's obvious I'm not used to this sort of thing. But it's also obvious your guys aren't as comfortable confronting mages as you thought. And your backup doesn't seem interested in being summoned like a dog. So maybe you should leave us alone, like I suggested."

The man grits his teeth but doesn't back down. "All right. So I don't have backup. But I do have a pretty good eye," he counters, looking at the gentle wind forming around my hands. "And it looks like, while I may have lost my magical reinforcements, you've lost your teeth." He smirks as several of his men realize the sparkle from my previous spell is missing. The quieter sound is a giveaway as well. I don't have much of an answer for that. He's right, and as soon as one person attacks me, it will be clear I am too shaken to be a real obstacle. I feel helpless, but a hand rests on my shoulder.

"It's all right, Ed," Sarafyna whispers. "You're doing great. Remember, I'm here too." I haven't seen Sara fight, but she did help Lillith with the king . . . She must be formidable. Although, if leaning on her would work, they probably wouldn't have needed me in the first place.

"Is this your woman, kid? Did you practice that spell on her face or something?" the leader taunts. "I'll admit you've got some assets, sweetheart, but I'm afraid offering them won't do much good. That face will give me nightmares, no matter what you have under your clothes."

"No," Sarafyna answers sweetly, "I'm not his woman. I'm the teeth you were asking about." With that, her face and neck split open from the front, and rows of sharp teeth line the folds. My face pales and I can't take my eyes off her. I knew she helped people with their bodies and shit, but . . . I'm going to have nightmares about this. I glance behind us and realize she has angled her body so the frightened crowd can't see the display.

"Fuck!" The leader recoils but doesn't run. It's all right though. It was a decent threat and the men nearby start to tremble again. More importantly, a weight lifts from my shoulders. Sarafyna was with Lillith in her fight with the king for a reason. She did this for me, so I would feel safe. I take a deep breath and the intensity of my wind picks up again. I summon shards of glass as well. I won't use it again. I don't think I can. But it makes a more effective threat, especially with the shredded body between the two groups.

There is a tense moment, but a previously quiet member of the gang breaks first. "Screw this," he yells before turning heel and running. For the first time, the leader actually panics as his men start to flee, one at a time, then all at once, and their numbers dwindle. Finally, he is standing alone in front of two people he clearly can't fight. It no longer matters if I have the spine to kill him or not. He is alone, and no one is afraid of him. He glares at both of us, shuddering when he looks at Sarafyna. Then he spits, puts his hands in his pockets, and turns.

"Fine. I did my job, anyway," he says. Then he yells at the crowd. "Don't be surprised if the people here are the only ones they managed to keep safe. I hope you didn't leave anyone you care about back home!" With those words, my eyes widen, and I flip around to see panic in the eyes of the commoners I have been protecting.

CHAPTER FIFTEEN

You Don't Get to Be Cowards

I t's easy enough to slip away while Ed talks to the gang. It's his first time dealing with this sort of thing, but Sara is there. She is sweet and meek a lot of the time, but she definitely has boiling blood underneath it all. The two will be all right. All I had to do was make my way to the back of the crowd, and a little light and sound mana covered me. It's not terribly difficult to sneak past a few street thugs who can't see mana. I don't know exactly where I'm sneaking to, but I am certain the goober in the dirty suit isn't the beginning and the end of the plan to deal with us.

A little upward force mana and my own physical strength allow me to jump to a nearby rooftop, where I lower my goggles and start scanning the roads in the surrounding areas. The average commoner tends to do one of two things whenever we are in town: hide to avoid trouble, or risk it and meet us for the supplies and whisper spheres we distribute. Street traffic is sparser than it once was in any case, since the wrong encounter is so likely to result in slavery now. All this together means that, when my radar spots a couple dozen people walking together a few hundred yards away, it's not exactly a mystery where I need to go.

With the different safe houses across town, each sheltering an access point to the Radiant Woods, I am not lacking in potent mana and am able to effortlessly fly from building to building. I am . . . slightly slower than I have been in the past. A girl only needs to collide with one rooftop before she learns a little caution. Before each leap, I extend a thin strand of grief mana to see if it disperses. It will make me a bit more visible to any mages keeping watch, but it also helps avoid any ambushes by snarky bards. It doesn't slow me down much, however, and even with my goggles up, I can soon see the group I spotted. Each is wearing the flexible mail armor of a magic knight, confirming my suspicions.

As I crouch on a roof across the road from the knights, my stomach churns a bit. I have trouble identifying the cause. Unfortunately, not because my health is so stellar but because there are competing sources. I have, over the years, grown used to the illness induced in me by powerful grief mana, since I am nearly always near the Radiant Woods in some form or another. Growing used to it is different from growing comfortable with it, however. It does still get to me.

This is, honestly, a relief. An unpredicted side effect of aspecting grief is that I have started to grow more numb to the feeling. It's not just grief mana, truth be told. Anything, once it becomes normal and expected, also grows acceptable. Or at least accepted. That includes the intense grief that saturates this world. The occasional urge to vomit when I'm hit with a wave of it keeps me grounded. Reminds me that I should never get too comfortable with it. Even worse, it empowers me. This allows me to act on behalf of the grieving, but . . . it also carries the very real risk of attaching a positive association to it. This is something I have found myself feeling at times. Relieved to have the power of grief nearby. That alone makes me sick to think about.

So it's good to feel that queasiness from time to time. As a reminder that all this grief is a symptom of a sickness in the world, and the power it grants exists to eradicate the source. Of course, I now have other concerns. The fucking cancer. And just like on Earth, the treatment doesn't make me feel like sunshine and rainbows. That potion of Henry's is no less sickening than chemotherapy might have been. I don't have time to decide which ailment is assaulting me, however. The knights are standing outside a large brothel, having something of an argument.

"Can't we skip this one?" a lanky knight whines to the irritation of the sturdy knight in the front, who has a blue ribbon around one shoulder, identifying him as the captain of the group.

"Look, Gabe," the captain snaps, "if you are feeling lonely, buy some fucking flowers for your wife. Lord Nathanial made it clear. The entire street burns. Every street burns if even one resident meets the rebels. Even your favorite brothel. I'm done with your complaints, now do what you are told before I decide I can spare a few men to shore up the slave shortage!"

Gabe, the lanky knight, straightens quickly enough to convince me this is far from an idle threat. He immediately gathers earth mana and erects stone walls in front of the door and most windows to the brothel. It looks like the plan is to make an example of anyone who agrees to meet me and accept our help. Not surprising, since the combination of the lord's actions and my aid has effectively cut off supplies from the nobility. They are surviving either with what slaves they can capture or by using the threat of slavery to force farmers and the like to produce for them.

But the nobility of this city took away the promise of cooperation. It's a bit like mass punishment in schools; when you can get the stick whether you follow the rules or not, the incentive to follow them disappears. This has always been the case to an extent, but the commoners are far more open about it now. Combine that with the greater communication the whisper spheres provide and the fact that, with aid, the people don't actually need the kingdom's money to live . . . Much of their incentive to provide the goods nobles need to live in comfort and excess is gone.

This violence is, of course, the natural next step. Prove that there are greater things to fear. The loss of loved ones. Violent deaths. Try to instill the distrust the church used to force into the minds of the commoners. Convince people to administer their own punishments, or ostracize anyone who works with me. I'm lucky the lord must have thought it would be most effective to do this while we were here.

He wants anyone who meets with me to return to their dead loved ones and ruined homes. He wants to intrinsically connect the two events in people's minds.

Which is why he bothered with the pitiful distraction while he sent the real threat here. I can practically feel the blood bubbling under my skin at the thought. Fine, Lord Nathanial. You want an example to be made? I can work with that. I'll start by making an example out of any knight who follows orders like this, then I'll move on to demonstrating what happens to men who *give* orders like this. I see fire mana forming around the captain, and I release all my aura at once as I jump from the roof, landing behind the knights.

It has been years since I fully unleashed my aura, and even I am surprised by the weight of it. It's like gravity has increased in the area. Every single knight visibly buckles under the pressure, and a couple fall to one knee. One even collapses entirely as if the wave of mana is physical. Even the captain is tense, struggling to look unaffected. He turns on his heel and the strongest of the knights form a semi-circle around me. Then the captain releases his own aura, enveloping his weaker men in it and allowing everyone to stand. "Impressive. The Mage of Mourning, I take it? I see our little ploy wasn't enough to fool you. That's all right. We expected it might not. Good move with the aura—your mana exceeds expectations. But we are two dozen trained knights. You may be able to fight any one of us with ease, but all of us? You won't hurt a single—"

My lightning descends on him in an instant. Without the dispersal circles and with the grief emanating from safe houses around the city, this spell is easy. With my mana all around us, he didn't even spot the spell forming as he threatened me. He and the two knights closest to him die on the spot, their burnt, crackling corpses collapsing in the dirt. There is a moment of silence. The knights previously protected by his aura begin to struggle again, and the rest stare at their leader's corpse in shock. I want to attack again, but I am immediately assaulted by a sharp pain in my spine. At first, I think a knight must have managed to attack me somehow, but they are all still staring at the corpses by the brothel. Another stabbing pain makes it clear the only attacker is my own fucking body. God dammit.

Before I can examine that, however, all hell breaks loose. These are in fact trained knights. It only takes a moment for them to get into a basic formation, even without a leader. I find myself surrounded by the knights in an L shape. The purpose for this immediately becomes clear as spells from both rows of knights assault me. They are trying to maximize their output while eliminating crossfire. They are also launching powerful spells by combining their aspects, one knight creating fuel for another knight's fire or another using wind to accelerate another's earth. This allows each to use the least amount of mana for the greatest effect.

It won't be enough. I may have been distracted for a moment, but they still aren't any match for the wrath of a thousand years of grief. I use force mana to repel every attack while using air mana to choke any fire. Meanwhile, I summon a steel blade that, in a moment, decapitates a knight who has been assaulting me with stone projectiles. I also use force and steel like a gun, tearing through the skulls of the knights on either side of him. The pressure of my aura slows all of them and I am already moving on to the next.

I start to form another lightning bolt and . . . my mana flickers. All my spells drop and a stone bullet tears into my side, then a powerful gust of wind throws me to the dirt. My face collides with the ground and I cough. I can't tell if the blood I leave in the dirt comes from my nose or mouth as I rush to regain my footing. My mana returns, revealing they didn't manage to trap me in a circle, and I am already firing bullets of my own into the knights, instantly killing five more of them. I create a flash of light and sound, then leap over the knights, impaling two more of them on a steel spear. Eleven left.

And my mana flickers again. This time, I'm not in the line of fire and I switch to purely physical attacks, gripping a knight's head and twisting it around, killing him instantly. The next knight I target has shifted to physical attacks as well, enveloping his fists in ice gauntlets. This doesn't particularly worry me . . . until that blackness returns to my vision and the sharp pain in my back stops me for a moment. It's all he needs, and a thorn of ice cuts a wide gash in my cheek. It might actually leave a hole. I grab his arm as his gauntlet is cutting into me, holding his wrist in one hand and forcing him to the ground with my other on his shoulder. I don't stop there, however. I push with all my strength, tearing his arm from his body. I don't give him time to feel the pain of the loss and crush his head with a single stomp as he falls to the ground.

I can feel my mana return and use pure force to crush three more knights to paste while I have it. The brutality of these deaths is the final straw for the remaining knights. Their professionalism breaks and one turns to flee. The other five follow suit soon after. I cough, spitting blood into the dirt beside me, then erupt walls of steel around the knights and myself.

"Fuck that!" I scream at them. "Fuck your cowardice! Look at that building! That building full of innocent people you walled off! You are lucky I'm kinder than you are! You were going to let them choke, and burn, and die slowly! Fuck. That. You took the ability to run from them before they even knew they were under attack, and now you think you get the luxury of cowardice? No! Fuck you. You are going to die here! I am going to kill you! No, get back here and fight, oh brave knights of Potestia. Fight me and be glad you had the option. Thank your precious Collector I am not you and your deaths will be quick!"

They don't come back and fight. One of them bangs his fist against the steel. Another falls backward, holding one hand up to me in a plea for mercy. The one nearest me falls to his knees and plants his face in the bloodied dirt. "Please," he begs, "we were just following orders . . ."

I grit my teeth. "You did not just fucking say what I think you said . . ."

CHAPTER SIXTEEN

Under Pressure

My head throbs as I fly through the city, leaving the corpses of every knight in the road, buried only under the remains of their own barricades. I'm hurt pretty badly, more badly than I should have been against a couple dozen knights. I have been fighting guards and knights for years, and outside of a dispersal circle designed for me specifically, they don't give me much trouble anymore.

This fucking cancer is a bigger problem than I thought. And, well, it's cancer, so that bar didn't start very low. And not only because I feel like shit. My mana is acting inconsistently. I have the cancer under control, through a great deal of effort from multiple people, but only physically. This fight revealed it is, I believe, a magical danger as well. Or at least, I hope the cancer is the magical danger in question. At least that would mean one problem with one solution. Truth be told, I'm not in love with the idea of yet another problem attacking my body from the inside. I'd really rather have as few problems to solve as possible. The only downside of this theory is that it means I have discovered not just cancer but magic super cancer.

I mean, that wasn't really in doubt with how quickly it manifested, but I did hope it was magical exclusively in cause and not effect. I can't let it slow me down, however. I still feel furious beyond belief at what this "Lord Nathanial" was planning to do. I still need to stop it before he gives another similar order. Yes, my loved ones are concerned. Yes, they want me to slow down and rest. And when I can, I will. But I feel the grief of the people in these cities. In the Radiant Woods. In the homes next to me. And I would have felt more if I hadn't killed those knights.

I can't get those images out of my mind. The House of Penance that was burned in Satusmor. Leo, broken and bloodied on the ground. A thousand other cruelties. Sarafyna is the only other person who could fight so many people at once, and, well, she is simply more important than me. Any role I fulfill, she can do when I'm gone. But no one can replace her. Not to me, and not to anyone else. I can't ask her to take over for me, and I can't stop fighting. I can't rest while this is still a danger in every city in this country. Not all the time, anyway. We will just have to compromise. Because I am not sitting out a fight only to find another home in ashes. I will not leave a single Leo to the same fate while I still have the will to move.

So I fly from rooftop to rooftop. From run-down houses to gambling dens, to ornate restaurants and finally sweeping, if somewhat neglected, estates. I'm feeling exhausted by the time I make it, but I arrive at the city lord's manor. I am sick and tired of this shit. No one should ever have enough money and power to wave innocent lives away on a whim. I plan to wrestle this power away from every slug of a human being who thinks they deserve it. I use steel mana to craft a great ax and tower shield. In my last fight, my cancer attacked me whenever I used massive, mana-intensive spells. Well, fine, I can work with that. Simple force and an ax will be enough to deal with this creep.

Based on my research, he is weaker than Baldwin, has no divine magic, and is something of a sniveling little shit. Well, all right, that last one is less research and more a generalization of fascists. The point stands, however. With my current mana and everything enhancing me, I should be able to kill him. I use gentle force to land directly in front of the main estate. Two guards on either side of the doors startle and point their spears at me, but I have little patience for them. Killing them doesn't even slow me down as I kick down the locked door of the manor and enter.

The pain and fatigue are catching up to me, and neither makes a great bedfellow for the cold fury those stone barricades burned into me. I am present enough in the moment to avoid killing any servants or slaves I pass, but not for much more than that. I barely remember ascending the stairs, slaughtering more guards, and searching different rooms. But I am on the second floor and the mansion is half destroyed before I know it. I find the lord's study, then his bedchambers, but he is in neither. I'm running through the hall with little care when a powerful wave of mana throws me through the wall. There he fucking is.

I quickly regain my feet, brushing off the splintered wood and plaster and gripping the massive ax in one hand, the large shield in the other. Neither has the integrity they would if a blacksmith made them, but they only need to make it through one fight. Some part of me begs me to leave, insists that what I am doing is stupid, but the part that got me here refuses. I know I can kill this man. I am certain I can. Another wave of mana I don't recognize flies at me, but I hold up my shield and plant my feet. It's something like force mana but feels less directed. It has a burnt orange color that varies a bit from my pale orange-yellow force mana.

Whatever it is, it is creating force but not so much that I can't withstand it. I take a step forward. "What kind of mana is this?" I ask. "It's not quite force, but not exactly distinct from it. Ah, pressure, is that it?" I don't really care that much, but talking helps me focus as I continue to push forward. Pressure or a similar concept makes sense. It must also take an immense amount of mana to keep up like this. Seeing as it is failing to crush me, it won't be the best tactic to keep up. I just need my arms to hold up until he realizes this won't kill me. This is not as reliable as if I didn't have bleeding wounds in my cheek and side, but it's reliable enough.

The assault maintains itself for another twenty seconds maybe, impressive for the average mage, but it does let up. I nearly stumble forward when it does. I'm not used to fighting mana with pure physical strength and it catches me off guard. But I maintain my footing and lower my shield to find a man in silken casual wear, with sweat running down his face and gasping for breath. "Lord Nathanial, I take it?" I ask while catching my own. "Clever plan with the knights." I pause for a moment as if in thought. "Well, no, no, it wasn't. It was the jackbooted plan of a rich asshole. That just seemed like the kind of thing I should say. Anyway, they are all fucking dead."

"Obviously," Nathanial scoffs, as if in irritation at having this explained to him. "And you thought you'd just march into my home and kill me. Arrogant bitch. I'd thought, after years of only targeting more vulnerable nobles, you had the survival instinct to stay away. Or at least try to be quiet about this. But no. What a disappointment. Or are you not the Mage of Mourning? I had heard she was a repugnant fool with half a head of hair, but you do look even uglier than described . . ."

"Oh no, you don't think I'm pretty?" I intone. "Then why do you keep trying to sweep me off my feet?" He actually chuckles at this before summoning various stones and rocks of random shapes. He throws them at me in a confusingly pathetic attack. He doesn't even use his—what I am assuming is—pressure mana to accelerate them like I would. They bounce off my shield and I furrow my brow at him. "What was that? Well, whatever." I have my breath back and start walking toward his smirking face, hand gripping my great ax. For anyone else, this would be far too heavy to wield one-handed, but he doesn't seem to notice. He just keeps throwing his little rocks and I keep walking.

As I walk through the ruined wall, stepping over its remnants and entering the hall with him, he suddenly shifts back to pressure mana. It's not a direct assault this time. Well, it is, but it's not only a direct assault. He is again expending massive amounts of mana to pin me down, but his mana is also behind me. I go to summon a steel wall, but I realize I am not the target. Not immediately, anyway. He seems to be using light amounts of pressure to gather all his stones in one spot. I look down and realize the burnt orange mana is walling me in on all sides as well. As what I recognize as fire mana starts to join the pressure around the rocks, I remember the capital.

The idiot bard who attacked me without any real plan. Who, absent effective spells, tried to shift to a spear. I don't know why he attacked me like that, but I think I have an idea now. He wasn't just doing his duty. He hated me. He, personally, wanted me dead. I must have killed someone close to him, or maybe he just really loved having slaves. But he attacked me as soon as he thought he had an advantage. No plan. Clearly no training. Just rushing in out of anger or some similar emotion. How can I guess this? Well, I have realized what Nathanial's plan is. It's not quite like on Earth, and I have never seen one in person, but I know how a pressure bomb works, and I am inside a giant one.

Because I was so angry. Because, with the cancer and everyone telling me to rest, I wanted to prove something to myself. Well, mission fucking accomplished, Lillith. There was a reason I didn't do this before. I didn't know enough. City lords are powerful, and some are even creative. Yeah, I couldn't leave him alone after that stunt or he would just do it again once I was gone. But I could have gone back to the group and made a plan. Had an escape route ready. And I was calling that bard an idiot. At least he had a way out.

I react the only way I can think of. There is no choice but to use a lot of mana now and hope it doesn't fail.

I pull back, letting the pressure from Nathanial's spell push me away from the shrapnel gathering beneath my feet. I then have to use force mana to push back against it and slow myself down before I am crushed between the two opposing pressures. I run through my options. I can try to counter the pressure in all directions, but that will increase the odds of my mana failing at just the wrong moment. I need to minimize mana usage while still surviving. I see the pressure building and realize I don't have time to plan more, and land on the first thing that pops into my head.

I gather powerful but condensed force mana between the now-burning shrapnel and myself, curving it backward slightly. I can't get rid of the magic bomb being formed in front of me, but maybe I can make it into a claymore instead of a pipe bomb. I pour all my mana into this and pushing back the pressure on my shield, which I hide behind. The pressure builds on all sides while I keep putting more and more force mana into the barrier I have built. I have stronger mana than him and should be able to win this with ease. He has to spread his mana all around, and I can focus it in one spot.

But if I use the full extent of my abilities now, it could flicker out at any moment. I have to be careful not to push too hard or I am dead. If only I actually knew where the dangerous threshold was, I could know exactly how much mana was safe to use. As it is, this is a huge gamble. But hey, at least I didn't get into this by being a rash asshole, giving myself over entirely to rage and stress. Then I would feel really stupid about this. Thank God for that.

Then the pressure reaches its peak, and my world lights up with fire and stone.

A Friend

Charlotte's Journal

For a while, I had a friend. The daughter of one of my parents' slaves. She was my age and she liked all the same things I did, when I shared them with her. It was a secret, that she was a daughter. A secret from my family, and a secret from hers. It was a secret that we were friends at all. My father hated when I talked to the slaves. He hated when I asked anything about them at all. He hated that I didn't hate them. And he would have hated my friend all the more.

But I would be dead without her. Without the secret that her name was *Amelia* and not *John*. Without the name she gave to the warmth that I felt when I loved the wrong things. I was afraid to choose a name like hers, but I was also so excited. So warm. Because like her, I realized I was a daughter as well. And, even if only one person knew it, I wanted a daughter's name. There were so many I loved. So many that made me feel so much more myself than I ever had before. I eventually landed on *Serenity*. Serenity and Amelia.

I had a whole plan. I would meet with Amelia any chance I got. When I became the lady of the Renatus house, I would free all our slaves, and I would marry Amelia. We would adopt other girls, or boys, who were like us. Given the wrong name. The wrong title. And we would raise them like our parents failed to. Fully in the sunlight. Comfortable. Themselves. It was a child's dream. I didn't know my parents weren't the only ones who would hate to see the sun on our faces.

Amelia took the risk first. She and her mother were close in a way I didn't even understand at the time. She trusted her. Amelia was nervous. She was terrified. But she loved her mother, and her mother loved her. And so I encouraged her because I knew that every person who used her name would bring her warmth. Especially if it was her mother. The last time she spoke to me was the day she planned to tell her mother that her name was Amelia. That she planned to make people treat her as who she was.

After that, she wasn't allowed near me at all. I could only watch her from a distance, but I could see the results of the risk she took. New bruises every single day. The guards were quicker with the whip on her than anyone else. They hit her harder, more frequently, and more publicly than anyone else. And then, one day, a priest was invited to her family's quarters. After that, I never saw her again at all, and her parents never spoke of having a child. For a while, I lost a friend.

CHAPTER SEVENTEEN

Stronger Together

What is wrong with you? Seriously, Annie, what are you doing right now?" Sara scolds in a quiet voice the second I open my eyes. My hand flies to my cheek, then my side. All healed. I'm wearing clean clothes and lying in my bed at home.

"What happened to Lord Nathanial?" I immediately ask. "Did he get away? We need to—" I am stopped short as I look at my girlfriend's face. I have seen her without form at all and with random limbs growing out of her body like Nico Robin. I have seen her split her body into a giant mouth with hundreds of teeth. I have seen her contorting into horrifying monsters and growing hundreds of mouths on tentacle limbs. The look on her face at this moment scares me more than any of them. She is furious in a way I have never seen directed at anyone but priests. All of it is directed at me.

"Shut up about the fucking lord," she says, still quiet, still calm. Sitting motionlessly in a chair beside my bed. When I woke up, I mistook that quiet for Sara's usual reserved demeanor. That was . . . a miscalculation. Because it is also cold. Cold and livid. I haven't had someone who I actually cared about this angry at me for a long time. I swallow. "Do you know what you looked like when I found you? Under a half-shredded shield, bits of stone embedded in your bleeding and burned flesh?"

Guilt begins to creep up my spine as I respond, "Sara, I know, it was stupid, I just—"

Her next quiet words boom over my protests.

"I thought you were dead, Annie. I thought you were dead for . . . longer than I should have. You don't have a heartbeat. You even felt dead to my divine magic. I thought you were gone *for hours*. It wasn't until you started coughing in the cart, halfway to the house, that I realized I hadn't lost you forever. So tell me, Annie. Why? Why did you rush into a fight you weren't ready for? Why couldn't you just rest? You told me you would rest! But you just had to push, and push, and push, like you always do. You got lucky. You should be gone now, do you understand that, Annie? You should be dead, and I should be mourning over your fucking corpse. Why? Annie, why?" Sara grows louder and more impassioned as she speaks, and water is running down her cheeks by the time she is finished.

I don't answer at first. Her tears are summoning water to my own eyes and my throat aches with an unreleased sob. I can't defend myself. She is right. And, while even in the moment I knew I had made a mistake, seeing the effect that mistake had on Sara carries its own gravity with it. The silence drags as she glares through glassy eyes, and I bite my lip. Finally, when I can't leave her in silence any longer, I speak. "I'm . . . I'm sorry. I was being an idiot. I just . . ."

"Just what?" She leans forward, elbows on her knees, inviting me to continue. I'm not used to being on this side of this type of exchange and I have to say, I'm not a fan. But I have to admit I belong here.

"I hate feeling helpless. I know, I don't have to tell you that. But it's the best I have. I hate feeling helpless, Sara. I hate feeling helpless to help. I can't stand watching horrible things that I can't change. I hate feeling grief I can do nothing to soothe. I hate that I found my friend beaten, abused, and mocked, and there was nothing I could do to make it better. Yeah, I killed the people who did it. And other people with the same power turned around and started doing it to other people immediately. I want to stop it all. I want to be everywhere, putting every fucking abuser and creep in the ground. It's what makes me who I am.

"And I was. I was doing everything I could, anyway. I finally felt like, maybe, I could stop all of it. Then this fucking cancer showed up. It showed up and tried to put a collar on me. It wants to chain me to the wall and force me to watch as comfortable, rich assholes wave their hands and burn homes to the ground to punish our efforts to organize. To help. To feed. I was so fucking angry, Sara. It was like I was at the academy again, looking down at Leo in the dirt and the blood. And again, I wanted to tear the culprit apart. So I rushed it. I'm sorry." It's not much, but it's true.

"Annie. You are not powerless because you are sick. Maybe you don't always get to be the big hero anymore, but you are not powerless. Or what have we been doing these past few years? All these communities we've built? All these whisper spheres we've distributed? You have always said you don't want to be the hinge the revolution needs to turn, so why do you have to risk everything you and I have as soon as you don't feel like you are that axle anymore? Do you know what Ed, your brother whom you used to complain about, pulled off while you were pulling your little suicide stunt?" Sara asks.

"He drove off the gang?" I guess. This isn't a huge surprise to me; it was what I left him there for. I knew he'd pull it off fine.

"Yeah, he did. It took a toll on him, but he did. But that's not what I mean. He pulled off what you could have, if you had come back instead of running off to fight the most powerful mage in the city while your body was trying to kill you. All those people who saw him defending them, then saw what the knights you killed tried to do? They reached a tipping point," she says, and I feel a sudden, small rush of adrenaline.

"He got more people to come back?" I ask, hopefully.

"No. He did the opposite. He convinced some of our volunteers to stay. Because the people there are ready to fight, not flee. After watching a regular mage defend them. After seeing what almost happened to their families. They are doing what you always said they would. They are organizing, fighting back. And Ed is the one who helped them put it together."

My breath catches. We have been helping and supporting cities all over Potestia for a long time. Freeing slaves when new ones have been captured and feeding anyone we can. But the commoners in each city have always chosen to risk the future or come to safety with us. If I understand Sara, however, it sounds like one city has actually decided to fight for their home.

"And people are going back there, to fight?" I ask. Sara nods.

"I've brought two caravans back already. They are ready to fight, Annie. Some of your ideas, and some of theirs, have already been implemented. The nobles in Tumult are about to get very uncomfortable as every laborer in the city begins to refuse them. They are standing together. This is growing beyond you. Because they are not alone, which means neither are you," she says.

"Really? Which ideas?" I ask, my blood pressure rising as I think about what this means. I have mentioned a lot of things from Earth that could replace the systems people here are used to. I don't know what will work best in a world of magic, so I just spread as many ideas as I could from Earth. The people in this country have spent their lives under mind control, convinced only one system of society exists. Even if they hadn't, it's easy to believe the current state of society is the best it can ever get. So instead of just ideas I like, I have been distributing everything I can remember about all sorts of theories and ideas. I am also not as good at this part as some of my friends back on Earth, but there are plenty of brilliant people here. The more I share, the more they'll be able to come up with their own alternatives.

This is what she means by *my ideas*, so I am more than a little curious how the beginning of this revolution is forming. She glares at me, making it clear this is not the time for questions. "They are refusing Potestian coin and using mana vouchers. Stop getting distracted, you can ask Ed all about this later. The point is that they are not powerless. They are not powerless, because they are fighting, together. So, you don't want to feel powerless? Come back to me. Make a plan. Talk to the thousands of people you helped bring together. And do not tell me how I'm 'too important to fight with you' unless you are willing to fight alongside everyone else. You aren't hiding your face anymore, Annie. You aren't trying to stay low-key while you sneak slaves out of the city. You don't have to fight alone."

I dip my head a little, properly chastised. "You're right," I reply. And she is. The truth is, I have grown arrogant. I have grown prideful, after killing the king. With my damn title like some kind of superhero. The Mage of fucking Mourning. "We are going to win. We are going to win because our enemies are powerful. They know they are powerful, and they are drunk on pride. And pride is just an uppity name for stupidity. But I wasn't being any different. I'm sorry."

"Yes. You were being stupid." She rubs at her temple. "Look, I'm not asking you to stop fighting. I know you won't. I don't even want you to, not really. I know you will be out there killing nobles and slavers in a day. But I refuse to watch you kill yourself because you want to do every single thing on your own. I . . . I love you, Annie." She waits for me to meet her eye before continuing. "I love you in a way I don't even understand yet, but it cuts into my chest and pulls my heart out. When I thought you had died, I was so desperate. I would have done anything to get you back! I was so hurt, so betrayed. Because we are just getting started, you and I, and you almost threw it all away. I could have killed you. Never again. Promise me you will never do this again."

"I don't know if I can promise I will never take a risk again," I begin, sparking a sharp, pained look on her face, "but I can promise I won't charge in like an idiot again. I will only risk what I have to, when I have to." I hold up a pinky, a gesture she recognizes by now, and she grabs it with her own. It's a bit funny, her conflicted face and the pinky promise. But even goofy, childish things can feel serious at times. She finally lets out a sigh and slumps over, resting her head on my legs. I adjust myself in the bed to make it more comfortable for both of us. She seems relieved, and she has shifted from my old legal Anne back to Annie, which was functionally my actual name on Earth. She must have been pretty pissed to use my legal name, which she knows no one but my mother has spoken since my . . . first childhood.

"He was dead, by the way," Sara finally answers. "I don't know what happened, but you seem to have taken each other out." That makes sense. Bombs tend to do that. Good fucking thing I had a similar mana to his or I really would have died. I sigh in relief, then something occurs to me.

"Wait, that is a lot of organizing for an afternoon . . . How long have I been out?" I ask.

"Two weeks." Sara sighs, and my face pales. Two entire weeks? Holy shit.

"Has Ed gone to the capital yet?" I ask again, and she nods. I am about to remark on this when my whisper sphere, the one connected to Godfrey, lights up on my end table.

CHAPTER EIGHTEEN

Family Loyalty

Edward

I take a deep breath as I emerge onto the road outside Lillith's old tavern. The city isn't quite like my sister described it, but it couldn't remain that way forever. There are people walking the streets, only a few who make or maintain eye contact. I do get a few glances as I look around with bulky goggles on. Sarafyna says Lillith designed these and some lady named Clarrise finished them. Supposedly they will warn me if some weird light that can make me sick like Lily is around, but I haven't seen anything. I'm not sure how light is supposed to do that or why I need goggles to see the special danger light but . . . I sigh. It still irritates me, but I don't really understand half of what Lillith talks about.

My sigh quickly turns to a traitorous yawn, then a scowl. I haven't been sleeping well since . . . well, I haven't liked my glass mana as much as I did at first. Lillith had suggested I be creative with my aspects, and I thought this had been a great idea. But now I can't close my eyes without seeing the man in the wind and the glass, and what was left of him when my spell ended. Even now, my stomach churns at the thought. But I told Lillith I would handle the capital and I intend to. Or at least I intend to find out what I can about the circles targeting her. I owe her that much.

Because, well, I am a fucking ass. Because I thought I had gotten over the damn pride that made me so, so angry at her. I thought, when I realized what she was actually going through, when I found a woman I loved who admired me in return, I could leave that coward behind me. The coward who used his brother as a distraction to run away. But when I had people relying on me, when I had to do what Lillith does all the time, I choked. I didn't have the stomach for it. I am still inferior to my own little sister. Which is why, when Sarafyna told me Lillith had died . . . a small part of me was relieved. No, a part of me was happy. Happy that she had failed and I had succeeded. That I would never feel like I had to look up at my shorter sister again.

I was upset. I was heartbroken. I couldn't accept that I had lost her. But I was also happy, deep down. Then she turned out to be alive, somehow. I don't understand it. Her body was shredded. Not quite like the man in the glass, but I barely recognized her. But she was alive, and Sarafyna was able to heal her. All but the scars she already had, which I struggle to understand. It makes me wonder if she keeps that scar on her eye on purpose, just to taunt me. Except the sickness is still there as well. And I was relieved. I was so happy, and a little disappointed. That sad little coward is still alive in me, and I need to crush him.

This is the first step. Go into the city that is safe for me, and dangerous for Lillith, and figure out how to make it safe for her again. If I can do that . . . if I can stand in the city where I am stronger than her, and give that up, maybe I can let go of all of it. It's worth a try at least.

So I make my way back to the circle I have been experimenting with. Or, well, the place I know there is a circle. Based on Lillith's description, I was able to identify it by the replacement of mana stones with torches. I also brought a stone enchanted with light mana. It basically just emits a soft light all the time. If it goes out, I know I am in an anti-Lillith circle. It will also let me know if I succeed in breaking one.

That thought makes me scowl. The Collector-damned Mage of Mourning. That is a way better name than *recovering gambling addict*, the only title I have earned. And she has the largest city in Potestia structured entirely around repelling her. The whole fucking world bends to her will, and she just shrugs it off before marching into some lord's house and blowing herself up. I have to shove those thoughts down as an old resentment boils up. I need to focus. I walk into the familiar neighborhood, and as expected, the light in the stone vanishes. I look over at the pit I have been digging for the past few days and groan.

At this point I want to just aspect earth mana, but I have been struggling to get any third aspect. Maybe I'll drop glass for earth. In any case, if the circle is underground, I'm not going to find it. And, although I am in a poor part of the city and anyone who does see me quickly turns away, I'm not going to be able to hide this pit forever. So I go through the same song and dance I have been through every day that I've come out here. I wonder where else the circle could be. It seems to actually run through the center of two buildings, and it's not in the sky, so I can't picture where else it would be. This leads me to the conclusion that it must, in fact, be underground. The same conclusion I reach every day.

I am digging right at the border where my stone light goes out and returns. I consider digging in another spot, but that simply doesn't make any sense to me. If this is the border, the circle should be on it. But I have already done a lot of digging. I idly start tossing the stone up and down in my hand as I debate my next course of action. I'm not making any progress. I suppose I could go back and get an earth mage, but . . . I don't know. I really don't want to rely on someone else. Sarafyna has cleared me of this "cancer" each time I've come back, so it should be safe at least. But doing that would feel like giving up.

I start tossing the rock higher out of frustration. I can't think of anything. I summon a little wind and start tossing it higher and higher, using the idle action to help me focus. The rock bounces up, I let it fall, then I lift it a little higher with the wind again. This is a little game I've played with myself to help master my wind magic, and it's beyond easy at this point. I haven't dropped or lost control of the rock in a long time now. Not until . . . today. I toss the stone up near the top of the building nearby and immediately drop it to the ground when it lights up. It dulls again as I drop it, and remains that way until it hits the ground. My eyes widen as I realize the problem.

It left the circle with elevation. Lillith explained these circles should affect the area both above and below them. She says they do have an upper and lower limit for range, but it's a long one. Longer than I should have reached with my little game. Then it occurs to me: we are entering the city using an underground tunnel. I figured Lillith never passed under one because we come out pretty close to the wall, but what if that's not the case? What if these circles aren't drawn on the ground, but on the walls? That would create horizontal columns and cover more of the city with fewer circles, wouldn't it? She did say the field hit her from the rooftops, which pours cool water over that idea at first, but . . . I realize it is probably both. Why not? This is . . . irritating, to say the least, but it does seem likely.

I need to get inside this building to test my theory. I am so excited about having a theory, I don't think much about how to proceed, and find myself knocking on the door before making a plan. It's not until after I knock that I realize, if my theory is correct, it could be any building next to this one. I also have no idea what to say to whoever answers. Well, whatever. It's not like Lillith was thinking when she got herself blown up. The worst case here is I embarrass myself. I am nevertheless relieved when no one answers. I jiggle the handle to find it's unlocked. So I shrug and walk in.

The building is empty; it's clearly been abandoned for a few years now. A few steps in and I can see why. It's a two-story building, but I can only guess what its intended purpose was. Any method of reaching the second floor has been removed, along with half the second floor itself. Mirroring this is the ground which has been dug out, foundation and all. Along one wall is exactly what I have been looking for. A large magic circle has been carved into the wall. I don't understand the runes like my sister does, but there is little doubt this is what I'm looking for. I tilt my head curiously as I look at them. Most of the runes are old and worn. I can see spider webs in a group of them. Only the center rune, which completes and activates the circle, and a few others I don't recognize appear to have been carved recently.

Someone has been drawing these for years. I guess that answers Lillith's question about how they reacted to her so quickly. She figured King Godfrey must have known a bit about what she was doing already, but this indicates a much greater depth of planning surrounding her. They were ready to shut her down fast, whenever they needed to. I shiver at the thought. It's nothing short of good luck her plan involved leaving the city when she did. We could all be dead now. I hesitantly approach the circle on the wall. I can't safely reach it on foot, as it is on the other side of the dug-out earth, which is too wide and deep to cross without excessive time and effort.

I quickly form a small but powerful gust of wind and fire it at the center rune.

The wood it is carved into is old, and all I need to do is break it. It holds up to the assault surprisingly well, so I pick up a stone and toss it into the wind. I use this stone to hammer at the center rune until, a moment later, it cracks, and the circle breaks. My feeling of triumph is very short-lived, and with it dies the part of me that thought maybe Lillith was the only one rushing into stupid situations. It turns out enchanting a stone to indicate whether a dispersal circle is nearby isn't an original idea. As soon as the rune breaks, stones, boards, and debris all around me light up like one of Lillith's blinding spells. In case that isn't enough, loud screeching noises assault me from all directions at once.

I stumble back, trying to regain my bearings as the alarm screams at and blinds me. A hand grabs the back of my shirt, and I feel myself being dragged from the building at speed. Collector's grace, I hope I am not being arrested by a bunch of fucking knights. That would be just my luck. I had one job and I got arrested immediately. Whoever grabbed me pushes me out a window, I think? They then drag me to another nearby building and throw me inside. Everything is bleary, my ears are ringing, and I'm seeing double. As the world hovers around itself and the doubles collapse into one, I look up to find a masked man glaring down at me.

"I see your whore sister has been rubbing off on you," he snarls. "The Ed I know never would have done something so stupid." My ears are ringing and my head is pounding. The Ed he knows?

"Do I fucking know you?" I ask, then I see him barricading the door with wood magic and remember something. Tall, masked, wavering aura, wood. "Wait, are you that bard? The one my 'whore sister' beat with a few baubles on a nightstand?"

The bard glares furiously at me.

"You used to be so smart and mature for your age. It breaks my heart to see you bowing down to your own kid sister. And here I thought Henry was the only eunuch in the family," he chides before pulling his mask off. "Well, it's nothing that can't be corrected."

My heart stops for a moment, then tries to beat out of my chest. I can't believe what I am looking at. "D-Dad?" I ask in a faltering voice.

CHAPTER NINETEEN

Benevolent

Typically, Sara will leave when Godfrey calls. Not out of any particular obligation, but she doesn't have the history with him that I do. Today, however, I don't have the energy for him alone. As the sphere gently vibrates, I share a look with my sweet girlfriend, my eyes pleading and hers confused. "Do you mind hanging around this time?" I request, and her face softens.

"Me? I . . ." She pauses. "I won't have anything to contribute. I don't want to distract you or anything . . ."

"I think you'd be surprised. It doesn't come out often, but when you are upset, or passionate, you certainly don't seem to have trouble finding something to contribute." I tease her.

"Yeah but . . . this isn't really the same thing as that," she says with a blush.

"No, but I don't need you to talk to him with me. I'm just . . . not done being around you yet. I'd like you to stick around just for support, if you're up for it," I say, and she blushes more.

"At least you're smart enough to ask for support this time . . ." she mumbles.

"Thanks, Sara." I chuckle. "Besides, if I convince him to give up his crown, he'll need suggestions for a new hat." She bites back a laugh at this, and I finally pick up the sphere, which stops vibrating the moment I do. "Lillith here," I say cheerfully.

"Collector's grace, Lillith . . . Where have you been? I thought you might be dead!" Godfrey cries.

I raise one eyebrow and share another look with my girlfriend. "A lot of that going around, recently. None of you should worry so much. I'm sturdy. A brick house. Mighty mighty, and all that," I quip.

"Lillith, you passed out mid-sentence and stopped answering my calls. What was I supposed to think?" he protests.

I actually snort. "I don't know. That the person half your city is structured around eliminating is gone? *Well, that's done* is what I might go with."

"Lillith, I don't want you dead, I just want your help. Those circles are to help you. To stop you before this gets out of hand!"

"I know, Godfrey. It's why you call, and it's why I answer. I don't suppose you are ready to take the crown off and get some real work done?" I suggest.

"Lillith. We can't take shortcuts here. Do you really think people can exist in the world you want to build? I'm old, and I've known a lot of people. A lot of commoners, a lot of nobles. And yeah, this country hasn't been kind to most of them. But they aren't kind to each other either. This country is filled with commoners like your father. Like all the slavers you have fought. Do you really think, if you take the crown from them, they will be able to exist in a society that depends on kindness? Generosity? That is going to fall apart. I am offering you a chance at change with structure!"

That one does bite a bit. Because he is wrong about the solution, but he's right about the issue. Well, sort of. My communities have been mostly doing well so far. Few of them actually work in a way that I would choose myself, but most of them are, truth be told, better off than I would expect. This is largely because they are composed primarily of the former dregs of society. The rejects and slaves who, before they left Potestia, already needed each other to survive. The wealthier and middle-class groups I've helped more recently, after the recent laws put them newly in danger, went and formed the shit pile known as the Kingdom of Endings. I'm glad to know Tumult is taking some steps forward, but there is some truth in Godfrey's complaint. They have thousands of years of poisoned worldviews to shake off.

"No, you're right," I respond after a moment. "Potestia, when we are done with it, will not look like the world I want. Not while I'm alive, anyway. I would be surprised if it ever did. Because you are right. Potestia has spent too long ignoring, dismissing, and crushing anyone and everyone who it found inconvenient. Commoners, like my father, are as guilty of this as nobles. Wherever they were, they always pissed downhill. And they aren't going to suddenly become benevolent when they don't have anyone to answer to anymore." I'm starting to sweat as the sickness protests my heightened emotional state. Sara wraps her hands around one of mine in an offering of comfort. She keeps her eyes locked onto mine as I talk to the stubborn king. I don't know what I'd do without her.

"So you understand," Godfrey starts, but I continue.

"But you know where else there were a lot of commoners like my father? In my own family. My father raised two boys who followed his example. Both grew into good, honest men. Because that's the thing, Godfrey. The people of 'your' country have been drowning in poison for centuries, but it's not who they are. It doesn't come from them. They can, and will, come up for air if given the opportunity. Enough of them will, anyway. So you are right. There is a lot of social change that needs to happen. The world they choose in the meantime probably won't be what either of us wants. But giving people options their fucking king didn't pick for them isn't the last step, it's the first."

Godfrey is quiet for a moment after this, but not because he is stumped. He simply wants to think before responding. Sara squeezes my hand again, offering her strength as we anticipate his response. Finally, his voice hums through the whisper sphere again. "That's not going to be good enough, Lillith. What about the ones who won't cooperate with any new way of doing things? What are you going to do about them? With no one watching them, no consequences promised for hurting the people you so badly want to protect? What happens when they start killing each other? How are you going to stop them?" he asks. His voice is calm and gentle in an almost irritating way.

"Well, I probably won't give them a spear and armor. I probably won't give them massive estates, servants, and authority."

"Quippy. Clever as always, Lillith. But it's not an answer," he replies.

"Isn't it though?" I challenge him. "Because it's not just a quip. It's true that the people in power, the people enforcing your new authority? A lot of the people you are worried about hold those positions. Because either way, they will want to do harm. But only your world actively hands them the tools to do it."

"Which is why I am here, Lillith. Because someone needs to take that power away from the wrong people and give it to the right ones. Someone needs to change this country while still leaving a country here to change! Give me time, Lillith! Help me! You are right, the way this works is wrong! I have only been king for a little while, and I've had to deal with more than a few other problems in the meantime. Half of which you caused! Don't you see? With your help, I can actually start fixing this *and* keep people safe in the meantime. Isn't that a good thing? What I want is achievable! Your goals are just . . . they aren't going to happen, Lillith!" he snaps back.

"Caused by me, you say. By freeing slaves. That's the problem, Godfrey. Your world is already falling apart without slaves. Any changes you make, you want to make slowly. Smoothly. More easily. For the people who are already comfortable. The problem you have is that the wrong people are being asked to suffer for a while as you fix things. The people who benefitted from the old world. And you know what? I already told you my world is a long way off. I will do everything in my power to get there as fast as I can while I'm alive, yes. But I know it's not the next step we are taking. I know the people of Potestia will choose something else. A republic, or a democracy, or something I haven't suggested.

"They are not going to stumble from a monarchy to anarchy. I know that. I can accept that, provided they get a choice. That is what I am fighting for with them. And it's something they can have if you just let go. But that's where we run into a wall. It's not the possible issues with what I want. It's that you want to be king. You can't accept anything short of that. And we will suffer no kings."

"You haven't even given me a chance to be a good king, Lillith. A good, benevolent king can solve all of this with the least loss of life! But you won't let me try! You are so determined to dismiss the idea that it's even possible!" he argues, the calm in his voice completely gone now.

I look at Sara and sigh. She gives me a sympathetic half smile, but remains quiet so I can continue my conversation.

"Fine. Let's say it is possible. Let's say someone with complete power over their people can, possibly, be benevolent. A theory I take issue with, considering how power is maintained, but let's just pretend. What happens when you die?" I counter. "When your grandson dies? When his grandson dies? A monarchy . . . any kind of absolute authority really, is the gamble that every king, for the rest of time, will be benevolent. It only takes one tyrant, Godfrey, to bring back all the worst bits of Potestia. Authority doesn't rely on the possibility of a benevolent ruler. It requires the *certainty* of benevolence, all the time, every time. Anything short of that guarantees atrocities."

"And your world requires the same of every single person! Which is more likely, Lillith?" he yells through the sphere, and I twitch. Something isn't right. That isn't representative of what I have told him, and Godfrey is less composed than usual. His arguments are worse than usual. He is upset, especially after my last comment.

"Godfrey," I respond, pausing for a moment, "why did you call me today? What's wrong?"

There is quiet for an uncomfortably long moment. Sara looks up from giving Suzume attention and tilts her head curiously. Finally, a calm Godfrey answers.

"Lillith, I need to know how your circle works. I know it's a tattoo. I need you to tell me how it works," he says. I pale as he finishes speaking and the room is silent again.

"Godfrey . . . you can't put my circle on anyone. It will kill people. Even if it doesn't, I don't know what the side effects are. I fixed it and improved it. I used it back home . . . Surely some students from Satusmor have arrived with it by now; ask them to show you. It's a safer version, and it's powerful. You can figure out how to use it. Even make it better. But . . . please tell me you aren't trying to use the one from my body!" I beg.

He is quiet again. I almost don't catch his response when he whispers.

"You didn't die, Lillith. Who is holding on to power now?"

"No, Godfrey . . . I was lucky—I should have died. I felt like I was going to die! I felt like I wanted to! If you put this on someone else, they almost definitely will. Even if they survive, without . . . what I know about the body, who knows how bad the side effects could be! Godfrey, please tell me you haven't forced this on people!" I plead. Sara grimaces at this, biting her lip and looking away from me for the first time since this call started. She actually opens her mouth to speak, but her breath catches and Godfrey replies before she can. I keep a curious eye on her as he speaks.

"I won't force it on people. But, Lillith, I need this. The country needs this, you don't understand. I only want to try it on a few volunteers. And it will be safer if you tell me what I am missing."

"Godfrey, there is no such thing as a volunteer for something like this. There is no way to communicate what they are going to go through. And the people in your city are desperate and scared! They want another option so badly . . . that's not volunteering. That's just . . ." I don't need to finish the sentence. Because I know he knows. And I now know why I upset him so much earlier. Because exposing people to torture and death, with continued fear and misery in one hand and power in the other . . . that's exactly what I have accused kings of doing earlier, an atrocity. And we both know it.

"Lillith, you want people to be equal. But you are hoarding power. You want me to give up my crown? Why can't you give up your own position? Your own authority? Your own power? Tell me how to make it work right!" he spits at me.

"No. The reason I didn't share this circle wasn't to maintain power. I have only ever used it to lift other people up. I understand what you mean, but I don't want power, I just wanted a tool to fight back with. And once I realized what I had done to myself . . . No, Godfrey. You know why I didn't share this circle. Because inflicting this on people, especially people with no understanding or ability to consent . . . that's the kind of thing I would kill someone for doing. It's the kind of thing I would deserve to be killed for doing. I don't know what you've already done, but please . . . if we were ever friends . . . don't do that to people. Please, I—" I cut myself off with a cough that splatters blood across the whisper sphere.

Shit, I've been asleep, so I haven't been manually managing the cancer. I open the drawer by my bedside and pull out one of Henry's potions, swallowing it and redirecting my mana to shave away at the hostile cells. Sara grips my hand harder and I feel her divine magic wash over me like warm water. She leans forward, desperation and worry in her eyes, and opens her mouth like she wants to speak again. Before she gets the chance, and just as I am composing myself, Godfrey speaks again.

"All right, Lillith. I promise I won't. I'm . . . I'm glad I asked you before I tried it," he says. Sara and I sigh in relief at the same time.

Godfrey

I stop channeling mana into the sphere and sigh over the body of the latest volunteer. I grit my teeth and clench the whisper sphere so hard my fingertips turn white. Stubborn little hypocrite.

"Bring in the next batch," I order.

CHAPTER TWENTY

Next Steps

My breathing shortens as the whisper sphere goes dark. He promised he wouldn't do it, but . . . if he actually saw it on me in the cell, there is no way he hasn't tried it yet. He would only ask me if he ran into a roadblock. I'll have to hope he ran into trouble activating it at all. He shouldn't understand the core concept of a universal center, but . . . the circle I shared uses that as well. It's only a matter of time before he figures it out. But . . . he's not a stupid man. He knows I'm trying to bridge the gap between commoners and nobles quickly. Obviously, if I could share my circle safely, I would have done that already and he'd have plenty of examples. I didn't because I'm not stupid. I just have to hope he isn't actually killing anyone with this.

"Annie, is everything okay?" Sara asks, the concern in her voice pulling my eyes to her and my mind back to reality. I shudder one last time, close my eyes, and take a deep breath. There is nothing I can do about this right now. I have to focus on what I can do.

"Yes, sorry. Just an old, arrogant mistake catching up to me. Hopefully, only me. Seems to be a lot of that going around these days. But I'm all right. When is Ed supposed to come back?"

Sara looks at me with concern but sighs. "I'm heading out in an hour to pick him up. But don't change the subject so quickly! I'm your girlfriend, right? Talk to me, you idiot."

I look at her for a moment.

"You're right, sorry. Force of habit. I've never really talked about this with you, not extensively anyway, but . . . you know how when I was younger—younger here in Potestia, not in my former life—I designed my own magic circle? You know all about the mess that caused with Baldwin and everything, but . . . I've never really told you what it was like. When I finished the circle, I mean."

She leans forward in the chair. "I know it changed you in ways you didn't expect," she says.

"Yes, but . . . Sara, it hurt. I don't just mean pain, I mean . . . it rebuilt me, cell by cell. It tore me apart and recreated me, not just as a mage, but as a magical space itself. It was . . . horrific, beyond words. I have never wanted to . . . hurt myself or anything like that. But when this circle was finished . . . I wanted to be dead. I wanted it over at any cost. For a moment, I was certain I was going to die.

Even now, there is no doubt in my mind that I should have died. I don't know if I was lucky, or if it was whatever force woke me up in this world the first time. But I shouldn't have survived it, and I don't think anyone else who tries it is likely to. The only thing this circle is going to bring people is an agonizing death, worse than I have delivered to any of the worst people in this country."

For a moment, Sara's face pales and she puts a hand over her mouth. I can see a thought flicker through her eyes before she closes them. I'm not sure what she is processing, but I have a feeling it is a step further than empathy and concern. Nevertheless, she eventually composes herself and speaks calmly. "And that's why you are so desperate to stop Godfrey from experimenting with it . . ." She taps her lip with one finger. "Just to be clear, this circle fundamentally changed your body. You think it should have killed you. Is there any chance it's the cause of the cancer? Why does it have to be something from Visenar?"

I sigh in response to this. "It's not impossible. Not unlikely, even, but it's at the bottom of my list of suspects for now. It's true I don't grasp all the side effects. And not just because that would be a pain in the ass. But the cancer hit fast, and hard. I've had this circle for years. If it's the cause, it changed years of behavior in a single day. It doesn't add up, not on its own. And, if that was the case, it would only ever affect me, at least until what I just learned today. We have mine under control," I say, and she gives me a half-lidded, unamused look. "All right, we have it mostly under control. The point is, it's more important to make sure others aren't at risk than to investigate that possibility."

"But now . . ." she guesses, and I snap my fingers.

"Right. If Godfrey has this circle, it could affect anyone who does actually survive it, if anyone. So we need to start looking into it as well. But we can do that when we move!" I announce, clapping. It's delayed a bit, but we have been talking about going to live near Clarrise. Sara wants to help research transportation and I have a few ideas myself.

"Right, and . . . you'll take it easy in the meantime?" she pleads.

"That," I announce happily, "depends on what you mean."

"Annie . . ." she starts, but I hold my hands up in surrender.

"No, I promise, I won't go charging into combat unless I have no other option. It's about time we took some other steps anyway. I have a new idea for equalizing power in the fights to come." Sara visibly relaxes at that, and as she slumps, I suddenly realize how exhausted she is.

"So, what are the next steps?" she asks.

"Well, we've got whisper spheres all over the country in the hands of regular people. The best thing to do is get them talking. Get them to tell each other what each city lord is doing, and plan ways to fight back. The next thing we do is give them the ability to do so," I say.

"You've been sharing magic for years, Annie, but . . . I don't think most people will stand a chance in a fight with a powerful noble. What's the plan here?"

"That's what I want to get started on. Because you're right. What I have been doing isn't enough to carry us forward anymore. People are angry enough now. To fight back. They are scared enough. The promise of safety if they follow the rules has been taken away. What they need is hope, and it can't just look like me. Or you, or anyone. They need a chance to fight back themselves, and I think I can give that to them. And not just with their own magic. I've been looking at a few ideas over the years. If I focus entirely on them now, I think I can finish. And if you succeed, well . . . Potestia is fucked."

Tension slides off Sara like mud.

"Thank you," she says. "That's exactly what I needed to hear." I smile gently at her, but something bugs me. Her relieved expression hides some meaning like a movement at night, just farther than you can really see. I decide not to press her. Whatever it is, she'll tell me when it matters. In the meantime, we have work to do.

"Nah, I should be thanking you. You pulled me out of . . . a dark headspace. And back from the brink of death, it sounds like. Thanks for having my back, Sara. I don't know what I'd do without you."

She looks at me seriously, that glint of a secret shifting in her eye.

"I need you just as much, Annie. Just . . . remember that next time, all right?" she says quietly as she stands. I can't think of anything quippy to relieve the tension from that simple request, so I just reply with a barely perceptible nod. "Thanks for coming back . . . I should go. I'd prefer not to leave your brother stranded. I just couldn't wait while you were still, you know . . ."

"Right. I'll start getting things ready for the move. I have to talk to my family about it, see if they want to come with us or stay here," I respond, and she turns around, closing the gap and putting her hand on my shoulder. She gently, but firmly, pushes me back down.

"I've already discussed it with them. Everyone is on board. They all want you researching instead of fighting too, for the record. Clarrise has rooms set up for us already. We'll start loading everything up when I get back with your brother. Get some rest, you've been through a lot," she insists. I want to grumble, but my body does feel a bit like someone filled a sock with quarters and went to town on it. So I just nod.

"I will need some food at some point . . . just saying," I protest.

She giggles a little. "I'll send your mom in on my way out. I would expect another lecture before you can eat though. She saw you when we brought you back too, you know." She turns to leave again as I pale. That's not going to be much better than Sara's lecture was. "I really need to get going now," she says as she pulls a frilly hat off a hook next to my door. She reaches for the handle and pauses. "Uh, Clarrise saved you room thirteen-twelve, like you requested. And before I go, I wanted you to consider . . ." She takes a breath. "I thought maybe, uh, if it's all right with you, and you can say no of course, but I thought maybe . . . I'd request the same . . . one . . ."

I actually blush at this, and she looks like she is actually trembling with nerves.

"Sara, I'd—" I start, but she rushes out of the room before I can answer her. The door actually swings on its hinges as she flees her last remark, and a grin splits my face. I pump my fist in the air in celebration, too distracted to notice the angry woman who has taken my girlfriend's place.

"Well. You look pleased with yourself," my furious mother remarks.

Sarafyna

It took the entire walk to the Radiant Woods for my heart to stop beating out of my chest. She'll say yes, I know she will. But it was still terrifying to ask. I want to get closer to her. Figure out how a relationship like ours should work, and truth be told, I want to keep an eye on her. This is what I was thinking when I had the idea, and building up the courage to bring it up was my primary concern until I did. It wasn't until I got to the beach that I even considered what other expectations might be attached to that.

So I spent the rest of the walk panicking about that. Realizing I am attracted to Annie is one thing. Fulfilling those . . . expectations is another. It was nice, worrying about those things, because now that I am at the Radiant Woods, I have to consider something else entirely. I hate going back into the woods. I despise it. They still talk to me every time I pass through. They still taunt me. And they hate letting me leave again. I am determined to figure out long-distance travel just to avoid this.

Thoughts of living with a woman who loves me, and has expressed physical interest in me, make me sweat. But facing down the woods? That still terrifies me. Something I have to be very careful to hide from Annie. She knows I don't like it, but if she knew how the woods still try to torment me, she may try to stop me from doing it. And I need to help. As terrifying as it is, I need to do it. A worse option I have been thinking about ever since I found her bloodied in that mansion . . . she might try to confront the woods before she is ready. She doesn't seem stupid enough to do this, but . . . she isn't the brilliant woman I love when she is pissed off.

I take a deep breath and step into the woods.

"How many more times do you think you'll manage it, Sarafyna?"

Then I am on the other side. In a cave outside of Visenar, and Ed is already waiting for me. He looks haggard and weary. His shoulders slump as he looks up at me. "Ed, is everything all right? Did anything happen?" I immediately ask.

He takes a deep breath. "Nah, I'm fine," he answers. "Just another failed trip."

Hope

Charlotte's Journal

When I was fifteen, I had hope again. The last few years had not been kind to me. I never forgot Amelia, and I never forgot the name Serenity. But I also never got to feel the rush of affirmation when someone used it to refer to me. I felt self-conscious about everything. I hated my body more and more with each passing day. It wasn't me. It wasn't my home. It was a lie I wasn't even allowed to acknowledge. I felt sick every time I undressed to bathe. I felt sick every time I dressed again in the wrong clothing. I always felt sick.

Then I met Lord Eric, my tutor. He was supposed to teach me to use my mana, but he did more than that. He was a kind man. He didn't really understand me, but he understood that I was miserable. It was months of quiet acceptance and gentle encouragement before I asked him to call me Serenity. Before I told him why. I was so afraid. So scared. But I needed someone to know that I wasn't Charles. That I wasn't my father's son, but his daughter. Eric didn't really get it. He was confused, and he asked a lot of questions. But he understood one thing. He understood that he didn't need to completely understand.

He called me Serenity. I didn't have another Amelia, to dream of the future with. To genuinely relate with. But I had someone who saw me. Someone who knew my name. Who taught me to use magic and treated me as myself. Who actually cared about me like a father should a daughter.

Then he accidentally called me Serenity when my mother was down the hall. She heard him, and it all ended. She searched my things and found my romance novels and my drawings of dresses. She found my hair clips. She blamed it all on Eric, and she told my father. They accused him of brainwashing me. Of lying to me. Of . . . other things. None of it was true. All he did was care about me. But their minds were made up. They had decided what they wanted to believe, and who to punish for it.

Eric was brave. He actually lectured them. He stood up for me. He told them who I was and that they would lose me if they rejected that. Eric was just a tutor. I was just a child who wanted to feel safe, and knew I never would, after what happened to Amelia. Neither of us had the authority to stand up to a man like my father. But he did it anyway. There was no priest this time. They didn't handle it while I was sleeping or distracted. No. My father wanted me to understand what would happen if I ever used the name Serenity again. This time, he made me attend the execution.

When we got home, all I wanted to do was cry. To hurt. To let the loss wash over me. But my father . . . my father had his own hurt. I had seen the whip used on the slaves. I never understood it. I knew, but I never *really* knew. Each hit stung, for me, and for Amelia. *Crack.* I felt the pain for both of us. *Crack.* I felt the pain for Eric. *Crack. Crack. Crack.* My father made me pay for choosing a new name. For choosing anything at all. I still remember his sneering. His quips about letting me have bloody sheets, if I wanted to be a woman so badly.

His message was clear. I was his *son*. This meant two things. I would never be his daughter. Not in his eyes. And if I were not his son . . . Eric's noose would fit just as well around my neck.

When I was fifteen, I lost hope.

CHAPTER TWENTY-ONE

Birds of a Feather

Ed was the only person in my family who didn't yell at me. Henry brought Autumn, who clearly felt a little awkward about the situation, and even Gil got mad at me. It must have looked bad, if Gil managed to notice. Ed, on the other hand, just seems upset. When Sara brought him back home, he was happy to see me recovering but had no new ideas about bypassing the circles in the capital. Nevertheless, he insisted he would make progress and asked Sara to bring him over for longer periods of time. Sara is fine with this, so I am too.

Honestly, I'm just happy he didn't yell at me about recklessness. I have now been so thoroughly dressed down that it's a wonder I have anything left to wear. With all that out of the way, it is time to finally move everyone to Clarrise's building. Well, everyone who wants to come. Sara and I will be staying together, provided she stops blushing for long enough to let me agree to her suggestion. From my family, Henry, Autumn, Mom, Ed, and Mariah will be joining us. Peter and Sara's dad will be coming along as well. Gilbert, August, Leo, and Charlotte are staying behind for now, at least until Leo is ready to face the world again. Gilbert has a detailed web of relationships he can't extract himself from, and August is staying with his parents, who, truth be told, have zero interest in following me anywhere.

I will still see them frequently, as Sara and I promised to help Charlotte transition physically. We have, regrettably, failed to do this with the consistency I had hoped, what with my now-famous fuckup leaving me unconscious for so long. I'm excited to actually get into it. I realized something while Sara was picking up Ed and I was packing up Suzume's toys. My problem is, essentially, that I have spent so long in a constant state of tension that I nearly forgot what it's like to, well, not be stressed out of my mind. I still have to be stressed, of course. We have mountains of ice to melt. But . . . I've helped build a good thing here. A safe place. A lot of them, actually.

People are in danger, but we are giving them options. Communication being key among them. There is a clear reason the church has been limiting it. It's got to be the most dangerous tool revolutionaries could have. And when the people are ready, I'll be right there next to them, fighting. But in the meantime, I actually have some breathing room. I can spend a little time with my family, who I am finally on good terms with. Start enjoying a relationship for the first time in this life. Do some fucking research for a while. Yeah, lives depend on it, which makes it high stakes, but damn. I missed just doing science without looking over my shoulder. Just a little science, as a treat.

"Is everyone ready?" Sara asks as we pull up a couple of carts to the border of the Radiant Woods. As usual, I feel queasy the closer we get, but I have gotten accustomed to the feeling. This is one thing I need to focus more on as well. Burning these fucking woods down. But I have no idea where to start.

"I'm Gucci," I reply.

"Where do you hear these strange words?" my mom asks before nodding in assent to Sara.

"Little Lily lives in her own little world," Henry says dismissively. "We are good over here!" Next to him, Autumn looks a little sick herself as she faces down the woods.

"Uh, y-yeah," Ed agrees. "We are ready." He looks down at Mariah's now-undeniable baby bump and gulps.

"Ready to go, Mom," Peter calls, holding his grandfather's hand tightly. It's cute how Peter started calling Sara *Mom*. The two have gotten extremely close over the years and I'm pleased she has fulfilled that role for him. Unfortunately, I suddenly start wondering what he's likely to start calling me eventually, and my face pales. All right, let's not follow that line of thought any further. Thankfully, Sara, satisfied that everyone is prepared, interrupts it for me.

"All right, everyone. Hang on to your hats," she calls, then puts her free hand on the trunk of the nearest tree. Just like that, as always, we find ourselves immersed, if briefly, in a strange forest. The tree she touched remains the same, but my nose burns with the pungent smell of a Bradford pear tree. I swear we have entered near one of those more times than makes sense, considering the biodiversity of the woods. It's like the Collector, unable to kill us while we are in the woods, is taunting us. Possibly me specifically, if it somehow knows about my correct opinion on pears. I dismiss that idea; it's not like anyone can eat the fruit of Bradfords. If it is intentional, it's likely just to assault us with the repugnant smell the plant is famous for.

Pretty goddamn petty for an endless nightmare forest, or an all-powerful deity, or whatever this little shit is. But what do I know? I'm just an interdimensional lesbian.

Before I can ponder the question further, Sara leads us back out of the Radiant Woods and into the mountainous terrain surrounding one of my favorite vertical communities. Everyone breathes a sigh of relief as we escape the uncanny smell of rotting fish the tree had been exuding. Well, everyone but Sarafyna. She has a scowl on her face, and not one that seems to be inspired by a foul odor.

I turn to count the members of our party, making sure no one got lost in the hell woods. Everyone seems to have let go of each other and is checking through their luggage. I sigh in relief. We've been using the woods as transportation for a few years now, but I still get a little worried whenever we pass through. Especially as the woods have possibly started to react to us. We are never there long enough that it can harm us, and Sara seems to be faster at moving us than the woods are. Nevertheless, I will be relieved when we have an alternate option.

I turn back to Sara, whose worry lines are trying to engrave themselves on her face. She is hanging back behind the group a bit and appears to be, quite literally, hanging on to her hat as she nervously pulls the brim down over her eyes. "Hey, Sara," I call out as I walk toward her. "Everything all right? You seem a bit . . ." I pause for a moment. "Not Gucci?" The question is awkward, but it helps smooth out the frown lines on her face.

"No, no, I'm all right. I just have a lot on my mind," she says.

"Is it about the room? Because, although you never let me reply properly, I would love to move in with you! I think it'd be great to see more of each other than we are now," I say. Then I worry that she is actually regretting the request and hastily add, "If you still want to, of course. If not, I'm happy to wait on it. I know your family will be pleased to keep you around."

She blushes as if something just occurred to her, then pulls her hat farther down over her face. "N-no, I still want to!" she assures me. "I'm looking forward to it! Although, I did want to clarify something about that. It does have, uh . . . two bedrooms. So . . ."

It's my turn to blush a little. We haven't talked about that particular topic much, since Sara is still sort of figuring herself out. I'd actually assumed that much. It does still give me goosebumps that she's revealed she's been wondering about it. I guess I understand why she has been off. It's pretty cute, all things considered. Unfortunately, I am a terrible person.

As such, my response is an intentional misinterpretation that turns her pink crimson. "Woah, kids? Already? Sara, I love you and all, but this is just moving too quickly. I mean, I'm sure you can figure something out with your fancy divine magic, but if you don't mind, I think you should take the other room for now instead."

She looks up at me with a look of sheer panic not seen on a woman's face since my best friend confessed his crush on me in middle school.

"N-no, I meant, I wanted—" she stutters, then her panic turns to true fear. Before I can process what is happening, her body starts to transform. Her mouth splits to her ears and boasts multiple rows of teeth while one arm tears through her blouse, expanding in size to make a massive chitinous surface.

I don't have the wherewithal to respond like I would if someone else was attacking me. All I can think is, well, this has got to be in my top ten worst and most unexpected breakups. Maybe in my top five, even. Unfortunately, it's not the only one on the list caused by a dumb joke.

Her massive arm swings at and then behind me. I flip around just in time to see a carbon arrow tear through her makeshift shield, her muscles contracting around it just in time to stop it from piercing my skull. Fuck. I don't know what the fuck is happening, but a lot of people we both love are all around us.

Thankfully, the group is all together and only a little ways ahead of us. Sara is literally hissing in pain behind me, and my eyes bulge as I realize her blood has splattered across my face. I want to soothe her, but there is no time. Another carbon arrow splits her chitin and flesh, and her hiss mixes with a scream just as I peek around her. The second I can see everyone, I put up a dome of force mana to protect my family. "Sara, they're safe, you can drop that and heal!" I yell as I flip around. The second I do, she is already letting her shield fall and the wounds are stitching themselves back together. The arrows fall to the ground like discarded garbage.

I pull her into a brief hug and whisper, "Thank you," before releasing her. We both run to check on our families first. We can respond to whoever did this when they are safe. They are all crouching behind the carts, uninjured, and Sara and I share a sigh of relief. "Where did that come from?" I immediately ask, and Sara gasps.

"I . . . I don't know," she replies, her arm fully healed and hanging from a hole where her sleeve once was. "I just . . . I looked up and someone was aiming at us. Annie, they were inside the woods . . ." she says, forgetting to use my Potestia name.

"Over there!" Ed calls a moment later, peeking over the cart and pointing past the tree line. "H-how is that possible?"

"Must be another divine mage," Henry guesses, hugging Autumn close to his chest.

"But . . . how did they know where to find us?" Autumn protests a moment later.

"It doesn't matter; we have to stop them, now," I respond.

"They look like . . ." Ed starts, pausing. "Lily, they look like some kind of giant . . . bird? Is it one of the monsters from the forest? Did any of them know magic?"

I raise an eyebrow. "I . . . I don't think so? Maybe the woods are changing them, to hunt us. Sara, we have to go after them, we—"

"I'll go alone," she argues. "Stay here, Lily. Keep this shield up. I'll get one of them. Trust me, and stay back."

I want to argue. I don't want to send her while I hide back here. I want to actively help. I don't want to fear for her while she is gone. But she is right. I can protect everyone here, she can't. She can move freely through the woods. I can't. And I promised her I wouldn't make stupid, arrogant decisions. So I nod. "Come back safe, all right?" I plead.

"I promise," she says. Then, before my eyes, her body melts like wax and forms into something not unlike a giant crow but with six wings, a red hue, and a lot more claws. I let her through the force barrier, and she disappears into the woods.

CHAPTER TWENTY-TWO

Hat Trick

Sarafyna

My eyes grow sharper with my claws and talons, and my ears keener. I fly directly into the Radiant Woods I was so desperate to escape for so long, and as soon as I do, it taunts me.

"Do you really think this will change anything?"

The moment I pass the first tree, I am aware of everything. I can feel the woods around me. They are endless and extend in all directions. From the outside, it feels like they grow in little patches on the planet's surface, like distinct areas. But once I am inside, the sensation nearly flips. Like the borders of the woods circle little isolated sections of reality. It gives me the same uneasy feeling it always has. The same sense of wrongness, like a sound whose origin moves whenever you approach it.

"This is reality, Sarafyna."

I focus for only a moment and immediately find my targets. There are three figures together. I can immediately tell they aren't part of this . . . hell. They aren't victims like me, but interlopers of some kind. I assume priests at first, but that doesn't feel right. The woods are moving them away from me, or trying to, at least. We haven't played this game in a while, but I have only gotten better at it. I am no longer the nearly mindless monster Annie pulled out of here. I can move through the Radiant Woods like I own them. Faster than they can move priests or whoever these people are.

"You can't keep her here."

It's something like swimming in oil, shifting through the woods. The filth of them slides across me as I move from one spot to another, easily tracking the fleeing trio. I wonder why the woods don't do as I would and take them directly to a border to escape, but my thoughts are quickly cut short as I fly over the trees and see two of them ascending to meet me. They don't feel like the victims of the woods, but they clearly aren't human either. They have wide, feathered wings growing from their shoulders, a joint that is shared with more traditional arms. Feathers decorate all their visible skin, sparing only their faces and hands, not unlike an ape's hair.

Their eyes are sharp and angled like a hawk's, and they have beaks instead of mouths. Before I know it, the one on the left, the one with brilliant emerald-colored feathers, begins to cast. *Those feathers would look lovely on a hat*, I think for an indulgent moment, until I see the same strange arrow that nearly killed Annie flying at me. Then I grow angry. Whoever that is, whatever species they are, they tried to kill Annie. I fly at them with the speed I've practiced outside the city for years, spiraling past the spell.

The other bird . . . person forms and fires the same spell, forcing me to veer out of the way at the last moment. Then both create some kind of mana barrier with a similar green tint to Edward's wind mana. It turns and flows around them, warping the air in a way I am wary of. It also catches their wings at odd angles, throwing them into sharp turns and impossible maneuvers I could never pull off in my current form. In the moment it takes me to analyze what they are doing, they have already separated and flanked me, one above and one to my side.

I don't have Lillith's general combat sense. I have mostly fought priests, who are unused to enemies capable of questioning them at all, much less fighting back. Whoever these creatures are, they are far more prepared for resistance. Something about the priest comparison sets off a red flag in my head, but I can't quite pin it down. The moment's distraction is a moment too long, however, and before I know it, both of my opponents have moved. And one of them is closing the distance rapidly. I barely manage to shift in the air and dodge as a blade of the same material as the arrows swings through the air I just vacated.

Dodging isn't enough to protect me entirely, as the complex wind barriers catch my own wings and throw me down toward the trees in a roll. The world spins and I feel a ligament tear somewhere at the ferocity of the sudden change, and I have to rush to heal it quickly. It took them a matter of seconds to completely disorient me. Thankfully, we are in the Radiant Woods. I know where everything is around me, all the time. Had we fought anywhere else I wouldn't be able to find them, much less react. But we aren't anywhere else, so I can see the second enemy descending on me with a massive javelin, preparing to skewer me before I can recover my bearings.

I can't right myself in time, but I haven't needed to in years. I abandon my current form, returning to something not unlike the formless monster Annie found wandering these woods. My flesh becomes smooth and translucent, and I expand it outward, leaving a hole in the middle for the bird creature to plummet through. I see its eyes widen as it does exactly that, abandoning its weapon to reach taloned fingers toward any flesh it can reach as it passes. This I don't mind at all, accepting their talons like I accepted the priests, dissolving them on contact and absorbing their mana.

A screech escapes its mouth as it withdraws its hands like it just touched hot coals, and it continues to fall through me. As soon as it is clear, I rapidly re-form my wings, then body, choosing to grow them so I start upright rather than rotating. I immediately begin flapping my wings slowly and deliberately, regaining altitude. It's a short-lived victory. As soon as I have avoided the first, the second enemy is throwing a new form of mana at me, this time in a sickly purple color. I have no idea what it is, but as soon as it hits me, the world stops making sense. I can't discern directions or distances, sounds are too loud, and everything spins despite the direction of my body.

At the same time, another wind attack assaults my wings and I feel myself lurching across the sky. Or down? A moment later, a massive branch breaks through my spine and erupts through my gut, painting itself with blood and bile. I cough and my own acid comes out. The world is still spinning. But it is only spinning for my physical senses. I clench my eyes shut and focus. Slowly, I am able to discern the layout of the woods again. I am able to spot all three of my enemies, two in the sky and one some distance away on the ground. I quickly modify my body, just to end the pain and aid my focus.

"Well, that was easy enough," a masculine voice jokes. "One chimera down. Think we still have time to take another crack at the queen?" he asks.

"Nah," a feminine voice replies. "She knows we're here now. We'll get her next time she moves." The two hover in the air, using both mana and wings to stay in the same spot without too much movement. They are next to each other now, right in front of the branch they impaled me on. They are smirking at me.

"Well, make sure it's dead," the masculine voice orders.

"Me? You do it! Did you see what it did to my talons? I'll need a fucking sage to get this healed! You do it!" she protests.

They believe they have won. But they tried to kill Annie. And they will try again. It's obvious why it seems like this is over. They can't see me healing. And I couldn't close the distance when I was moving freely. Even if I could, I couldn't get around their wind or whatever other disorienting mana they are using. But I don't need to. I am in the Radiant Woods. As soon as I am done healing, I shift through the world. Here, moving small distances is as easy as long ones.

Before either can react, I am directly between them, my leathery wings colliding with their feathered ones and sending us all toward the forest floor. As both my enemies struggle to free themselves from me, I extend arms-turned-tentacles toward them both, growing quills and spines to bite into them as I wrap around both their waists.

"It's . . . it's a fucking sage!" The feminine voice comes from the cobalt creature while the other caws in pain. Immediately, I feel the pain of their arrows piercing my body from all directions, but I bite back the cry they try to summon. They tried to kill Annie, and I am going to find out why.

I feel blood building in my throat, but I simply re-form my body around it. I grip the two more tightly and immediately feel crunching. Their attacks grow more desperate for a moment, but I have them now. It was too easy. My tentacles begin to grow around them, enveloping their bodies in flesh.

"W-what are you doing?" the cobalt one pleads. "W-wait, we can—"

Neither of us gets to finish what we started. None of our wings are free and we all collide with the forest floor with a sickening *splat.*

I feel my own flesh separate and scatter with the impact. My blood immediately paints the surrounding flora and I feel several of my own bones crack. It hurts, but I have been the complete master of my body for a long time. The wounded bones melt into nothing as my body returns to a gelatinous shape. My formless flesh spits out the remains of the strange arrows that tore into me, and I quickly form a human head and arms from the top.

I look down to see both of my opponents dead where we landed. They were . . . oddly fragile when I finally made contact. Their own blood decorates their clothes, and one large, snapped feather on the emerald one seems to be releasing more of it than any other body part. The thought of the brightly colored feather adorning a hat is no longer enticing. Instead, I am starting to feel a bit sick. They weren't monsters of the woods. They have clothes, even. They spoke to each other. They knew the exact same spells for some reason. And if they hadn't been here, in the Radiant Woods, they would have been able to outmaneuver me entirely. They weren't priests either. These were people, and not ones who were desperate for death.

But they were people who tried to kill Annie. I set my jaw, then turn as I feel the third approaching. I don't know why this one didn't fly up to help, at least not at first. I feel their mana before I see them, and I tense. They are moving quickly, far faster than I have seen anyone but Annie move. When they emerge from the trees, I shift, allowing them to find their dead friends. Or rather, allowing her to find them. This one isn't the same as the others; no feathers, but she isn't human either. She has an obviously feminine build. From the sides of her head grow ears like Suzume's. They grow from the same place as anyone's but extend to the top of her head, pointing up. She also has a tail and strangely shaped legs.

She howls as soon as she sees the mess of her friend's bodies, then flips around. Her back arches and fangs present themselves from her mouth. I don't care to find out what kind of mana she has. No doubt she can throw me around as easily as the others, and I want to bring her back alive if possible. Something courses through my veins whenever I am here in the woods. An instinct to kill. Something I cultivated when I was alone and it hurt to allow myself to think. But I bite it back. I need to ask why. I step on a twig and she turns and runs in my direction immediately, but I shift the woods around us.

She recovers her footing astonishingly quickly, running on all four limbs, but I am no longer in the spot she's approaching. I make another noise and she turns again. I shift. Again and again I do this, until finally I make a noise and she fails to respond. I shift us again and make another noise, then another. We have flown past cacti, massive trees, fields of flowers, and deep rivers, and she is already distraught. I can hear her breathing deeply. I can see her eyes bulging. Then I shift only myself so I am behind her, and I immediately envelop her head in gelatinous flesh. I don't dissolve it, however. I just deprive her of air.

Her struggle is immediate, claws tearing into me furiously. It doesn't matter; she might as well be tearing at water. I heal faster than she can damage me. Her struggling grows more desperate the longer she goes without air, all four limbs nearly breaking themselves in their attempts to wound me. Finally, she begins to slow. Instead of attacking, she pushes two hands into me and tries to force her head out. I just allow the flesh to give, enveloping her to the elbow and denying her leverage. Her struggles weaken, then slow and finally stop.

It's time to take her to meet my girlfriend.

CHAPTER TWENTY-THREE

Cat Girls and Mean Girls

I look down at the unconscious woman, bound to a steel chair in a pair of Clarrise's own flavor of mana-restricting cuffs. Once we got her back to the main building and got her mask off, we discovered the nose, mouth, and fur of a cat to match her ears and tail. They aren't quite right, as they conform to a more humanoid skull, but it's very clear they're feline. It was very clear to Suzume as well. She is usually the sweetest ray of sunshine to descend upon either world I have lived in, but a single whiff of this woman and she was hissing from the wagon the entire way here. All of this to say, what I am looking at is a cat girl. Finally, some proper isekai adventuring.

Of course, this particular cat girl tried to kill me with the help of some bird people and an ancient, unknowable hell forest, so we aren't off to an amazing start, but time will tell. I'm sure I simply need to demonstrate the ability to walk in a straight line and say, *Hey, girl, I see you,* and she'll be head over heels for me in no time. I sigh as the comical scene plays out in my mind, then look up at my companions. Most of our families are unpacking, but Sara and, for some reason, Edward want to be here to talk to our new friend when she wakes up. "I'm more attracted to eldritch girls anyway," I mutter.

"Eldritch?" Sara questions.

"Girls?" Edward adds, and I remember I haven't actually been clear about the nature of my and Sara's relationship with everyone in the family. With the drama of displaying it in front of the stewards of the Kingdom of Endings and making no effort to hide it in front of Clarrise, it has slipped my mind. Especially since we are sharing a room here, but I suppose in Potestia few people would assume two women alone in a room were interested in each other. Ugh. I have so many things to do. So many stressors. And now, apparently, I have people coming out of the damn Radiant Woods to murder me. Moving people around is going to get complicated if there are more than those three enemies after me.

"Uh, I'll explain later. Suffice to say it just means something incomprehensible, possibly maddening," I answer. Sara and Ed look at each other in confusion.

"You mean eldritch?" Sara asks.

"Girls?" Ed asks again.

"Yes," I respond, again not clarifying to whom. "You, uh, really knocked her out, huh?" I deflect instead of getting carried down that rabbit trail. Cat girls aside, this is extremely serious. The woods have found a way to fight back.

Sara blushes. "I may have gotten a little carried away," she admits. "But . . . they were powerful and well coordinated. I don't know if I could have won otherwise."

I nod. I wish she had grabbed a sample or two from the bird people; I'd be fascinated to study them. But I am glad she came back in one piece. I did not care for my time as a goalie while she did the fighting.

"Do you think we can wake her up?" I ask, looking with interest at the white whiskers protruding from our captive's cheeks. I can't figure out what they are actually for. They're too short to extend past the sides of her head. She also has none over her eyes, and if there are any on her arms or legs, they are covered by clothes. They are either entirely vestigial, used for something completely different than a normal cat's, or a result of something I don't understand.

"Uh, yeah, I think I can do that," Sara says, approaching the chair. She places one hand on the woman and closes her eyes. A moment later, the captive's eyes fly open and she immediately hisses at me before looking around with wide, panicked eyes. Her pupils fill the majority of her eyes in an unsettling way and her tail actually bushes up like a raccoon's.

"Hey, girl, I see you," I try, and her gaze snaps toward me. Her head flicks up and down, first to my hair, then to my eyes. Her hair seems to actively frizz as she looks at me and she only responds with another hiss. "Well, it was worth a shot. Let's start over. My name is Lillith. You may know me from that time you tried to shoot me in the head. This is my girlfriend, Sarafyna. Really takes your breath away, doesn't she? She's a sweetheart, but she does have something of a temper, so sorry if she made a bad impression. And finally, my brother Edward. He's a nice guy, however he might smell. And you are?"

Her breathing is heavy and rapid like a wounded animal's. She bares her fangs at me, and I just wait, smiling at her. She looks at Sara and me with clear fear, then Ed with confusion. "Lillith has no brothers," she protests quietly.

I look over at my brother with a raised eyebrow.

"Well. That is alarming news. Which one of us is adopted, do you think?" I ask. Ed looks at me with bewilderment. "I don't know, we look pretty similar. I think I might have brothers. You didn't answer the question. Do you have a name or should I assign one?"

"No one has ever mentioned a family," she says again, glaring at my brother.

"Felicia it is. If you don't mind, Felicia"—I sigh—"I'd love to know exactly who failed to share my apparently alarming family registry with you. Who, and why. Whenever you're ready."

"What kind of question is that?" she snarls in response. "The whole world hates you! What do you mean why? Now let me go!"

I look at my two companions. Ed shrugs.

"You aren't exactly popular right now, Lil," he says. He's not wrong. There is certainly a type of person who finds me more than a little unpleasant.

"I like you," Sara counters with a blush, and I grin. She smiles back.

"See that, Felicia? Sarafyna likes me. So the whole world doesn't hate me, do they? I'd love to narrow it down some. Like, say, who specifically told you about me?" I press. "And what do they specifically want?"

"I didn't mean your chimera pet! My mother told me about you, who else? I don't understand what you are asking me!" she yells.

My mouth opens in confusion. That is . . . not the answer I was expecting.

"I'll admit this isn't the first time a girl has taken issue with me at her mother's insistence, but, uh, I have to say I don't think I've actually met yours. And your mother sent you to kill me because . . . ?"

She growls. "My mother didn't send me to kill you! How does that make any sense?"

We examine each other with bewilderment. Again, I look back at my companions. Sara just tilts her head and looks at the cat woman with consternation.

"Don't ask me; neither of you is making any sense from where I'm sitting," Ed says.

"All right, we aren't getting anywhere. Why don't you just tell me your story, Felicia? Where are you from, and why did you come here? Can you do that?" I ask.

"Why would I?" she spits.

"What does this room look like to you?" I ask, spreading my arms. She looks around with confusion. At the bed, then the large windows and the trees growing through them, as well as the kitchen through the door to the room. This gives her pause.

"A . . . home?" she answers, and I nod.

"Right. It's a home. Not a cell. Not a dungeon. Just a random empty home. It may be a tactical error, but I'm going to be honest with you. That'd be because we don't have a dungeon. No jail. No prison. I'm a bit sour on the whole concept, truth be told. That does present a few concerns here and there, but only one of them matters to you. That is, I am not going to keep you captive. You and I are going to decide if you are dangerous to innocent people, or not. If you aren't, well, we can move forward from there. If you are, well, we won't.

"Now, I don't know much about you. I know someone with you tried to kill me, but I don't know to what extent you were involved. I don't know why. I don't know if you will do the same to anyone else. It would be a pretty good idea for you to fill in those details. If you won't, I'm not going to hurt you. I'm not going to torture or interrogate you while you bravely withhold what information you have. I'm just going to come to a decision, right here and now." I stare at her, and Ed stares at me. She sets her jaw while Ed shudders.

"You aren't very practiced at interrogations, are you?" she sneers in response.

"Nope," I reply immediately. "Like almost all people, I have zero experience interrogating my own attempted assassins. I'm pretty cool with that, truth be told. I haven't gotten nothing from this conversation though. I know you aren't from Potestia. Admittedly, the ears gave it away. We do speak a common language, which is interesting. But I also know you have strangely selective information about who

I am. You know enough to call Sara a chimera. A bit rude, but it does imply you know more about me than almost anyone here. But you didn't know I have brothers, which everyone in Potestia does by now.

"You hate me. Apparently, everyone where you live does, although I don't think I've ever been there. In other words, I'm fucking famous in a country I've never been to. Don't get me wrong, I get it. I'm hot. I have cool hair. A voice like an angel, or so Sarafyna tells me. But I haven't been on TV in a while, so I'm not really sure why you know all that. And here's the thing: if I am famous, then it's not even a damn secret, is it? So just tell me what I'm so famous and reviled for that you'd want me dead! Is that so hard?"

Felicia and Sara both gape at me for different reasons. "I've never said she has the voice of an angel . . ." Sara murmurs under her breath.

Finally, Felicia responds, ignoring Sara. "You really have no idea why I am here? You, Lillith, Harbinger of Endings? The demon queen here with a chimera sage in the middle of an invasion, and you have no idea why we would want you dead? I thought you were just playing games, but you really are clueless. We are here to end your invasion! To kill you before you can start the war we have spent our entire lives dreading! How sick are you? Of course we are going to fight back!"

I blink. I look at Sara and blink again.

"What? Demon queen? Bitch, I don't even like Dairy Queen. What the fuck are you going on about? I'm, like, eighteen, dude. I'm involved in a revolution in Potestia, I'll give you that, but that's it. I'm not invading anywhere!" I am truly at a loss now. *Harbinger of Endings* is alarmingly close to my actual name, and the intent behind it. The demon queen shit is obviously propaganda, but why? Who have I pissed off outside of Potestia? My best guess is the Collector. But that crotchety, old asshole hardly talks to anyone and hasn't been doing much with his priests. He has, in fact, been suspiciously docile. I had been prepared for much more pushback when I decided to use the Radiant Woods in my plans.

I suppose this must be why. Instead of fighting a battle he had little control over, he went out and started spreading rumors behind my back to people I hadn't met yet. The Collector: ancient, evil god and resident mean girl. Well, fuck you, Regina.

"You are invading," Felicia challenges. "You have crossed borders and set up military outposts all over the world. You are bringing your demonic soldiers from the third plane to the first, and you are showing no sign of slowing down. A demoness from the third plane starts moving armies into our territory and you want me to believe you have peaceful intentions?"

"The third plane?" Ed cuts in, asking the question for all of us.

"What, like . . . hell, right? You think we come from hell? I'll give you it's full of rich people, so I understand the confusion, but no. We are just from a shitty country," I say.

"I know where you are from, Lillith. Everyone knows where you are from, and what you are here to do," she replies.

I look back and forth between everyone in the room and sigh.

"You know what, this is a bit of a risk, but we are going to have to make a decision about you one way or another. Perhaps if I give you context, you'll more freely give me some. It's not like this setup is free from spies anyway. How would you like a tour of my demonic military outposts? We can continue this chat afterward," I suggest. I'm not certain how safe travel is going to be between communities now. I'm not sure how safe individual communities are, even. And I need to know. So I'll start by clearing the air with the cat girl, and see if she will be more open then. "What do you say, Sara? Are you up for that?"

"Yeah, I don't mind," she says.

"I, uh, I'd like to join you," Ed requests.

"Sounds like a party." I shrug. "So, Felicia, what about you? Would you care for a little context about my demon army?"

She glares at me, her pupils narrowing in a predatory way.

"My name is Ember," she finally replies.

CHAPTER TWENTY-FOUR

Curiosity

Sara and Ed are resting while I show Ember around. We are starting with the community we are currently at, for obvious reasons. The two are taking a break before we hit the Radiant Woods again. Everyone is understandably nervous about that trip. So I am handling this bit alone, with Sara's approval.

"And this," I announce, gesturing to my brother's lab, "is where my brother makes drugs. The guy with the messy hair is Henry, my youngest older brother. The pretty girl is Autumn. They're special friends. Hey, guys, this is Ember. If all goes well, we aren't going to try to kill each other soon."

Autumn blinks at me while Henry's focus is on some kind of herb he is grinding. I am honestly amazed at how quickly he got this lab set up. And at how attentive Autumn was to his work before we arrived.

"Um, hello," Autumn responds. "Nice to meet you. Are you a, uh, cat?" This question is more successful in grabbing Henry's attention and he finally looks up. I guess people try to kill me too often for him to take special note.

"Huh," he says after a moment. "Are you?"

Ember growls. "I'm an ailur, not a 'cat.' No more than you are an ape."

Autumn and Henry share a look.

"Why would Autumn be an ape? She doesn't look like an ape," Henry says.

"That's a long story," I respond. "One I am interested to learn our new ailur friend is aware of, actually. Suffice to say she is a person. But we can talk about that later. You mind telling Ember what you're working on? I'm trying to give her a decent idea about the type of community we have here."

Henry puts his mortar and pestle down before rolling his right shoulder, massaging his wrist at the same time.

"Yeah, all right. I assume you've seen the plants growing all over the building, poking into everyone's homes?" Henry says easily. Autumn looks at him like he's insane, but Ember doesn't seem to notice.

"Obviously," she answers.

"Right, well, these are largely protected from insects and other hostile influences using mana. My little sister there designed an artifact that scares them away with sounds people . . . er, humans can't hear. Our friend Clarrise created one that uses various scents. Some people use little barriers around them, but that's pretty mana intensive. We have a lot of little tricks like that to maintain them, but I'm trying to design an alternative. A mist-based potion to protect all the plants. They are our primary food source right now, so redundancy is never bad," Henry explains.

"An insecticide? Those are toxic," Ember says, and I raise an eyebrow. I grow more curious about her culture the more she speaks. I suspect it has not stagnated at nearly the same level as Potestia's.

"This one isn't," Henry says dismissively. "Well, it won't be when it's ready to actually use, anyway. That is an interesting name for it though. What's it mean exactly?"

"It means something made for killing bugs," I answer. This time Ember gives me the quizzical look.

"Huh. Well, it's not for that," Henry answers. "Not trying to kill the little guys, just scare them away. I'd be interested in how the ones you mean are made though. Or are they made? I guess if they are toxic, you probably have little use for them, right?"

"I could think of a few uses for them," Autumn mutters, and I let a smile paint the corner of my mouth.

"And what are you hanging around here for, Autumn?" I inquire.

She jumps a bit but straightens her back.

"Well, I didn't exactly have much of a plan for my future a few years ago. I was supposed to get decent at basic magic and enter a political marriage. That's changed now. So Henry is teaching me alchemy!" she says.

Oh, of course he is. I hadn't pegged Autumn as the type to find alchemy interesting, but I guess I hadn't pegged her as the type to find anything interesting, really. Nobles sort of have an air of . . . do-nothing, about them. Perhaps not fair to apply to people like Autumn who willingly gave up their noble titles.

"Oh, that's awesome, he's a good teacher. Taught me to read once upon a time. Very patient but knowledgeable at the same time. I've heard recent rumors he has inappropriate relationships with his latest students though," I joke, and Henry scoffs while Autumn blushes.

"Patient my foot. It took you less time to learn your letters than it takes Gil to get dressed in the morning." Henry laughs.

"Figures," Autumn says. "It's honestly rude how quickly you picked up mathematics."

Ember's examination of me only intensifies and I remember why I brought her here.

"Well, I had a head start in some ways. Anyway, we have a lot of stops to make today. We gotta go collect Sara and Ed; I want to give her a tour of some other settlements," I say.

"Already? After you got attacked on the way here? Are you sure that's safe?" Henry asks, worry suddenly tainting his voice.

"Yeah, I know. Don't worry, I won't push myself. I've got Ed and Sara. No one is getting past Sara in the Radiant Woods. I don't have to push too hard while I'm there either, truth be told. Besides, I thought we'd head back and visit Charlotte first. She may not be interested in fighting Potestian mages, but I suspect she is a dangerous person to attack anyway," I say.

"Still, be careful," Autumn adds.

"I promise. Take it easy, you two. Don't do anything I wouldn't do," I say. Finally, I nod at Ember and we start to head back to the room I am now sharing with Sara. "So, what do you think? Of our first big evil military outpost of demons? That kid with the prosthetic was particularly scary, right? Wait until you meet my buddy Ozzy. He's got the heart and temperament of an angry lion."

Ember looks at me appraisingly as we walk. Her focus is so intense, she doesn't notice the people staring and pointing as we walk by. At my leisurely posture, at her black fur, at the cuffs she now wears in front of her body, and at her digitigrade legs. Maybe they are just looking at our stark height difference. I'm a bit short and she is . . . definitely not. Which biologically makes sense considering the aforementioned legs. In any case, it's all lost on her. We are in front of my new room before she finally answers me.

"I want to see all of them" is all she says. That's progress I can do . . . oh, god dammit. All means all. I pause before opening the door.

"All of them . . . as in . . . all, all?" I ask.

"Yes," she says with a glare. "The Nexus has shown us everywhere you travel, so I know how many places you have invaded. I want to see all of them."

I groan. I'd very much like to avoid visiting the Kingdom of Endings. *No, no, I'm not the demon queen, Harbinger of Endings! These people, referring to me as the queen of endings? No, that's unrelated.* Yeah, that'll go over well. Whatever, I can save them for last. Maybe she'll come around before then. I decide to change the subject for now.

"The Nexus?" I ask. "What's that?" She looks at me with narrowed eyes before clicking her tongue and looking forward. After a moment of silence, I decide she isn't going to answer me, so I open the door. I have to smile when I walk inside. The place is a mess. Half-unpacked luggage is everywhere, with almost nothing in place. Almost nothing. On one wall, at least two dozen hats have been neatly displayed on various hooks and nails. I walk into the next room and find my two favorite girls on one of two beds. Sara and Suzume are both fast asleep, sprawled out, side by side, and both on their backs.

As I walk in, Suzume is the first to notice, trilling and looking up at me without rolling over, until she notices Ember behind me. Then she immediately regains her footing and hisses. This wakes up Sara, who looks at me with hair that resembles a half-styled afro of tangles. "It's all right, Suzie," she whispers before looking at me with bleary eyes. "Time to go?"

"I mean, you can get the jungle on your head sorted first, if you like," I offer. In response she shakes her head a little and, with the aid of divine magic, her hair is perfectly styled and smooth a moment later. "Well, that's not fucking fair," I say, and she grins at me.

"One second," she says before running to her hat wall, scanning it for a few minutes, then selecting a feathered bycocket. If it were green instead of black, I'd think she looked like a femme Robin Hood. "Ready," she announces. "How did she like the place?"

Ember growls at this and I pout back at her in a slightly mocking way. She isn't saying anything to indicate she is receptive, but I think somewhere, deep down, she is. Having her preconceptions challenged is having an effect, if not a visible one. Because however she looks and growls, I can feel the tiny seed of grief she keeps trying to fight off.

It doesn't take long to collect Edward and get provisions for the trip. Half an hour later and we are headed toward the Radiant Woods again. "All right, Ember. Now is the time. I need to know how dangerous this is. Are we going to be ambushed as we approach the woods? Will there be more people waiting to kill us? Tell us now. The only chance we have at sparing them is if we see them coming. The only chance we have at sparing any of you is if we aren't surprised," I say, looking directly into the taller woman's eyes.

She pauses for a moment, then shakes her head. "N-no. No, I don't think so. We . . . weren't supposed to attack you at all. We were scouts. It was . . . It was Skia. She saw you undefended and thought she could be some kind of fucking hero. No one is supposed to attack you unprovoked," she admits. That certainly does explain some things. And is a point in favor of *not a danger to innocent people*. Short-term, anyway. Scouts can be pretty dangerous. Still, if that's true, she didn't actually try to kill me herself. She just . . . didn't stop her friend from doing it. Yeah, all right, that's not amazing either, but there is still a lot I don't know.

Ed asks the next question before I get the chance. "And if any other scouts see you, cuffed and accompanied by an infamous demon queen?"

"I . . . don't think they will just attack. It depends on who it is. And how dangerous they are. But . . ." She pauses, not wanting to give military secrets away but hesitant to give up on seeing more. She has already seen enough to have more questions, and she probably doesn't particularly want to die. It's true some soldiers are willing to do just that, but not nearly as many as the movies imply. "I don't think so," she finally repeats. I look at her appraisingly for a few moments. Then I give Sara a questioning glance, and she gives me a gentle nod. Finally, I create a shield of force around all of us.

Here, so near the Radiant Woods and the intense grief contained within, my mana is completely invisible. It also takes very little effort, so the risk of my cancer fighting it is relatively low. We should be safe even if Ember is wrong or lying. "Well. All right, then. Let's go meet some more friends," I announce, and we approach the Radiant Woods.

CHAPTER TWENTY-FIVE

Changes

Leo

My hands tremble as I stand at the door to my room. Lillith is back already, showing our community to some woman from outside Potestia. Again she is being too trusting. But she isn't just showing her where we live. No, she is letting this stranger watch while Sarafyna helps Charlotte. I want to be there as well, to see how possible it really is. Sara has started, but she needs Lillith to make real progress, apparently. I don't really understand how that works.

But I want to be there. I want to support Charlotte like she supported me, and I want to be there as myself. As Leo. But, dressed as myself, I can't bring myself to open the door. On the other side, Charlotte is going through something we have both talked about for years. Something I should be by her side for. But when I look at the handle, all I see is a group of nobles, rich and cruel. Looking down at me. Beating me while I can't do anything but beg them to stop. The woman who actually did stop them is there too, and I don't know how to face her.

I don't want to be saved. I don't want someone else flying in at the last moment and making me safe. I want to be able to open this door and just . . . be allowed to exist. I don't even want to have to fight for myself. I don't want to earn it. I don't want it to be given to me. And I don't want it protected by my friends. I want to just . . . have it. At least to the same extent that everyone else does. But I don't. Part of me wants to believe I will if I do what Charlotte is doing. That once no one can tell I ever looked any different, I'll feel that safety. But I know I won't. Part of me will still be stuck on the ground, aching and in pain in that empty lot at the academy.

Part of me will always believe that when people look at me, they don't believe I really count as the man I am. Because changing will make me feel comfortable, but it's not about that to them. I will still have stepped out of line, out of their vision of who I am supposed to be. And I won't be safe. This is part of my reluctance to go through with it. Because once I do, how will I know who I am actually safe around, and who I am safe around until they find out who I am? If I can't walk through this door as I am now and know that I am safe, then I will never be safe. And I can't.

I lower my hand back to my side, turn around, and sit down with my back to the door. Not today. Not with a stranger there. I glance up at my vanity for a moment.

I could get dressed like they want me to. I could put on the dress and the makeup, and walk out there. But I can't bear that anymore. Not right now. I have done it a few times now. But it carries with it a different kind of danger. A danger closer to home. I know some men here have been wearing makeup, but that doesn't make it feel any better to put mine on. They didn't have a mother, so excited to share it with them the first time, and so disappointed when they hated it. It doesn't feel like a lie they were taught to carve onto their face their entire life. Until Charlotte, at least.

And that's the final piece of the puzzle. The part that keeps me locked up in my room. Because I hate the feeling of danger. The eyes on my back. The hatred. But I hate the pity too. The sad look in my friends' eyes when I do come out, dressed to protect myself. It's not the same as the fear. I don't even blame them for it. But that doesn't make it bearable. I've had to present as nothing more than a masculine girl for a long time, and everyone seemed to understand. But here, where it's supposedly safe to do otherwise . . . Well, no one has said anything, but it feels like there is an expectation to present the truth openly. And I'm just not ready. So instead, I rest my head against the door and listen.

"Ember, was it?" Charlotte asks curiously. "You are . . . amazing. Who did that for you? I have to assume it wasn't Sarafyna."

This is met with a low growl. "No one made me this way; I'm an ailur. I am who I am because my parents are ailur. The same reason you are a human," an unfamiliar woman says.

"Really?" Charlotte responds with interest. "Where are you from? I've never heard of your people before."

"What are we doing in this foolish man's house?" asks the new woman, Ember apparently, instead of answering.

"Foolish woman's house," Lillith corrects. "And we are here to do some magical HRT for her. It's one of the many services offered by our obviously militarized outposts of invasion. Are you ready, Sara?"

"Yep. Charlotte, do you mind the company? We can do this more privately if you like," Sara offers.

"No, no, absolutely not. I want to hear everything about Ember here," Charlotte says.

"I don't have anything to share," Ember growls.

"Ed, do you mind heading out and guarding the door? This could get a bit graphic—no boys allowed," Lillith says, and I hear a sudden thump followed by a man groaning.

"I, err, right, no problem. Ow," the startled Ed agrees. I hear him walk across the room before a door opens and closes. The room is silent for a solid minute after that, and my heart pounds. This is it. They are going to really, really help Charlotte.

"Oh, that . . . that feels strange," Charlotte says. "How peculiar . . ."

This is interrupted by a sudden, loud hiss.

"You're changing his body!?" Ember spits, horror coloring her voice. "That's . . .

that's monstrous! That's unnatural, what is wrong with you? The local sage doing it to herself is one thing, but this man too? It was all true, you are demons!"

I feel a pang as she yells this. She's right. It is basically blasphemy. It doesn't matter if I care, because other people will. And this is exactly what I am afraid of. We can do everything right. We can change ourselves so our clothes and names don't offend anyone. But the way we got there will still disgust them.

"Oh, fucking Christ, tell me you don't worship the damn Collector where you're from! That's just some petty bullshit, no need to raise your hackles about it," Lillith cries.

"The Collector? You mean the Nexus? Of course we don't worship it! But everyone knows you don't manipulate people's bodies! A sin is a sin no matter who you worship! The other sages will kill you when they find out! We are what we are for a reason!" Ember lectures.

I feel sick. "We are what we are for a reason." That's true, but . . . it doesn't mean what she thinks it means. I can't listen to this for another minute. I don't know what Lillith thought bringing this woman here would accomplish, but it was clearly a terrible idea. It was great learning there was a whole other country I'd never heard of and . . . they fucking hate me too.

I stand and walk away from the door. The arguing turns into muffled voices and I allow myself to collapse on my bed. Charlotte's transition was supposed to be amazing. It was supposed to give both of us hope. Instead, I just feel more hopeless than ever. I don't hear how the rest of the conversation goes. I'm sure Lillith gives a very harsh speech. Or maybe she just smacks Ember around a little. Either way, I now know what is waiting for me beyond the borders of Potestia. And it's not safety.

This little community feels more transient than ever. It's impressive that Lillith managed to get it set up. It's amazing that so many people, the dregs of society, have a chance to explore a new way of life. Lillith even says there are other men like me. Other women like Charlotte. Even one woman who often volunteers to go back to Potestia alongside Lily and Ed. It's a beautiful promise. But people will always be people, and people will always find someone to hate. And that someone will always include me and Charlotte. I will have to keep wearing the dress. But every dress feels like the one I was forced into that night. I can't live like that. I feel like I'm treading water in the middle of an endless lake. Like nothing will ever be right. Not for long.

After a while, the voices fade. There is no more arguing. I think I hear the door at least once, then there are no voices at all. It's quiet, until a soft knocking interrupts the brief peace. "Come in," I call. I don't look up, but I hear the door softly open, then close.

"Are you all right, Leo?" Charlotte asks. Her voice is the same as it was before, indicating that they haven't finished their work yet. I wonder if they were interrupted by the argument, or if it was always going to take multiple sessions.

"Fine," I answer. Neither of us believes that for a moment. I haven't been fine in a long time.

"How much of that were you listening to?" she asks.

I pause for a moment, consider lying, then sigh. "Up until that Ember lady started yelling about how evil you are for changing your body," I finally reply. I look up at her guiltily and my breath catches. They did more than I thought. Her face itself is . . . different. She still has a sharp chin, but its angle is . . . I don't know, narrower? It's odd; she looks like exactly the same person but completely different. Like a reflection in rippling water. She even has the beginnings of cleavage now, which feels . . . right. She has a glow to her.

"So. You missed the part where she explained that Lillith was a demon queen intent on subjugating her people, then," Charlotte guesses, and I blink.

"Demon . . . queen? Like in a children's story?" I respond. That is . . . more than a little silly. Lillith is a lot of things, but none of them end in *queen*.

"Much like a children's story," Charlotte agrees. "I wouldn't take her too seriously."

"Why did Lillith even bring her here?" I ask.

Charlotte smiles at me. "It's complicated, but . . . I think she is trying to introduce Ember to us. Not you and me specifically, but all of us. Everything these communities stand for. And who you and I are . . . that's part of it."

That thought does make me happy, if only for a moment.

I roll back over, looking away from my mentor. "Yeah, well. It doesn't change the fact that she hates us already," I say.

Charlotte is quiet for a moment. "No," she finally agrees. "No, it doesn't. But you know what? That won't stop us. It's all going to be all right, Leo. Trust me, please?" She always says this to me. Trust her. She'll make sure everything is all right. She just always fails to mention how. I'm not a child, and that isn't what I need. But my trust is what she needs, so I nod.

"I trust you, Charlotte," I reply quietly. I want to talk about something else, so I change the subject. "Where did everyone go?"

"Hm?" she replies, then realizes what I asked before I can clarify. "Oh, I guess Edward disappeared somewhere while we were working. They are off tracking him down."

"You can help them, if you want," I suggest. She is quiet for a moment, but she gets the message.

"All right, I'll leave you alone for now. Is there anything you want for dinner?"

"Anything is fine. Um, thanks, as always, Charlotte."

With that, my mentor leaves and I am alone again. As usual, I have a lot to process. I still have a lot to heal from. And I get about fifteen minutes to do it. After that, a quiet voice speaks to me from . . . the drawer next to my bed. I sit up and look at it. The muffled voice continues. I blink. Then I open the drawer and find the sphere Lillith gave me when I moved here. I didn't answer it. I have never actually used it. But . . .

I pick it up and listen. Not one but two men are speaking, and my sphere is picking it up.

"What else do you know?" one voice says.

"Not much. But she is definitely from another country I've never heard of. She isn't even human. More than anything, she definitely hates Lillith," the second voice responds.

CHAPTER TWENTY-SIX

Invaders

This is not going as well as I had hoped, but it is going better than I expected. Ember's revulsion to the magical altering of the body surprised me. It also connected a few dots. I don't know who or what the Collector, or the Nexus as Ember calls it, is. But either its influence extends past Potestia, despite the lack of worship it receives, or its taboo on changing the body has a common source. It could be a coincidence—it's not like people responded universally well to transitioning on Earth after all. But it feels the same.

As far as I can gather, tattoos and piercings don't elicit the same strong reaction. At least, Ember didn't react to mine or anyone else's. And it wasn't the lack of respect for gender as a law of reality that seemed to throw her. It was the very concept of changing the body from its original design. Except in Sarafyna's case, because she is a sage, apparently. I have to assume this refers to her divine magic. Her mention of other sages concerns me, especially since I get the feeling they are the rulers of her country in some way. It was bad enough when the national religion had mind control powers, but if all the country's leadership does? Well, I wouldn't want to live somewhere run entirely by Baldwins.

And of course they have some sort of special exemption from the taboo. Still. Her outrage had the easy tone of a child echoing their parent. Like a belief wedged into her like thorns, but lacking roots to hold their place. This is important. We have visited a couple dozen communities now. Places with elected leaders, others that chose leaders by drawing, and my favorites, the ones with organizers but no established authority figures at all. It takes days to visit all of them. But I promised to show them to Ember. I have shown her all kinds of places, played all kinds of games, and eaten different kinds of food. We spend the night in some of them, check in back home with the whisper sphere, and move on to another. I have introduced her to people all over the world now. Former slaves and Mages of Penance. Dozens of different ways of life that people have been allowed to choose.

One thing she hasn't seen is a military force. Anything to indicate we are invaders. She has seen people living their lives for the first time. Listened to their stories. She had nothing kind to say to any of them. Not a word of comfort or a hint of compassion. Outwardly, she was nothing but hostile. But I am hopeful. Because this entire time, she has been fostering a deep grief. One I could only feel a hint of when we first met. But the longer she spends around Sara and I, the more it resonates through her bones like music. It is a rope, knotted around a wooden stake. It's a stake she has held through her heart for so long her flesh has grown around it. Into it. But I can feel it. If I grab that rope and pull, I can tear it out.

It will be painful. It will be bloody. And it will leave an open, empty hole behind. But it will be something that can heal. I don't know what she is comparing everything she has seen with. I've never seen her home, and I've never met her family. But I know that what she has seen is not what she was told she would find. It's so easy to believe strangers are invaders. A malignant force creeping into your home. It is sickeningly easy . . . until you meet them. Until you meet their children and hear their stories. Until the foreign monster is revealed to be just another person.

She has resisted this every step of the journey. This is always the way. To find excuses to dismiss their personhood. To vilify them and curse them. To justify fear in any and every way available. But I can feel it failing. I can feel the truth burrowing into her. So this isn't going as well as I hoped. But yes, it's going better than I expected.

"There is one more," I hesitantly admit. We walk through the green field near one of the more democratic communities in the middle of an open plain. "I'll be honest with you, it's not our best. In a way, it is more depressing and pathetic than anything you have seen so far. In another way, it will be the closest to what you were expecting. You asked to see all of them, so I'll show it to you. But truth be told, I'd rather not. I think you know enough to understand what I stand for, and this last place . . . it's not what I stand for." I leave it at that and Ember is silent for a while. She actually lowers herself slowly to the ground and sits, her tail flicking behind her. It's an impressive feat with her hands bound.

Again, I look at her legs and wonder why a bipedal creature would still have that structure. It explains her height; she'd have to be that tall just for balance. Then I examine her face for a moment, shrug, and sit down next to her. Ed and Sara share a glance and join us so we are all sitting in a circle, flattening the tall grass. "You are still invaders, you know," Ember says.

"Invaders, are we?" I scoff. "On all this unused land. Providing for ourselves. Asking for nothing but a safe place to live our lives. What are we invading, Ember?"

"You crossed our borders and built entire cities on our land. That's exactly what an invader is. A fucking colonist," she retorts.

And sure, I guess we are literally colonists, but not in the way she wants to believe.

"We aren't what you've been told, Ember. We aren't the forces of hell. We aren't the first wave of some superpower here to drive you from your homes and take it for ourselves. These people are refugees, occupying unused land because their homeland wants to enslave them."

"Occupying our land, past our border," Ember corrects me, and I roll my eyes.

"We crossed your border so we are invaders? What, you drew a squiggly line on a paper somewhere and if anyone crosses it, they are an evil demon you have to drive away? That's a child's game, Ember. You play that in a sandbox and then you grow the fuck up. You don't base decisions about actual people's lives around it!"

Ember scoffs. "You're hardly objective about this. But we aren't getting anywhere. I want to see the last one. I don't care if it's your least favorite. Show me," she says.

I sigh. Well, fuck. But I suppose we weren't going to get anywhere with half the truth anyway.

"She was going to see them eventually, Lil." To my right, Ed shrugs.

"Uh, can I wait outside this time? I keep getting weird looks when we go there," Sara asks, leaning back on her hands.

"What, they don't like sages? Is that why you don't like it there? I don't care about that; plenty of people don't like the sages," Ember says.

"That is actually very interesting," I say. "See, it's not that bad, just telling me a little bit about where you're from. But no, not sages. Assuming I understand you correctly, I don't think I am a *sage*. That's all Sarafyna. No, it's lesbians they don't like. I kissed her in front of them on a recent visit when they were trying to set up a marriage for me. Anyway, one thing led to another and I couldn't exactly go with her on the next visit. Sorry about that, Sara."

"Wait, what?" Ed startles. "You two are . . . courting?" Oh, right, I keep forgetting to talk about that with them. The relationship is still new and I was planning on coasting for a while longer, but I guess we aren't doing much to hide it.

"Yes, Ed, we are courting. Don't worry about it," I reply. I'm about to elaborate, but I see Ember staring across at me with a previously unreached intensity. "Uh, hey, girl. What is it? Don't tell me you have a problem with it too, do you?"

She blinks, then shakes her head. "N-no, I don't care about that. It doesn't . . . The stories never mentioned the chimera being intelligent, much less romantically involved with you, but it doesn't matter. I suppose prophecies are always vague. But . . . you aren't a foreign sage, are you sure?" she asks.

"Prophecy? Seriously? You have been talking about some bullshit prophecy this entire time? Come on, man, that's an even worse reason to hate me than the squiggly paper line! But no, I'm not sure. I can only guess what you mean by *sage*, so I suppose I'm *not* sure I don't qualify. Care to share with the class?"

Ember looks back and forth between us, her mouth closed and calculations running across her eyes. Finally, she lets out a breath.

"A Nexus sage. Someone who can control and manipulate Nexus energy. Weren't you both using it to . . . Weren't you both using it back there?" Ember asks. So she does mean divine magic.

"No." I shake my head. "I was just using regular mana. I use it to help direct Sara. If that magic is what you mean, then yeah, that's all Sara. I'm just the trophy wife." Ember examines me even more intensely at this. Then something occurs to me. "Wait, why did you assume I was a 'foreign' sage and Sara was a 'local' sage? What's that about? We're from the same country."

She looks at me for a moment. She opens her mouth to respond, pauses, and I can see her expression shift as she changes course. "You just talk like a foreigner," she says finally. What does that mean? I talk like a foreigner?

"What? Do I have an accent? Wait, we both talk like a foreigner to you," I protest, but she looks away stubbornly. "I don't talk any differently than anyone else here. I mean, I say some eccentric things, I'll give you that, but . . ." And then it hits me. I do, in fact, speak differently than anyone else here. Or rather, I talk about different things than anyone else here. It's obvious, really. She is in contact with the woods, or Collector, or Nexus, or whatever you want to call it. The same entity that tortured Sarafyna and told her she was in hell.

In a way, Sara is local in a way I am not. They all are. They may have been born across different borders, but I am the only real foreigner here. The way I trail off doesn't go unnoticed. Sara's eyes widen as a similar realization dawns on her. Ember's eyes narrow as she watches me work out what she means. Ed, still reeling from my casual coming out, slackens his jaw as he tries to figure out what everyone else is reacting to.

"I thought you said you weren't a sage. Why lie about that?" Ember questions, and I hold my hands up in protest.

"I didn't! I don't have divine magic! Or Nexus powers or whatever. I just . . . look, what do you mean by foreign? Are there 'foreign' sages in your country?" I ask as she examines me.

"What's going on?" Ed interjects, but no one turns to respond. Sara's scars begin to grow more pronounced and her fingers lose their shape as she prepares to defend me as our guest grows more agitated.

"I think you know what I mean," she accuses. "I have never heard any local speak like you do. About the things you do. But I've heard plenty of it from the sages. But I don't know why I should be more open while you continue to lie."

Well, fuck. That is about as much confirmation as I need. I'm not the only one. There is someone else like me here. Multiple people. This only introduces a million questions. Are we all from the same place? How long have the others been here? How many of them are here? What does she think I'm lying about?

"All right," I say. "I am a foreigner. I'm not from this world. I'm older than I look. I had an entire other life in another reality. All cards on the table here. So. Will you tell me about your sages now?" Edward looks at me like I just spit up on myself, but Sara only looks concerned. Ember looks hostile.

"Yes, I figured that out," Ember replies. "I've suspected it since I first woke up. But you are still lying. I know this because every foreign visitor is a sage. If you couldn't control the Nexus, you couldn't come here. So why are you lying to me?"

CHAPTER TWENTY-SEVEN

Trade-Offs

'm supposed to have gotten here by divine magic? I suppose that does make sense. Magic may be real, but nothing I know about mana indicates it can bring a mind across worlds. The workings of divine magic, on the other hand, seem far more nebulous. If anything brought me here, it seems obvious that would be it. Still, I don't have it. If I did, I certainly wouldn't be fighting the urge to vomit at the thought of one more drink of Henry's medicine. Ember glares at me with an intensity and certainty so severe, I wonder for a moment if I'm wrong.

I hold my arms out to my side and half shrug at her. "If I could do what Sara can, I would be doing it, babe. I'd be a real menace to Potestia with that under my belt. But I can't. All I've got is mana, comfortable shoes, and a tendency to bite. I promise you, I don't have divine, err, Nexus magic," I say.

She narrows her eyes. "I'm not an idiot. Foreign sages can't change their bodies. How do you think I knew Sarafyna was local? You're going to have to do better than that," she counters. That is . . . interesting. My hand absently moves to the scar on my cheek that Sara has never managed to heal. My mind wanders to the cancer we have struggled to fight. All the time Sara has been unable to help me with my own changes. In fact, all she has really been able to do effectively is heal me to the same state she had found me in. In fact, she isn't the only one.

Baldwin tried to change my body too. And what had he succeeded in doing? Nothing but reverting my own alterations. She is wrong about my ability to change my body, but she is right that I can't use divine magic to do it. All my life I have been resistant to divine magic in one way or another. "Why?" I ask, forgetting entirely about her suspicion and focusing on the implications of this claim. She shakes her head like I just sprayed her with a water bottle.

"What? I don't know why, you tell me! What does that matter? Look, you can't leave one world and enter another without manipulating the Nexus. So you have that ability—what's the point in hiding it at this point?" Ember asks again.

"An excellent question. What would the point be? Think about it, Ember. Why have I done all of this today? Why have I shown you everything a scout could possibly want to know about me? Every dangerous secret and vulnerability of everyone I care about?" I ask. "Sure, I want information from you as well. That's obvious. But it's also a Hail Mary. Or, uh, a huge gamble. I'm trying to save your life. I'm trying to find out if I can afford to."

She scoffs, although it feels half-hearted. "You can't kill a restrained prisoner. That's a war crime. Besides, I saw everything you showed me today. I'll admit, you aren't quite the monster from the stories. If anything, you are soft. You let these people walk all over you. Take advantage of you. You offer them whatever they want in exchange for nothing. You don't have the stomach to kill someone who surrendered. Someone with no chance of fighting back against you. You overplayed your hand on that one."

I share a look with Sara, then shake my head.

"Damn right, I'm soft. I love people, and I love when people are safe and comfortable. As you've seen, I'll do a lot to give them that opportunity. But none of them had that chance before, Ember." I lean forward, the grass still tickling at my legs. "You heard how some of them grew up. They didn't win this life by luck. They fought for it, and I fought next to them. I will do a lot to give that to them. I have done a lot. You think I won't kill you because of those cuffs? Because you 'surrendered'? Well, you're right that I don't want to. I don't kill unless I know someone needs to die. But I don't let people walk away from me if I know they are going to cause pain when they leave. And we don't have a fucking prison. There is no convenient dungeon to usher you into.

"I am showing you all of this because this is all or nothing. I met you because your friend, as you claim, tried to murder me. Because you came here treating refugees as invaders. That's not a lot of points in your favor. But I don't know you, or your country. I don't know if you actually wanted anyone dead. I don't know what your job actually entails. I don't know enough yet to be sure that if you walk away, you will cause pain. That's why you are alive. Not because I won't kill you in those cuffs. Because I won't kill you yet. And because, however you present yourself, I can feel your grief. So no. I don't have a reason to lie to you. Because you are either safe, or you are a danger to these people. And if you are a danger, you are dead."

A stiff breeze blows through the meadow and Ember's eyes remain fixed on mine. The tension in the air is oppressive and I see Sara fighting the urge to lash out against this woman. Finally, Ember speaks. "All right," she says. Her voice still carries an edge but it has dulled significantly. I can see in her eyes that this, at least, she believes. "I'm sorry. If you are not a sage, can you tell me how you made it to our world?" She is more demure now but clearly set on getting to the bottom of this. I guess I am essentially the boogeyman to her. Which is . . . weird to think about.

"I have no idea," I reply. "I died. Twice, I think." Sara flinches at this, and my eyes flick to her but return to Ember. "First, in my old world, then in this one. When I, as Lillith, died as a child, I . . . woke up. I woke up and I remembered the lives of two women. A Potestian child and an American woman. I don't know if you have any reincarnation myths, but that's what happened to me. I am both women. I think I always have been. I have no memory of moving from one place to another. I certainly haven't used any 'Nexus magic.'"

She gapes at me, and she's not the only one.

Edward looks like I got a solid grip on his underwear and pulled it all the way over his head. "What in the third plane are you talking about, Lily?" he asks. "Died? Twice? When did you fucking die?"

"When I was sevenish, I think. When I got sick, remember?" I answer casually.

"I remember thinking you had died, but . . . Wait, is that why . . ." He trails off before catching sight of Sara idly playing with her hair with one hand. He immediately begins to interrogate her on her lack of response while I focus on Ember.

"You claim you died," she says. "So you, as you are now . . . This is a different person than who you were before?" She has either accepted that I'm not lying, or recalculated the position she is in. Either way, I am happy to get as much information as I can. She has clues I have wondered about for years.

I shrug. "Different body at first. Lord knows if I had done it on purpose, I wouldn't have gone through puberty twice. Your turn. None of your sages got here this way? How do they use the Nexus?" I interrogate her, and she begins to scratch at the fur behind one ear while thinking.

"No one really knows, but . . . they are all sages. What I know is they use Nexus magic to step from their world to ours. I don't know why and I don't know how they find us. But I've never heard of one dying first and having a new body here. How did you die? Are you certain that's what happened?" She has completely moved on from her suspicion and hostility now. There is a look in her eyes I can't interpret, but the throbbing grief has started to fade as well.

"Pretty fucking sure. I wasn't hit by any truck. I was pushed from a high-rise. Not sure there was much of me left to magically move myself here. I definitely died."

"What's a high-rise?"

"Tall building."

"You could survive that."

"No, like really tall. Splatter height, I think is the technical term. I'd also already been shot."

"With what, a spell? Arrow?"

"Bullets. Like faster, angrier arrows."

Ember looks at me and I look back. Both of us seem to have forgotten that I was threatening her life a moment ago and that her friend threatened mine earlier. For the first time since meeting, our interest in the same topic allows us to resonate. We also, apparently, forgot my brother was in the middle of a meltdown. In the awkward silence that follows the angry-arrow comment, I finally look over to see my brother staring at me, genuine hurt in his eyes.

"Lily . . . who are you?" he asks, and I gulp. I suddenly feel like an absolute asshole. I am so used to handling the insanity of my life with flippancy, I didn't consider how this would hit him. In a way, this is the root cause of years of discord between us. The change in me when I died. The secret I kept for so long. Of course it would hurt him, and I wasn't even talking to him when I revealed it. I am a little disgusted by how thoughtless I'm being.

"Oh, uh, listen, Ed," I begin, but he just shakes his head.

"You know what, we'll talk about it later," he says, irritation clouding his voice like smoke. "I think the rest of the family should be able to hear what you have to say. Just . . . keep unloading on this stranger who tried to murder you instead. I need some air." He stands and storms off, muttering to himself.

"I'll make sure he's all right," Sara offers, standing herself. "Be careful, Annie." Then I am alone with Ember, whose eyes are locked on me like the jaws of a predator.

"All right. So you died," she continues, somewhat rudely ignoring the drama that just started in front of her. "You aren't a sage. So let me ask you. I have heard a lot of stories in the past day, but little about how people went from slavery and abandonment to here. Can you tell me about that?"

I nod. Ed is right. I should talk to the entire family about this. I should have a while ago. Once they learned about the Radiant Woods and my plan to kill the king, they could have handled it. I was stupid. I'll finish handling this and prepare myself for that later. "It's simple enough. I got here and discovered the people in charge thought their subjects were things. So I killed them. And I kept killing them, while Sara helped me bring their victims here. Everywhere, really. And I intend to keep doing so."

She stares at me, her pupils narrowing to thin slits. "And your king? He didn't try to stop you?" she questions.

"He just tried to keep himself safe and comfortable. He didn't care about anyone else. Killed him too," I say. Something clicks into place for her as soon as I say that. I feel the numbing grief return in force and her face softens, her pupils growing wide enough to nearly fill her eyes.

"I want to make a deal with you. I will tell you anything and everything you want. I will guarantee I am safe. I will stay wherever you are, if you like. I will help you with your revolution if you need it. I'll even wear these cuffs every day," she offers, and I raise one eyebrow.

"In exchange for . . . ?" I prod.

She takes a deep breath.

"Help me kill the sages."

CHAPTER TWENTY-EIGHT

Out in the Open

I couldn't promise to kill the sages for Ember. I don't know enough about them, their positions, or their culture. The same reason I wouldn't kill Ember once she wasn't an active threat, really. All I have is Ember's assurance the sages are evil. Ember also panicked at the evil of a woman's medical transition, so I'm not ready to cut my hand and swear her in as a blood sister I'd kill for. She is, in fact, a bit of a . . . well, little shit. Still, I won't just dismiss her offhand either. She hasn't told me why she hates them, but if someone reacts that way to someone else, you don't ignore it. I wouldn't have in any case, but the level of grief she felt when talking about them . . . I intend to learn all I can about these "sages."

Fortunately, that was enough to make the deal. Just the promise that I intend to see for myself and will help her kill them if they need to die. If they are what she seems to believe, keeping her here may be more like sheltering a victim than anything. Either way, she is safe from them and we are safe from her relaying information about us. She didn't even make me go back to the Kingdom of Endings after all. We can move forward now, and with more information. Truth be told, I would have been happy with one completely dysfunctional country to overthrow. But I can add this to my fucking backlog if I need to.

We have left the sunny meadow behind for the evening mountains where we met Ember. As we finally walk back to our new home, I turn my thoughts back, as ever, to the first dysfunctional country on my list. I need to figure out how to help just as much without fighting on the front lines. I need to give regular citizens the ability to fight back without me. And I have to act while our enemies are still distracted by their own internal power struggle. After all of that is over, well. They are going to have a lot of focus leftover for the woman who killed the last king. Her and all the free labor she stole away with. Apparently, the fucking Collector will help them find us too. That is the biggest concern Ember revealed, just by showing up.

She isn't a divine mage. As far as she claims and Sara could tell, neither were her avian friends. Our greatest advantage has been location. The enemy couldn't reach us because only the priests could move through the Radiant Woods, and they were headless. Now I know that's no longer the case. Once Godfrey or Darian has handled the other, coming for us will finally become an option. I can hope it's only these other countries and their agents being granted access to us, but I am not going to hang my hat on that hope. Sarafyna would never forgive the disrespect to it.

But that means we are on an even tighter timeline than I thought. The plan has always been to provide aid to the other cities first while the conflict in Visenar distracted the big players. But people aren't as ready to fight back as I'd hoped. It's taking too long. I need to put my all into leveling the playing field for them. And perhaps, as a side project, designing a weapon I can use without mana. Maybe Ember can help, with knowledge of her culture's magic and enchantments. Or her knowledge of Nexus magic, whatever it is.

I need to get to work. In a respectfully restful way. Goddamn magic fucking cancer shit. Such a pain in the ass. Of course, I can't even get to any of that yet. Edward's stare as we walk makes that perfectly clear. The first thing I have to do is face the music with my family. I can't believe I got so caught up I just . . . said all of that in front of Ed. Keeping it a secret in the first place is one thing, but dropping it all on someone else in front of him like he didn't matter was, well, thoughtless. And there it is. My first act ever that could be called indelicate.

Ed is walking behind Ember and me, glaring while Sara whispers to him. But hey, that's a bonus. He seems far more concerned with the world-shattering revelation of my origins than with my proclivity for women. I mean, that does seem like the obvious priority list, but some men just really don't like the idea of women who are sexually unavailable to them. Although, I suppose that's not an issue in this specific instance anyway, unless he had a thing for Sara. Any flavor of bullshit can feel more important than the knowledge of . . . what would he call me? An invader in his world? In his family? An alien anarchist? An otherworldly revolutionary? Well, something like that. It doesn't matter; I'm spiraling. The truth is, I'm scared.

I have been lying to my family for a long time. It's terrifying to think I am going to be completely upfront with them now. Years after I stopped having a decent excuse. Will they reject me? Will they think I'm a changeling? Ugh. I'm not used to worrying about stupid shit like this. This is why I didn't say anything for so long. Give me regicide over family drama any day.

By the time I resurface from my thoughts, we have made it home and Clarrise is greeting us.

"Lillith, there's a message for you from the relay station. It's . . ." She trails off, glancing at an annoyed Ember.

"It's fine. She's gonna stay here for a while and help us out. What's the story?" I ask.

Clarrise nods at that, failing to ask any further questions. "The Kingdom of Endings is short of supplies; they are requesting a delivery today, if possible."

I rub my temples in frustration. "How? We gave them so much! For fuck's sake, if they collected all the resources so they could withhold them, I am going to go apeshit on them!"

Ember throttles a laugh in her throat. "Apeshit, I like that." She chuckles.

"Fine. Sara, I know this is asking a lot, but is there any way you can do a supply run? I'd go with you, but I kind of . . ." I glance at Ed.

Sara bites her lip but nods. "Yes, I don't mind. I just hope they don't stare so much this time . . ." I maybe could have thought out the public kiss as well. I'm starting to think my tunnel vision can lead me to hasty decisions sometimes. Naw, that's probably silly.

"Sorry about that," I apologize. "I'll make it up to you, I promise."

She smiles at me and adjusts her hat. "Don't worry about it. I got this." She turns to leave, pauses, then looks at me. "I . . . I guess everyone here is going to know soon anyway . . ." she says. Then she hops forward, wraps her arms around my neck, and kisses me. I don't have the wherewithal to take in the reactions around us as I wrap my arms around her waist and kiss her back. Finally, she backs away and smiles. "I love you, see you soon, Annie," she says.

"I love you too, Sarafyna. Be safe, all right?" She nods before going to find volunteers for her impromptu supply run. "I'm glad we didn't go there already. Would have been a huge waste of time. All right. Clarrise, is there any chance we can get Ember here set up in her own room? Thirteen-thirteen if it's empty."

"Sure, I can do that," Clarrise agrees, less taken aback than the first time she learned about my relationship with Sara.

"Ember. I'm trusting you here a bit but . . . not that much. I'm not the only one here who can kill you in a moment if you so much as try to hurt anyone. I'm just the person who will do it the most painlessly. If you are trustworthy, you'll be fine. But stay trustworthy," I warn.

"I get the picture. Go deal with your housekeeping," she snaps.

I stick my tongue out at her and she rolls her eyes.

"Clarrise, if possible, can you get her some cuffs that aren't connected so she can move her arms?" I say. The continued cuffs were actually Ember's idea. A way to earn our trust and make people feel safe, which relieves me because, truth be told, I am nervous about her. She claims she wasn't the one to attack me. She claims none of them were supposed to. But time will tell. This sort of community doesn't come without risk, however. I trust Clarrise though. That will have to do for now. It's time to have a chat with my family.

Collecting them is easy enough. Ed goes to get Mariah and Mom, because significant others are included in this, I guess. I handle Henry and Autumn. Gilbert will have to wait until our next visit to his community. His significant others would be something of a distraction anyway. Who has time to keep track of all of them? I'm amused to find Autumn's stuffed animals have overtaken their bed. Henry is actually holding Wilbert the stuffed cow as he sleeps, which is charming enough to calm my nerves.

Autumn has to help me get him out of bed, but eventually the entire family is sitting around a large table in one of the common areas. We had to ask for privacy but received no pushback; there are plenty of alternative spaces. I take a breath as everyone stares at me, some groggily, others expectantly.

"Go ahead, Lillith. Tell them. Tell them how you have been lying to us all these years," Ed instigates.

I wince and receive a raised eyebrow from Henry, a look of concern from Mom, and a furrowed brow from Autumn. Mariah glares at Edward instead. I take a deep breath and nod.

"All right. A long time ago, when I was seven, I died. When I woke up, everything was different," I begin.

Sarafyna

I feel amazing. For once I am not thinking about the fight. I'm not thinking of the need to kill people. I'm not even thinking of the Collector's taunts. This kiss was different than the last one. Validating, in a way. Like I made a choice to be who I am. Being seen with Annie just feels good. If I doubted my sexuality before, that moment alone would have been enough. It was like a warm bath, or the first time Annie convinced me to try soap.

I have more energy than I should after such a long day. Even the stares in the Kingdom of Endings don't bother me. Hell, I kind of wish Annie was here so I could kiss her again. Let them see how their stares affect me. The stewards here were irritated Annie didn't come with me, but it's for the best. It turns out they didn't run out of resources, they cooked them all at once. This was supposed to be some royal feast. The queen's failure to show up didn't help whatever they were going for, and it's a little funny to watch them arguing under their breath about it.

I wish Annie had come. She would have been *furious*. She doesn't like to tell people what to do with the resources other communities share, but she still would have given them a dressing-down for this. There is something about her when she is really angry at someone. It's so different from me. Either when I am calm and demure, or furious myself. For her, it's more . . . passion. I like it.

"Ms. Sarafyna, we have something we'd like to discuss with you, in private," one of the stewards says, pulling me from my thoughts.

"Huh? Oh, uh, sure. I don't mind," I agree.

"You may want a drink," the other says, startling me. "It's not going to be easy to hear." They poured me a glass of wine some time ago but I haven't touched it yet. I haven't touched any of the food, really. I only stayed at this dumb feast to work through my thoughts. They are looking at me with such expectations, I feel a bit awkward about it now. I don't think I am in any danger of getting drunk. Anything short of Annie's venom will be easy to eliminate from my system. I pick up the glass and take a polite sip, which is met with a nod of approval.

"Right this way," the first steward says, gesturing to a nearby doorway. I follow her inside and immediately hear the door close behind me. A shifting shadow in the next room catches my attention, but a blackness edging into my vision immediately distracts me.

"W-what did—" I start, but my breath catches. I try to transform my body, to flush whatever I just drank out of my system.

"The queen," the steward in front of me says, her voice far too calm, "will give us a king."

I feel my knees buckle. My divine magic isn't responding. Even my regular, uncontrollable mana isn't responding. I catch myself on a table as I struggle to stay awake. I reach into my bag looking for my whisper sphere, and my hand is caught by the second steward. My eyes dart frantically around the room as I collapse to my knees. My breathing is labored and slow. The darkness closes in. Just before I black out, I catch a glimpse of two new figures entering from the next room. One has the wings of a bird, the other the ears of a cat.

CHAPTER TWENTY-NINE

Family Meeting

My family stares at me in silence. As I finish telling my story, the air is heavy with silence and I feel unusually aware of my hands. What do I usually do with those? Eyes stare at me for far too long as the people I love process what I've just said. I awkwardly rub the back of my alarmingly sweaty neck. *Come on, Lillith, keep it together.* I've been less nervous in fights to the death. That's not really comparable, of course. I can act in a fight to the death. That's a competition of sorts. A winner and loser. Facing down a family you spent years lying to is . . . different.

"Well, that certainly explains some things," Henry says, tapping the table with one hand. "Can't believe you've been holding out on me. A 'biologist,' was it? You must have so many ideas other than these potions for your cancer! And no wonder you knew what you were sick with. I've always wondered how you understood the things you did. I figured it was just noble knowledge you read at the bookshop. This is a way cooler explanation!"

I blink at him, as do Ed and Autumn. Mom keeps her gaze steady on me.

"I, uh, well, I wasn't a medical doctor, but yes, I know some things that can get you started. I've been trying to record what I can in something like a textbook, but it's not an easy undertaking. I wasn't exactly holding back . . ." I trail off and Autumn suddenly snaps.

"Oh!" she exclaims. "No wonder you rejected August so quickly! Oh, Collector, we must have been like children to you when we met! We were children to you!" She immediately starts blushing as she thinks of our various interactions.

"That's one reason," Ed comments under his breath.

"Right, I left that bit out," I respond. "I'm gay as shit. I'm only attracted to women and am in fact courting Sarafyna. August never had a chance, I'm afraid." Autumn only turns a brighter red at this, and Henry leans back in his chair.

"Huh," he says. "Well, I have a couple of friends looking for an introduction who may be disappointed."

"Oh, poor August . . ." Autumn whispers.

"Oh, he knows that bit, actually. Has for, like, four years now, I think. Thought it would soften the blow of my, uh, disinterest. He responded pretty positively, actually," I assure her, and her eyes widen further.

"That little prick! He never said a word to me about it!" she complains.

"That was actually pretty respectful of him. Not a lot of people can be trusted to keep private shit to themselves, especially when they have a twin. He's a good guy, your brother," I say.

"How is everyone so normal about this?" Ed whines, scooting his chair back from the table. "She lied to us. She has been lying to us since she was *seven years old*. You are all just fine with that? Lily, you aren't the only one everything changed for! I thought I was some kind of idiot child! My little sister, the girl who used to follow me around like a puppy, suddenly learned everything faster than me! Do you know how small it makes you feel, when a child suddenly seems ten feet taller than you? I have struggled with this for so long. Even after I realized how poorly I reacted to you, it still haunted me. It still made me feel so fucking insignificant.

"I know. I know it's not your fault. You are who you are. You couldn't just be a child again. But you could have said *something*. You could have said *anything*. Anything would have made me feel less worthless. Just knowing there was something else going on could have changed everything for me!"

I have to process that for a moment.

"Ed. Your value never had anything to do with me. You shouldn't have been measuring yourself based on me! Based on anyone! It shouldn't have mattered what I did! Whether I looked up to you or not. That was never going to make you feel like a person. You can't live your life like that, Ed. It's not like you exactly earned my trust!" I protest.

The next voice surprises me. "Lillith, you know your brother isn't good with words," Mariah says. "He is terrible at saying what he is feeling. Honestly, he is terrible at parsing what he is feeling. It doesn't matter whether he should have measured himself against you or not. He was a kid too. Maybe not the whole time, but he was. And you're right. It probably wouldn't have made him feel better. You're right that he didn't deserve to know. I'll even say what you aren't. No one would have believed you, before all this. And that matters. It does. You were a victim of the way he treated you, more than he is of your dishonesty. But you understand. He feels hurt. He feels lied to. Because, well, he was. You don't need to respond to the rest, in this moment. There will be time for that, and Ed knows that. But please, for now, just respond to that."

I bite back the retort that comes to my tongue.

I look at Ed and see she is right. Ed shouldn't be comparing himself to me like that. He never should have been. But I can see in his eyes now. Mariah is right. He doesn't need an argument with me right now. What he needs is simple. I look down and clench my fists. "Ed . . . I'm sorry. I'm sorry for lying to you. I'm sorry I saw you hurting and didn't do anything to help. I'm sorry," I say quietly. Because it doesn't matter, in this moment, who is right.

It's true I couldn't have told him right away. It's true he wasn't safe to tell for a long time. I wasn't wrong to withhold it from him for much of the time I did. And I don't need to apologize for that bit. But I could have told him a long time before now. It's hard because he really was an unpleasant little shit. And people who behave like that have no right to expect sudden trust. In fact, people who are sorry for that shouldn't expect to be trusted. They should expect not to be trusted and accept it.

But this isn't quite that. There was an undefinable change in our relationship some time ago. A vulnerability that I allowed him to believe had been reciprocated. I didn't tell him I still didn't trust him. I think that's what he means by wanting to hear *anything*. He would have accepted that. But I kept this from him, all while trusting him, risking him, with my own plans.

If nothing else, I can understand why that hurts. And that? That I don't mind apologizing for. Yeah, we will have to talk about the other side of it. The way I was treated and the reason he needed to be lied to. But sometimes it's all right to handle one thing at a time. I should have at least been clear. Communicated as much as I expected him to. Especially after the last few days. He crosses his arms, but gives me a brief nod, sniffing and wiping one eye on his sleeve. It's going to take him some time to process. But I think that really was all he needed.

Meanwhile, my mother is still staring at me, her arms folded neatly. She doesn't have the same anger Ed did. She doesn't have the nonchalance of Henry either. She looks . . . cold.

"Is my daughter dead?" she asks suddenly, and silence falls on the room like a tempest. The color drains from my face.

I gulp. "No," I respond. "No, Mom. It's me. It's still me. I am who I have always been!"

"You're not though. Are you? You are this . . . other woman. This Annie. You're . . . Collector, you're older than me. How can you say you are my little girl?" she challenges me. Still quiet. Still calm. I feel tears forming in the corners of my eyes.

"Yes. I am Annie Beckett. But . . . I'm also Lillith. I am *more* Lillith now. Mom, I don't . . . I don't know how to say it, shit. I am your daughter. I love you. You're my mom. The best mom I ever had, truth be told. I remember everything. I remember asking you for an extra serving of dinner when I was five. I remember begging for another story when you tucked me in at night. I remember walking around in your shoes, pretending to be you because I couldn't imagine anything better than that. I remember throwing a tantrum when you asked me to clean my room. I remember you holding me when I came to apologize.

"That was all me. Those are *my* memories. No one else's. They belong to me. They are *precious* to me. And so are you. So are all of you! Yes, when I was seven, I had an entire other life dumped on me. All the baggage and trauma of another reality. But it didn't hollow me out to make space. It opened a door that was always there to a life I had always lived. I'm not someone new. I'm just more . . . me," I say pleadingly, tears gently running down my cheeks.

"How . . ." Mom says, her voice finally catching as the ice cracks a little, "how do you know that? How do you know those aren't just inherited memories? The memories of my daughter. Of the girl you usurped? How can you know that for sure?"

I lean forward and let a deep breath out, then look up at my mother. My mascara must be a fucking mess.

"Because," I answer simply. "The moment I opened my eyes and saw you, I loved you. I admired you. I ached for you. I didn't *remember* caring about you. I didn't *remember* looking up to you. I didn't *remember* feeling safer because you were there. I *felt* those things. I still do. I didn't inherit them. They are how I have felt about you my entire life. Before I got sick as a child, and after. Mom, I love you. That's how I know." I am practically sobbing by the end of this. Everyone else in the room has various looks of concern and awkward energy, but none of that matters. I look my mother in the eyes. The same crimson eyes that have always defined me. And she collapses.

Not literally. But the tension dies and her muscles slump. A moment later she is sobbing too. I could have sworn we were sitting on opposite sides of the table, but within a few breaths, she is wrapping her arms around me. Things get messy from that point on. Emotional in a way I am used to suppressing. Joking away. But since I started dating Sara, that layer has been slowly peeling away. We do get to a point where we can joke, most of us. They have a lot of questions. Mom is still struggling to grasp it. To accept it. But she knows I love her, and she still loves me.

There is a lot of healing to be done. This revelation hit her harder than anyone. I am actually a little older than her, in a way. But she is still my mom. That dynamic will never change. I eventually have to retire early. It has been an incredibly long day, and I want to do something before Sara gets back. My family isn't satisfied with this, but it's important to me. I take only Autumn with me and head up to our room. She has been practicing earth magic and I'll need her for this. She kisses Henry goodnight and promises to see him once we are done, then comes up to the room with me.

She actually blushes a little when we reach the door, but I roll my eyes and tell her to relax. It's not like I jump on any woman I see. The work I borrow her for takes about an hour, but that is much faster than it would have been on Earth. Autumn is a good sport about it and I promise to make it up to her later. But as she leaves, I smile. I have remodeled the room a bit. Instead of hats hanging on one wall, Sara now has her own studio. Rows of shelves line the small room, displaying all her hats. A desk sits in the center of the room with her father's hat block in the middle. She is going to squeal when she gets back.

Speaking of which, she actually should be back by now. I thought I would run out of time before she made it. She must be at least a half hour, forty-five minutes late by now. Idly, I take out my whisper sphere to call her. It hums gently, the light slowly fading in and out, until she answers and the light steadies.

"Hey, beautiful. Everything all right? I want to show you something when you get home," I say as soon as I see a connection has been made.

"Hello, Queen Lillith," replies the voice on the other end.

CHAPTER THIRTY

Time to Scream

I have to suppress an exhausted groan as the voice of one of the fucking stewards comes through Sara's whisper sphere. April, I think? It has been a moment since I learned their names, and I am fucking tired. "Is this April? Why do you have Sarafyna's sphere? Can you just give it back to her?" I ask. The fatigue is clear in my voice and I really hope this lady doesn't want to have some debate about her shitty little monarchy right now. My hackles rise as I hear her clicking her tongue on the other end.

"I'm afraid she is . . . indisposed, at the moment. You'll have to talk to me instead, *Your Majesty*," she replies. The words *Your Majesty* are dripping with condescension. I feel a low, humming anger ripple across my skin as I guess at her meaning.

"Indisposed *how*?" I coldly demand.

"We have been discussing you a lot, recently, Rebecca and I," she says, ignoring my question. "You and your . . . unconventional relationship choices. In fact, there has been some discussion about it all across the kingdom. Since, in your wisdom, you chose to display it in public, in front of all your subjects. Well, you'll be pleased to hear this. The general consensus is it doesn't matter who you choose as a . . . concubine. However frankly disgusting that choice may be. Several prominent betrothal candidates have actually shown increased interest since your proclivities were revealed, it would seem. But your duty remains, and your people need the leadership of a king. I'm afraid we must insist that you provide us with one."

I nearly crush the whisper sphere in my fist as she explains this. Her comment on "increased interest" trickles across my skin like wastewater. I'm certain this is perfectly visible on my face, but I'll have to communicate disgust through voice alone. "Where. Is. Sarafyna?" I repeat.

"Sarafyna is in our custody, for now. It was decided she should not be allowed to . . . distract you, for the time being," April replies. "After the wedding, or perhaps once we have a suitable heir in line, you can speak to your husband about her release." My stomach churns. This woman is going to die. She is going to die the second I can get my hands around her throat.

"Are you fucking stupid?" I say. "What is your fucking plan here? We need her to travel through the Radiant Woods. Even if I wanted to pick one of your nasty little candidates, how would we even get to each other? More importantly, how do you plan to survive if we do bridge that gap?"

"Well, I'm glad you asked." Her nasty smile is evident in her voice. "First of all, there is no need to choose anyone. Considering our respective positions, I took the liberty of selecting for you. My son, Michael, will be your fiancé. As for how you plan to get here for the wedding, well. I suppose you'll have to figure that out. You're a resourceful woman. I believe you can do it. And, if you want your concubine spared, you'll do it peacefully."

"And your precious resources? You produce less than every other community. How do you plan to feed and clothe people, you moron? Sarafyna is the only one who can deliver supplies. Are you hoping your self-satisfaction will keep everyone fed? Because you are the only one I plan to fucking feed it to," I snap.

She has the gall to laugh at this.

"Oh, sweetheart, we don't have to worry about that. Weren't you wondering how we even managed to capture her? We have some . . . friends. We'll make it to the other communities just fine. In fact, everyone else will need the Kingdom of Endings to travel between communities as well. Your husband will be able to set some new . . . rules for resource management," she explains, and the blood drains from my face. Ember's fucking people. I need to speak to her the second this call is over. Did she know about this? I hastily pull my glasses out of my bag and put them on. Facing the wall separating our rooms, the radar enchantment reveals a tall, ailur-shaped woman moving around inside. So she is not doing anything to anyone right now, at least.

"I see. So you plan to come to me for this shotgun wedding, then? You know the fucking Collector won't let your 'friends' retrieve me. Only Sarafyna can move me to your precious kingdom. Only someone who can control the woods themselves, not a group that is simply allowed through with the wood's permission."

"Shotgun?" she whispers, but regains her composure quickly. "No, no. The wedding needs to be in the capital city, of course. Your most loyal subjects, the new nobility, will want to attend! Nowhere else will do. Of course, if you can't find a way to reach the Kingdom of Endings . . ." She trails off for effect. I can feel her glee seeping into my skin at her next words. "Well, then, it is a good thing you have such competent stewards, isn't it?"

And the penny drops. She's never fucking cared if I got married. I was only ever a name to lend her authority. I've been too easy on these morons. I wanted them to see how quickly monarchy fails without the threat of force behind it. This "kingdom" is made up of people who escaped an abusive monarchy and immediately wanted to build a new one. I figured that was the only way to make it clear to them. That was a mistake. Because they used me. They used what I had done to prop up their own authority. And some part of me really believed they just admired me enough to want me as a ruler.

But I knew. I knew no one ever actually admired their ruler. No one who isn't gifted prestige themselves based on said ruler's existence, anyway. I never should have given these stewards the benefit of the doubt. Not for one fucking second.

They are fucking using *me* as a prop for authority. Christ. I was just so certain it would collapse before it got too bad. So certain, and distracted, and, well, goddamn arrogant. I was arrogant and it felt just a little good to be called queen. To be called queen and reject it; to be above it.

I could have made it clearer I wasn't anyone's queen. I could have ended it once and for all if I'd really wanted to. I didn't. Whatever I said, part of me wanted that admiration. And I thought ignoring it would be a sufficient solution. Pride and stupidity are the same fucking thing. You can't ignore a royalist. A fascist. A power-hungry asshole. If you ignore them, if you think they'll fail on their own just because you took their support away . . . But even the weakest and most pathetic of them can't really be ignored. When people are that proud, that hateful, that desperate for power . . . they always, *always* have claws. And even as they fall, they will tear at any precious thing they can reach.

And here we are. I glare at the sphere. Blood starts to trickle from my nose, down to my lip, and into my mouth. "I see. So this was the game the whole time, huh? Keep me around to use my name, to prop up your own authority, forever? You are still a woman, like me. They still want me, not you, as a queen. Don't you think they'll ask questions if I just . . . never show up?" I ask.

She fucking laughs again. "No one wants you as queen, you sanctimonious bitch! Everyone just wants to be king and they know they'll be able to fuck the most powerful baby into you! You are nothing but a sack of too much mana who is in over her head! Will they care if you never show up? Sure. But they'll also know that, as long as you are unmarried, there is still a chance for them to get you on your back and make themselves king. They'll just be happy you haven't married anyone else, until Rebecca and I have made enough changes and laws that they forget they ever had anything but stewards. That's how you start a new kingdom, Your Majesty," she sneers.

Blood drips from my lips and makes small puddles on the floor, barely missing the whisper sphere as it falls. Sara was supposed to be back by now. She was supposed to help me manage my cancer. I need her. That I can handle. But she needs me too, and failing her would be too much for me. My next words are ice. "You are right. I suck at politics. I can't play these games all the time. I can't wrap my mind around the thoughts of snakes. But I didn't tear down Potestia by playing politics, did I? No. I did it with violence, April. I am not Lillith of Clever Little Games, I am Lillith of Endings. And you know what? If I were you, I would hope, and pray, and beg on my knees that I find my way to you. Do you know why?" I ask.

She chuckles. "Very scary, stuck in some other city, too scared to walk through the woods to find us. No, why should I pray that you manage to find me?"

"Because I kill quickly. I won't give you time to feel the pain. If I make it to you, you will be afraid, but you will simply die. But Sarafyna? My future fucking wife? Well, see. She has some unprocessed trauma. I've been trying to talk her through it whenever I can, but it's a lot to unpack. See, she was trapped, imprisoned you might say, for quite a while. She was trapped by people she was supposed to trust. And she was hurt while she was there. For years. And the only way she found to fight back against that imprisonment? Well, it was violence. It was the fucking hunt. The hunt of the people who hurt her.

"She didn't kill people to stop them from existing. She killed them because she was in constant pain. In constant fear. She tracked them down and hurt them like they hurt her. Yeah, she is usually quiet. Demure. Happy making her hats and chatting with me. But that's all still there. Under the surface. Boiling. Waiting for someone to light the fuse. The last time that happened, a man was eaten alive. Chewed up, slowly, and spit back out. And what did you do to her? You told her she could trust you and you imprisoned her. Trapped her. Hurt her. So yes. I want to kill you. And I will as soon as I have the chance. But that's why you need to pray that I do.

"Because she is going to find a way out whether I get to you or not. I will kill you in a blink. But if I'm too slow, and my girlfriend escapes first? She will give you time to fucking scream," I finally finish.

April doesn't laugh. After a moment of silence, I hang up. My nose is bleeding too much; I spent too long on that call. I'm starting to lose my vision. I need to confront Ember. I pull one of Henry's potions out of my bag and drink the entire thing. It tastes like sewage and goes down as easily, but it'll steady me out. I focus all my mana on the cancer. Shaving it away. Then I channel my mana into the whisper sphere again, this time willing it to call my brothers.

CHAPTER THIRTY-ONE

Again

The urgency in my voice is enough to get Ed and Henry to my living room quickly. I watch Ember through the wall the entire time, gritting my teeth. I don't know if she is involved in this or not. I don't know if I can trust my judgment in either direction. I wipe the blood on my hand, then my shirt, and finally groan. It won't stop. With irritation, I form a needle of mild, focused lightning mana and shove it up my nose. After a short, sharp pinch, I manage to seal the vessel and finally stop the bleeding. I slump over in my seat, anxiety twisting my muscles with tension.

It takes less than ten minutes for a knock to finally sound at my door, but it is an agonizing ten minutes. I feel weak as I stand, but not as weak as I did a few minutes ago. Henry's potion is doing its work, and I've had time to shave away at the cancer. It takes so much focus to keep it under control on my own; I can't allow this to go on for too long. I can't survive Sara's absence. And, bluster aside, I can't allow Sara to hurt someone like that again. I need to get to her before she has to.

My body throbs with fatigue as I make it to the door. I can cast more powerful magic with less effort than walking across the room, but fighting cancer in my own body is precise and has a toll all its own. Finally, I open the door.

"Exactly how many times are you going to wa— OH SHIT, Lily, what the fuck happened to your face?" Henry says as he sees the blood on my face, staining my shirt.

"I'm fine, just a nosebleed," I reply. "That's not what matters. I need your help, both of you."

"What's wrong?" Ed asks, looking around like he can spot the source of my stress.

"We need to talk to Ember again. Ed, I need you to back me up if I need to fight. Henry, did you bring more potion?" I speak quickly, grabbing Ed's shoulder to steady myself as I grow dizzy. I am getting stronger, after the potion and all that work, but just the amount of blood I lost is leaving me lightheaded.

"Uh, yeah," he says, fumbling through a messenger bag for a few more potions. "You shouldn't be out yet . . . Where is Sara? Has she not helped you yet?" He too looks around, trying to find my missing girlfriend.

"She's not back yet. And we are going to have to make those stronger for a while," I respond, and he furrows his brow.

"Is that safe? You said your contributions to the formula were basically trying to kill you as well, didn't you? They just kill the cancer faster?" he questions.

"Some of it, yes. But I can fight those bits myself. Right now, it's less dangerous than the alternative. That is a good question to ask though. I'm going to need your help with something else for a while," I reply.

Henry and Ed share a glance, then look at me skeptically.

"What's that?" Henry ventures.

"I need you to stick with me, in case I need a sanity check," I say.

"Well, I can answer that now; you are crazy as fuck," Henry says. I chuckle a little at the levity, but I lack the emotional energy to reward him with much more.

"No, seriously. I need you to make sure I don't do anything . . . rash. I might make some questionable choices in the coming days, and I need someone to tell me when it's insane," I say.

"You are always doing crazy shit, Lil," Ed interjects. "I mean, it's worked out for the best. But why now? Because of the thing in Tumult the other day? Or did something else change?"

"It is pretty late at night for a sudden choice like that," Henry agrees. "What happened?"

"Sara's been captured," I say. "I don't know how, except they had the help of a third party. I'm thinking Ember's people. They deal with divine magic and these 'sages' more than any of us have. If any third party could wrangle her, it's them. I need to know if Ember knew about this, and I need to know now."

"What, wait, who captured her? Is she all right?" Ed asks, genuine panic in his voice.

"Your cancer, Lily! Fuck, that's why the potion needs to be stronger, isn't it? What are we going to do?" Henry asks with distress.

"I don't know. But we start with Ember. Whether she knew this would happen or not, she'll have information we need. Let's go," I say.

"Wait," Ed says. "No offense, Lillith, but if you want to do something stupid out of anger, Henry isn't going to be able to talk you out of it. You know that, and I know that."

Henry looks relieved when Ed brings this up and I sigh.

"I'm not worried about doing something stupid because I'm angry. I, well, maybe I should be. But that's not what I'm talking about. Look at me," I suggest, and they do.

"I mean, you should probably clean up before talking to Ember, if that's what you mean . . ." Henry says, and I pause. I actually didn't consider that. Which . . . terrifies me. Because anger isn't why I want him helping.

"Thank you, that is exactly what I am looking for. Someone who will notice things that I should but don't," I say.

"Wait, you were really going to talk to her like that?" Ed asks, bafflement taking over his face.

"Breast cancer doesn't give you nosebleeds! But there are a few kinds that do, and most of them are above the neck. So yeah, I missed that. I was going to walk into her room covered in my own blood," I snap. "So yes. I am going to overlook things, and yes, I need to be fucking minded until we get Sarafyna back! Can we please just go? I can answer all your questions afterward!" I insist.

Henry understands what I mean before Ed does, but both quickly grow silent as they do. I give a quick nod, glad to finally be on the same page. I move to leave when Henry grabs my arm. "Wait, Lil, you're still . . ."

"Fucking god dammit!" I curse before marching to the kitchen, channeling mana into the water stone over my sink, and scrubbing at my face for a moment. I try to scrub at my shirt as well, but after a moment of frustration, I grab my collar with both hands and just tear at it, revealing a hint of my tattoos. Immediately feeling stupid, I march my dumb ass back past my brothers and into my bedroom to replace my new V-neck with a clean shirt. This typically routine endeavor is challenged by an uncharacteristic clumsiness, brought on by a growing sense of frustration and helplessness. I even manage to ignore Suzume as she asks for attention. I practically growl as I finally manage to force my arms through the sleeves and join my brothers in the living room. "Are we good?" I ask, more vitriol in my voice than they deserve.

They both nod, and I march past them to the door. Ember better not have gone anywhere during all that. I feel a little bad about snapping at my brothers. Especially Henry, who has been incredibly understanding all day. And who I am planning to lean on for the foreseeable future. I shouldn't be snapping at them, but it just . . . comes out every time. They follow me next door, and I knock, hard. I had intended to convey how serious the issue was, not splinter the door. I *intended*. I curse again as a few sharp pinpricks of pain identify the splinters I just gave myself.

It does also have the intended effect, however, as Ember very quickly opens the door, a look of irritation contorting her only vaguely humanoid face. "What the hell, what's fucking burning down?" she demands, but I immediately grab her by the collar and pull her head down to my level.

"Did you know?" I ask through clenched teeth.

"W-what? Know what? Shit, how fucking strong are you?"

"Don't fuck with me, Ember. Did. You. Fucking. Know?" I jerk her toward me again so her eyes are only a couple inches from mine. Her pupils narrow to slits, and her eyes scan me. A hand rests on my shoulder.

"Lily, you aren't going to get anywhere doing this. You're too angry. You need to let her go and explain what you mean . . ." Henry whispers to me. I come very close to snapping at him for telling me when to be fucking angry, but a little voice in my head stops me just in time. The voice that reminds me that this is exactly why I asked him to come with me. Ember continues to stare at me. I take a labored breath through my nose and slowly release my fingers. They shake and resist like those of a corpse, but I do manage to let her go.

I take another deep breath, then glare at the taller woman as she straightens to her full height. "Sarafyna went to the Kingdom of Endings earlier today. They managed to capture her," I begin, and Ember's eyes widen.

"She's a Nexus sage! How did your people manage to—"

I shake my head. "It wasn't just *my* people. They had help. I am thinking—likely from someone who is more familiar with this 'Nexus' bullshit. *Your* people. So I am asking again. Did you know?"

She doesn't answer right away. Her mouth opens a little, in surprise rather than in preparation to answer. And there it is. The one thing I needed to release the tension in my shoulders. Not the surprise on her face or in her posture, but the spike of sorrow I feel as the realization of what happened dawns on her.

"No . . . fuck, you need her to travel through the Nexus, don't you? *You* of all people certainly can't go in alone. Which means . . ." She practically whispers this part to herself. "Lillith, this 'Kingdom of Endings,' that's the one you didn't show me, right? The one that is hostile to you? How widely known is that?"

I look at her, a bit taken aback. I am a rapid pendulum between panic and fury at the moment, and the splash of relief followed by the question leaves me dizzy. I just kind of look at her for a moment, and Henry answers for me.

"She has been pretty openly antagonistic. Or, at the very least, she has very readily rejected their expectations of her," he replies.

"Shit. If it's that obvious, the Council may have sent ambassadors. They would definitely know how to trap a local Nexus sage . . ."

Shit.

"What would they do with her, if they were the ones who took her?" I ask.

Ember begins to answer, then frowns. "Well, they would usually feed a sage to the Nexus, but . . . if she can move through it freely, they will likely consider that too dangerous. How did you find out she was captured?"

"Feed her to it?" Ed cuts in before I can reply.

"Yes, feed her to it. The Nexus . . . collects sages. But I don't think they'll do that this time. Not right away, anyway. How did you find out?" she repeats.

"The stewards there told me. They want to negotiate. They are trying to use me for . . . They want the next king to inherit my mana. They are using her to manipulate me," I reply quietly.

"Fuck, I'm gonna be sick," Henry mutters.

"Then, we'll have to hope that's their actual plan. In the meantime, is there any other way you have of traveling through the Nexus?" Ember replies. Her demeanor, despite the grief this apparently brings her, is helping to calm me.

"No. All I have is Sara. We were working on transportation, but . . . I don't know how to find them. I don't actually know where the Kingdom of Endings is. I have amateur drawings of my guesses at constellations and how they look from different places, but that's it. I don't—I don't know—" And here they fucking come. The goddamn tears. *Come on, Lillith. You are Lillith of Endings. The Mage of Mourning and the terror of the nobility. You invented vampire mythology in this country. You are the actual boogeyman to this woman, and you are on the verge of a breakdown in front of her. Lock it up, Lily.* I set my jaw and sniff, water gathering in my eyes but failing to fall. "Can you move through the Nexus?" I finally ask.

Ember looks at me with calculation. "No. The Nexus decides where I go. Only a sage can move us through it. Besides, after traveling through it with you so many times, it will certainly turn me into one of its experiments if I try," she replies. "What do you want to do?"

I clench my fists, driving the earlier splinters farther into my skin. "We have faith in Sarafyna. And we experiment. Starting tomorrow, I want to spend every fucking day experimenting. I want to know everything you do about the Nexus. I want to know what you know about how this 'Council' catches sages, and I want to find a way to reach the Kingdom of Endings and kill everyone involved in hurting Sara. She will fight again. She will make it out again. And I will end the people who hurt her. Again."

CHAPTER THIRTY-TWO

Trapped

Leo

I pace back and forth across my room, anxiety forcing me into movement I lacked the energy for before. When I first heard the call on my whisper sphere, I was confused. I didn't know the spheres could work like that, picking up on other conversations. I've never heard of it happening before. Then I couldn't understand why anyone would do something like betray us. I couldn't tell who either speaker was. One voice was hushed and the other entirely unfamiliar to me. I have my fears here, but I have to be afraid everywhere. Who would want to go back to the way things were before?

The best I can guess is it's someone from the Kingdom of Endings. Some deal to return their business, or home, or even be elevated to nobility if they agree to help bring everyone who escaped back. But that doesn't make sense. They talked about the people we just met. Surely the Kingdom of Endings doesn't even know about them yet. Or for some reason, they knew about them before Lily did. Ultimately, I realized it didn't matter who it was. Not in the moment, anyway. No, what matters is alerting Lily as soon as possible. If she knows there is a traitor, she can at least make a plan. She might be able to identify the speakers as well.

I'm not an idiot, but I've been locked up in my room for weeks. I haven't left this one settlement. I'm not going to be able to identify any spies who haven't recently been inside my home. My gut reaction was to call Lily right away and tell her what I heard, but . . . well, if I could overhear a call, who else could? I don't want to call her just for whoever the spy is to bolt or go quiet as soon as she knows to look out for them. That would be better than her not knowing at all, but worse than her knowing without alerting the spy.

Eventually, however, I realized she would come back soon. Before going anywhere near Potestia. Charlotte said Lily promised to come back and help with her transition again tomorrow. All I have to do is wait, and I can warn her without anyone being the wiser. I don't have to risk anything else. I just have to wait. This knowledge fails to relieve my anxiety. My skin itches in that unique way that feels like an insect burrowing under it. I keep panicking, thinking something has just bit me. My plan is simple and easy and requires nothing from me until tomorrow. But it doesn't feel right. It feels like it's not enough. If I can't tell Lily tomorrow, I'll call her anyway. Risk be damned.

The problem, of course, is both of these plans mean there is nothing I can do *right now*. Which means I will continue to feel this anxiety. It's hours past sundown, but I still feel energy pulsing through me. When the quiet of the room is interrupted by a gentle knock, a sharp pang rings through me and I jump, my heart beating out of my chest until I realize it must be Charlotte. She visits me all the time, like she has a sixth sense for my particularly bad days. Still. It's hard not to jump at everything these days. Even once I realize who it is, I struggle to control my breathing and heart rate. I take a deep breath and redirect my pacing to the door. I open it slowly to reveal it is, in fact, my mentor.

"You all right in there, Leo?" she asks, and I sigh. I should have just talked to her about this from the beginning.

"Not . . . really," I reply. "Come on in." I open the door for her and return to pacing. She sits down on the bed.

"The nightmares again?" she guesses.

"No," I say before pausing. "Well, yes. But . . . no. It's something else." I stop and she raises an eyebrow at me. I take another deep breath and let it all pour out. "It's my whisper sphere . . . I heard something on it. Something not meant for me. Someone is spying on Lily." Her eyes widen at this revelation, and I continue to recount the entire thing as best as I can remember. Charlotte doesn't interrupt once, listening attentively. She shows clear concern when I tell her when I heard the conversation, especially when I mention the information shared about Ember. I tell her everything I can remember, and she sits in silence for a long while.

My heart is beating in my chest like I just confessed to doing something wrong. Charlotte stews for an agonizing amount of time before looking up at me. "Leo, this is serious. It's good you said something. We need to let Lillith know as soon as we can. It was smart of you, not to use the whisper sphere right away, but . . ." She pauses.

"But?" I prod, desperate for her to tell me everything is going to be fine.

"But . . . I don't know if it will be safe to tell her tomorrow either," she finishes.

I freeze. "W-why not?" I stutter.

"You said the call came in a little after we all separated, right? Just after Lillith met Ember. That timing is . . ."

I fear I know what she is going to say. My theory about the Kingdom of Endings doesn't make sense. They wouldn't have been making a report about Ember's people for the first time immediately after Lily met her. Even if they made contact separately, the timing would just be too coincidental.

"I see you understand what I mean," she says. "It must have been someone who was here. Someone in this community, the first she visited. Probably someone who wouldn't have had the chance to report on it until . . ."

"Until they were alone. Someone who had been too close to Lily all day, until that point," I finish. "Edward." She nods gravely. "I should have known. He was always so . . . off," I lament. "So jealous. So angry at her. But Lily . . . You don't understand. She wants her family to be good . . . She wants it so, so badly. This will crush her."

"And," Charlotte adds, "he will probably be with her again, when she visits next. We need to make a plan. A plan to distract him, while the other warns Lillith."

I nod, if only to hide the tremor in my jaw. Everything about this makes me feel sick to my stomach. It's all so wrong. It's true I have had trouble facing Lily lately, but I still love her. She's like Charlotte. Like the family that didn't reject me. I don't know if I can be the one to tell her that her family is trying to hurt her again. Charlotte seems to understand this. "I'll do it," she says. "The part that frightens you so much. I'll talk to Lillith. But you need to be strong. You need to keep Ed away from her. Can you do that, Leo?"

I nod. For Lily, I can do that.

Sarafyna

My head throbs as I finally wake up. My cheek rests on cold, dirty stone. My hands are tied behind my back, and my clothes have been replaced with some kind of burlap dress. Everything hurts and my limbs don't move like I want them to. It feels like the morning after too much physical labor. Annie says it has something to do with . . . tearing your body and acid, I think? Whatever the case, it hasn't been much of a problem for me since I was a child. Not since my nine years in hell. I can always just heal that kind of thing.

The thought panics me. I try to re-form my arms to escape the cuffs. It works, a little. I can feel the muscles and bones shift around, but they move like old molasses. They aren't responding like they usually do, and it hurts. It hurts like no pain I've felt since I was first thrown into that wagon as a child. I push through. I don't know how I got here, but I need to get out. I need to get out now. But . . . I can't. Before I can get myself free, my arms stop shifting. They defy me. I feel like I am no longer in charge of my own body.

My heart starts beating faster. I can feel the veins in my forehead pulsing. My breath grows shorter. I try to flex my mana, usually useless for anything other than suppressing other mages. I'm desperate enough to try. But it too is entirely suppressed. No. No no no fuck no. "Help, HELP ME! IS ANYONE OUT THERE?" I scream. No one answers. I scream again. And again and again. I can't be trapped again. I can't be gone again. I can't be away from Annie. I can't let her . . . Not again. I can't do this again.

I struggle to rise to my feet and fail. My muscle weakness and tied arms fight me, and I fall to my face again. I am in the woods, with a hood over my head, drowning in the river. My vision clears, and I realize I'm not. I'm in some kind of cell. I cry out—I feel like I scream for hours. Maybe it is minutes. I don't know. But my voice is hoarse and fading when the thick steel door to the cell finally opens, and Rebecca walks in.

"Oh, quit making a fuss, you're embarrassing yourself," she chides.

"W-what am I doing here? Why did you do this? . . . H-how did you do this?" I beg.

"Patience, Sarafyna. Patience. All will be answered. A . . . special guest will be coming to visit soon. You just need to sit tight until then." I roll over to my side to get a better look at her. "I'd like for us to be friends. To get along. Until our queen comes around, at least. Even more so if she doesn't, actually."

"You don't understand. She needs me," I say.

"Don't you worry about that, sweetheart." She shakes her head. "We've got her love life . . . arranged, should she ever wise up. She doesn't need you. If she wants to engage in . . . unnatural relations, there are plenty of other women. Women—well, I don't want to be rude, but women who don't need a wide-brimmed hat to hide the ugly bits. Your value is in what you can do for the people."

"No, you don't understand, without me, she'll . . . she'll . . ." I can't say she'll die. I can't accept that as reality. And I can't just say that to this woman. "She needs me," I repeat.

"The people need you. The people of her kingdom. Now, you know Lillith better than I do, Sarafyna. Would she want people to go hungry just because she can't have you to warm her bed at night? No. She would want you to make sure everyone could get where they needed to go. She would want you to feed the hungry, wouldn't she?"

I bite my lip in frustration. This woman doesn't understand Lillith at all.

"Of course she would want me to help people. She would want me to keep everyone safe," I whisper.

"Good, so we are in agreement." She smiles.

"No. She wants all that. But she loathes the idea of taking it at the tip of a sword. She loathes it. I was helping. I was making use of my sickening connection to the Radiant Woods. But if Lillith thought anyone was safe, and fed, and comfortable at the expense of the people they stepped on . . . no. The woman I love wants all these communities safe and protected. But she wouldn't want me accomplishing it in chains," I spit.

She frowns at me. "Well, I don't want you to do it in chains, exactly. Just with a little . . . encouragement to behave, is that so bad?" I glare at her. "Well, no matter. You have time to decide. Our distinguished guest is taking the long way around, it seems. I'd like you on our side before then. See, they are helping us in your stead but . . . well, it never hurts to have a contingency. Something 'the woman you love' should have considered. Think about it. In the meantime, it's time for dinner." She snaps her fingers, and a man, maybe a year younger than me, carries in a plate of fruit and bread.

"I . . . I can't eat with my arms tied like this," I protest.

"Oh, I wouldn't worry about it, sweetheart," she says. "He'll make sure you eat it all. Wouldn't want you going hungry, would we?"

My eyes widen as he approaches me. I understand on an instinctual level what he plans to do. I won't eat it. Not like that. It must be how they are drugging me. But I won't eat it like that.

"No," I whisper. "Please . . . just, no. I'll eat it off the floor if I have to. Just drop it. But . . . no," I beg. She says nothing, and the man approaches. He fixes one hand on my jaw to force it open and grabs a piece of fruit with the other. My heart is beating so quickly that I can hear it in my ears. I am in the Radiant Woods again. And the food I need is being offered. Bile rises in my throat. I rapidly turn my head and bite as hard as I can. I can't do enough to free my arms, but I can at least sharpen my teeth.

It's almost too easy, the way I shear through his index and middle finger. The taste of copper floods my mouth as my assailant screams. He leaves the two digits behind, and I spit them out. Rebecca watches me with gruesome fascination. The man screams and drops the tray. "I told you no," I growl, and the woman in front of me shrugs.

"Very well," she says. "Off the floor it is. But be certain to eat it all." She turns at that and whistles, then cries into the hall, "Get a healer here, quick as you can." She tries to hide it, but there is a slight tremor in her voice, and she marches out of the room just a little more quickly, more rigidly, than she entered.

CHAPTER THIRTY-THREE

Reality Check

Sarafyna

I don't know exactly how long it's been. It's difficult to keep track of the days with only ambient light making it into my cell. The stewards don't visit often. Every few days, I think. Although food arrives twice a day, the one thing they have been nearly religious about. It isn't hard to guess why. I only needed to try it once to feel the effect. The pain in my muscles got worse and my joints grew more difficult to bend after eating only a few mouthfuls. Every meal is poison. Even the water turned the world to mud through my eyes. I try to deny myself as much of both as I can, but it isn't doing me any good.

I have sores on my wrists now. Cuts and bruises all over my body. My hair is tangled and matted with . . . things. A constant aching torments me. I could handle all of it, I think. Every indignity of this cell. Every self-assured comment from Rebecca. I could handle all of it if I could close my eyes and visit happy Annie, safe Annie. If I pictured the home we're supposed to be living in. But instead . . . I can feel her. When I close my eyes, I feel her fighting. Worrying. Dying. All of it. Instead of an escape from hell, I get a reminder that she needs me and I can't help her. And she feels the same. Desperate and helpless to save me.

I hate it. It's like thorns in my throat. Every movement and moment a reminder of my helplessness. It's exactly like the Radiant Woods. Except I don't know how to move through this place. Anger isn't the right word for how I feel when April or Rebecca visits. When they try to convince me that helping them is what Annie would want, given the circumstances. The feeling cuts much deeper than ordinary rage. It touches an old, raw vein. One Annie has been talking to me about and helping me with at every opportunity. But they cut me off from her. They locked me up and tore the scab off. So what I am isn't angry, or enraged, or furious. What I am is fucking feral.

This is why, as I hear the door open too soon after the last meal was delivered, I use what little power I have to maintain the sharp edge of my teeth. I am ready to snarl at whichever steward is visiting this time, but I stop short. My new visitor is neither steward nor anyone with a plate of food. Instead, a young boy in a robe examines me, holding his hand on his chin in thought. He can't be any older than twelve or thirteen.

"Are you certain?" asks a familiar woman's voice from just behind the door.

He looks in her direction. "I'm quite all right, thank you. Please, close the door behind me," he requests. There is a moment of silence before April, I think, responds.

"Very well. We will be right here, if anything goes wrong," she says. When the boy fails to answer, it is quiet for another moment, and the door slowly closes, echoing in the cold room as a latch clicks into place. That unique and totally opaque darkness of a previously lit room clouds my vision for a moment, but I can still see the boy. I can see him by his mana and by his divine magic.

"Hello, Sarafyna," he says. "It's a pleasure to meet you. My name is Rune. I'm the Scholar Sage from the Council territories. How have you been?" He smiles at me and I blink. I missed the moment it happened, but the room is completely lit again. He is using not his mana but divine magic. I have no idea how, but I can . . . feel the intent behind it. "Ms. Sarafyna?" he repeats.

"I'm . . . not doing great," I answer in confusion.

"No, I suppose you wouldn't be," he muses. "Well, that's to be expected. Still, nothing to worry about for long. You'll be out of here in no time. I'm very sorry you had to be kept here in the first place, but I suspect you'll understand, in time."

I glance at the door with apprehension. "You're going to help me?" I whisper.

He holds up one hand and wobbles it in a so-so gesture.

"I'm afraid not. Not exactly, anyway. I'm going to tell you how to leave if you want. You'll get there eventually, of course, but I'm on something of a schedule. I'd prefer you not take quite so long as last time. In fact, I must apologize for how long the trip took me. I had to go the long way around," he explains nonchalantly.

"I don't understand. Who are you exactly? You want me free? Why did they let you in? What do you want from me?" I interrogate him in a whisper.

"Slow down, slow down, one question at a time." He chuckles, holding his hands up in mock surrender. "I told you who I am—I'm Rune, the sage. I am a counselor. To answer your other questions, yes. I want you free from this cell. They let me in because . . . well. Truth be told I am the one who helped them capture you. I know, not likely to ingratiate me with you. But I'm all right with that. Your opinion of me isn't really all that important. And what I want from you? That's a little harder to answer."

I stare at the door the entire time as he makes no attempt to lower his volume. I can see the mana on the other side of the door, practically pressed against it to listen.

He looks over his shoulder, then laughs. "Oh, don't worry about her. I know she plans to turn on us eventually, of course. She can't hear a thing. You should be able to sense that; is the dosage perhaps a little high?" he ponders. I gape at him, then focus. He's right. I don't understand it, but . . . I can feel the reality of it. The sound and light in this room belong to this room and only this room. If I were to focus on it, I might be able to figure out how to do it. Well, normally. Right now it feels like trying to describe the shape of a rock I can feel under a foot of mud.

It's at this point that his last words sink in. "I . . . haven't been eating. I think they have adjusted the dosage to compensate," I reply idly, still trying to get a grip on his magic.

He clicks his tongue. "Those idiots. That's what happens when you work with children's playthings." He curses. "Well. No matter, you'll be fine. I'd planned to keep you on a lower-than-normal dose in any case."

I blink at him. "What's going on?" I ask.

Instead of answering, he asks a question of his own. "You know the Nexus tried to hide your existence from us? He succeeded, for a little while. Quite the breach of our . . . understanding," he says, only confusing me more. I no longer feel feral. Instead, everything is surreal. Like I am in a fever dream. I can't catch up to him, largely by his design, it seems.

"What understanding?" I ask, and he shrugs.

"You know, even an increased dosage shouldn't work on you. From what we saw while you lived in the Nexus, your resilience, your downright stubbornness, and above all, your power . . . this poison shouldn't even be enough to slow you down. You could have been out of here on day one if you dropped the weight around your neck. Of course, you've never done things the easy way, have you? Killed another sage without ever meeting him, in a way, and all while sleeping on the job. You're an amazing specimen, Sarafyna. But not amazing enough. Not yet," he says, leaving me more confused than ever.

"P-poison?" I ask. "I thought it was just . . . drugs. I don't understand . . . You want to free me, but now you want me dead? What did I do, exactly?"

The boy chuckles. "I don't want you dead. No, quite the opposite. You are in no danger; poison is just our only option. A sleeping concoction alone would never slow down a local sage. Poison, however—well, that limits your use of the Nexus. You can only do so much to one person with Nexus energy. Even the threads of reality themselves have limits before they'll snap. But you have already displayed that it takes more than a little poison to stop you, haven't you?" he prods.

I sit back against the wall. "What does that mean?"

"Well"—he tilts his head—"it's how the Nexus controlled you for so long. Or did you think it had a fetish for force-feeding? Still, didn't stop you, did it? You fought it better than any sage ever has, in fact. That's the answer to your question, by the way. What I want with you. What all the sages want with you. We want a weapon against the Nexus. And you . . . you fit the bill."

My jaw slackens as I look at him. "You drugged me . . . no, poisoned me, locked me up, and left me worrying about my trapped loved ones . . . in the hopes that I would help you? What is wrong with you? I have people who need me!"

He's already shaking his head. "Not at all. I sent people to put you here to make you stronger. Or to force you to trim the dead weight. Either way, you'll be more formidable when you escape this room. As for helping me, well. I honestly don't give a shit if you help me. I don't care if you hate me. What matters to me is that you hate the Nexus more. I don't need your cooperation. I just know that, once you can fight the Nexus, you won't leave it alone just to spite me."

"I'm confused. You're a sage, so . . . you work with the . . . cat and bird people. Haven't you been sending them *through* the Nexus? Isn't that how you captured me? Because you . . . want me to fight it?" This kid is insane. Or maybe he is just a kid with too much power. Then again, Lillith is older than she looks. Maybe he is too. In any case, he isn't making sense.

"Like I said, we have an arrangement. And if it can hide things, so can we. You don't need to worry about that. You just need to figure out how you are getting out of this room. I think we can agree on that, no?" he says, uninterested in fully explaining himself.

I sigh. He's right. All I care about is making it back to Annie. Whatever game he's playing . . . Well, I'll ask Annie about it when I'm back. But first I need to get out of here.

I sigh, slumping my shoulders and hanging my head. If he knows how I can escape, I need to know. Annie, Peter, and Dad are all that matters to me right now. "All right," I agree. "Is that why you are here? To speed up the process of my escape . . . from you? How?" I'll play along if it gets me free. At least I have someone to negotiate with this time.

"Do you know why the Nexus . . . collects people? Why it changes them?" he asks in response. I stare at him blankly, then shake my head. "It's because it wants to grow. It wants more power. More Nexus energy. It's a glutton for the stuff. It can never have enough. It's why most of us sages can't enter the Nexus. It will overpower us. Devour us. Only one sage has ever entered and left alive," he says. I look at him in bafflement.

"Why would torturing people . . ." I trail off and he answers the unfinished question.

"There are two ways to become a sage, whether local or foreign. One is to consume, literally, another sage. Or a bit of them. This is how your 'priests' earn their little minor Nexus abilities. It's also how the Nexus, and you, grow their abilities," he says. I wince at that, feeling more aware of my scars than ever. "The other way is simple. Need. That's all it is. A need that exists like a stake inside you, burrowing through your heart, and stomach, and mind. Something that you would break the world to fulfill. Ambition. Loneliness. Desperation. Any of these, in the right heart, can create a Nexus sage. Someone with the ability to grab the threads of the reality Nexus and pull.

"And once a sage is created, they can keep pulling. Some more than others, and everyone in a different way. Everyone has a limit. Everything you try to change has a limit. Foreign sages can't alter their bodies because existing in this world already takes too much constant and active Nexus energy. Even local sages run into barriers and limits. Some people have seemingly arbitrary limits. But in all cases, a true Nexus sage is created through need. And that's what the Nexus does. It creates desperation. The desperation of being trapped in hell. Trapped in your own body. Of being alone. Whatever it might be. The Radiant Woods, as you call them, are a farm. To create and grow sages, then consume them when they can grow no further. All to feed the Nexus and allow its powers to grow."

I stare at him in horror. I almost question why he is telling me this, but . . . of course, he wants me to fight the Nexus. Me and Annie, I suppose. I almost think he's lying to ensure this result, but . . . it's true. I know it's true. Because I lived it, and he's right. Something else falls into place at the same time. "And you're doing the same . . ." I mutter.

He grins. "That's right. And it's working. I can see your desperation. Your loneliness. You'll grow here, until you are too strong for these . . . toys to contain. Or you'll stop wasting your Nexus energy on useless baggage. Either way, you'll escape. And the Nexus will be even more frightened of you," he agrees.

"And why tell me all that? Why tell me your whole plan?" I ask.

"It's simple, really. You mastered the Nexus itself when you didn't know what your power was. With context? You are going to be terrifying. And you are going to go after it much more quickly. I am fascinated to see the results." He grins.

"And when we finish with the Nexus, and come for you next?" I ask.

"Oh, honey. You're not going to kill the Nexus. You're not that strong," he says mockingly. "But you'll try. It's in your nature. And you'll try to make it hurt while you do. That's all we need from you. It will be enough." He turns and knocks on the door three times. Before it opens, he looks back at me. "Why do you keep those scars, by the way? I have always wondered." I look at him in confusion. He shrugs. "Well, you should think about that too. I promise you, even if people act like the marks aren't there, even if they say they don't notice them . . . they do. Something else to work on while you are trying to escape."

I glare at his back as the door opens and he starts happily chatting with the steward outside. I feel that feral rage growing in my chest again. Then the door closes, and I am again in darkness.

CHAPTER THIRTY-FOUR

Fight the Sickness

... wouldn't go in there if I were you," Ed warns from the other side of the lab's door. "She's not feeling her best. She can be a bit hostile. Very quickly and with little provocation."

I grit my teeth. I can hear you, asshole. It may not quite be like my strength, but my hearing is nothing to scoff at. If that little shit warns people about my temperament one more goddamn time . . . I audibly growl, and Autumn and Henry look at me with awkward trepidation. Ember, the final person in the room, just shakes her head in irritation.

"I don't want to bother her, I really don't." It's Peter's voice. "But . . . it's Sam. I don't think he's doing so well since Mom . . ." I feel a pang of regret. That poor man. This isn't the first time he's lost Sarafyna. I'm honestly afraid to face him. It's been nearly a month now, and I am useless. Just more and more sick. More and more furious. I am fucking useless to the woman I love and to everyone who relies on her. And I am useless to her father. "He just needs someone to communicate with him," Peter continues after a moment.

"I understand," Ed replies. "I just want to warn—"

"Christ, just send him in, Edward, he deserves that much," I call through the door. Raising my voice forces me to cough, which splatters the circle I am designing with speckles of red. Autumn and Henry look at me like I'm crazy.

"Who are you talking to, Lily?" Autumn asks, and I just roll my eyes. I didn't actually request two people for sanity checks, but I can't exactly begrudge Henry for bringing his girlfriend along. He basically spends all day, every day with me. It's not reasonable to resent him and his happy relationship, nor my friend for keeping him company. But I haven't been in a reasonable mood lately. I feel like, well, absolute fucking shit. I've been sleeping less than an hour each night, and when I do, it literally feels like dying. I should know.

I don't bother answering Autumn, as Peter does it for me a moment later. I feel an irritating mixture of regret and annoyance as his eyes dim when he sees me, but Autumn and Henry visibly relax when they realize I was actually responding to someone. It makes me regret ever telling them I might be mentally compromised by this. Of course, that's exactly why I had to tell them when I did. I suppress an exasperated sigh and force a weak smile. "Hey, Peter. How are you holding up?" I ask. He looks awkwardly to the side, gripping one arm with his opposing hand.

"Hey, I'm really sorry to bother you, I know you've been busy . . . trying to help," he frets. "Maybe this wasn't such a good idea." He glances at my face again and grimaces. I know exactly why. I look like I feel. My hair is thinning, from medication or anxiety, I don't know. Probably both. The dark circles under my eyes grow a little puffier every day, and I am quickly becoming the whitest woman this side of Potestia. I've lost weight as well, which I really didn't need to lose. Food makes me feel sick and tastes like . . . nothing.

I feel like there is no right answer. I want to rest, for Sarafyna. Because she wanted me to rest. But when I do, it doesn't help. I can never sleep. And I feel like I'm failing her. I can't do anything. Anything at all to help her. Of course, when I do work, it still doesn't help her. All this time and I have no idea how to get to her. It's a fucking mess. I have to bite my tongue to stop myself from snapping at this poor kid looking for comfort while his adopted mother is missing. It takes me a little too long to respond, and he starts to turn before I speak. "No, it's all right," I say. "It's good to see you more. Sara would like us spending more time around each other. What's on your mind?"

"It's . . . it's Sam. He's . . . well. I think you understand. He's taking this hard. And you've been so busy. Constantly working, and I know that's because you want to get Mom back, but I thought . . . I thought you would have a moment, eventually. And when you had a moment, you could visit Sam. For more than a minute, I mean. To talk to him. Reassure him. Reassure me. But . . ." He trails off, and I understand. Looking at me, no one is going to feel reassured. The only thing I can do is . . . present what little hope I can as an exhausted, dying woman. He doesn't have to say this. I don't have to say this. Everyone in the room understands. Thankfully, Henry speaks up on my behalf.

"You know, I spent some time, back in Satusmor, trapped like your mom is. Longer than this. Lillith pulled me out of there. I, uh, I can talk to Sam, if you want?" he offers.

Peter's eyes brighten in an almost imperceptible way. He's not happy, but he's . . . relieved. I get it. He's like me. Desperate to do something, with nothing to do.

"That would actually be really great," Peter agrees. "Thank you . . ." He stands around awkwardly for a moment while I look down at the circle I was drawing. At the steel spike in the middle of its own circle that Ember is quietly directing unaspected mana into. The silence drags on for a long moment before it grows unbearable and Henry speaks again.

"And you know what? Now would actually be a great time for that. Autumn, do you mind hanging back?" he requests. Autumn and Henry try to share a subtle glance, and I roll my eyes.

"She won't let me do anything stupid, all right? You're good to go," I say, dismissing my brother and breaking the awkward moment. A deep throbbing radiates from the back of my neck into my head. I want to scream, except that would make my head throb more.

"Right. Sorry, Lil," Henry says. "Uh . . . never mind." At this, he joins Peter and begins to speak to him quietly.

Before they leave, Peter gives me an apologetic look. "Thank you, Lillith. I, uh . . . Let me know if I can help in any way, when the time comes. To get Mom, I mean. Please," he requests.

I muster a nod, and they walk through the door. If I strained, I could probably hear their whispering or whatever they say to Ed as they leave. I don't have the energy for it, however.

"He's really worried about you, you know," Autumn says once my brother is far enough away. "He's hardly sleeping any more than you are."

". . . I know," I whisper in response. And I do. It is wretched, how much I do. Because no matter what face he, or anyone else I love, presents to me, I can feel it. Their grief is acid running through my veins. I can even feel it from Autumn right now. "He's a good man."

"He is," Autumn agrees. "Do you think . . . you'll be all right?"

I pause, still looking at my drawing, then take a deep breath. "I don't know, Autumn. I'm sorry. But, if it gets too bad, if I don't think I can push anymore, I'll make sure he knows he did everything he could. I won't let him do anything stupid either. I promise," I say, answering the question she was working her way toward. She looks down, a little embarrassed but grateful. And with that out of the way, I can finally fucking focus on what I am doing. I will find a way through the woods if it literally kills me. Better than just dying without doing anything.

Luckily, Ember is still focused on her own project. "It's stabilized," she announces.

I look up with a raised eyebrow at the feline woman. "Think this one will work?" I ask.

She shrugs. "I told you I've never made one before; it might still take some trial and error. But I've seen them used for riot control before. It feels closer to those this time," she replies, handing the spike to me before offering her wrists to Autumn to replace her mana-dispersal cuffs.

"Thanks," I say mechanically. "Might as well leave them off for now though. It'll be easier to tell if this works. Let's go."

With that, all three of us begin to head outside. This can't really be tested indoors. Ed falls in behind us as we leave the lab, following along, of his own accord, to keep an eye on Ember.

"You seem pretty good at enchantments, for a scout," Autumn muses, tilting her head at Ember as we leave the building and head toward an empty field.

"I was going to school for enchanting before I enlisted," she explains with boredom. "Didn't Lillith tell you this?"

"Figured your personal details were personal." I shrug. Ember has been telling me all about her culture over the last month. But I haven't absorbed much of it. Usually, I would find it fascinating, but my mind is so murky. I feel like I'm constantly wading through Jell-O. And it's hard to focus on history when all I can really think about is Sarafyna. What she needs. How she's being treated. How to bring her home.

Ember clicks her tongue but looks toward Autumn. "A lot of people join up for different positions around the Nexus. Just to get away from sages, for one reason or another. It's the only place they refuse to go. Well, it's the only place they'd be insane to go anywhere near. I can't believe Sa—" She cuts herself off, realizing she is about to step into dangerous territory. "Anyway, a lot of us have different skills and abilities. Besides, basic enchantments are an elective in school. Military enchantments are a specialization as well."

Autumn nods. "I suppose that makes sense. What is this one anyway? You and Lillith keep stabbing it into the ground, but it never does anything. You just mutter about it together afterward. What's the point? You said it's for . . . riot control? What's that?"

I answer this one. "It's like the mana-dispersal cuffs Ember usually wears but stronger. And external," I explain. "Essentially, it's like a portable dispersal circle. Pump it full of mana, stab it into the ground, and it'll eliminate all mana in an area. Even mine, I think." I'm not so sure about that last part. I made some minor changes to Ember's design. I know Godfrey is working on spreading my circle, and I know he has a nonzero chance of success. Not a high one, but he's smarter than the average noble. I can't count on his failure. "If these are going to be effective, they have to be effective against everyone. As such, they don't just disperse mana, they absorb any mana that tries to gather. This means anyone near one of these spikes—I'm dubbing them riot spikes—will just be a normal person. And with someone like me around them, the spikes will actually last longer."

"What do you mean 'someone like you'?" Ember cuts in, and I curse internally. Shit. This fucking brain fog. One of the things I've been trying not to share with her is the workings of my circle. I sure as hell don't want another situation like Godfrey's, with someone thinking about recklessly testing out my circle on other people. I'll have to come up with an excuse later. For now, I'll change the subject before anyone says something more revealing.

"Aren't you worried someone will use this against you?" Autumn asks. So much for that. I sigh.

"Yeah, I am," I reply in resignation while Ember's eyes track me with suspicion. "But it's a tool uniquely useful against me in that way. What we gain from everyone in Potestia having the chance to level the playing field far outweighs the risk to me alone. It's a trade I'm willing to make."

"Oh. OH!" Autumn exclaims. "I thought you were making some superspell weapon or something, but that's not it at all! You are taking the nobles' advantage away! With enough of these, if they work, it'll just be like fighting the guards!"

I nod. "Better, actually. When was the last time you saw a noble with a sword, spear, or any kind of weapon? Even a magic knight? We put weapons in the people's hands and spread these around and we'll be the ones with an advantage," I tell her.

"Sounds . . . scary. Our people don't know how to fight either, for the most part. Will that be okay?" Autumn asks.

"It'll be dangerous. I wish that wasn't the case. But if it comes to using these, well. We'll have numbers and grief on our side. At that point, enough people will be too angry for a few guards and knights without magic to effectively stop them," I answer.

As we reach the middle of a nearby meadow, the Radiant Woods taunting me to one side and the towers small enough in the other, Ember and Ed start laying stones with light and sound enchantments in a practiced way.

"And the noble families, like mine, that haven't changed their minds yet?" Autumn asks, audibly casually but with visible strain on her face. It's back to this again, of course.

"Well. That's one reason we have been all over Potestia all this time. We've been doing all we can. To give people options. To tell people they aren't going to get their luxuries back. Their slaves and wealth are gone for good. Whether they actively participated or passively benefited, it's over and it's not coming back. All they have to do is accept that," I reply. I examine the spike for a moment and continue, "And of course, to organize. To keep people together. Create a united front rather than aimless violence when the time comes."

"Is there no more peaceful way to change minds?" Autumn tries while I clear the ground where I want to stab the spike.

"Sure. But anytime people try, the guards and knights brutalize them. Round them up. Enslave them. Potestia doesn't exactly have free speech, you know. Even if they did, how many times are we supposed to ask nicely to be treated like people? *Peaceful* often just means *quiet*. Ignorable. Eventually, you have to do something that can't be ignored. Because I'll tell you what. Sitting comfortably in your mansion while the knights burn down a brothel to punish commoners? That's violence," I answer.

I'm speaking far more calmly than the first time I had an argument with Autumn about this. Almost idly, like the conversation is in the background. Largely because Autumn has changed a lot, and I've changed . . . a little. Also because I have a hard time focusing on all that. Because none of this is what I want to be doing. What I want to be doing is storming the Kingdom of Endings and burning their fucking "palace" down. I want to be saving Sara. But these pointless arguments and designing weapons I can't give to people is all I can do. At least they distract me from my complete lack of ideas for saving the woman I love.

"What if more powerful mages come along? Like Godfrey or Kallon?" Autumn asks, changing the subject. "They can move fast, and honestly, there are a few ways around these . . . Couldn't both sides end up getting killed for nothing?"

"The idea is to do it all at once. Maybe not at exactly at the same time, but within a couple of weeks for every city. As for Godfrey and Darian and the others, I—"

"We're ready," Ember cuts in.

"Hold that thought," I say to Autumn. This conversation went a long way in distracting me from . . . everything. But I have a new distraction now. "If all goes well, none of us will be mages in a moment. It can be a little strange if you've never been in a dispersal circle, Autumn. But it won't hurt or anything. Everyone ready?"

Ember rolls her eyes and Autumn nods. I feel nervous. I don't know why. I won't be able to distribute these yet. They won't get me any closer to Sara. They will effectively be useless for now. Still. It feels like, if I can't even do this . . . I need to be able to do something. So I need these to work, however useless I may still feel afterward. So I push a little mana into the spike and drive it into the ground.

I wake up in my bed, Henry sitting next to me and Ember leaning against the wall, tinkering with something. My mouth tastes like copper. My muscles are sore. And . . . I feel pretty good, actually. Like I can think clearly. The walls that were closing in on me have backed off. I still feel more pressure than a helicopter mother behind my eyes, but comparatively speaking, I'm doing okay. "Henry? What happened?" I ask, causing him to nearly jump out of his skin.

"Shit, Lily! Are you fucking good?" he asks intensely, examining me with the wide-eyed look of the thoroughly startled.

"Are you an idiot?" Ember cuts in before I can answer my brother.

"That is a common sentiment, yes," I reply. "Any particular reason it only just now occurred to you to verify?"

"Was that snark? Shit, you were right, it does work!" Henry literally claps.

"I knew you were sick," Ember says. "I knew it was affecting your mind. But none of that made me regret our deal. Knowing you were insane long before you got sick, on the other hand . . ." Ember rubs her temples with her index fingers.

"Insane I may have always been. But slow to get to a point? Well, yeah, that too sometimes. Still. It's annoying, so what are you talking about?" The words come out before I even think about them, in a way they haven't in weeks. In a way I lacked both the physical and emotional energy for. A switch seems to have flipped in my head. Not only do I feel better, for some reason, I feel less hopeless about Sara. I still lack any ideas to get to her. But . . . it feels like I just saw her.

"I finally saw your magic circle is what I mean," Ember growls. "It's impossible. You should be dead. I thought you *were* dead when you collapsed out there."

"I did too, for the record," Henry adds. "The lack of heartbeat makes it very confusing. You're lucky we've seen this before, or Ed woulda told Mom and then you'd be dead for sure."

I smile at my brother, but my focus is on Ember.

"What's impossible?" I ask.

"You can't survive turning your body into a magic space. Not unless you are a sage, and a more powerful one than average at that. Which you insist you are not. You should have died the second you finished the center rune. And don't get me started on the level of magic permeation you've baked in. You have your damn bone marrow storing mana? No wonder you're sick! What kind of a person designs a circle like this? This design should have killed you years ago! Fucking insane," Ember lectures me.

"Then, why didn't it?" I respond.

"How should I know? But I'll tell you what, you absolutely cannot go anywhere near another dispersal circle. I assume you went inside one just before getting sick? One that powers some other kind of enchanted artifact?" she guesses.

I snap my fingers in realization.

"Oh. Well, shit," I answer.

"What?" Henry asks, looking back and forth between us.

"It's the drain. The part I added to our spikes. Right?" I say.

"That would be my guess," Ember replies. "Hard to say, since no one has survived this long with either idiotic mistake you made with your circle. What the fuck were you thinking?" Her glare is half anger, half bewilderment. Shit, how was I supposed to know it was so dangerous? There is a reason I didn't try it again on anyone else.

"Uh, you only live once?" I offer. Then I pause. "Wait . . ." I really am feeling better. That stupid joke would have refused to enter my brain before. "So . . . why do I feel better?" I ask.

"Oh, she made these for you," Henry replies, raising my own arm to present to me. It has an unfamiliar bracelet and several rings.

"You shouldn't feel better," Ember replies. "Those are artifacts that are collecting the mana trying to feed your cancer. They slow it down, but they don't improve its state. A treatment discovered to help people only half as stupid as you. Keep them on, and you should at least stabilize. Better, on the other hand? I wouldn't count on it anytime soon. Not without your little Nexus sage around."

Usually, I would snap at her for that comment. Make her feel small for referring to Sara that way. But I am distracted. So it's my own fucking circle killing me. This is amazing news. I've considered it as a possibility but didn't know how to really investigate. But if that's the case, everyone else is safe. That's not all. Because Ember is right. Slowing the cancer down wouldn't make me feel better. Just stop it from making me feel worse. Not until I was able to treat it. Sure, it could just be a night of sleep, but I don't think so. Because I feel better about Sara too.

I don't understand it. I don't know how. But . . . it feels like Sara is responsible for this somehow. It's knowledge that wraps around me like firelight. I don't know why I am so certain. But . . . I know she is safe. I feel so relieved, like I just had my first glass of water in days.

Until a knock comes at the door. Henry happily answers it, and he seems to know too. I can feel his grief subsiding after just looking at me. He speaks with someone at the front door briefly. I hear Clarrise's name come up and feel a sharp stab of agonizing grief from whoever is on the other side of the door.

As Henry walks back into my bedroom, I have returned to a panic. "What is it? Is Clarrise okay?" I beg. He is reading a letter apparently dropped off by our visitor.

"She . . . she's fine," Henry replies with a hitch in his voice. "But . . . Lily, we have to get back to Potestia, now. They . . . they . . ."

Ember snaps the letter from his hands.

"Shit," she mutters. "Here, you'll want to read this. Seems like the time to start your revolution in earnest has come. Good thing that fucking spike works. Maybe you can tell people how to make it via sphere." She hands the letter to me and I accept it, a sharp pang of anxiety coursing through me.

As I read it, my blood runs cold. This? Because people started taking care of themselves? Fucking *this*!? "I am going to kill them all," I say as soon as I finish reading.

Fight

Charlotte's Journal

When my parents died, I tried to fight. I knew I wasn't alone. It didn't matter how many people tried to tell me I invented the fight. How many people insisted no one before me had ever felt uncomfortable in their skin. Had ever felt elation at a new name. I knew I wasn't alone, because I had met Amelia. I knew then that our childhood dream of marrying and starting a family could never be. Not in Potestia. Not with a king and a god who wanted to wipe us from history. A slave could never marry a noble. A woman could never marry a woman. And the man they would insist I was could never marry the man they would insist she was.

I understood once I grew up. There were mountains in the way of my dream. It was just a childhood crush in any case. But it still weighed on me. It wasn't a dream that should be impossible. Some things are too simple to remain unachievable forever. So I searched. I was of the house of Renatus; I had the power to look. I searched until I found others like me. Slaves. Commoners. Minor nobles. Men and women who looked in the mirror and knew what they were seeing wasn't right. Even one person who would accept neither label. And we each fought, in our own way.

We all had Erics. Amelias. Deaths and banishments of the ones we loved. Accusations of abuse, spit at anyone who cared about us and coming straight from our actual abusers. And we were all determined to stop it.

I tried to petition the king but was never granted an audience. My father would have been seen. But the only person anyone was interested in listening to was Charles Renatus. And I wasn't him. I didn't understand how I could be acknowledged and dismissed at the same time. I would never be a woman in their eyes. I would only fit in the role they had designed for me.

But at the same time . . . they did acknowledge me. They did treat me like a woman. Or the same way they treat women. With contempt. Dismissal. I had to live in the body they demanded or I was challenging the Collector himself. I had to use the name they gave me, wear the clothes they assigned me. In the ways that made me loathe myself, I was a man to them. In the ways that made them loathe me, I was a woman. Not to be entertained. Not to be listened to. To be treated as an ornament of their power.

I could not change things. Or . . . if I wanted to change anything, I needed to give up on myself. I still hadn't hurt enough. So we had to fight. Just to be seen. Just to be heard. Just to exist, every single day. We had to weather interrogations, glares, sneers. Contempt from all directions.

I hired doctors and alchemists to help us. It looked like something could be done. Like there was some way to move closer to bodies that fit our souls. Sadie, a friend and former servant, was the first to try. A potion was supposed to start the change. But . . . everything fell apart. Just as everyone was starting to come together. Just as we started to hope. The more public we were, the angrier everyone else was. And if we were happy? Well. That only upset them more. Sadie was the first to die.

That was when a silent war broke out. I had a friend named Rose with fire in her blood. Fire, and rage, and grief. She killed Sadie's murderers. And it was too late. Violence and counterviolence. Sadie inspired all of us. But I was the only one who could really fight. One by one, our friends died following her plans. And then Rose died. And I was alone again. And no one even knew we had been fighting. No one knew my friends were dead. Because no one cared. And anyone who did cared just enough to make sure it was silenced. Forgotten. Everyone was forgotten. Everyone but me, and I would only ever be heard if I used a name that slid off my tongue like bile. When my friends died, I stopped fighting. I'd seen what it would lead to.

CHAPTER THIRTY-FIVE

Incentives

Dominic

I sit in my new room with my head in my hands, waiting for Grandfather to finish his meeting. I don't understand how this could have happened to Visenar. I left to help a few lords sort out their cities and redistribute long-range whisper spheres where they had seemingly gone missing. I knew things were bad even before I left, but they were progressing in that direction steadily. Slowly. I expected to find an anxious but functional city when I returned. Instead, I arrived and my home was under siege from the inside.

One of Grandfather's bards had to sneak me into the palace this morning, apparently through the same escape routes Grandfather has been using to keep any semblance of control over the city. He's been sending bards and knights out under the cover of darkness just to keep his people fed. His people who cower in their homes every day instead of meeting their friends, going to their shops, and living their lives. I was surprised to find him ruling at all, much less in this state. Too much happened while I was out of the city.

I can't help but feel furious at all our allies. The allies Grandfather protected from the Mage of Mourning. With his advice, they stayed safely off her list for four years. With their help now, he could end this sickening stalemate. I hear yet another barrage hit the barrier around the palace. The rebel king alone couldn't do that. Not constantly. At least our allies are contributing mana to this spell. Still, it must be exhausting Grandfather. Of course, these supposed allies are comfortable offering support as long as they feel safe. As long as they feel comfortable. The minute they have to put their necks on the line? Nothing. How long has he had to keep this up? The bard who brought me here barely had time to catch me up.

Well. Whatever the case is, it changes now. I am back and I am quite possibly the most powerful mage in the country. I have no idea how long this rebel king spent in his circle, but I know it wasn't the royal circle. And I have an entire generation on Kallon despite our similar ages. I won't let my grandfather . . . no, I won't let *the king* fight alone any longer. I am going to stand beside him. And if that isn't enough to get our allies off their asses, well. Who cares? The two of us will tear this country back from the rebels. No more hiding behind a shield. We are getting to the people and giving them their lives back.

A sharp knock comes at my door and I open it after a single breath. The bard on the other side blinks in surprise before clearing his throat. "His Majesty is ready for you," he says. I straighten my shirt and nod. He then begins to escort me to the throne room. The halls of the palace are quieter than I expected. We are harboring a large number of the more powerful nobles in the city. I suppose we lack the supplies to support their usual frivolity. I would nevertheless expect a little more life in the building. It's nearly as quiet here as it is in the city. The first people we pass are a group of four, all dressed in heavy woolen cloaks that obscure both face and figure. Three of them are unusually tall, nearly a pace and a half over me, while the fourth seems petite.

The taller members of the group walk in a strange lilting fashion, while the shorter seems to quickly shift focus between everything they pass. I try to place them, but I'm certain I've never met a noble of any station at that height, much less three. I don't actually think I've met anyone of that size before. As they pass, I swear I see a taller one's eyes light up, not with mana but on their own, under their hood. I follow them with my head as we pass each other, nearly walking into my escort. It's distracting enough that I nearly don't notice when we arrive at the large doors to the throne room barely a few breaths later. I look around a bit and realize there are few other doors near here, and most are typically used for staff of one variety or another.

More importantly, no one else came from this direction. Grandfather was in a meeting when I returned, and it seems the members of the strange group were likely the other attendees. Interesting. The bard pushes the door open with less ceremony than the previous king would ever allow, then steps out of my way. "His Majesty is inside," he says, nodding toward the gap.

"Thank you." I nod in return, and he turns to leave. Grandfather isn't running too strict a hierarchy I see, which is one thing I have always respected about him. Once inside, I see him sitting tiredly at the head of a long, wooden table that has been brought into the large hall. It wasn't here the last time I was in this room, and I suspect he uses it to meet with the other nobles on something closer to equal ground. There are other rooms for this, but choosing the throne room sends a message about what *king* will mean moving forward.

He looks exhausted, as I expected. Heavy bags mark his already aged face, and his long hair is wiry and unwashed. Even his clothes appear ragged and hardly becoming of a king. Despite it all, he has a soft grin on his lips. "Welcome back, Dominic," he greets me happily.

"Grandfather." I bow. "I'm sorry I failed to return more quickly. Had I known the situation, I would have rushed back to your side."

He shakes his head at me. "No. You were doing important work. Did you deliver the intercity spheres to all your assigned cities?"

"Yes, Your Majesty. The church seemed to struggle in every city, as a result of either unwillingness or inability to produce the spheres as they were needed. As such, I used more of the supply I was sent with than I anticipated. I . . . also struggled to stabilize the economy in each city. I don't know how, but it seems your, uh, apprentice somehow reached them as well. There wasn't much I could do," I report. He waves his hand at me.

"I'm aware. It seems she has found a way to move freely through the Radiant Woods. It's no matter, we will see to that in time. So long as we can communicate. You did well, Dominic. And please, call me Grandfather. None of that 'Your Majesty' nonsense. Not among family," he replies. "Please, have a seat."

I nod, a soft smile on my own lips now. As I approach the table, I see a shallow, long box on the table, nearer Grandfather's end. I approach and see there is a tall, ornately jeweled staff inside.

"What do you think of it?" he asks, catching the look in my eyes.

"What is it?" I reply curiously as I sit.

He looks at it with something not entirely like consternation. "A risk. And a last resort. One I was starting to think I was going to have to use, but am relieved to keep as a backup plan," he answers.

I blink at him. "Grandfather," I say with a blank stare, "that is not even sort of an answer to the question. What does it *do*?"

His eyes smile at me when he looks up. "You're right," he agrees. "I am getting long-winded in my old age, I'm afraid. It is an . . . artifact of the Collector, I am told. A divine artifact designed to 'set things right' in a way. No matter whose hands it is in, it wields powerful divine magic. Divine magic that can help us rebuild everything that is falling apart."

I give him a skeptical look. "Just like that?" I press. I glance at the staff again, then back at my grandfather. "And where does the last resort bit come in?" That sounds a little too easy for me. And he included too many references to information from a third party. As much as I would love a divine artifact that builds our cities, feeds our people, and satisfies our nobles . . . I have difficulty believing anything but hard work is going to accomplish any one of those things. There is also a . . . hollow look in my grandfather's eyes. Something just behind the smile, like mold under new paint. There's more to this. It gives me the feeling of something that should never be focused on.

He lets a deep breath out through his nose. "Well, for one, it is apparently most effective and safest when used by a powerful divine mage. And ours is, well, dead. If I use it . . ." He trails off and the weight of the silence tells the rest of the story. I understand immediately. It will kill him. But . . . that can't be it. If that was all, I'd grab it right now and give everything to help Grandfather fulfill his dream. He would too. There must be more than that. But that is the second time he has dodged my real question. It's clear he won't be sharing the rest. Which is all right; I can wait.

"You said you could keep it as a backup plan?" I ask. At this, his face . . . brightens? I'm unsure. He has an excitable energy about him, but he also raised me. I can taste the poison in this excitement. I'll have to press him about it later.

"That's right. You wouldn't know, would you? I'm sure you have much to report about the country at large, but I have something else to announce, and not just to you. But I can tell you a bit. It's about Lillith's strange magic circle," he begins, and it's my turn to brighten.

"You finally found where she was hiding it?" I ask.

He shakes his head. "She had it with her the entire time. She somehow figured out a way to carry it with her, tattooed onto her body. Completely ignoring the need to find the center of a designated space. She has never left her circle. And I saw the design, when she was in the dungeon," he reveals, and my eyes widen. That shouldn't be possible. No one can do that. "Not only did I see the design, but—" There is a loud knock at the door, which is still ajar, interrupting him. "Enter!" he calls. "Well, it seems the rest are here now. Allow me to show you."

At that, a stream of affluent nobles begins to file into the room, each taking a seat along the large table. I have to hold back a sneer at all these so-called supporters. I could get away with it if I did, considering how hard each is working to avoid making eye contact.

"We have come as requested, Your Majesty," one man says while bowing slightly, just before taking the seat opposite me. "However, if this is about confronting the revolutionary army, we still fear it would be unwise while we have other options. Even with the aid of your grandson. Welcome back, Prince Dominic, of course." He adds that last bit with the haste of a man who forgot his anniversary.

"Worry not, Lord Anders," Grandfather says. "I didn't call you here to rehash old conversations. At least not . . . without incentive. Please, present yourselves." He then turns in his seat and gestures to two men emerging from Grandfather's private office at the back of the room. One of them is clearly a beleaguered priest, the weight of overwork hanging around his neck. Few people notice this, however, as everyone's eyes are firmly fixed on the other man: a tall commoner with mana swirling and gathering around him as he walks, no magic circle in sight.

"Now. In exchange for sharing this circle with your houses, do any of you feel confident enough to put down this fucking revolution now?" he asks the silent room just as the new mage stops at the table.

CHAPTER THIRTY-SIX

Understanding Sacrifice

Dominic

Everything has changed. Everything. Nobles who wouldn't lift a finger to repay a debt will absolutely put their necks on the line for more power. If not to get ahead, then to avoid falling behind. They don't have a choice really. Not after seeing a commoner gathering more mana than any of their circles ever have—and with freedom of movement. If only one noble agreed to help us, they would likely become the most powerful noble house outside of royalty in a single generation. Even if none of them did, Grandfather has the circle. After a couple generations of *only* the royal family having it? They would be further behind us than ever. Eventually, their support will be entirely unnecessary and pointless.

And so, here we are. With actual support, standing in the palace courtyard on one side of a massive yellow barrier of mana. The gardens around us are dead. The fountains are dry. What was once a beautiful welcome to the finest estate in the country has fallen to neglect, all of our spare mana contributing to our protection rather than upkeep. Finally, for the first time in weeks, the onslaught has stopped and the air is electric. I stand next to my grandfather and a dozen of the most powerful mages in Visenar. Behind us, twenty or so bards in full combat attire prepare different types of mana. Several carry various instruments, actually living up to their name for a battle of this scale. Others use different means to create the emotional responses they seek—pain, anger, indignation. Many remain unarmed and rely on snide comments alone. In any case, it is unusual to see them fully prepared in this way. And of course, at their head is Ansel, finally recovered from his apparent encounter with the Mage of Mourning.

On the opposite side of the shimmering sheet of mana stands the false king Darian, smirking at us. Next to him is Kallon, his seething focus entirely on my grandfather. About four powerful nobles are lined up beside him, alongside nearly a hundred nobles from weaker houses. Overall, it seems like we have a more powerful force. It is just too difficult to overcome the gap between a powerful mage and a weaker one. If I fight Kallon and Grandfather handles Darian, the others will fall into place. The rest of his force doesn't stand a chance against ours. They did before I got here. And they would have without the rest of the nobles on our side. But now, no. They can't beat us.

They seem to remain confident, however. For one reason. Well, two, I suppose. The first reason is that Darian doesn't care about any individual city. He will burn Visenar to the ground so long as the throne is left intact, and he knows we won't. So he believes he can fight more freely than us. The second reason is, well. He doesn't know how my grandfather's magic works.

"It's time to surrender, Darian," Grandfather says. "Your little game is over. You know those people behind you will die if we fight. All of you will."

"We will never fucking surrender, usurper," Kallon replies coldly. He misses the dangerous glance he gets from Darian.

There is no sign of danger in the challenger's voice when he speaks, however. Not for Kallon, anyway. "No. We really won't. For one simple reason. I am stronger than you, Godfrey. You and your grandson. As a mage, yes. But that's not all there is. I know how to sacrifice. Well, I suppose you do too, in a way," he prods, sending a chill down my spine as he winks in my direction. "But it's not enough. You still asked for 'volunteers.' You still want to believe you are a hero. You won't be able to give up enough to beat me," he taunts. "Now, tell me, where is the actual king?" His comment about volunteers makes Grandfather wince and I raise an eyebrow at him.

"Volunteers? For what?" I ask.

"You know the answer to that. Let's say you are right," Grandfather replies to Darian, ignoring me. "Let's say you do beat me. What happens then? You step aside and give the throne to Kallon here? How exactly does this alliance work?"

Kallon bristles, but Darian simply grins.

"Perhaps you should worry about your own allies. You wouldn't bring your dear grandson out here without telling him how you made it happen, would you?" Darian taunts, fixing his eyes on mine. "So, did he tell you? How he got this whole party together? How he got the support he needed to brave this fight?"

I blink at him, then glance at Grandfather, who maintains his forward focus.

"He discovered a new magic circle," I say dismissively, setting my jaw. I don't know what he's implying, but it's not going to make me turn on my grandfather.

Darian gives me a wide smile. "You were right, Kallon. He is soft. Too soft even for the pretender king. Why don't you share the body count behind this discovery? Tell your poor, naive grandson how many of his precious commoners you sacrificed, just for a carrot to dangle in front of your supposed supporters. Or did you not think I knew about that?" he pushes, grinning a little too widely at both of us. It's pathetic. Grandfather is the one who taught me to respect the commoners. The one who suggested sharing magic with them. Moving the country forward. He's a compassionate man. I glare at Darian and wait for Grandfather to spit the slander back at him.

And I wait. And Darian's grin only grows wider, until I am forced to finally look at King Godfrey with wide, hopeful eyes. He continues to avoid eye contact. I swallow, my heart sinking into my stomach with dread. "What does he mean, Grandfather?" I finally ask. He doesn't look at me, but he does wince.

"Everyone involved in the development of the new royal circle participated voluntarily," he says. "I sacrificed no one. We took risks, together. On equal footing, to win this country back from your sick revolution. To earn a life back for the people of this city. How dare you try to reduce their . . . dedication to a weapon to hurt Dominic?"

His words are wind through chimes. I can hear their attempt at music and the hollow truth behind them. Kallon sneers.

"Oh yes," Darian chuckles. "My mother volunteered in the same way once. To serve the country and the king. I'm certain you walked them all past the mass graves in what used to be the palace gardens. Introduced them to the volunteers who came before them. Offered them magic, wealth, and renown even if they turned you down. Certainly you, the supposed king of the country, didn't make a request of the people you rule and believe they could truly say no? Right? If not at first, certainly after the first dozen died? The first hundred? The first thousand? No?" he chides, then directs his attention to me.

"You're here to support your favored king?" he asks. "To stop my revolution for the people's sake? Boy, I am the people. I was discarded and lived among them. I struggled alongside them. Lived like them. I started at the same level as any commoner. I earned my position. My power. I am the representation of the people. Of what they all dream of achieving. Godfrey here? He's the same as every king who came before him. More concerned with appearing benevolent than being it. More worried about *feeling* kind. But people like me? We remain tools to him. Ask to see the mass graves, if you live through this. See how far his noble dreams reached."

I spit on the ground, just shy of the barrier between us.

"Bullshit," I challenge. "You expect me to believe he sees commoners as tools while you represent them? You, who have kept them locked in their homes, sneaking out to gather food and too afraid to visit their families? You, who have terrorized every citizen in Visenar in the name of revenge? And look at your allies! Slave owners desperate to regain their comforts! You'd kill or enslave every person in this city if it got you what you wanted. You want me to believe you will be delicate with these people, and you cover it with lies about the better king who got the throne you covet?"

Darian sighs and shakes his head. Godfrey remains terrifyingly silent. "You misunderstand me, child," he says condescendingly. "I never criticized your dear, aging grandfather for understanding sacrifice. If he didn't, I would be sitting on the throne already. You're right, I understand it too. I will sacrifice whatever I need to. No, Godfrey's problem is he is too ashamed of it. He wants to sacrifice without losing the love of the people. Without losing you. So he came to a battle counting on the loyalty of a child. A child who believes in a fictional version of him. Yes, Kallon told me all about you, Dominic. You truly do love the people. You don't understand the burden of the crown at all. You really want the commoners as equals. But if you are here to put down everyone like me, who will do whatever they need to do to seize this country, well . . . you don't have a single ally on the field."

I look at my grandfather. "I'm sick of listening to this shit. This fucking slander. Grandfather, please explain to him that you have never hurt anyone. Tell him you are ruling this country for the people, not by using them like he wants to do. Stop letting him smear your name!" I beg.

Grandfather lifts his chin and finally looks at me. "He is trying to divide us. To make us doubt each other. What matters here, at this moment, is that this is an evil man who cannot be allowed to rule this country. We will catch up on the rest once we have the breathing room to do so. Once this despot has been removed as a threat," he replies.

There is something chilling in that answer. Because he is right. He is absolutely correct. Whatever happens, I have to stop Darian from taking the throne. If that happens, we will never succeed in spreading magic. Everything he said was true. But what he didn't say? That's what runs through my veins like ice. He didn't say, *No, of course I sacrificed no one*. He didn't deny a word Darian said. I have to believe he just needs me to focus, but . . . there is something in his eyes. Something in the way they keep flicking away from me.

Nevertheless, I nod. I put my hand on my grandfather's shoulder and whisper, "All right, Grandfather. We'll talk about this later. But . . . I need him to be lying, do you understand?"

He gives a nearly imperceptible nod. He understands that if there is a grain of truth in Darian's words, my grandfather cannot be the king for long. That we need someone who the people can trust if we are ever going to get them back on our side. "I think we have discussed enough," I announce more loudly. "Why delay this any longer?"

Darian steps back and bows. Kallon glares at Grandfather, eyes boiling with hatred. The revolutionary nobles gather mana. Some of our bards stretch casually. One with braids puts a violin under her chin, creating a strangely calm juxtaposition against the environment. Following suit, a woman next to her raises a flute to her lips. One bard literally sticks his tongue out at the opposing force. Grandfather starts to move his oppressive, yellow mana. He and I both stop suppressing our auras at the same time, allowing reality to nearly crack around us. Darian's lesser nobles nearly crumple under the pressure, until he and Kallon release their auras as well.

Kallon, as I suspected, has a slightly less impressive aura than me. But Darian. Darian's aura far surpasses my expectations. I don't have to look at our allies to know panic has started to leak in. His aura is a deep crimson red. Nearly brown, like dried blood on cloth. His followers immediately regain their footing.

"So, King Godfrey, the wise and kind ruler who only murders volunteers . . ." Darian mocks. "How do you plan to fight me here, in this city? How do you plan to end a revolution without killing your own people?"

Grandfather doesn't answer. He sets his jaw and, in a breath, expands his yellow shield across everyone on the battlefield. The color fills every sense, the heat of his aura seeping into our skin, possessing our minds. When we can see again, we are over an open field. Visenar is still visible, as Grandfather's space mana can only move us so far. Something about the nature of space that he has explained to me but I failed to grasp. He moved two small armies into an open field in an instant, a feat only a royal could ever do. I find myself face-to-face with Kallon. Shit. When he saw Darian's aura, Grandfather should have left him to me. But he separated us into four separate unique conflicts.

I face Kallon. Grandfather faces Darian. Our key nobles face the revolutionary nobles. And the mob of lesser nobles is left to the bards. That is about as much time as I have to take stock of the situation, however, as a tsunami of water forms behind Kallon.

CHAPTER THIRTY-SEVEN

Noblesse Oblige

Dominic

Water towers over the battlefield, enough to drown everyone present if nothing is done. But not enough to stop me.

Cold mana erupts from me, assaulting the water in a massive wave of its own. It takes time but little effort. My mana saturates the wave, spreading ice like a stain on cloth. It's only a few moments before a massive wall of ice casts a shadow over the entire area. It was a pathetic attempt. A massive amount of mana, just to distract me for a moment. As I turn, I see why Kallon even bothered. The little prick doesn't want to fight me alone. Weeks assaulting the palace, and the asshole runs the second someone on his level comes to fight.

Instead, bursts of familiar pink mana flash beneath his feet: his signature explosion mana he has always been so proud of figuring out. It does make him fast, each explosion not only elevating but accelerating him rapidly through the air. I can't help but feel impressed. The amount of precision needed to use the force of little blasts like that . . . He has to perfectly apply each explosion to push his body in the correct direction at the correct speed. A slight miscalculation and he would spin like a top in the air. Speaking of which, it would be best not to let him beat me to the bards he is currently racing toward.

I use wind mana for this. Not a lot, but enough. I first launch myself after him, controlling the wind to accelerate me while also redirecting resistance around me. As I get close enough, I push mana out ahead of me, creating a little wind vortex just where I think his next explosion will go off. I miss once or twice, but I only need to get it right once. He is getting concerningly close to the bard with the flute, but my plan works in time. Just as a massive amount of pink mana prepares a surely deadly spell and the bard woman fails to form a defense, I hit just the right spot.

Kallon's foot is pulled into the wind just before his explosion goes off. Instead of setting off an explosion in her face, he trips in midair and collides painfully with the ground just as I fly past him. I can't help but laugh. Despite how serious the situation is, it's good to see the arrogant prick eat dirt. Before he can recover, I surround him with pale green wood mana. Roots spring up around him like a liana tree's, pinning him against the ground. This doesn't prevent him from casting unfortunately, and his explosion still tries to kill the bards he'd been targeting.

I grow another root to force his face into the ground and stymie any further spells. Meanwhile, I push the bard out of the way with wind and use a wall of wood to intercept the explosion. It does splinter, but it absorbs the majority of the impact. I easily catch the disoriented woman as we both descend to the ground. "Get your hands off me, freak," she protests, pushing me away as soon as her feet touch the ground. Harsh, but I don't mind so much.

"Um, that's the prince, Viola," another musical bard warns. This one has a violin and braids, and she's looking at her friend with embarrassed concern.

"Don't worry about it." I laugh. "She's right, I didn't have to catch her like that. I'll admit to showing off a little; that one's on me."

Both women look at me with something of a charmed surprise, which I am used to. Even some bards are unused to interacting directly with royalty, and I suppose I am the prince now.

The flautist, Viola, I think, scoffs. "We don't have time for this. Come on, Octavia." The woman with the braids watches me for another moment before following her friend, the surprisingly heavy tones of their music beginning to augment their mana with their opponents' and allies' emotional reactions to it. What a charming way to fight.

As I return to the root trap, I curse. A tunnel into the ground reveals that Kallon has traded one of his aspects for earth mana. I smile. He is too predictable. I casually step to the side just as earth erupts in front of me, Kallon rapidly emerging where I have just been standing. Pressurized water helps propel him more quickly as blades of stone fly through empty air where he'd hoped to find me.

I laugh and use my cold mana to freeze his water around his feet. My mana easily overpowers him, especially as he tries to throw one of his stone blades at a nearby bard. The man easily dodges to the side and sneers at him. "Come on, Prince—er, sorry, *former* Prince Kallon. Don't get cold feet, attack if you are going to attack!" he jabs. His aura immediately flares as he successfully draws the desired emotional response from Kallon. He'd be in danger but I quickly swirl my wind around Kallon to prevent any retaliation, which only empowers the bard more. There is little Kallon can do here. His superiority endoaspect should make it easy for him to kill most people on the battlefield, but it's a poor match for my protection mana. As long as he is targeting someone else over me, he will be at an even greater disadvantage.

"I'm going to fucking kill you," he snarls at me.

I glance behind me before pointing at myself.

"Me? You're planning to kill me? Well, all right, I guess, come on over and give it a shot," I say. "Oh, come on, don't freeze up on me."

He practically bares his teeth as deep blue mana erupts around him, creating a pillar of thick water around him. He's panicking. The idiot is literally panicking. How many times is he going to make the mistake of using water against me? I immediately bombard it with cold mana, freezing it around him and only further trapping him. I'm trying to decide what ice pun will annoy him the most when I see the pink mana inside, shimmering through the newly formed ice. Is he insane? He is more desperate than I thought.

I quickly summon as much wind as I can to catch the shards that erupt as Kallon's spell shatters the ice and sends it in all directions. It's trivial, considering the obvious color of his explosion mana. He's lucky I don't kill him now. I can just barely see his desperate mana flaring beyond the wind and ice. If I collapsed this spell on him now . . . I could shred him to pieces. But he doesn't deserve that. He's just a spoiled child. Besides . . . as much as I hate to admit it in this situation, it's a little fun fighting like this. We haven't sparred for so many years. And it gets my mind off everything Darian was saying before the fight. It would be better to incapacitate him, then help Grandfather with the actual enemy.

"What the fuck are you doing?" a woman screams behind me. "Fucking kill him while you have him there!" I turn to see the flautist woman from before, Vi-something.

"It's fine, I have him under contr—"

A loud explosion, and the earth shifts beneath my feet. I stumble but don't fall. "Behave yourself in there!" I call, turning back to the spell behind me. Except Kallon's mana is gone. I look around with a sigh. Where is he this time? How irritating. I expect him to come from below again, but as I look down for more shifting in the ground, a man's cries redirect my gaze upward. Kallon is descending on all of us, huge clumps of stone raining down alongside him. He is forming explosion mana behind each in order to create more shrapnel and spread it farther.

"Shit," I whisper under my breath. It's fine. I can handle this. First, I summon wind in massive quantities, sharpening each gust like a blade. I spread it out over the entire battlefield, protecting both my allies and his from this insane attack. As my wind tears through his stone, my protection mana flares, aiding me in the destruction of my opponent's mana. At the same time, I grow a massive tree in the center of the battlefield with a huge wooden canopy to absorb as much of the impact and rubble as it can. It's not perfect, the cover being formed of tangled branches. But it works. Nothing terribly dangerous makes it through.

We can all hear heavy impacts above us and see flashes of pink light through the cracks. But we are safe in the shade of my spell. It takes a few moments, but eventually, the impacts stop. Terrified combatants on both sides of the battle crouch and look up. We have a nearly kind moment of camaraderie as everyone sighs in relief. But Kallon isn't done. A moment later every single crack flashes with vibrant pink light, and a massive explosion rings out above us. The shock wave knocks most people off their feet, and the wood canopy bursts into terrifying flames. Even my heart skips a beat as I see it.

But fire is no more dangerous to me than water. More wind mana fills the sky, its darker green contrasting with the red firelight in an almost beautiful way. I pull from the fires, moving the wind and air to choke them before the canopy above can collapse and hurt the combatants below. And after so many spectacular spells in a row, the battlefield is silent. No one fights. I can understand why. I take a few steps toward the bard who screamed at me before. I give her my most winning smile. "See? All under control."

She shakes her head in exasperation, then looks around her as I offer a hand to help her up. "Where is my flute?" she asks, ignoring me. I look around myself. It is almost surreal how quiet it is. The way the display of magic has calmed the conflict. It's heartwarming. While we were all in danger, we forgot which king we supported. We simply supported each other.

"Funny, looking for a flute on the battlefield." I chuckle as she searches desperately.

"Where is it? Fuck! Where is my—"

I open my mouth to stop her from panicking when the world turns red and my mouth floods with copper. There is something in my eyes—I don't understand, what's in my eyes? Is it water mana? It must be water mana, but why does it burn? I rub my face with one sleeve to see the girl spluttering, reaching out for me in desperation with one hand and grasping her flute with the other. Her flute, which is now lodged deep in her throat. She silently coughs. Blood spills over her lip.

"What's in my eyes?" I whisper.

CHAPTER THIRTY-EIGHT

The Power to Protect

Dominic

Viola!" another woman screams. The woman with the braids runs past me as the woman in front of me, Viola, uses ice mana to try to close her wounds. What is that taste? "What happened to her? Who did this?" asks the woman, now cradling Viola's head as she splutters. I stare at her, then look down at my tunic. What is this, oil? What's happening? The braided girl, Octavia, looks at me with that same charmed surprise she offered earlier. The look makes my stomach churn. It's wrong. Her friend is hurt. Why is she . . .

"DO SOMETHING!" Octavia screams at me. I remain frozen. Something doesn't make sense. Fuck, what is this oil all over me? Why is it red? Why is it so warm? Viola stops spluttering. Octavia screams again, this time without words. She is forced to abandon her friend as she creates a massive flare of light to blind a group of lesser mages trying to take advantage of our distraction. Collector, what is all over me? A creaking sound followed by a number of explosions resound above me. Branches from my spell have started to fall. No longer protecting people from shrapnel, it has become the danger itself. Large branches, reignited by the explosions above, fall onto the onlookers below.

Red. It's red. Viola's body has finally stopped twitching, and her blood is pooling inside her own ice. I try to brush the hot liquid off me. My hands are red like the woman on the ground in front of me. I can't think about what it is. I can't, I can't, I can't. I was right there. The most powerful mage here. My protection mana withers as the realization settles on me. Is blood supposed to be this warm? What happened? Who killed her, how did they— Octavia bears down on five mages, pouring all her rage into heat mana. Paired with her light, she uses it to boil all of them alive on the spot. Their skin pops, filling the air with a sickeningly sweet smell.

I have to look away, but there is nowhere safe to look. As the enemy mages flee the falling branches, every direction carries the same brutal realities. Bards, my allies, don't allow them to flee. They all seem to have gone feral, like with Viola's death the entire reality of the fight changed. Steel chains wrap around one mage, pulling him limb from limb. I swear I can hear the tearing from where I stand. Another bard beats two mages into the ground, ragged and sharp stone clubs colliding with their heads again and again and again and again.

Nearly twenty enemy mages corner one of my bards and harass him with smaller spells. He could kill any of them, but they are unrelenting. Fire. Steam. Stone. They chip away at him, piece by piece, pulverizing him until I can't tell if he is alive or dead. These scenes repeat no matter where I look. My own spell crashes around me with the sky. I can't move. A charred corpse catches my eye and I can't look away. I want to look away, but I can't. Why this one? Why is this the one that I can't look away from? I force my eyes shut, but I still see it. No matter what I do. Like it's in the corner of my eye.

Because . . . it is. While I chased Kallon. While I saved the bards from the first explosion. While I trapped him in ice. While I chose not to kill him, because part of me was having fun. This ruined body was there the entire time. It must have been there from early in the battle. I see Octavia's face. Her look of *charmed surprise*. I feel sick. I almost break free from whatever is holding me in place, just to scream at her. How can she take this so . . . lightly . . . And it dawns on me. Is that really what that was? Was I being charming, ignoring a charred body to flirt with a couple of pretty bards? No. She's been looking at me with horror. With disgust.

"Fucking move! We need you out there!" Octavia screams at me, and I jerk back to the present. My eyes fly open. The blood has begun to dry on my lips. Or are my lips themselves dry? I can't tell. There are still explosions. Still screams. Are those new? Why couldn't I hear them before? Have these people really been dying the entire time? "I SAID FUCKING MOVE!" The scream comes again, and just in time. She's right. What am I doing? People are dying and I exist to protect them. Kallon is after the bard who taunted him a moment ago. Finally, finally, my body listens to me.

Kallon is trying to drown the man. I won't allow it. I send cold mana after the water and wind after Kallon. I try to draw on my protection mana, but it flickers. Kallon throws up another wall of water to catch the cold, and stone to stop the wind. His water freezes perfectly, creating a transparent wall between me and his victim. His first water spell makes it to its target, enveloping him entirely. I cover my fists with heavy blocks of wood and throw myself at the ice wall, closing the distance and hammering it with wind-enhanced blows. Closer now, almost close enough to touch the bard, I see little pockets of pink mana being forced down the man's throat.

"Kallon, stop this! You don't have to—" I stop as a muffled popping sound comes from the other side and I can no longer see through the wall of ice. Thick, chunky liquid runs down the other side. I can't. I can't I can't I can't. I need help. I can't do this alone. My protection mana is weaker than ever, and Kallon's aura is growing. I look around desperately for Grandfather. The two of us against the two of them. I can do that. With him, I can do it. I have always been able to push through with him around.

I sigh in relief as I spot the battle in the sky, completely forgetting about Kallon. I just need to . . . Darian is throwing Grandfather around like a rag doll. Like he's playing some kind of sick game. His deep red mana forces Grandfather down at breakneck speeds, then shifts so his victim flies directly toward him. Grandfather does his best to escape, jumping rapidly through space whenever he gets a break, but the power gap is just too large. Wherever he goes, he finds himself assaulted by that red mana again. Always pushing him toward Darian or toward the ground.

He can't help me. And I can't fight back alone. I can't. Kallon doesn't wait for me to get my bearings, and the earth opens up beneath my feet to trap me as he propels himself with explosions again, aiming for more of my allies. I just . . . let him. I can't respond. I'm terrified. I'm a failure. The viscous liquid on the ice wall begins to pool at the bottom. The woman with braids is screaming for some reason. I . . . I can't do this. Why did I think I would make such a difference? Like my presence would end this whole thing? They are going to die, they are all going to die. Shit . . . I can't . . . But I have to. Because if Grandfather can't help me, I have to beat Kallon and help him.

I have to cut at the earth with razor-sharp wind. It's agonizingly slow, and Kallon has a man's head between his hands by the time I succeed. I launch myself forward painfully, no longer caring about anything but stopping him. I almost make it. Almost. Kallon smirks at me as the pink mana forms and the bard's head is turned into wet mist. My mana falters, I use too much wind on one side, and it's too sharp. I cut into my own flesh and crash into the ground. *Come on, Dom. Please. Please please please get it together.* How many people have I let die now? How many people has a *weaker* mage killed, right in front of me? I can't see that again. I can't. The world starts to blur together. The pain in my side taunts me.

I find myself in front of Kallon again. We are on the other side of the field now, among the nobles of the highest rank. I don't remember how I got here. I catch another wave of water, this time with wind. Why did I choose wind instead of cold? I step to the side and run into a wall of ice. One of my nobles is half stuck inside, a stone spear pinning his head to it. Did I . . . did I freeze it while he was inside? Did I trap him for Kallon? I can't. The wind catches the water, but the flood is bigger than I realized. Does he not have any allies left over here? Why would he do this? Instead of catching the water, the wind creates a whirlpool.

Two mages, absolutely powerful ones, attempt to fight the water pulling them in, but Kallon crushes their attempts with pure mana. They are pulled helplessly into the center, where pink mana waits for them. The explosion is muted. Or is there more than one? They seem to go off over and over, until I can no longer tell which mage was which. Bile rises. I can't.

I need to stop him. I can't. I'm stronger than him. I'm too weak. *Grandfather, I need your help. But you need mine.* I can't.

We are surrounded by bards again, and a few dozen of the weaker revolutionaries. How did we get here? Kallon's back is facing me. Does he not know I am here? I can stop him. I can. I form a spear of wood and create a powerful gust of wind to propel it into Kallon's back before he can turn. It flies faster and smoother than an arrow. I start to feel like I can do this, until I catch sight of the fight between the army leaders. Darian seems to be holding one of our nobles and laughing, but Grandfather finally has a chance to respond. He is forming two walls of ice around his opponent, and they begin to collapse into each other. But . . . Darian has a hostage, he wouldn't— Darian suddenly launches himself upward with his mana, dropping the hostage and leaving him to be crushed.

Did he just . . . ? No. Grandfather wouldn't. He couldn't. The man who raised me would never sacrifice a hostage like that. He would never. Not someone who was counting on him. It doesn't matter if he needs a hit on Darian. He wouldn't attack if it meant killing the wrong person. He wouldn't make a sacrifice like that. He wouldn't. He wouldn't. "We remain tools to him," Darian said. I hear a spluttering and realize my attack hit. I'd forgotten I attacked. Did I actually kill Kal— As I look toward the pained sounds, the blood drains from my face. The dying man before me isn't Kallon. It's another bard. One of my grandfather's best. A man named Harper, I think. He has a bugle at his side and fire mana dissipates as the light leaves his eyes. It's my spear impaling him.

I can't. I didn't. I can't. I didn't.

I look around in desperation. There must be another wood mage here. Someone else. Someone on Kallon's side. I couldn't have done this. I couldn't be responsible for this. I can't be. I find no one. I hardly find anyone fighting at all. I hardly find anyone living. Only a few people remain around us at all. Octavia, bleeding badly from a stump of a leg and sobbing over Viola. A revolutionary mage, crawling through the mud with one hand. Harper buckles to his knees before falling to one side. Kallon is nowhere to be seen. What happened here?

I look up at the fight again. Grandfather is terrified. He is using space mana on anything he can to distract Darian. Stones. Debris. Bodies. One of the bodies starts to scream as it flies toward Darian, desperately casting to defend itself. I fall to my knees. I can't. How did this happen? I can't do it anymore.

A booming voice echoes across the bloodied field as sound mana floods the area. "You can all run. You can run as fast and as far as you like," Darian announces. "It won't save you. Neither will 'King' Godfrey's little circle. He wasn't open about that with you, was he? When he offered it? Did you know it killed over a thousand subjects before he got it to work on one? Did you know he needs *multiple* priests constantly channeling divine magic to keep one mage alive? No. He told you none of that. I know he told you none of that. You won't find a cure for your ailments with him, because he is a liar and a coward."

No. That's not my grandfather. He didn't kill anyone for that circle. He didn't. "Ask to see the mass graves," Darian said. Then Grandfather killed that man. And thoughtlessly sacrificed the other. I look at Harper next to me. Crumpled over. Clearly dead. By my hand. No. Grandfather is better than me. He's better than me.

"No. He can't put this country back together. This country his own apprentice tore apart," Darian continues from up in the air. Grandfather is trapped beside him, immobilized by his mana. "But I can. My own apprentice is taking care of that now.

Because you cowards, fleeing from your king on both sides, are not to be appeased. You are to be controlled. You will do as I say, or you will die. You will control your people, or you and your people will die. And I will prove it to you. See, Prince Kallon, my heir, has already left." Where is Kallon? I look around. He's nowhere to be seen. He's gone. "Thanks to the former Prince Dominic, we have reestablished communication with some nearby cities. And what did we discover? Tumult is in open revolt. Well. They were. When Kallon gets there, there will no longer be any such place. The city lord there is a failure. The nobles there are failures. And the people? Well, they are no longer of use to us.

"So. Go ahead and run. It doesn't matter. Because soon you will know that you will either fall in line, or you will die. Every city in this country will know that soon. You want your labor? You want your food and your luxuries? Well. I'll bring them back despite your best efforts. And no one will ever take them again," he finishes.

The sound mana dissipates, and my eyes go wide. Only a few stragglers remain on the battlefield, the rest not stopping their flight to listen to Darian. Only four people who can fight are left. Me, Darian, Grandfather, and Ansel. That is three against one, and Ansel is our strongest bard. I need to chase Kallon, but if I do, Grandfather will die here. I am torn, but I can't let Grandfather die. I obviously can never be king. The world needs him.

I launch myself at Darian with wind. He smirks and flicks his red mana at me, but Grandfather sees me and extends his aura to augment mine. Our mana together is enough to crush the red mana. This protects me and frees Grandfather. I form dozens of wind blades in front of me. Darian raises one eyebrow and a brighter red appears, summoning molten rock directly over me. Grandfather doesn't allow it—his yellow mana surrounds me and jumps me forward just a bit. Just enough for me and my mana to bite into Darian's arm, tearing it off. My mana is still unstable.

I can't keep myself in the air and maintain perfect control over my attack at the same time. It tears savagely at my opponent, but it hits me too. I feel my own wind biting into my right hand, tearing, and cutting, and screaming through my own flesh and bone. Before I can end the agony induced by my own spell, three of my fingers fall to the ground, my own blood joining Viola's on my face. As I recoil in horror, Darian's fist collides with me, forcing my body further into my own wind. The pain in my hand fades as my focus is forced to the side of my head, a sickening tearing vibrating through my skull as an ear is sliced off.

The yellow mana envelops me again, and I find myself on the ground. "Get Kallon, you fool of a boy," Ansel says, startling me. "I'll help the king. You stop Kallon from doing something irreversible." He's right. I can't wait any longer. I look off in the direction of Tumult and see bursts of pink in the distance. He is already too far. I nod at Ansel.

"Keep him alive, please," I beg. He nods in return, and I push through the pain. I have to stop Kallon. I have to stop him no matter what. Once again, I throw myself into the air with powerful wind.

CHAPTER THIRTY-NINE

Preventing Downfall

Dominic

My head aches. My entire right hand feels raw despite the tight bandages I've applied. My arm is badly swollen, and the blue, black, and yellow of the bruising leaves it nearly unrecognizable.

I hardly notice any of this anymore. The pain has long since given way to a deep, unrelenting exhaustion. Kallon hasn't stopped. He hasn't slowed. I don't know where he finds the energy. For a week he has failed to pause for rest. Failed to falter in the slightest. He hasn't even looked behind him a single time. Were it not for the pink of his explosion mana shining through the night, I would have assumed he'd collapsed long before now. I am running entirely off my own mana at this point, as my body has long passed the point of uselessness without it.

Pursuing Kallon is all I can think about. It's all I can focus on. It's all I will allow myself to focus on. Because that battle, no, that butchery I witnessed . . . the disregard for life. By my enemies. My allies. Grandfather . . . Had I not emptied my stomach over the road on the first day, I'd vomit again just thinking about it. The flautist bard, what was her name? Viola? I have to remember her name. I learned it; I owe it to her to remember it. The image of her death is seared into my mind. All of them are. The ones I failed to save. The ones I killed. The ones Grand—Godfrey killed.

How could he do that? How could *he* do that? I can't think about it. I can't, I can't. I fucking can't. Kallon. I have to stop Kallon. So many people need me to stop him. I can't let him get to Tumult. My only choice is to continue pursuing him through the air despite the way my arm throbs in the wind pressure caused by my mana. I can't tell if the filth where my ear used to be is just blood and dirt, or insects and pus. None of it matters. None of it fucking matters. Because if anything else matters right now, I am a pathetic failure. The people of Tumult need more than a failure. They need more than an arrogant prick who watches them die. Who hurts them with incompetence. Who learned everything he knows from a callous coward.

I bite my lip hard enough to draw blood, just to pull my mind to the present. The pink mana in the distance has finally stopped. My heart begins to sink as I realize Tumult is in view. It's distant, but I can see it. It should have taken at least a month to get there, but at the speed we've been going, without rest . . . And if

Kallon has stopped . . . I have to push even harder. I have to get to him before he can hurt anyone. I have to fucking do something, anything to feel like there is light left in the world. Like I can do anything at all. To get Viola's eyes out of my head. To erase Godfrey's . . . fear. I abandon efforts to prevent wind resistance and plaster myself against my own mana, trying to close the gap. Terrified with every moment I'll see the signs of a massive spell I'll be too late to stop.

One second passes, then two. Three. Four. I refuse to hope. But I also refuse to stop. I have a fever. I am exhausted. I don't know if I will survive this. But if I can stop this one thing, this single thing before I die, I will be all right. I will have mattered. The explosion fails to come and I almost miss why. As I approach the city walls, I feel Kallon's aura below me. He is . . . standing in the middle of an open field. Waiting. So close to the city. He could have done unspeakable damage by now. But he is waiting. I pause, apprehension overwhelming me. I look around for any traps, but he really is simply standing. Alone in the middle of the field. Just barely too far to attack the city. But I can't let this opportunity pass. If it's a trap, well, my spell will fall into it.

I don't bother approaching him. Instead, I cast two spells at once from a few dozen feet above him. Finally, there is no one he can use against me. No one I can hit on accident. Nowhere to hide any last-minute tricks. I have to stop him here and now, and I can't hold back. I owe it to . . . everyone. My wood mana erupts around me, surrounding me in makeshift but sturdy armor to absorb any upcoming impacts. I can't let Kallon slow me down. At the same time, I work my wind mana into a furious tempest around me, swirling the air with enough force to ravage the landscape and tear down stone walls. But that isn't enough. I need more.

I mix in the winter-colored cold mana so just touching the wind will bite and freeze and kill. It's still not enough. I focus on every turn of the tornado around me and I press the mana. I speed it up. I feed it so each gust carries a razor-sharp edge, capable of cutting stone. Finally, I plummet. Directly toward Kallon. It still feels too weak. My protection mana should be empowering this spell even beyond its current destructive power, but it does nothing. Kallon is here to massacre an entire city and it does nothing. Part of me wonders if this is why he stopped, so my mana wouldn't recognize this as protection.

But that's not it. Of course it's not it. The truth is, I don't know if I'll ever use my endoaspect again. I don't know if I can. I started to lose it when that bard died. And more at every failure after. How can I embody protection after watching a massacre I couldn't prevent? This will have to be enough. I'll just have to pour every ounce of mana I have into it. Everything I have left. My life if I need to. It feels like my blood is being pulled from my body as I drain the remains of my already weary reserves. My muscles burn and my eyelids try to force themselves closed as the mana keeping me awake is spent on this attack. This is all or nothing.

Below me Kallon prepares his defense, erecting a spire of earth around him, changing the landscape with a defensive mountain. I can't see him through my storm, but I still glare as the earth closes over him and spears toward me. It won't stop me. The only shields he had that could protect him were human, and he left all of them bleeding and weeping over their friends. My wind connects with his stone a breath later and begins to shred. Stone joins the wind, freezing as it does. Light bounces off the icy surface of the earth as it is further pulverized by the blades of wind. Frost begins to gather on my wooden armor, but nothing slows me down.

My tempest fills more and more with frozen stone until I can no longer see through it. It looks like I am surrounded by shards of stained glass, the light from above changing color as it bounces and reflects across the shards. I can see faces in it. Blood from Viola's mouth as she splutters. Disregard on Godfrey's as he kills his own ally for a shot at Darian. The shock on Harper's as my errant wood spell impales him. I will kill Kallon. I will fucking kill him and then . . . then perhaps I won't have to see them anymore. Just as I think this, the first sparks of pink mana appear, too late for me to react.

As my wind cuts into stone, pink mana erupts to my left. The massive explosion is caught up by the wind, the pink mixing with the different shades of green and blue. Shrapnel carried by the wind is blown inward toward me, colliding with my armor and slicing into my clothes and skin at the joints. I don't feel the pain. I don't care if I'm reduced to nothing but shredded meat, so long as I live to end Kallon before he can destroy Tumult. Before he can kill even one more person. I keep pressing. More explosions come. My world is nothing but magic and color and death.

I see the faces. I feel my phantom fingers twitch. I close my eyes and push. My bones feel like they will break under the pressure. I try to focus on the fresh cuts just to keep myself conscious. Pain is all I have to keep me moving, and moving is the only way to prevent real pain. My body is an empty well, trying to draw water from long-exhausted dirt. I push it further, the wind shreds, the cold freezes, the light blinds, and the blood pours. Finally, the stone breaks and I can see Kallon's aura through all of it. I've made it. A few more seconds, and he will be dead. Everyone will be safe.

All the colors turn to a deep, inescapable red. Pressure like I have never felt descends on me from above and I am pushed at an increased speed. My body is forced through my own dissolving spell, the earth, ice, and wind cutting through my armor and leaving me open and bloodied. The force snaps my head back. I can't see. I don't understand what's happening. My mana dissipates entirely, leaving me powerless. My body slows a breath later, just before I collide painfully with the ground. Again. It happened again. I did everything I could and failed. No. I have to get up. Too many people need me to get up. I can't. I can't. I can't even move my arms.

A foot kicks my side, then wedges itself under my ribs and rolls me over. I see the open sky above through the tunnel of ruined earth I passed through to get here. In the center, a one-armed Darian slowly descends on us. Standing next to me is a furious Kallon, sneering down at me. No. No no no no no. I can't, I can't fight them both. The red mana pushes on me more as a laughing Darian finally reaches me.

"Don't mind me," Darian taunts. "Just here to collect something you owe me." At this, he draws his sword, a weapon few mages of our level bother to carry at all. He swings it down on my right shoulder, cutting deep into my flesh. I try to scream, but my voice is too exhausted. I feel the cut into my bone, but he fails to sever the arm entirely. He puts one foot on my shoulder and yanks, tearing at me and flicking sinew from the blade. "Sorry, I don't use this too often. Give me a few more swings, I'll get there." He chuckles. And he swings. And pulls. And hacks. Over and over and over. I don't know how many times, until my arm finally matches his. I cough up blood as I try to speak and nothing comes.

In the meantime, Kallon works at removing one wall of earth, giving me a clear view of Tumult. "Hurts, doesn't it? But now there should be no hard feelings," Damian says. "Keep an eye on him, will you?"

"Happy to," Kallon agrees once he is done with his spell. He then moves and sits next to me as I pant for breath. I am completely numb now. Darian doesn't linger long, launching himself toward the city with the same deep red mana as before. It is finally quiet. "You did this, you know," Kallon says as Darian disappears. I roll my eyes over to him, as I can't move my neck. "Let me help you with that." I feel the earth rise beneath my head and the view of Tumult grows clearer. "You and your grandfather. With all your scheming. All your ideals. All your filthy love for your little pets. You did this. And now you get to see what it leads to."

I want to respond. I want to deny it. I want to deny the part I played to myself. But I can't say anything at all. I can't move. I can't feel. All I can do is watch. Watch as the much more vibrant mana floods the sky above Tumult. As the molten rock begins to rain on the city. I am losing too much blood. I see the fires and the smoke. Distantly I think I can hear screaming, but it's too far. I wouldn't be able to hear it from here. Somehow, I still feel like I can. The pain. The accusations. *Prince Dominic, why are you letting him do this?* The city burns and I can't move. Viola splutters and I can't move.

The deep red mana joins its brighter counterpart. It hovers there for minutes, it feels like. For long enough for the first spell to cause as much pain as possible. It's not until the entire city burns and the walls can't be seen past the molten earth flowing over them that the deep red mana does its job. When it does, it only takes a second. Tumult stands tall, proud in its death, and then it is flat. Like it was never there.

Something inside me bends, then buckles, and finally shatters. Crushed like the city I came here to save. I feel nothing anymore. Because I can either feel nothing, or I can acknowledge that this failure isn't one I can ever overcome. I close my eyes, and Kallon scoffs, kicking me in the head before everything goes black.

CHAPTER FORTY

Give Them Hell

Annie

A city. An entire fucking city. One I just visited a month ago. I spoke to people there. Fed them. Protected them. I fucking hate feeling helpless. Helpless as the world crumbles around me. As it crumbles around everyone. I can't live like this anymore. The woman I love locked up somewhere in the world, out of reach. I cannot live with the atrocities of the entitled. There is so much I need to do, and I've isolated myself from all of it. I feel sick. I feel so fucking sick.

I'm sick.

I'm sick.

I'm sick.

I don't remember falling asleep. I remember nothing after reading that letter. The note that failed to contain the misery of thousands of deaths. That simple ink and parchment that carried more grief than I could ever bear. I am supposed to be the spear of that grief. The claws that remind the powerful that they should be afraid too. Instead, I am a dying woman, locked in a fucking tower. These artifacts of Ember's, they could let me fight again. If I could get to the people I need to fight. The people I need to fight for. I don't remember falling asleep.

It's been nearly a month since I dreamed of anything at all. Sleep has felt far more like death than rest lately. So when I find myself half conscious in a dark room, it takes me a moment to realize I am dreaming. I must be dreaming. This isn't my home. My and Sara's home. It smells of filth and neglect. In front of me is a steel door with a closed flap at the bottom. I'm in a cell. I suppose it's appropriate, as far as stress dreams go. I am in a cell. People are dying. People's homes . . . cities are becoming mass graves. And I am trapped. How fucking clever of my mind to manifest it this way.

"Annie, you're here," a hoarse voice says behind me. I freeze. It's tired. It can barely be described as a voice at all. But I recognize it in an instant. I feel it. But . . . I don't feel the grief it should carry. I can hear it, but I can't feel it. I can't feel any mana at all, actually. I feel like I did back on Earth. I turn slowly, fearfully, and find Sarafyna. Chained to a wall. Tired. Sick. I feel sick. Even her scars have a white pallor, and she has lost weight. Too much weight. More than a person should ever lose, and too quickly. Even more than me. And I look . . . fine. This last bit confuses me as I realize it is true. I look perfectly healthy. I understand this in a way only a dreamer can.

"You look good this way too." Sara smiles. It's genuine and it melts me. I have failed her for so long, and she is smiling at me. I can't hold myself back. I run to her and try to throw my arms around her, to kiss her, to tear those filthy chains off her wrists. Her eyes carry disappointment long before my arms pass directly through her. "You're not here, Annie. I'm sorry, this was the best I could do," she apologizes as I collapse to my knees. I have to fall backward and sit to look at her broken smile again. I blow a curl of hair out of my face in frustration. She is so close.

"Is this what we are doing now? Dreaming of even greater helplessness? If I want to feel powerless and hurt, I can just wake up," I lament.

Sara laughs like summer birds. "This isn't a dream, Annie. I'm here. You're . . . well, you are here a little. I've . . . wanted to see you," she says. It feels like a dream. But she does feel real at the same time. The chills of a fever torture me. But as I look into her eyes, her smile, her sorrow and joy as she sees me, I know she is right. This is no dream.

"H-how?" I ask, and she closes her eyes.

"I don't know, exactly. Divine magic . . . It was described to me as more like reality magic. I don't know what that means, but I know it connects me to you. I don't know the rules. I don't know how it works. But . . . I know it connects us," she explains. That is . . . less than a satisfactory answer. But I have other questions that matter more.

"Are you all right? Are you hurt? What have they been doing to you? Do you know how I can get to you?" I interrogate her.

She smiles warmly at me. "I love you too, Annie. No. I'm not all right. I'm really, really not. But I will be. As soon as you are," she replies, clearly fighting to keep her voice steady.

"What is that supposed to mean?" I ask, shaking my head at her. "I need to get you out of there! I need to find a way to get to you, to really get to you!"

She opens her mouth to respond but hesitates. When she does speak, I suspect she has left something out. "I told you, my magic . . . it's connecting us. I don't know what changed, but I can feel that something has. It's why I was able to reach out to you tonight. You've found another way to fight the cancer, haven't you?" she guesses. I look down at my right arm in answer. The bracelet and rings have disappeared, replaced with the buttoned sleeve of a white blouse. But I can still feel their effects.

"To stop its advance, yes, but not fight it, exactly," I reply. "How did you—?"

"But that's not all. Something else happened, didn't it?"

My face turns to stone. Not blank and emotionless but hard, with an edge that cuts. "I thought so. I could . . . feel it. I've never felt anything like that from you before, Annie. It . . . it scares me."

I take a deep breath. "I'm sorry. I don't . . . I don't know what's happening. How I am here, how to get you out, or how to stop . . ." I trail off. I feel sick.

"It's all right," Sara promises. "It's all right. I can . . . I can help you now. I'm getting stronger. I can help you. And . . . apologize to you . . ." she says.

I hold up a hand to touch her cheek, remember I can't, then just . . . hover it where it should be.

"You have nothing to apologize for," I insist. "It's my fault I haven't found a way to you. It's my fault I relied too heavily on you. I should be the one apologizing."

She shakes her head. "No, not for that. I just . . . I didn't realize, until today. Until I felt that . . . tearing from you. I wanted you to rest, to keep you safe. And I still do. But we were both wrong. You were being reckless. You were hurting yourself, and me. I was right to be angry about that," she says, and I nod.

"I know. I know you were. And I have been. Until I can find you, at least. I've done everything I can, but I haven't pushed too hard. But . . ."

"I know, Annie. I forgot. What it's like to feel completely trapped. To feel helpless. I fell in love with a woman like fire. A woman who felt such grief from the people around her that she burned it into her soul and turned it into a sword. A woman who found me and pulled me out of hell. I fell in love with you, Annie. And I realize now. While your body needs rest . . . too much is like another kind of cancer to you. I can feel it, eating at you as surely as your body is. You need to be out there, fighting. It's who you are. I'm sorry I didn't realize that," she says. With each word, I love her and hate myself more for letting her come here.

"It doesn't matter," I say. "It's not your fault. It's mine. You were doing everything you could, and you ended up here."

"But I can help now," she whispers. "I can help now, and I want you to know, I understand that you need to fight. I understand why. I'm getting stronger here, Annie. It's sick, but it is working. And right now, I want to help you so desperately . . . I can do it. I know I can do it." I feel my heart beating faster inside my chest. She can do something?

"You can help me get here? To you?" I ask, hope lifting my voice. She shakes her head and my heart sinks into my stomach. Something about that doesn't make sense, but I don't have time to think about it.

"I can, but . . . not yet. There is . . . an obstacle. The timing isn't right. But I can get you back to Visenar. I can get you everywhere. I can do that at least," she assures me.

"This is where I need to go, Sara! I need you! Once I have you back, we can face the rest together. We can face all of it. Just get me here and I will tear you away from these people. Please . . ." I beg.

"I love you, Annie. I'll keep you alive. Do what you need to do. And give them fucking hell," she says.

Lillith

The vibrating of the whisper sphere wakes me up. Everyone is gone. Off to make their own plans, I suspect. Or to make more riot spikes. I don't know how long it will take to make it to Potestia, but we will want to be ready. Every city needs as many of these as we can put together. I sit up to answer the sphere and pause. The dream was so strange. On impulse, I reach to one wrist to check my pulse. It remains as still as ever. It felt so real. Like I actually got to see Sarafyna. Like I was actually Annie again. Finally, I reach over and will the sphere to connect.

"What is it?" I ask groggily.

"Um, this is Lady Lillith, right? Lady Lillith of Endings?" a man's voice asks.

"She doesn't like being called lady, you idiot," a feminine voice chides before I can answer.

"But she is a lady; what else would I call her?" the first voice protests.

"She's a lady, sure, but she's not a *lady*, you know? She hates that nobility shit as much as we do!" the second says.

"I mean, yeah, but—"

"This is Lillith. You can call me Lady, Lillith, Lily, or that skinny balding bitch for all I care, but I'm tired. Can you tell me why you called?" I ask.

The man clears his throat. "Um, right. Uh, Lily. So, the thing is—"

"She didn't actually mean to call her Lily, asshole," the second voice valiantly interrupts. "Do you think she actually wants to be called a skinny balding bitch?"

"I literally don't care. I'm sick, people. Please. Have mercy on me," I beg.

"You were right, she is funny," the first voice says.

"Well, are you going to tell her or not?" the second replies.

"I was, but you kept . . . Ugh, never mind. Um, Lady Lillith, it's the patrol on the Radiant Woods. Clarrise asked a few people to post up out here and keep an eye on it; I'm sure you know that. Um, anyway, uh . . . something is happening," the man finally says.

At this, I wake up completely.

"What, what's happening? Where?" I immediately prod.

"Give me that, you dork," the second voice says. "Sorry about my brother. The woods are . . . opening up. I don't understand how, but a massive path is splitting the tree line in two."

Adrenaline takes over. "I can help you now," Sara said. "Give them fucking hell."

"Stay there," I say. "I'm on my way." I immediately pull myself out of bed and start to get dressed. Then I realize I already am. I don't recall getting in bed. Maybe I passed out. But I never undressed for it. Then I realize I feel even better. I look at the bracelet and rings on my right arm. Ember said this would only stop the progression. But I feel better. Stronger. Alive. I close my eyes and examine the cancer internally.

The tumors are smaller. Maybe because of the potions. Maybe because of what I have been doing. But . . . "I can help you now. Give them fucking hell." I flex my mana, letting just a little of my aura out. It's not like Godfrey, but it almost looks like reality bends around my hand. That was no dream. I'm not back at one hundred percent. But I can definitely find this Darian character and put him in the fucking ground.

Thank you, Sara. Thank you for this. I just wish I could go to you first.

CHAPTER FORTY-ONE

The Ones We Love

Are you sure about this?" Autumn asks, nerves clear on her face. "Henry, aren't you supposed to stop her from taking this kind of risk?"

Henry shrugs.

"I'm supposed to stop her from doing stupid shit because of her cancer brain. Not from doing stupid shit because of her Lily brain," Henry says, lying in the grass and flipping through an alchemical book. "This is definitely something she would have pulled when she was, I don't know, thirteen. Well within the normal Lily margin of error. Not our job to stop it."

"But . . . this is insane," Autumn protests.

"Like I said," he agrees.

I roll my eyes.

"I'm gonna make you pay for that later, Henry," I promise before turning to look at Autumn. "He's right though. For one, I'm in pretty rapid remission, thanks to my excellent taste in women. For two, this is entirely necessary. I have to know if I can fight inside a riot spike, or the whole plan falls apart."

"But isn't this what gave you the cancer in the first place? What if this test makes it worse again?" Autumn protests.

I sigh. "I got the cancer from one of Godfrey's fucking circles, which I can only assume have a similar draining effect, since he has seen the way mana gathers around me. Basically, I got sick because the horny old grump has been watching me way more closely than I thought for the past four years." Henry looks up at me with a baffled look. "Yes, I heard it, I heard it. I mean he was way more aware of my extralegal activities way earlier than I expected. Not the other thing, I don't think. Anyway, I am going to be inside a dangerous circle regardless, and we need to know how I'll respond to it *before* I am in a fight to the death."

Autumn still seems concerned but looks down and nods. She actually feels a little spike of grief, which is honestly very sweet. Henry, on the other hand, only feels warmer and warmer. Just seeing me cope with humor again seems to have done a lot to heal the entire family. Well, except Gil, I guess. His happy ass was in another community, largely unaware of my worsening condition until I started getting better.

Done with prep, I take a deep breath, take out a riot spike, and channel mana as I stab it into the ground. Immediately the world through my eyes dulls, grass and flowers losing their vibrance in an undefinable way, like a color has suddenly been deleted. My access to mana is cut like an ax through rope.

I feel dizzy, then suddenly mana floods my body again. I can't channel it, I don't think, but the sudden fatigue fades and my vision clears. My bracelet and rings glow like metal over fire, although they remain cool against my skin. "Huh," I say.

"What? Is everything all right?" Henry asks suddenly, his facade of disinterest washing away in an instant. I look up in confusion before remembering how frustrating a lack of information in this type of situation can be.

"Oh, I'm fine, I'm fine. Just surprised, that's all," I explain.

"Why, what happened?" Autumn asks.

"Nothing bad, sorry. It's these artifacts Ember gave me. They aren't just keeping me stable; they seem to be feeding me mana to keep my body balanced. The same mana they have been draining from me to avoid the growth of new tumors," I reply, examining them curiously.

"Maybe they are supposed to do that?" Henry says.

"It would be a weird detail for Ember to omit," I counter, and he shrugs.

"Maybe it has something to do with your weird circle?"

I examine the glowing artifacts curiously for another moment, then sigh.

"Well, while it is true that guessing at the side effects of my circle has literally never had negative consequences, I think we'd better ask her," I reply. I flex a little, then jump, just a little higher than the average person could. Not with all the strength I have available, but enough to demonstrate I will maintain at least one advantage while inside a riot spike's sphere of influence. "Let's give this another ten minutes or so. See what happens. If nothing, we should be ready to move tomorrow. We got volunteers raring to go, more than ever before. I think it's high time Potestia joined the ranks of fallen empires and monarchies."

It's been two weeks since the genocide in Tumult. I don't know what Darian was thinking, but if it had anything to do with ruling through fear, well. He forgot that you have to offer safety in return for obedience. An animal only runs in fear when it has somewhere to go. But when it is cornered? It will bite. People were already desperate. They were trading food to survive. Hiding to avoid slavery. Every single option was taken from them, and he massacred them for living on anyway. He forgot the carrot. So yeah, people are terrified. No one knows if their city will be next. But there is no behavior change they can make to avoid it. All of them. Commoners. Nobles. Priests. He backed everyone into a corner.

If he was hoping this would pacify people or bring them to submit to slavery, well. The choices now are to fight back and risk death, or hide in their homes and risk death. I suppose he assumes this will be no problem since even the newly magical commoner class can't hope to fight nobility. Not without these riot spikes, in any case. As it stands, I am not the only one ready to march into the safe place the nobles have left and raise hell. Especially if someone can distract the heavy hitters while the common folk take their cities back.

Godfrey and Darian think I am the head of a revolution? They set up Visenar specifically as a trap for me? They think everything will collapse without me? Fine. I'll use that. No better way to keep them all in one place than to give them their favorite fake figurehead to chase around their little kingdom. Meanwhile, in every other city, everything they hold dear will burn. And with riot spikes? They will be the ones surprised to be without magic. I'd love if I could just talk to Godfrey, but Darian? Darian died with Tumult; he just doesn't know it yet.

Especially now that Sara, that magical, beautiful, sexy fuckin' angel, managed to reach across the goddamn planet and tear a hole through the literal hell forest to help me get there. And that is exactly what she has done. She connected every community and city with the roads she opened up. She didn't take the long way around either. It takes maybe five minutes of walking to find a shimmering wall on each path, and a step inside leads to, well. A hub of sorts. A beautiful, charming hub with exits to every other location we could want to go to. People have been sharing resources again faster than we ever could before. Shit, I love that woman. She is so amazing, in the most perfect ways. The things I would do to thank her, if only . . .

If only the one exit she didn't give us wasn't the Kingdom of Endings. I don't know what she is waiting for, but it is going to drive me insane. I want to claw my own skin off. Leaving her in that fucking cell makes my blood boil. Whatever reason she has for leaving that exit off, I have to trust her. Makes me want to puke, but I trust her. I will just have to focus all that anxiety on this plan. All this anger on the murderers I can reach. And I have plenty.

"Lil, you all good?" Henry asks. I come back to the present and nod at him.

"Yep, this is working perfectly. I think we are good for tomorrow," I reply, pulling the spike out of the ground and letting it deactivate on its own.

"That's good to hear. I'm glad you are all right, kid. But, uh . . . Mom was hoping to talk to you without me around. She just called on the sphere while you were, uh, blushing quietly to yourself," he informs me apologetically. A mild anxiety itches at the back of my neck, but I smile and nod.

"Sure. You mind cleaning up here?" I ask. Autumn and Henry agree, and I leave them to pick up the various glowing stones and notes we were using for the experiment. Things have been a bit awkward with Mom since I told the family about my past life. But like I promised her, I still love her. I still consider her my mom. I enjoy the gentle mountain breeze as I walk back to the building my family has moved into. It's chilly, but I don't mind. I have been regaining the sickness weight remarkably quickly. I kind of feel warmer all the time right now.

My mom is waiting for me in her room. I knock on the open door, and she looks up from her tea and book, then adjusts her glasses.

"Hey, Mom, Henry said you wanted to talk about something."

She winces a little but gives me a smile. "Thanks for coming so quickly, Annie," she says, sending a pang through my chest. She has exclusively called me Annie since finding out about my past. It's not like when Sara uses the name. For Sara, it's almost like it's something she always knew, or understood on some level. Like the name fits me better, to her. But she knows I am me. The choice of name is almost intimate on her lips.

But when Mom says it . . . We love each other. She understands I love her and think of her as a mother. And she loves me. We have been through too much together to feel anything else. But she calls me Annie not because it feels right, but because she is rejecting the idea that I am Lillith. The little girl she chose a name for. She calls me Annie to draw a line. Because she believes that *I* believe I am Lillith, but that doesn't mean that she does. She doesn't look at me like the woman who killed Lillith either. But she looks at me like Lillith died of pneumonia when she was seven. It hurts. But she does still love me. That's enough for now.

"No problem," I reply, stepping inside and closing the door behind me. "Is something wrong?"

She sighs and folds her hands over each other. "I know you have to do what you are going to do tomorrow. I'm used to the risks you take. And you've changed all our lives for the better. So I get it. You'll never be able to rest until you've done the same for everyone. I understand . . ." She trails off.

I cross my arms almost defensively in response to the apprehension in her voice. "But?"

"But my . . . your brothers," she says on a sigh. "They aren't as prepared as you. I want you to ask them to stay behind. I can't lose them, not again. Please. They won't listen to me, but if you ask, they'll stay behind."

This request hits me like boiling water. I bite back the immediate response that floods my mouth like poison. It won't help heal things. It was silly of me to think a cry and a hug together would completely convince her. She likely doesn't even realize some of the ways she has changed when she speaks to me.

"I . . . can't. They are grown men. And they care. If they want to help, I have to let them help. Or I am asking everyone else to risk something I'm unwilling to," I reply.

She looks down, water gathering in her eyes. "Annie, please. I . . . I don't want to lose my children," she whispers. Her words are ice in my gut.

"Don't worry. Henry won't be entering the city. Just providing support. Same for Gil. And Ed, I'll look after him. I will do whatever I can to keep him safe. I don't need him for the dangerous part. I'll send him away from the worst of it when that time comes, all right?" I promise.

She bites her lip. "All right," she agrees. "Thank you, Annie."

Don't say it, Lillith. Come on, hurting people never pays off in the long run. This isn't going to help anything. Her confusion is understandable even if I think she should believe me, should trust her daughter. But saying this will only hurt both of us. Don't say it. "Don't worry, Mom. I'll make sure all your real kids make it back alive."

God dammit, Lillith.

CHAPTER FORTY-TWO

Suffer No Kings

While things between my mother and I are smooth like sandpaper, all other preparations are going extremely well. We couldn't make as many riot spikes as we'd like, but every city should have more than enough to keep people safe from domineering mages. I'd like every person to have multiple, but we don't have time for that. No, we are moving today. The only thing that could buy Darian a goddamn extra hour on this planet would be a way to get to Sarafyna first. But I don't have that, so I hope he is enjoying his final breakfast. Well. That's a lie. I hope it's full of maggots and pears.

As I head up the group walking into the path through the Radiant Woods, I can't help but focus on Sarafyna. I dreamed of her again last night. Or rather, I visited her. This path I'm walking on is proof enough that these dreams are real, somehow. That alone is more healing than anything she is doing to handle my cancer. In a way, anyway. It was going to be so amazing, sharing a home with her. It's still going to be, once I get my hands around those fucking stewards' throats. I want to get her out of there so, so badly. But every night she tells me to wait a little longer. Trusting her is easy. What is not easy is finding something to do with all this violent energy I get when I think about her in a cell.

What she has done here is amazing beyond words. From a cold, dark room where she has to shit in a corner, she reached across the planet and connected every city in Potestia to me, and anyone else who wants to visit them. She felt my need, our need, and while I failed to help her, she tore through reality to make sure I had what I needed. Throughout all this, she is only growing stronger and keeping my cancer at bay in the meantime. I adore her so fucking much. I owe her everything, and I will force the world to stop mistreating her if it costs me my life.

I need to focus. Almost four dozen people want to go back to their respective homes and help wrestle them away from the nobles in charge. To take them back and let them know destroying us won't keep them safe. But to maintain any victories we earn today, it'll be necessary to not just distract but kill Darian and Kallon. I can't afford to be unfocused. I don't even want to think about the inevitable meeting with Godfrey. It was easier to play at being friends from a distance. But neither of us has had the time to argue with the other for long. I doubt he was involved in Tumult's destruction, but . . . it's never safe to assume anything is too cruel for a man with a crown on his head.

Even if he wasn't involved, I can expect a finger pointed at me so stubbornly I might as well be north. I already know how my actions will be blamed for this atrocity. Well, perhaps not. It's hard to get a read on Godfrey sometimes. However it goes down, it's going to be extremely unpleasant. But for now, I will focus on the man I know is responsible for a massacre. These fucking riot spikes better work on Darian. There are still little patches of the Radiant Woods inside the city that will empower me, and my mana is feeling far more stable, but . . . that won't be enough. A battle of magic will almost certainly end in my death. But if I can get Darian and Kallon inside a riot spike, well. Then I can do some percussive maintenance.

Finally, the group arrives at the rendezvous point. We stand in front of a shimmering wall. It looks much like the Radiant Woods behind it, the unnatural trees blowing in nonexistent wind. But unlike amid the threatening foliage to either side of us, the air is thick and light reflects at just the wrong angle. It looks almost like a desert mirage. The path to the world of Sarafyna, which will take us anywhere else we need to go. I look behind me, at all the volunteers. People I barely know, Henry's goofy smile, Edward's nervous confidence, Autumn's bit lip. I give them all a massive smile, then I back into the portal.

Immediately, I feel the warmth of the new environment. The shift is immediate, just like when I touch a tree from the woods, but my surroundings look nothing like the Radiant Woods. The constant midday sun remains in the sky, but it shines through a ceiling of glass. In all directions, there are shelves, stools, and racks lining an endless maze of walls around wide passageways. On each of these are hats of every variety I can imagine. Or, well, every variety Sara can imagine. I don't know how it works. I recognize several from drawings I've made for her. I fucking love it here. It is so wonderfully Sarafyna. It still carries grief that saturates the air. But where it fills the Radiant Woods like humidity, here it's like sunlight. Gentle. Calm. But still relentless.

I love her. I pick a woman's tricorn hat with a feather lining along the brim and put it on. *I'm coming for you next, Sara. I'm coming and I'm pulling you out of there. In the meantime, I'll carry you with me as far as I can, in whatever way I can.*

In the Radiant Woods, once you enter, you enter. There doesn't seem to be a massive correlation between where you enter and where in the woods you end up. This is different. In the, uh, Radiant Hat shop? I don't know, I'll wait for Sara to name it. Anyway, in Hats "R" Us here, however wide and endless the space may appear, everyone shows up in the same spot. Well, everyone from the same place has the same entrance. Kind of like, well, normal places. It's more magical than that, but groups similar to mine start emerging from different exits. I am not the only one who is angry, and an electricity fills the air as collective fury gathers in one spot.

I scan the crowd. The room seems to be opening up somehow as more people arrive. Making space. This room feels like war. I can see it. In every twitch of the hands, every silent glare. These people are ready to fight. I approach the middle of the room while Ed, Henry, and Autumn start to help distribute riot spikes to different wagons and bags. Every eye in the room is on me. All of them are ready. A few faces present surprise me. Even Leo came to help. Leo and Charlotte.

I almost want to cry seeing them at all. But seeing Leo, out of his room and ready to fight back . . . Something must have happened with him in all that time. He looks nervous and still presents . . . differently than when I met him. But he is here, and that is amazing. I'll have to see if he is finally up to talk to me before we go.

But first, I have to try to rally a crowd before we burn the country they grew up in. I am better at putting the fear of, well, not God in people, but fuck it. I'll lean into that.

"Thank you, everyone, for coming to help," I begin. Then I realize I am still wearing a silly hat, consider taking it off, but simply tip it up to reveal my face instead. Let Sara join me in this. "Everyone knows what happened. Two weeks ago, Tumult was destroyed. People's homes. Families. Children. A massive home turned into a mass grave of ash. To teach us a lesson. Me, you, even the nobles ruling our cities. To teach us to submit. To prove that standing up is too dangerous. That the only safety we can ever expect, ever deserve, is one we beg for at their feet." I spit on the ground, which quickly cleans itself. Oops, sorry, Sara.

"Darian knew this would hurt us. Not just the people still in danger, but all of us here. Everyone across the world who escaped them. He didn't just want to beat us into submission. He wanted to punish those who left. He wanted to punish every single person who ever told him no. He wanted to crush our will to live our lives without groveling at his feet. But you know what? Fuck him. Fuck him, fuck Kallon, and fuck all their little friends. They have so much power. So much strength. Enough power that they've never felt unsafe. Have any of them ever asked what might hide in the darkness? Why someone might follow them too closely at night? What prowls in the tall grass?

"Of fucking course not. They don't know the instinctive fear of living in a world of predators. They don't understand fear at all. They think it's a lack of satin, or sugar, or women to pour it in their fucking mouths for them when they're too tired to gorge themselves on *our* labor with their own hands. Their greatest fear is a cold fucking bath. So easily they crush. So easily they tear. They beat us, they take our homes, and they don't know fear. They put collars around our necks and brands on our skin, and they don't know fear. They take our names and our minds, and they still don't. Know. Fear. They think if they push just a little harder, threaten us a little more, if they massacre our loved ones and taunt us with their corpses, that we'll finally bend the knee and beg for forgiveness? That we'll be too afraid to fight back? They think they can rule us with fear, while they don't know it themselves?

"No. No. Fucking no! They want to find out how far fear can get them? How far they can push us? Well. Let's teach it to them. Throw it through their ornate windows. Burn it into their extravagant gardens. Paint it in the streets. No man with a spear will tell us whether we deserve to eat. No knight will barricade our doors. And no lord is going to decide on our laws. Absolutely not. *We* will teach them fear.

We will teach them to cower. We've long since learned how to be afraid. They spent their lives, *your* lives, teaching it to you. Well, we learned. And every weapon they used to do it? Every tool of power and death and control? We'll choke them with each and every one. It's our right.

"As for the kings? Not just the current kings, but every man, woman, or anyone else who tries to put a crown on their head and call themselves our ruler? We'll show them too. What happens when they put their boots in the wrong place and press too hard. We will suffer no fucking kings."

The speech doesn't exactly inspire a cheer, but these people are too angry to cheer. Too sick with grief. And I don't need a cheer. I need people who are prepared for incredible violence. And this group is. But fear remains behind their eyes. A man speaks from the crowd, cutting the furious, nervous energy. "They are right though. They are too powerful for us to fight. Few of us know any combat magic. Few of us know any combat at all. Show us these 'riot spikes'!" he demands. There are some murmurs of discontent, but I nod.

"No, you are right. You're as right to be scared as you are to be angry," I reply, looking through the thick crowd for the speaker. I can't find him. "I'm sorry, I don't know who spoke, but, uh, the commentator is right. You are all right. So let me show you."

At this, I flare my mana. Even in Sara's space, we are still within the Radiant Woods in a way. And so the grief of the area, the grief of all these people, Sarafyna's grief—I feel it all flow through me, enhancing my aura. Around my right arm, the mana bends the light almost like Godfrey's does. But this is the aura of their grief. It can't hurt them. Instead of oppressing them, each person in the crowd stands just a little taller. Not with pride but as though a weight has been eased.

"This," I announce, pulling a spike out, "is a riot spike." I channel mana into it, and in a blink, the aura vanishes. "With these, if you can reach them, you can make them bleed."

CHAPTER FORTY-THREE

Trust

Riot spikes, real weapons, and people willing to use both. Everything we need to offer our help for the fires waiting to burn across the country. Ed, Henry, and Autumn help introduce the resources to their users while I look for Leo. I ache to speak to him again, and seeing him out here has lit a little bit of hope inside me. He got lost in the crowd while I was speaking, so it is difficult to pin him down. I begin to grow anxious, looking through the crowd, when finally, I spot him speaking to Edward. I move to greet them both, but a hand grabs my arm.

I turn to find Charlotte, a concerned look on her face. "Do you mind if we speak privately?" she requests. I give one last look to Leo and sigh before turning back to Charlotte.

"Happy to. Let's head to one of the endless private corridors here," I agree, smiling. She nods, looking back at Leo in apprehension herself before following me.

"We've actually been trying to get in touch with you for a while, but every call ended up at Edward instead. Is everything all right?" she asks.

I rub the back of my neck and sigh. "Yeah, it's been tough, but I'm trucking. Been feeling sick, so Ed has been fielding most calls for me. You could have just left a message, you know," I say, and she shakes her head. We aren't quite in private yet, so she changes the subject.

"Yes, you do look a bit . . . pale. Better than the last time I saw you though. Your arm even has a royal aura now, which implies an impressive amount of mana. I've never seen it on exclusively one arm, however. How did you manage that?"

I look down at my bracelet and rings. "Oh, it's these artifacts made by, uh . . . the rude woman from before. Sorry about her, by the way. She's got some cultural hang-ups, but she's working on them. Anyway, they help manage my illness and let me fight effectively in mana-dispersal circles. They seem to have an interesting feedback effect with my mana as well, hence the localized aura change," I explain. She looks at the curious jewelry for a moment longer, but her focus is clearly on finding privacy. We take a few turns, confident Sara's magic won't let us get lost, and find a fairly secluded area. "All right, what's up?" I ask. "Everything all right with Leo? I saw he came today. Any chance he's ready to talk again?"

Charlotte shakes her head. "No, this isn't about Leo. I mean, it is, but it isn't about that. He's doing better, but he didn't come just to fight. We came to warn you," she explains.

A warning. Not my favorite thing to hear right before something like this, but not entirely unexpected either. Fortunately, I have no heart rate to rise, and this environment is very calming for me.

"Well, I'm glad he's doing better. But I was wondering—you never seemed too interested in, uh, joining us for the grisly bits. What did you want to warn me about? Why couldn't you have left a message with Ed?" I ask.

Charlotte's hands clasp each other and fidget with anxiety. "Well, that's the problem. Edward is the one we came to warn you about. Lillith, you can't trust him. He's turned on you," she finally says.

I examine her face for a moment and cross my arms. "I . . . see. Can you elaborate?" This is really, really not what I need right now. Or ever, truthfully. But right now especially. But I have to hear her out.

"It was the last time you visited. Just after you met Ember, and you and Sarafyna started . . . Well, that's beside the point. After we all separated, Leo's whisper sphere activated on its own and he overheard a conversation. A call between Edward and another man. Lillith, he's reporting on you. He told them about Ember the second he had a moment alone. You need to send him back. You can't go into the city with him—you'll be killed!" she insists.

I blink. Reporting on me? A call being intercepted by the wrong sphere? Whisper spheres don't work like phones or radios. There is no signal to speak of. They work on the same magic as this endless hat shop. You decide who to call with intent alone. They shouldn't be intercepting each other unless I am wildly mistaken.

"What . . . what makes you believe Ed was the one who called them?" I ask. There is something going on with the whisper spheres that I need to understand. How could Leo have picked this up?

"Lillith, it was *right* when you'd met Ember. And the very first moment you were separated from Edward, someone called the capital to tell them about your interactions with her. There are not a lot of ways to interpret it. Please. Do not leave your life in his hands. Leo may not be ready to face you yet, but he still loves you like a sister. If you die because he couldn't get this to you soon enough, I don't know what will happen to him. Please. I can't see him hurt like that again. So don't trust Edward. Just call this whole thing off," she begs.

I let a breath out of my nose, and I think about my brother. His love of impressing me when I was a child. His spiral after my change. The way he smirked at me before Baldwin beat me, and his shame whenever he looked at my scar afterward. The way he is still nervous around Henry, for some past slight neither has shared with me. The hurt when he learned about my life as Annie. Mariah and the child he'll soon have back home. I sigh and shake my head. "Ed has had a . . . complicated life. I know that. He has been confused, and hurt, and let his pride control him. He has hurt me in the past. He's hurt Henry too," I say. Charlotte seems to relax, but I hold a hand up.

"But . . . he's more than what he was as a child. Edward is a good man. More importantly, he is a man who expects to be treated like he did something wrong. Not a man who apologizes and expects his sins to be forgotten. Who grows angry when they are presented to him as a reason to deny him trust. No, he knows what damage he has done and owns it. That's the first sign of genuine regret. And you know what? I do trust him. I'm sorry, but I do. And I need him. I can't do this without him," I finish. I mean every word. Even when Ed did get upset . . . it wasn't because I didn't trust him. It was because I told him I did and still lied to him.

I do have mixed feelings about that. But I can understand the sting. Of believing you were granted something that you knew you didn't deserve. Of feeling grateful for it, feeling hope because of it. And then finding out that, in reality, it was only partially granted. I don't know if that is entirely fair as a representation of what I did. But I do understand what it must have felt like. And at the end of the day? I just trust him. He is a good man and maybe one of the most dedicated allies I have. I appreciate Charlotte's concern, but I need to trust Ed.

"You're making a mistake," Charlotte protests. "Please, Lillith. Don't do this. I'm sorry we couldn't tell you before you made this plan. I know a lot rides on it. But please. We can still go back. Plan something else. Something they don't already know about, because if we are right, they *do* know what your plan is. It won't work."

"Well, that's the good thing about this plan. It will mostly work whether they know about it or not. At least the basics. If they learn about the riot spikes too early, that could cause problems. But not as many as if they know about them already and have time to plan counters. Either way, we have to move now. I'll warn people to keep an eye out for that. But everyone knows spies are possible already. It's almost guaranteed with recruitment like this. They are here anyway. But I am certain Edward is not one of them. Delaying because of him could, well, destroy everything," I say.

Her face displays full-on panic. "You can't do this. I'm serious. You can't. All of these people will die. Everyone you care about. Everyone *I* care about . . . Lily, they will win. They always win. And they will take everyone and everything away. We can still go back. Everyone can still survive this. But if you go through with this, you will lose everything. We don't have to lose everything."

I examine her face. Her worry. For me. For Leo. For everything that Sara and I promised her. I feel a deep, well-worn grief like cliffs carved by centuries of water. And I make a decision.

Leo

"Yes, but don't you think a bow will work better?" I ask in desperation. Edward is growing more irritated with me as I keep flipping back and forth, but I have to give Charlotte a chance to warn Lily. For over a month, every single call reached nowhere but this man. I don't even know how sick Lily has actually been. For all I know, her brother has faked that just to stop anyone from contacting her. I feel like ants are crawling all over my skin. Like everyone around us is staring at me. Hating me. Waiting for a chance to lure me into another alley and punish me for existing as who I am.

"Man, you just said you didn't know how to use a bow a few minutes ago," Ed says. "I promise you it is not a good idea without practicing first. Trust me, without practice, a spear is your best bet. Lots of reach, lots of distance, and the easiest to use without experience. Take the spear." He turns to leave, everyone else having already accepted a weapon, and I start to panic.

"W-wait, I have more questions!" I cry.

He stifles an irritated sigh and smiles at me. "I understand. I'm scared too," he says. "It's a terrifying thing to do. It was brave just to come this far. With what you've been through . . . with what you've been through, no one will blame you for going back home. But I don't think you want to do that. I think you want to fight back. Lily . . . Lily has a lot of empathy. But she doesn't always understand the rest of us. How hard it is to face danger like this. She's been some kind of demon of death since she was . . . well, for as long as I can remember. There is a whole mythos around her back in Potestia. You know some people think she can't enter a home without being invited in? She's like a storybook monster.

"But we aren't. And when you don't have that in your pocket . . . this is scary as hell. The fear of dying. The fear of killing. I am terrified of both. I shudder at the thought of both. But we have our own reasons to fight back. I want redemption. You want . . . I don't know what you want, I'm sorry. But I can see it. The same look I have. You want to fight back with your own hands, just like I do. So take the spear. Grab one for Charlotte; she'll be limited by the spikes too. And fight. Not for Lily. For Leo. And please, let me go. I have to do something else for Lily, and I am running out of time."

I look at him in shock for a moment. I begin to doubt Charlotte's theory. That was . . . well, an attempt at being kind, even while he was annoyed with me. I think I actually like him a little. I don't want him to be the traitor. Just that and I think it will hurt a little if he is. Because he's right. I do get it. Part of me wants to say a small prayer to no one in particular. *Don't let him be the traitor.* He takes my silence as leave to go, and he is already walking away when I come back to myself. And he is heading deeper into the maze of hats, shit. I hurry to follow him. As quietly as I can.

He makes nonsense turns. Is he heading to Lily? Is he going to catch Charlotte? Is he going to hear? One moment of empathy aside, I know what I heard. I follow him around one turn, then another, and another. I have no idea where I'm going. But I keep him in sight until he finally stops and sits on a bench behind a freestanding shelf of hats. I crouch around the other side as he shuffles around. My heart sinks as I hear him speaking into a whisper sphere.

"Yes, Dad," he mutters. "Yes, she will be with me. I'll make sure she is there. Kallon and Darian just need to wait."

Fuck. How could he say all that to me and then do this? How could he hurt Lily like this? Does he hate her so much?

"Make sure to find an excuse to separate from her before then," a man's voice responds. His father, I have to assume. Lily hasn't spoken about him much, but I get the feeling they aren't on good terms. This more or less confirms it. "And be certain you have all of these 'riot spikes.' We don't want to risk her having anything to fall back on when she gets there. Where are you most familiar with in the capital? I'll meet you there."

"Near the circle I broke. In the abandoned building. I'll meet you there with the spikes," Ed promises.

"Thank you, son. You're doing the right thing. I'm proud of you," the other voice says.

"Dad . . ." Edward replies, but the connection ends there. "I love you," he finishes anyway.

Shit. This is bad. Lily is walking into a trap. I have to get to her. I creep away as quietly as I can, only to freeze as Ed passes me. If he knows I heard him . . . I hold my hand over my mouth to cover my breathing. He walks slowly, and sweat drips down my head. But he passes, and I am able to breathe. I try to follow him back, but while I was hiding, he managed to vanish somehow. I panic, worried I am lost, but after only a few turns, I find myself back at the center. Definitely fewer turns than I took to get where I was.

The only problem? People are already filing out their respective portals. Wagons have already moved out, and only a few people remain. "Where have you been?" Charlotte asks, putting her hand on my shoulder. "We are the last group to head out. Is everything all right?"

"No. No, everything is not all right. Please tell me you managed to warn Lily," I plead.

CHAPTER FORTY-FOUR

Family Drama

Badass speech back there, Lil. Did you practice it in front of the mirror this morning?" Henry teases as we walk past the unsettling trees of the Radiant Woods. I look back with a wry smile. It's a universal fact that anything you say with complete sincerity will look at least a little silly to any siblings who love you.

"No need. I just adapted my old Suffer No Brothers speech," I quip. "Just had to drop some of the more violent, hurtful bits to be fair to the genocidal nobles. But the rest transferred pretty well." Ed and Henry snort at this, but Autumn looks at me with concern.

"You all know we are walking toward a fight with the most dangerous people in the country, right?" she asks.

"Yeah, we know," I reply. "But hey, I'm Lillith of Endings. The Mage of Mourning. The demon queen of children's nightmares. The original vampire. The death that lurks in noble halls. And Ed is . . . well, he's scrappy too."

Henry laughs out loud and Ed rolls his eyes.

"Lillith, you don't even like half those titles," Ed complains, and I waggle one finger back and forth.

"No, no, I don't like those titles being used as a vector of authority. I loooove rubbing them in my brothers' faces as an explanation for why I was always Dad's favorite," I say. Both Henry and Ed chortle at this. Autumn looks between us and I laugh. "Oh, come on, if August were here, you'd do the exact same thing. Brothers are to be kept in check, especially in serious situations."

She gives me a half smile.

"I suppose so," she agrees. "Still . . ." She pauses as we exit the path into a curiously dark cave. The cave Sara lived in for some time. We finally emerge to see the walls of Visenar and that's not all. A wall of ice surpassing them in height stands in the distance. I can practically taste the blood in the air. Her point is taken.

"This is just how we handle stress, Flower," Henry assures her. "We are taking this seriously."

She nods hesitantly. "All right, I get it. I'm just . . . scared," she replies. "I don't want to lose anyone."

"I can understand that. They'll be careful though. You can trust these two," Henry assures her.

"And even if you can't, well, you two will be here to get us home, and we trust you," I add. She nods her head slightly but seems unconvinced. We walk in silence for a while after that, until I turn around and look at Henry again. "Flower? Really?" I ask. Henry sighs and rubs the back of his neck while Autumn blushes and Ed laughs.

"Oh, shut up, Demon Queen Lillith," Henry retorts. "Sorry if autumn flowers don't strike fear into children's hearts. Not all of us hide under beds to grab ankles as they pass by."

"Fucking hate that title," I grumble. The air is cold as we make our way to the city. Likely on account of the giant iceberg just . . . chilling in the southern fields. It certainly doesn't help with the goosebumps when we reach the hidden entrance to our tunnel.

"Be careful in there, both of you," Autumn says.

"Seriously. If you need anything at all, let us know. We'll come help. It's dangerous for you in there. More than for us, in a lot of ways," Henry adds. "You too, Edward. I know we've had something of a . . . rocky past. But I love both of you. Come back safe."

"We'll do everything we can, Henry," I promise. "And when we are done, everyone will be safer. Everyone. I love you too."

Ed looks down. "I failed you, in the past," he says. "I'm so sorry. And I won't do it again, I promise. I love you too, Henry."

"And let's not forget everyone's second-favorite twin!" I joke. "Keep my brother out of trouble while I'm gone."

"I promise," Autumn agrees. After a round of nervous hugs with three pounding hearts and one still, Ed and I enter the city. Autumn and Henry have brought various medical supplies and will come in to help if something goes wrong and it looks like civilians need help evacuating the area. Ed and I are the front liners. We are quiet by necessity as we sneak into the city, where the streets are surprisingly more active than the last time we visited. Still not bustling, but there are a few people out and about. One of the kings must have decisively won in the last exchange. That could be troublesome if a magic fight breaks out. Thankfully, it is late at night and people haven't entirely returned to normal life yet.

As part of the plan, Ed and I have to split up right away. We wordlessly nod to each other as he hurries into the dark. I count slowly to ten and take a deep breath. Then I follow him. Far enough back, with sound and light mana masking my presence where I can. I have to avoid the irritating anti-Lillith circles, which are apparently horizontal and not vertical in many areas. But I manage to keep myself hidden until Ed quietly enters an old, abandoned building. My mana seems to work in the area, so I lift myself with force mana to enter the second-story window.

The stairs leading to this floor have rotted away, and I don't suspect the floor is much safer, so I keep my footing in the window and look down. Edward is meeting with a man I haven't seen in a long time. Well, not exactly anyway. Richard. My father. A bard now, apparently, if not a terribly talented one. My uniquely invisible mana allows me to replicate the sound waves below near my ear without drawing attention to myself. At the same time, I lower my goggles and use the X-ray enchantment to examine the area for anyone else nearby.

"Edward, it's good to see you," Richard says. "Do you have the riot spikes?"

Ed nods, pulling the bag off his shoulder and tossing them to him.

"Just like you asked," Ed answers. "They're not going to hurt her, right?"

"I'm sorry, Edward," Richard answers. "I know this is hard. I know you love your family, and it's not easy to do something that you know will hurt them. But you are doing the right thing, son. You're doing the right thing, I promise."

"I . . . know. I hate it, but I know. But if there is a chance that no one has to get hurt . . . Please tell me you aren't planning to hurt her," Ed asks again.

"I love her too, Ed. But you've seen what she's done. What she and her friends have done to this country. The same thing she did to our family. Tore it apart. Hurt the people involved. You have to understand, we can't move forward while she . . . You're a good man, son. I'm sure you understand," Richard insists.

Ed sighs. "I do understand. I do. It hurts, so, so much. But I understand completely. Now even more than I did a moment ago. I'm sorry, Dad. I do love you," he apologizes.

And that's my cue. I'm now certain none of my father's allies are nearby. They are still waiting for me near the palace, where Ed told them I was heading. This will work. I jump down, landing in the middle of the room and startling my father.

"Hello, Dick Endings," I say. "So sweet of you to plan my death like that. I guess I understand. You didn't get the role you were hoping for in my wedding; I do suppose my funeral is the next best thing."

He looks between me and Ed a few times.

"Ed, what . . . ? Hurry, we need to fight her together, she—" he starts, grabbing Ed by the shoulder, but Ed pushes him off and summons his own wind mana to push himself away.

"No, Dad. You and I are not going to fight her together. That's not what I came here for. I'm sorry. But it's like you said . . . you have to understand," Ed says. And the penny drops. I see the moment the realization hits and my father's face hardens.

"So you are like your younger brother. Brainwashed. Whipped. A servant of your own kid sister, is that right? After what she did to this family? She managed to twist your mind like the rest of them. To lie to you. To turn you against me," he accuses, straightening up and attempting to project an air of confidence.

"No, Dad," Ed responds. "Lily didn't turn me against you. You did. I can't close my eyes without picturing the glee on your face when she came back bloody and bruised. The satisfaction when she was taken to be beaten. It all made me feel so . . . ugly. Sick. And even now, you tried the old familiar tactics. The old compliments. Offering your pride in me like poison. It was always a lie. The only way to really earn your pride is to be like you. And . . . I don't want to be like you, Dad. But I was hoping you weren't trying to kill Lily. It was the last hope I had."

Richard scoffs. "So. That's what this entire thing was, Lillith. You left me hiding. Running from my own flesh and blood for years. Always looking over my shoulder, wondering when I'd be found and killed for putting a roof over my daughter's head and expecting respect in return. For helping elevate this family to a position of authority. For finding a powerful noble house for you to thrive in. For trying to protect you the first time you assaulted a noble. You turn my last son against me and lure me into a trap, destroying so many lives along the way? Were the years in hiding not enough? The loss of my other children, of my wife?"

He says so many absurd things in a row in this lecture my head almost spins like a loose screw.

He certainly has an interesting version of events bouncing around in his head. Neither Ed nor I miss the way he immediately dismissed his son when he realized the manipulation was failing. I want to explain each and every detail to him, but when someone is so convinced of so many silly things, there is little you can do to persuade them of the truth. So I focus on the one idea that seems to most support the others.

"You think this is about you? Seriously? You think I've been scouring the country for you? Looking for my revenge? I guess I did say I'd kill you after you tried to hurt Mom. But seriously?" I can't help but laugh. "Dad. Richard. Dick. You didn't have to hide from me. You didn't have to look over your shoulder and hide your face. You didn't have to do anything at all. You are a man remembered only by your petty cruelties. I don't know how to tell you this, but there are far greater cruelties in this world. I wasn't looking for you. I forgot about you. You've been playing chess against yourself. Looking for enemies in every dark corner when you should have been looking for someone to give a single shit."

He looks like I slapped him across the cheek, and his face is overtaken by red. "Then what are you doing here? As usual, your words and actions aren't lining up. These greater cruelties of yours are waiting to be fought. But here you are, slinging mud at your father. Explain that," he sneers.

I look at Ed, but he's already said all he can.

"Same thing Ed was doing telling you about this visit in the first place. Same reason he told you about the riot spikes, my allies, and Ember's people," I explain. "I know he's not the only spy anyone got through. But I needed him to be the most reliable. The closest to me. He told you anything a lot of people would know. And most importantly, he told you I was coming here today. For your master's sake. To ensure they would be here to kill me. And now that you have helped with that, you are going to help bring them outside the city, where I can fight them without anyone else getting hurt."

Ed is staring at me in confusion while Richard glares at me.

"And why would I do that?" my father asks.

"Because you are a coward," I answer offhandedly as I look toward Ed, who is still confused about something. I send sparks of electricity across my arm to emphasize the threat. "Remember the years looking over your shoulder while no one was chasing you?" Richard practically snarls at that, but I already have force mana covering the exits. "What's wrong, Ed?" I ask. I mean, I know he just turned on his father, who he admired his whole life. But confusion isn't the emotion I was expecting. At least, not this type of confusion.

"Nothing, I just, I never told them about Ember's culture. I figured anyone who told them about her wouldn't know that much. Thought it was odd that you listed it, that's all," he replies. Well, that makes sense, I suppose. He's right; he was only supposed to share the minimum, and it's not like Ember was running around posting a history of her country and military. But . . . Leo overheard a call somehow right after I met Ember. If that wasn't Ed, then . . .

Before I can follow that thought to its conclusion, two things happen. My whisper sphere goes off, and an oppressive mana collapses on us, forcing all three of us to the ground.

CHAPTER FORTY-FIVE

Betrayal

Leo

I actually feel . . . something close to comfortable. Not what I used to feel around Charlotte and Lily, but . . . something not entirely different. My hair is too long and a lot of things are wrong. But I am dressed half comfortably in public for the first time in a long time. A little like Lillith, actually. And no one has even glanced at me twice as we walk down the empty path through the Radiant Woods. No sneers. No comments under their breath. Everyone has bigger things to hate than my clothes. I am marching toward a city with a spear on my back, ready to fight for my life and those around me, and I am the most comfortable I have been for a long time.

Because *I* am the one going. Leo. Someone like him, anyway. Closer to myself than anyone here but Charlotte has met. And as far as everyone with me is concerned, that's all there is to it. Maybe they are all too focused. Maybe they are all too afraid. Maybe Charlotte has been out in public so much they've gotten used to the idea. Or maybe the church has been disposing of and hiding our existence for so long that they just never had a chance to learn they were supposed to hate us. Probably all of the above. But the result is this. I am almost happy. I might even remove my makeup before we make it, finally let my face touch the open air again.

It doesn't hurt that a massive weight has been lifted from my shoulders. For weeks I have been in a near panic about Lily and her brother, for no reason. He's been part of a trap the entire time. So that when they were ready, they could lure the royal mages away from the city. Or so Lily finally explained to Charlotte today. If Charlotte hadn't been close to announcing the danger to the room and fighting to stop this entire plan, Lily probably wouldn't have said a word even then. I can't blame her, exactly. It did keep Ed safe, and it's the reason this plan isn't, frankly, insane. If I hadn't been so worried about Edward, I would have been worried about this instead.

Our enemies may want Lily dead, sure, but they don't care who else gets hurt, and there was no way to guarantee all of them would be in the capital when she showed up. No way to get them all in the same place. Unless, of course, they had someone on the inside. Or, as Lily was apparently planning, unless they could capture one of our opponents and use them to draw the royals out. It's how she knew it was a safe time to attack, and it's how she's going to fight them without anyone else getting hurt. Not a terribly complex plan, but effective. Considering the certainty of other spies existing, considering our open recruiting method, it was the best they could do. Give them the information anyway, from someone actually close to Lily. It makes me feel more confident. Charlotte is clearly still worried. She still seemed to want to get everyone to just turn around. But it's a high-stress situation, and I have confidence in Lily.

Two terrible walls of horror line our path. Fire and violence lie at the end. And I feel . . . light. I've left my room in more ways than one. But . . . something still bugs me. Some instinctive fear I've cultivated from years of needing to fear every time I need to buy groceries or go to the bathroom. Like standing on a precipice with only loose pebbles to secure my footing. The fear of heights where the heights follow you to the ground, offended you ever dared to climb to them in the first place. I give another cursory glance to the group around me. Still, no one watches me. No one smirks. No one does anything but march forward, carried by rage.

Perhaps it's the lie I still carry. The lie that offers me external safety while inviting the most dangerous thoughts late at night. I decide I need to wipe the makeup off. If I'm safe now, I will still be safe without it. I try to convince myself of this, repeating it to myself again and again. If the threat isn't external, perhaps it's internal. I look toward the front. Charlotte is outpacing all of us by a significant distance. Two hundred paces maybe? I tried to keep up with her at first, but she told me she wanted to fight off anyone who might attack us before they could reach anyone else. It makes sense, so I have been hanging back. But she'll have a handkerchief I can use.

She won't mind if I catch up briefly. I feel lighter with each step, as I feel safer presenting myself. Maybe I'll ask her to help cut my hair on the road too. It won't look nice, but . . . it will feel like breathing. Still, that sense of danger lingers. Like that anxiety you get just before begging for food or money. Just before meeting someone powerful who you know will hate you. That pounding in my heart that makes me want to find somewhere to flee. To back out. But I don't know what I need to back out of. Maybe I am just scared of making it to our destination. I've never fought before. Not effectively, anyway. And not when I had anyone on my side.

But that doesn't feel right. If anything, the idea of having people fighting by my side, fighting back and standing a chance of winning . . . it only makes me feel more free. It's something else. Something failing to line up, like clothes that are too small. What is it? If Lillith knew about it the whole time, why did Ed wait until Lillith wasn't around to report about Ember? I know he was who I heard now. I know Lily knew it too. I get a little closer to Charlotte but slow down. Well, they certainly wouldn't want to do it in front of Ember. That's probably why they split up in the first place. So Lily could watch Ember while Ed reported. Yeah, that makes sense.

I pick up my pace again. It still isn't following. What was the rush? If they didn't want Ember to hear their plan, they could have just waited for privacy. Wouldn't Lily have preferred to screen the information shared first? Yeah, they went ahead and shared things they would rather keep secret, but that was because some things were going to leak anyway, like a giant furry woman with a tail wandering around. But details of Ember's country? Her allies? Surely Lily would have preferred these details remain private? Why wait for the first moment he was alone and immediately tell his contact everything? It doesn't make sense.

I pick up my pace, beginning to jog to catch up to Charlotte. That's it. Ed was playing both sides. He *is* a traitor; he must have been using the plan as cover so he'd have an excuse if he was caught. It has to be him; Charlotte is right. Only a few of us had that information. Ed and I were the only men there, and it was a man's voice I heard. I have to warn . . . My heartbeat speeds up. A possibility I refuse to acknowledge presents itself. I take a few more steps. I pause. Was it a man's voice? Or was it just a deep voice? I know better than anyone that the sound of your voice doesn't make you a man or a woman. I take a few more steps, more slowly this time.

It's hard to mask your voice when you speak in a whisper. Why would my whisper sphere pick up Ed's conversation anyway? It doesn't make any sense. A sphere calls who you *want* to call. Why would Ed want me to hear that? The only reason my sphere should have picked it up was if the caller wanted me to hear what they were saying. Or maybe . . . maybe if just some small part of them wanted me to. No. There was no chance. Why would she? She loves me. She relies on Lillith. There is absolutely no reason Charlotte would turn on us. I'm being silly. I need to stop letting the upcoming fight get in my head. I can trust no one like I trust Charlotte. Not even Lily.

But . . . what if she did? Lily told her . . . everything. But why would Charlotte relay it all to me? Well, I would have followed Lily if she didn't. And Charlotte does love me. Why else would even a small part of her have wanted me to catch her? It's that last thought when I realize it. I believe it. I don't know why, but somewhere in my chest, I do. I think Charlotte is the one who called them. And Lily told her the plan. All of it. Charlotte is so far ahead. To protect us? From whom? This road didn't exist two weeks ago. Any danger that can reach us can come from the woods beside us as easily as in front of us. No. No no no no.

My heart tries to beat out of my chest. Water runs down my cheeks, and I begin to walk heel to toe. Quietly. Suppressing my mana. Please. I have to be wrong. It is agony, trying to close the distance this way. Charlotte seems to be hunched over as I get closer. Snot begins to run out of my nose. My heart is beating too fast; my head is starting to pound. No. No no. I get close enough to hear whispering. This can't be happening. Why? Why would she? Why? I finally get close enough to make out words.

"Thank you, Charles. You have saved King Godfrey a great deal of trouble today," a smooth voice says.

No. Why?

"It's Charlotte. You know that, Ansel. And he'll keep up his end of the deal?" she responds in a whisper I recognize all too well.

"No," I say out loud before I can stop myself. Charlotte whirls on me with a look of horror on her face.

"Wait, Leo," she says, reaching out for me with one hand.

"W-why?" I plead.

Her lips jerk briefly into a hard frown, like one might have while fighting off a sob.

"It's not what it sounds like. It's for you. And Lillith. I'm trying to keep everyone safe, Leo, please," she begs. I reach toward my side, looking for my whisper sphere. I have to warn Lily. "It's . . . it's not there. Please, hear me out," Charlotte says.

I turn on my heel and run back to the group behind us. I feel her begin to chase, her aura releasing and nearly knocking me off my feet. She won't hurt me, but I run like my life depends on it anyway. I feel pure mana trying to stop me, but if she restrains me too directly, everyone else will notice something is off.

I have one chance. I throw all my mana into a sound spell to amplify my voice. "Warn Lillith! She's running into a trap!" I scream into the spell. The second I do, everything falls apart.

"Leo, don't do this. Don't you trust me? No one is going to get hurt! Godfrey isn't going to harm anyone! He's offering clemency!" Charlotte insists. What is she talking about? Her mana finally catches up to me and forces me to the ground, knocking the air out of me. "Listen. You will never be safe in Lillith's world. I like her too, but surely you must see that. We will never, ever be safe and accepted. The best we can hope for is the strength to protect ourselves. You will never be able to leave your room again. Even if we both change completely, there will always be someone who remembers, and someone who hates us for it. We will never be people to *anyone*. But we can protect ourselves, in the right world. Please, Leo! Listen!"

No. No, I can't accept that. I understand what she is saying, but she is wrong. I need to tell her she is wrong. I understand it now. But again, I am forced into the dirt. Forced to submit. Forced to comply by someone stronger than me. Charlotte . . . this won't make us safe. It already failed me! I struggle to move as Charlotte hovers over me, pleading, begging me to understand. I don't even know if she is speaking to me or herself. And she is forcing me into the ground again. Again. Not again. I have to fight back!

Just when something in me is about to break, like wood under too much pressure, her mana disappears, and all the pressure with it. As the force releases, my struggling throws me too hard in the air for a moment, leaving my head to crack against the ground as I land. Everything spins. Physically and mentally, my world turns upside down. Reality is wrong. It's wrong. When I finally get my bearings and pull myself to my feet, Charlotte is wrestling the others.

"Stop her!" a man yells.

"Tie him up," another demands.

"Get the sphere back!" a woman cries. I look around and spot a riot spike in the ground. Sure enough, my mana is gone. At least four people are wrestling Charlotte, who is looking pleadingly at me, makeup running down her cheeks. Her hand is reaching out between her assailants, still begging me to understand. I step forward, reaching toward her. I still love her.

"Don't hurt her," I beg. They continue to wrestle. Has anyone warned Lily? Or did Charlotte somehow take everyone's spheres from them? I step forward, grabbing Charlotte's hand, only to get jerked forward. There are too many people trying to restrain her at once; we are moving too far. The road isn't wide enough for this.

"I got it," someone yells, and I see the woman next to me grasping a whisper sphere. Of course, they have to warn Lillith. I hold Charlotte's hand tight. She didn't want to hurt anyone. I believe that much. "Shit, I dropped it—stop that," the woman cries as the sphere falls to the ground. It rolls away and the woman dives for it alongside another man. I move into the empty gap to hold Charlotte closer. I need her to understand. Her more than anyone. I need her to understand. The woman picks up the sphere and immediately tries to call someone.

Charlotte lunges to stop her, while I and the one man still trying to restrain her lunge after her. We all collapse into the woman, and into the Radiant Woods.

Gray

Charlotte's Journal

My adult life has been dull and gray. A shadow of the loss in my past. I didn't try to attend court anymore. I'd already been given an answer about everything that mattered to me. That answer being: I was lucky to be alive. I was lucky to be safe. I was lucky not to be beaten. I was lucky not to always be treated the way they treat women. It was no answer, really. It was a threat. Because with less mana, to them I wouldn't be worth the food I ate. So I aspected earth, water, and air. The aspects needed to keep our city clean. The aspects of service. Of value. Aspects that would justify my existence to the other nobles of my station. My father would have turned in his grave had he seen the fall of our house.

Until I met two men. The first was a young boy with eyes like mine. Abandoned like I was. Desperate like I am. A boy who needed my help. He brought color back with him. And hope. I wouldn't repeat my mistakes. Not with him. I didn't have Amelia, but I hadn't forgotten our childhood dream. Children who could bask in the sunlight. I would do whatever I could to be that sunlight for him. To be that safety. And to keep him safe from the world that hated him. With him, I chose a new name. One that felt right but was close enough to my old name to feel safe. Close enough to be denied if the wrong person heard it whispered down the wrong hall. I would be Charlotte, and he would be Leo. And I would love him like a son.

The other was Duke Godfrey. A man often taken lightly himself, but with position and power that surpassed even mine. And he offered me his hand. His help. His authority. He wasn't the king, but he was too powerful to ignore. Too strong to balk at. With a word from him, the Renatus name carried weight again. With a word from him, lesser nobles were too afraid to hurt me or my son. I still wasn't respected. Not really. I knew I was hated. I knew neither of us was really safe. But we were both safer than I had ever been before. We had a chance at a life.

My heart stopped when Leo asked to go to school. When he asked to prove our value. But I understood. And I could protect him, since meeting Godfrey. So I agreed. I bought him clothes he would love. Paid for an inn he could sleep at when they insisted on the wrong dorm for him. I put all my hopes for the future in him. I wouldn't let him make the same mistakes I had.

My heart stopped again when Godfrey asked for my help making him king.

But I had tried fighting without him. And with the king we had . . . I knew Leo would die. Even if Godfrey was only a duke, he was a powerful one. With Godfrey as king . . . I finally had a chance at real change. I would finally have a voice at the top that listened to me. I could finally exist without begging for permission or losing a fight to win the right. So I agreed to him too. He was a good man. He didn't understand me, but he understood that he didn't need to understand. And he could offer Leo a real future.

And finally, Leo and Godfrey both approached me, at separate times, asking for help with the same girl. A girl with a fire in her blood. Leo said she could heal our bodies. Make our skin fit. Godfrey said she would get my son killed. My son and so many others. Godfrey could offer us a future. And I had seen what Lily could offer, and where it led. I decided to gamble on the man who offered a future. I chose to keep my son alive. I would not repeat my mistakes again. I would not let the world turn gray.

CHAPTER FORTY-SIX

Crippling Defeat

Deep red mana forces me to the ground like the planet itself has suddenly grown more attached to me. I flare my own aura to counteract it, but my mana cracks and shatters under the power of my opponent's. The spell is entirely undiscerning, pushing me, Edward, and Richard down all at once. I have to rely on my actual physical prowess to move at all. I am barely able to lift my head, just enough to turn my eyes to the sky, and I see two men descend on all of us, both elevated by the same red mana that assaulted us a moment ago.

At first, they are black spots in the night, barely visible as more than a blur. But as they grow closer, two things jump out to me. The larger man is missing his right arm, and the smaller man is familiar. I forget his name, or if he even gave it to me. But the last time I saw him, I was striking him with lightning. I thought he was dead. The apparently living bard lands first, violently pulling Ed's bag from him before patting him down and pulling his spare riot spike from his jacket. The burgundy mana seems to flow around him and shift directions as he needs it to, but it comes from the larger man. I have three guesses who that is, and they are all Darian.

The mage restraining all of us smiles at me as he finally lands, the mana around him rippling like water as it flows out of his way. He releases his mana around Richard, allowing him to stand. The bard moves on to me, using a knife to cut my pack off my hip. As he continues his search, I make furious eye contact with Darian, ignoring my father's glare behind him. I wince as I feel my own spare riot spike pulled out of my boot. Darian doesn't look away from me as he issues a command to his subordinates.

"Bring those back to the palace," he orders. "Both of you."

"Your Majesty, please. I'd like to share a few words with my children before we go," Richard requests.

"You'll have the opportunity to meet them on the third plane if you hesitate to follow my commands," Darian growls. Richard grimaces, then offers a half bow. The quiet bard, satisfied he has found all the riot spikes, joins Richard and directs him to the door. I get one last glare from my would-be father before they depart. They can't fly like Darian can; that's good. I can work with that. I don't see Kallon anywhere.

"Ed," I groan as the pressure tries to prevent any movement at all. "When you get that chance, follow them. Get them back, before they reach the palace. Before they find . . . Kallon. I'll . . . keep this one busy!" Each word grows harder as the pressure increases on my body. Ed doesn't respond at all, lacking the physical strength to do much more than survive. It's like my force mana but more . . . directed. More, I'm not sure, universal. Like this spell is reality itself. Darian raises an eyebrow as he looks down at me.

"The Mage of Mourning indeed," he muses. "I've never seen anyone move like this while under my gravity mana. Then again, I suppose I have had little opportunity to use it before recent weeks. I am impressed, nevertheless. With your fortitude, and with your confidence. Your brother isn't getting a chance to pursue my soldiers. The only way either of you leaves here alive, in fact, is if you agree to help me get my slaves back. You've caused quite a mess, I hear. All across *my* country. And after I so generously offered you real power within it. Fortunately for you, I am a generous, forgiving man. And while your headache annoyed me, it annoyed Godfrey more. So I will give you one chance now."

"One . . . chance?" I ask. "To . . . what? Pretend I . . . am . . . afraid of . . . a coward . . . like you? And what . . . you'll let me . . . live?"

He laughs. "No, of course not. You and I understand the same thing, I think. Leaving the wrong people alive is dangerous. And you are the head of a very dangerous snake, Lillith of Endings. However trite your name is. But your brother here? All your little soldiers marching on all my cities? I can leave them to flounder, once you have helped me subdue them. So? Are you as loyal as your subordinates? Willing to sacrifice yourself to spare your army? Or are you every bit the coward you claim I am?" he taunts. Mana forms around my right arm. Around my rings and bracelet. The only place where I can create a royal aura if I try. "Oh, my apologies. You must be finding it hard to answer," he suddenly adds, easing up the pressure around my head.

It's not gone, but I can look at him again. The mana continues to gather. Thankfully, with the Radiant Woods still buried all over this city, it remains invisible to Darian while the effect of the artifacts just barely allows me to form the spell against his oppressive mana. "You seem to be doing well for yourself, for someone with no fucking clue what's going on," I chortle. "But I'm glad you don't. Your confidence in your infallibility is why you are going to die today. Your obsession with authority and competing against everyone else who has it. That's why I'm going to be able to kill you." The spell forms as he smiles at me.

"I'm sure. I'm sure you have a foolproof plan to kill me, with your meager, common mana. With your lovely circle that killed so many of Godfrey's little elevated commoner pets. Your special circle he bought all those terrified nobles with, only to watch them die or flee in the face of a supposedly weaker power. Although I'll admit his use of the priests was fairly clever. But that's beside the point. Bluster won't get you out of this one. Nor will a sharp tongue. You've been outmaneuvered. Your clever little plan to trap your betters failed this time. Now tell me what I want to know, or your brother dies he—"

I loose my spell in the middle of his threat. As soon as it forms outside my body, his mana crushes mine. But I only needed a second. Once the spell was formed and aimed, it was too late to stop.

Thunder cracks through the empty building as my lightning collides with Darian's chest, knocking him off his feet and releasing us both from his mana. "Run, Ed! Get the spikes back!" I scream. I don't need to, however, as my brother is already running out the door. I don't hesitate either, immediately pulling my ax from my back and swinging it down on Darian's body. He wants to commit fucking war crimes? Let's see how he feels about double tapping. I flex my arms and swing with force mana enhancing my already powerful strike on what I hope is a corpse.

But this fight won't be so easy. The man's eyes fly open, and his gravity mana throws him out of the way just as my ax lodges itself in the stone below him. His tunic burns and he tears it off to reveal a rapidly healing scorch mark beneath. Fuck. Fuck fuck fuck. A divine mage? Another one? No, he's still missing an arm. If he could heal himself like Baldwin or Sara, why would he leave it like that? I have to kill him now. I surround his head in invisible air mana, trying to create a vacuum around his head. The mana makes it to him, but he crushes the spell the moment he feels something off about the air.

I throw myself at him with force, forming bladed tonfas with my steel mana. At the same time, I flood the room with as much water as I can and pull the heat from it a moment later. The ice and weapons form, and I nearly make it to him to stab into his face with my first punch. He moves only his head, easily avoiding my attack while catching me by the throat with his remaining hand. I try to force my other tonfa down on his arm, but his gravity grabs it and forces both arms and weapons rapidly to my sides before either can reach him. The blades bite into my legs, causing me to grimace as he chokes me easily with one hand.

I can't even flail as his gravity pulls me down, straining my neck against his grip. He shouldn't be this strong physically, but I can feel his gravity mana, counteracting and enforcing itself in just the right spots to grant him strength comparable to mine.

"So you really have invisible mana. Fascinating. I was almost certain that was just part of your legend." He smirks. "And so many aspects too! Wonderful. You really would have made an excellent officer, were you a little smarter. Perhaps Godfrey isn't entirely a fool, bringing women to the battlefield. But it's not going to be enough to save you."

I start forming a lightning spell again, but he throws me down into my own ice, following it with a sound spell of some kind.

I form a bubble of mana around my head to protect my ears, but his spell is so powerful it creates a concussive blast that cracks both my ribs and the ice beneath me. His gravity mana forces me against the ground again. I am no match for him. Not without the riot spikes. Not while he can heal from even a lightning bolt in a moment. How did he do that? How can he heal himself from that but not his arm? I haven't felt that aching in my blood that comes with an attempt to take my mind either. Is he a divine mage or not? I have to do something. I have to fight him somehow. How is he healing? If not with divine magic, then . . .

"Someone told me that you are very sick, but you seem all right to me. It must be true. Your little jewelry is helping you out, I hear. Well. We don't want you making another mistake, do we? Let's see what we can do about that," he says, examining the bracelet and rings on my right arm. He awkwardly draws a sword from his right side with his remaining arm. "I am sorry about this. The sword is primarily meant for display, and, well, I have only recently become left-handed. But I'm sure you understand. Sometimes, a little clumsy destruction is just easier than more precise efforts. And, truth be told, I haven't quite taken out my anger over the loss of my own arm yet," he laments.

My eyes lock on the sword as he clumsily raises it over his head. I try to form my lightning bolt faster, but he swings the sword down, biting into the leather armor at my shoulder. He frowns, putting one boot on my collarbone and yanking the sword out before raising it again. "Looks like I need a little extra help. One moment," he says apologetically. He then swings again, this time the sword backed by his gravity. This time I feel the blade cut into my flesh and I have to bite back a scream. I lose focus on my spell for just a minute and frantically try to form it again, but he expects it this time. Despite the invisibility, he surrounds me with mana and crushes any spell I try to form.

Again he presses against me with one foot, rocking the sword back and forth painfully to break it free, and again he swings it down. He misses the first cut, biting into unbroken skin and bone with this one. A deep scream escapes through my clenched teeth as tears start to run down my cheeks. Each time he pulls his sword out, he first saws it back and forth, drawing an involuntary whimper from me and tearing as much of my shoulder as he can. He is slow. He is deliberate. He hacks at me again, and again, and again. Hot blood splatters against my face as I fail to hold back a closed-mouth shriek of pain.

Each time I try to cast a spell, I feel my mana collapse under the pressure of his. I can't focus on it anymore. My own blood fills my mouth as it splatters against my face again, and again, and again. Eventually, he begins to find old cuts, and part of me feels relief. Relief that he is finally getting closer to his goal. That he is closer to severing my arm and stopping the fucking torture. I can take pain. I can take pain. I can take fucking pain. I can I can I can I can.

I don't know how long it takes. But eventually, finally, the sword bites all the way through, and my arm falls to the broken, bloodied ice beside me. Tears and blood mix on my cheeks. I am not sobbing yet, and that is the victory I have right now. I am not sobbing, because I have only grown more furious. More determined to kill him. I hold the blood in my mouth. Waiting for a chance. He said something about the priests. During the pain, during the torture, that was all I could think about. Divine mages who lack the power to heal an arm. Either he was given divine magic like them, or more likely, he has a few nearby to heal him. That has to be it.

"Now. If you want me to tell Kallon to spare your brother, you will call off your dogs," he says. "Or I will go to them directly and kill them myself."

I try to summon a spell, and my mana turns on me. The bracelet and rings are on my severed arm, doing nothing to protect me from my own body. I can feel the tumors drinking in the mana. I've also lost too much blood. I have to do something. I can't die here. I open my mouth as if to speak, but no sound comes out.

"What was that?" he asks. I do the same again. He crouches down next to me and leans in. "Come on, now. Speak up, or they all die. And I will make it hurt. A thousand times more than I just hurt you. Now speak. Up."

As he gets just a little closer, I turn my head and cough in his face. My blood paints him, drawing a look of irritation. His mouth is half open, and he spits, confirming I managed my desperate plan. Now I just need him to touch me. And he does. He grips my face in his only hand. "You just killed your brother. Now. Call the rest off, or he won't be the last." I just close my eyes and wait. It's not long before he notices the change. The pain and twitching in his hand. "What did you do?" he snarls.

"Killed you, I fucking hope," I reply.

He looks down at his twitching hand and . . . clenches his fist. The twitching stops. The priests are still healing him.

"Well. Not everyone's hopes come true. Looks like you will need a little more convincing," he says. I see the discoloration and bulging veins trying to return. It's not enough, but . . . maybe it will be like with Baldwin. Maybe the next person to fight him can outpace his healing now that he's been poisoned. It's all I can manage. "I guess an arm wasn't enough," he laments. "Well. We'll just take a little at a time until you do as you are told—or die."

He picks his sword up and stands again. As I feel the steel cut into my right knee, I can only think of everyone else. *I'm sorry. I did all I could. I love you all. I love you, Mom. Ed. Henry. Gil. Leo . . .*

The blade cuts.

Sarafyna.

The blade cuts.

I love you.

The blade cuts.

I don't think I'm going to make it any further than this. I did what I could. I trust you all to finish what I started.

The blade cuts, and I finally let the sob escape.

CHAPTER FORTY-SEVEN

Confronting the Past

Edward

I don't know if I'm chasing or fleeing. I am doing exactly what Lillith asked, begged me to do. What she risked everything to give me the chance to do. But . . . I still feel like I'm a terrified child, running while Henry is taken. Because the man I am leaving my little sister with is more dangerous than the men I am chasing. I could feel it in the air even without his mana on me. Even as he fell to the ground with his flesh charred and his tunic burning. I could feel it. He wasn't dead. He was still dangerous. And Lillith is going to be fighting for her life.

And I am powerless to help her. Even if I stay, it will just waste her efforts. But I can't get the image of that coward out of my head. That arrogant child, leaving his little brother behind. Hiding behind bravado when I thought he was dead. I need to focus. The best way to help Lily is to get the spikes and get back to her. I can't think about who I'm chasing. I can't think about my father. I just have to catch the other man and get the spikes back. I can't fly like I've seen Lillith do, but it doesn't seem like my enemies can either. Instead, I create quick bursts of wind behind each step, pushing me farther and faster than I'd be able to manage otherwise.

Unfortunately, both men I am pursuing have their own tricks. Dad looks over his shoulder at me before exchanging words with his companion, then abruptly stops. He turns and waits, and I groan. I really don't want to do this. My wind pushes me forward anyway. He is glaring at me with a deep disdain I know I could never climb my way out of. As the gap closes, my heart pounds and my stomach twists, like I'm a child on his way to be reprimanded. When I am ten paces from him and his red mana forms into hot flames, I create a huge burst of wind beneath me to vault over him, hoping to avoid the confrontation altogether.

I tried so hard with him. I really wanted it to all be a mistake. I knew he was working with Darian. I knew he was angry. But I wanted my memories to be wrong. The genuine happiness when Lily was hurt. The moment I realized I admired a small, sad man. Or at least the moment I began to suspect it. I spent my entire childhood waiting to be my father. Worshipping him. Emulating him.

Twisted branches of wood try to tangle around me as I leap over him and I have to knock all of them away with wind.

I wanted to be my father so, so badly. He was my entire world. A pillar my life revolved around. He was what I wanted to be for Lily. A mountain to provide shade and protect her from the winds of the world. I didn't respond well when she grew taller than me. Not literally, but . . . I knew I would never provide her with shade again. I modeled my response after my father's when he realized the same. Petty attempts to hammer her back down. To maintain my status above her with excuses and insults. I thought it was all right. Good, even. I thought I would someday be vindicated in all of it, because my father thought the same. Because he was above reproach. Because he couldn't be wrong, and if I was careful to step where he had stepped, neither could I.

Then I saw his face, after he tried to marry Lily to the man who beat her behind a church. I saw his smirk at her blood and her pain. And I saw his rage at Mom. And I felt the filth of my admiration rising up my throat and crawling across my skin.

A wall of wood is waiting for me as I make it through his first spell, and I am finally forced to stop. I have to cushion my impact against the wall and then cobblestones with wind. I stand in front of it and pound a frustrated fist against the side. The image of the first man I killed flashes through my head. I can't do that to my father. I can't. I don't know if I have the stomach to do that to anyone.

But as I turn, fire surrounds him and I see that same look of disdain. And Lily is fighting for her life. I can't waste time on him. I need to end this all in a single spell and continue chasing the riot spikes.

"I was so proud of you, Edward," my father says. "I wanted to be proud of you more than anything. To watch you grow into a man. You will never understand the disappointment you have left me with. The emptiness when you turned on me, in favor of the child who destroyed our family. You were so promising. So bright. And you had a chance to bring our family back together. To do what even I couldn't. And now . . . now I have to . . . You'll never understand."

I have to fight the quivering that tries to take control of my lip. I wanted the same thing he did, really. A chance to bring the family back together. I knew I would fail, but if he hadn't been so determined to kill Lily . . . I don't know. I hoped he could be convinced to let go. I was. Part of me still wants to believe I can convince him myself, if I could just stop him long enough to really talk. But Lily's life depends on me. For all my worries about inferiority, for all my panic about not being trustworthy, she did trust me with our lives. With her life. And, unfortunately, Dad's allies clearly didn't trust him as much. However impressive he thinks his fire is . . . his mana is weak. They gave it to him as a collar, not a weapon. He is with them to trap Lily and me, and nothing more.

So I am able to overpower him. Not easily enough. I still have to fight for it. And the last hope I have for him dies with that. He's not weak enough to subdue but spare, at least not quickly. Not powerful enough to delay me without it being willful on my part. My mana climbs from the ground and strangles his. "I wanted you to be proud of me too, Dad. I loved you so much. Admired you so much," I reply. He summons all his mana, which flares with the water running down my cheeks, but remains too weak. My glass aspect forms all around him. "You are wrong. I understand that disappointment. It is etched into me where my pride once stood."

"What are you doing? Stop this now, Edward! Stop this now!" he demands. He still sounds like he is lecturing a child. And the glass solidifies. Not in a thousand shards, but in a single, uneven pillar. I couldn't leave my father like shredded meat. Instead, he dies in the glass. Still. Unmoving. Forever looking down his nose at me. Forever waiting for the respect he is owed as my father. I was like him, for a while. I was just like him. But he lived and died the same way. Frozen in time. And I couldn't live like that.

I turn and leave him there. I have no time to grieve what I've just done. No time to clear the tears from my eyes. I have to keep moving. Maybe, in some small way, I can at least feed Lily's mana a little more now.

Henry

Autumn and I run through the city, twisting down alleys as fast as we can. I barely know how to find the building Ed told us about, but we have no choice. The plan has already gone wrong. "Is anyone still trying to contact her?" I ask the sphere I grip tightly in one hand as we run.

"Yes, but neither she nor Edward is answering!" cries the woman on the other end. Shit. Shit shit shit. She was so careful. Ed was so careful. And then she tells someone about the plan at the last minute? Shit! Whose side is the spy on?

"It's Godfrey, right, Autumn?" I beg. "The fucking traitor went to Godfrey, right?" If Darian catches wind of this somehow . . . Godfrey will at least want Lillith alive. Maybe. It's Godfrey, it has to be Godfrey. I know Autumn doesn't know. I just need reassurance. She looks down quietly instead of responding. She has been quiet since we got the call. Something is wrong, but we don't have time to address it. We stop at a four-way intersection in the road. Where did Ed say it was? Where did . . . Right, that way. Toward the wall. I grab Autumn's hand and run as hard as I can. As I do, I realize I need to rely on Ed's crap directions less and less. But it's not a relief.

I look back at Autumn and see it on her face as well. The pressure. We are approaching a powerful mage. A mage powerful enough that Lily never would have willingly fought them in the city. The pressure grows like a sweltering summer day and it becomes difficult to run. Eventually, we can't anymore, but we do find our destination. Not only does it look exactly like Ed described and emanate that foul aura of power but . . . there seem to be a few men hiding nearby. Not just any men but . . . priests? Fortunately, their focus is on the building itself rather than anything in our direction or they would have spotted me immediately.

So not guards, then. Autumn and I duck behind an old restaurant nearby. "What do you think they're doing here?" I whisper. She looks at me with wide eyes.

"I—I don't . . ." She is having trouble focusing. I am scared too, but there has to be something under all of it. Neither of us is exactly "punchy," as Lily would say, but . . . Autumn is somewhere else entirely. I put my hands on her shoulders and look her in the eyes.

"Please. Autumn. I love you. But my sister needs help, and you know more about things like the church than I do. Please. Why would they be here?" I ask again. Her breathing is heavy, and her eyes flick back and forth for a moment before finally locking on mine.

"I . . . priests are healers. They may have brought them as healers," she finally replies.

Well, that wasn't a part of Lily's plan, so . . .

"So they are here to, what? Heal any wounds they get in a confrontation?" I ask.

"M-maybe? I don't really understand divine magic. What do we do?"

"I don't know. Knock them out maybe? If the owner of this aura wants them here, we don't, right?"

"W-what if they are here to heal Lillith and Edward, like . . . to take them prisoner?" she suggests.

"I don't know. I don't think they would do that, right? Shit . . . I think . . . I think we have to make a call here," I reply. "Sitting here isn't going to help anything. We have to guess . . ."

"And then do what? You'll hit them with acid? Kill a couple divine mages? There could be more than the ones we see, Henry," she counters. Shit, she's right. At least she is present now.

"My mana's not really that kind of acid, I can't kill anyone with it. But we have to do *something*!" I answer. I have water mana as well, but . . . I am not practiced in combat. I use magic for alchemy.

"What about a potion, then? Anything to knock them out?"

I mentally catalog the potions I brought with me. "I, uh, I have an anesthetic, but it has to be ingested. And I have green mist," I suggest. The response to this is the most ordinary *Autumn* she has been all day.

"Why in the third plane did you bring green mist? What's the plan? Get them too high to heal?" she asks. I shrug.

"It's got Lily's poison in it. We can't activate it, but she's used it to kill people before. Maybe we can use it to give her an advantage!" Autumn looks like she is going to protest, when the door of the building literally flies off its hinges and a furious, bloodied man with one arm storms out. The priests jump and run to meet him. As Autumn suspected, more than the few we could see end up swarming around him. Eight in total, it seems.

"You said you could keep her alive longer than that!" he snarls, to the priests' terror.

"We have been trying, Your Majesty," one of them begs. "It's not working on her! We don't know why!"

"Do you know how hard it's going to be to stop this fucking rebellion without her?" the man snarls. That must be Darian. "Get in there, all of you, and bring her back!" he snaps. Back? What does he mean *back*?

"Your Majesty, the Collector gives us power, but bringing back the dead . . ." the priest says.

"She wouldn't be dead if you hadn't convinced me of the wonders of your damn magic. So go fix your mistake, or join it," Darian orders. "Except you four. She did something to me, and you and every other priest in the church are going to fix it!" Without waiting for a response, he releases an explosion of deep red mana, launching himself and several of the priests into the air, leaving only four behind. My heart tries to beat out of my chest as the remaining priests rush into the building in his wake.

"No, they're not . . ." I whisper. Autumn bites her lip and I look at her desperately. "Please . . . please can you . . ." I trail off. She looks at me in terror but hesitantly nods. She sneaks up to the side of the building, and I follow. We make it to a window, but neither of us wants to look inside. I give Autumn another desperate look and she clenches her eyes shut for a moment, gripping her blouse with one hand. Then, slowly, she gets up on the balls of her feet and peeks through the window. The strangled shriek she chokes back hits me like a landslide.

She falls backward and holds one hand over her mouth in horror. My heart is in my stomach. I have to see. "Wait, Henry," she protests in a whisper as I peek inside myself. Ed is nowhere to be seen. But the priests huddle around a woman I know well. Lillith lies in a pool of water and blood. Her right arm has been brutally severed at the shoulder. Her right leg is the same at the knee. I see her left foot, casually thrown to the side in its own pool. A sword protrudes from her gut, pinning her to the ground. She is completely motionless, and her open eyes are empty. She is dead.

CHAPTER FORTY-EIGHT

Rejecting Reality

Sarafyna

It happened again. But it's worse this time. She's in pieces. I can see her. Broken. Bloodied. Dismembered and impaled. It keeps happening. With whatever she did, I had hoped it wouldn't happen again. But this was more than her cancer. This was a far darker malignance. This was torture and I felt every stab. Every slash. Annie screamed out. She sobbed. She wept with pain and I was too far to help her. I hate it when Annie is in pain. I hate it when she feels helpless, just as much as she does.

"You know you can't keep this up. Day after day. Hour after hour. Minute after minute. You have to rest eventually."

One more time. Two more times. As many times as it takes. I will not leave her. I will bend and break the world to keep her safe. To keep her alive.

"Why are you so certain she even wants this? Don't you think this hurts? Don't you think this is miserable for her? Exhausting? What if you are hurting her?"

Nearly every night since I have been here, this has happened. The cancer has caught up to Annie again, and again, and again. And each time, I have fought it off. Each time I have brought her back. Until that night she came here and visited me, this happened to her every single night. Twice on that last day. It felt like it would never end.

"You know it will have consequences. There is a reason sages only push the world so far. There is a reason her body resists you when you try to change it more. There is a cost for this."

I realized it, back in Tumult. When she fought the city lord. And I became certain when I found her at her desk. I had always felt connected to Annie. From the moment I met her. Before that, really. The moment she got anywhere near the Radiant Woods, I knew she could save me. I knew she *would* save me. And with the realization came the images. The insistence of reality that I was wrong. Every single time I have brought her back since, I have been assaulted by the images. I push at the boundaries of the world. I push at reality, and I reject the vision. I will not let Annie go. I will never let Annie go.

"Don't you wonder why she remembers the first seven years like they are hers? Why she considers herself Lillith? Do you really think that doesn't matter?"

I tell the world no, and it shows me the reality. It demands I acknowledge the truth. Annie is dead. She was beaten. Hacked at. Killed. Her cancer came back when she lost her arm. The fabric of reality shows me, tries to prove to me, that she is dead. I reject it. So it shows me another image. Her corpse in bed. Exhausted. Overworked. Overstressed. Taken by cancer. I reject it again and it shows me this image over and over. On different days. Different nights. The details shift: the way she's lying in bed, where Suzume is in the room. But one thing is always the same. Annie is always dead.

"It's because she is Lillith. She has always been Lillith, and she has always been Annie. What do you think that means? What do you think that implies about what you have done to her? About what you keep doing to her?"

I reject all of them. So it keeps going back. It keeps trying to force me to acknowledge what should be true. The scene finally shifts to a new room. A room back in our old community. It shows her collapsed at her desk, a whisper sphere in a pool of blood from her mouth. Godfrey shouting from the other end. She is dead. I reject it. Again the vision changes. Her body is on the floor of a mansion, torn to shreds by shrapnel. Another man lies near her. Some kind of explosion has gone off, killing them both. She is undeniably dead. I reject it.

"We are supposed to move on when we die, Sarafyna. We are supposed to move to something new. Something better. A new chance to live again. We are not supposed to keep fighting. We are not supposed to be relied on by the living."

Now she is in the Radiant Woods. I feel a stone in my gut as I see it. She has been impaled by some kind of stinger because I failed to protect her. She should die. This should kill her. She should not be able to survive this. But I am there, by her side, and I reject it. I put her back together. Now she is on campus. There is so much blood around her. So much anger. Sinew runs down her chin. She is impaled on a spear of bone protruding from a corpse's arm. She is dead. I reject it.

"We have new lives waiting for us. She has a new life waiting for her. A better life. Without the death. Without the suffering. She could have started it so many years ago. But you are holding her here. Holding her captive."

She is a child now. Crumpled on the floor. Pain is etched into her rigid face. Her hand is gripping a needle and she lies next to an open bottle of ink. She is dead, and mana swirls mockingly around her corpse. I refuse. She is in bed. Surrounded by her younger family. The sweat of a fever decorates her head and soaks her pillow. She fought as hard as she could, but she couldn't beat the sickness. It was too much for a child her age. A tragedy, but a familiar one in commoner households. It's simply not plausible to keep every child healthy into adulthood. She is dead.

"How much Nexus energy does this take you? To bring her back, over and over and over again? To sustain her? To keep the blood running through her dead veins? To grow her into a woman? How much could you do for other people with this power? Wouldn't she want that? Wouldn't she want the massive amount of Nexus energy to be used to feed the poor? To fight the nobility? To end suffering, instead of wasting it on her?"

She is dead.

She is dead.

She is dead.

She is dead.

No. No no no. She is Annie Beckett. She is Lillith of Endings. She is the Mage of Mourning. She is the hope for the people in the world. She is the savior of so many people. She is my savior. She is the woman I love. And she. Is. Alive. I will not accept a world where she is dead. I will not accept it and I have the power to deny it. Annie is not dead.

"How much power does it take to sustain her? To let a corpse grow, and age, and change, and bleed? How much are you wasting to make the world pretend she is still alive? You know that's all it is, don't you? Pretend? She is nothing more than a moving corpse. Nothing."

She is on the ground. Ground like I have never seen in a city I don't understand. People in clothes that make no sense surround her. She is . . . unrecognizable. Not because of her curled hair. Not because of her brown eyes. And not because of her differing build. Because of the impact from her fall. She is unrecognizable. She is dead. No.

"How soon could you have escaped from the Nexus, the Radiant Woods? If instead of reaching out and demanding the world send you help, you used this power yourself? You were only there for, what, a year when you started spending your massive power on this? Begging for help? Bringing a child back from a peaceful death with memories she shouldn't have? Feeding Nexus energy to her body so she could age and eat? I know you were a child. I know you weren't even aware of what you were doing. But don't you see what a waste that is? You spent eight more years in the Nexus, waiting for your pet corpse to come and save you!"

"Shut up!" I finally shout. "I am trying to focus, and I have nothing to say to you, Rune!" The boy shakes his head at me as I try to focus on Annie again. I can still see her. There are priests surrounding her for some reason. They think they get to decide her life, but it is out of their hands. It almost feels like cramping through-out my entire body as I wrestle with the world. Rune was right; I am getting stronger. But he is also right that this gets harder, and harder, and harder. I feel like I am folding in on myself and lifting a boulder at the same time. Like my skin is growing too small for the rest of my body and I have to struggle to move.

"Drop. The. Dead. Weight," Rune insists.

I refuse. I am not the one who needs to move. Reality is. The Nexus is. Anything that insists that the woman I love is dead. She is not deadweight. She is not dead *anything*. I will not allow it. I don't care if they tie me up. I don't care if they lock me here. I don't care if Rune keeps watch on me so it is too dangerous to bring Annie here. I don't care if they feed me poison day after day and refuse to give me a place to shit. I will use everything I have to deny a world where Annie is dead and I am alone.

I push. I bend. I break. And I feel the breath enter her lungs again.

I look at Rune. "No. I do not care about you. I do not care about your plans. No. Annie is not deadweight. Annie is everything. And without her, this power is nothing."

He sighs and straightens up. No longer leaning against one wall, he brushes off his jacket.

"Then you were a waste of my time. I have more important duties to attend to than a lovesick child and her meat puppet girlfriend. Rot here until you learn to let go," he spits back in disgust. Then he knocks on the door and unceremoniously leaves. I only smile. I did it again. Everything about reality tried to stop me, but I did it one more time. And I will keep doing it, as long as I need to. Annie is alive. And I can feel how angry she is. I would hate to be the man who did that to her.

And if Rune is serious, if he is finally giving up hope on me . . . I would hate to be the woman who put me here. Because Rune is wrong. Annie is not holding me back. She is not deadweight. Getting back to her is the desperation that pushed me this hard. Harder than that child's taunting ever could. She is why the poison is holding me back less and less.

Annie is why I am now able to shift and mold my arms into slick, formless flesh and slip from my restraints. As soon as I can't feel Rune's presence anymore, Annie will be why I was able to break free.

CHAPTER FORTY-NINE

Dead or Alive

Edward

I'm almost there. Dad . . . the man I killed managed to slow me down a little, but some aspects are simply better for speed than others. I am closing the gap on the remaining bard. The wind at my feet pushes me forward with all the urgency I can force into it. I need to give Lily a chance. The palace is in view now, and time is running out for both of us. The man ahead of me seems to glide through the air in a way I don't understand whereas I am jumping forward in quick bursts of speed.

When I am finally close enough that I think I will finally catch him, he seems to respond to my aura and pick up the pace as well. Worse, silver mana similar to Lily's steel forms in little bursts behind him, and I barely react to the shards of shrapnel before flying directly into it at full speed. I am forced to create a spell in front of me to redirect the razor-sharp metal. This works well enough at first, until we pass an intersection where one of the few people out on the streets has to duck out of the way of a weapon meant for me.

I wince at the mistake I nearly made. I can't hurt someone else while defending myself. I'd forgotten that people were starting to venture out of their homes again. I use a burst of wind to throw myself high into the air again, avoiding the attacks and giving myself time to form a shield of thick glass. It's a bit hard to hold as I sweat with exertion, but as I come back down, the steel lodges in my shield instead of flying to the sides. The spiderweb cracks that form with each impact gradually make it more difficult to see my target, but my shield holds.

It slows me down a bit, however, and I am forced to form more glass on the front in a wedge. This helps cut the resistance and deflect the projectiles with fewer cracks. This protects me, but his lead is growing. I am just about to throw my shield to the side when a burst of flame shoots from behind the other man, colliding directly with my glass. It's hot enough to make the glass glow red and bend, but not enough to stop me. Lily taught me a trick for this, and I can do it with wind.

I can't crush this spell like my fath—like that other man's fire, but I can suck the air away from the flames, choking them. This isn't foolproof, but so long as the flames aren't fed by mana constantly, they will die. Just as Lily said, the fire dissipates instantly. But as my vision was obscured, we have closed on the palace. It's right in front of us, and my opponent doesn't seem concerned with making it to the main entrance.

He is practically running up a pillar, headed straight for a window on the second floor. It's high, but I can make it with a leap. I jump in the air, create a pocket of high-pressure wind, and launch myself toward the window on a collision course with my enemy. His face is perfectly still as he launches fire and metal blades at me. I try to deflect some of it with wind, but defense can't be my only goal. No, I will soon be close enough to touch the bag on his back. In one hand I create a knife of glass while I keep my eyes on the bag. My defense isn't strong enough to protect me. This man's aura grows and wanes like my . . . like the other enemy, but it's so much stronger.

Hot metal shards cut through my clothes and into my flesh as I get closer, but I am able to deflect them from anywhere too dangerous. They embed in my legs and forearms and cut deep gashes along my rib cage, but I fail to take any fatal damage. And finally, we collide. I see my quarry forming a long knife to stab me with, and I form a barrier of glass between his arm and my throat. I can't hold it in place, so it only buys me a moment. But in that moment, I cut deep into the burlap of the bag he stole from me. A moment later, we both crash through the massive stained glass window.

We slide, tangled up together across a wide marble floor. Everything hurts. But the other man is still trying to kill me. I roll over onto my back and grip one of the cold, black spikes that scattered from the ripped bag. As my opponent tries to stab at me, I kick up at him to redirect his knife, meanwhile countering his mana with my own. Until I manage to push a little mana into the spike and activate it.

Fire and wind disappear in an instant. The vibrance of the world dulls. The pain all over my body sharpens. My opponent staggers, having failed to entirely regain his feet before his mana disappeared. I manage to land a kick on his face and knock him backward. I groan as I climb to my feet, fighting all the stinging pains and protests of my legs. I am about to move to stop my opponent when a voice interrupts us.

"What is this, Ansel?" a bored voice asks. I whip my head around to find two men. One is sitting on a small but elegant throne while the other is . . . chained to the side. The speaker toys with what looks like a letter opener while his prisoner, a one-armed man with nearly empty eyes, simply examines the cold floor he kneels on. The chain is attached to a metal collar around the captive's neck. The man I was chasing, Ansel, hurries to his feet and bows.

"Apologies, Prince Kallon," he says. "I . . . have not quite recovered from my fights with the Mage of Mourning and the false King Godfrey. I was unable to shake this . . . boy. He isn't strong, however. I will dispatch him shortly."

Kallon raises his eyebrow. "Is that so? Isn't that one of these . . . riot spikes in his hand? How do you plan to kill him from over there without your mana?" he challenges. Ansel bows his head further.

"He is injured, my prince. It will be no matter. I apologize for bringing this embarrassment before you. It's . . . unsightly. I had intended to kill this rabble earlier, but I judged the risk that he acquired a spike and returned it to the Mage of Mourning was too high. I was also ordered to bring these directly to you. I acknowledge my failure in allowing this mess. It will be handled shortly, on my honor," Ansel insists. I look back and forth between them, a little flabbergasted at this conversation happening in front of me. The chained man catches my eye and pours desperate determination over me like a waterfall. That single look sends energy through my veins, begging me to act.

"I expected no better from you," Kallon says dismissively, glaring at me instead of bothering to look at Ansel. "Your failure now is more minor than your failure to properly monitor Godfrey. Or to stop that bitch before she killed my father. Yet you live. Failure is expected. I will handle this child." He puts down the letter opener and interlocks his fingers, leaning forward while maintaining eye contact with me. I decide in this moment that I don't want to talk to him. I begin to make my move, but he flares his aura, nearly knocking his prisoner to the ground. It curves around a spherical area as it dissipates. I look down at my hand and groan. I am holding a smaller spike. Lily wanted spikes with varying ranges, which made sense before this moment.

I glance at the other spikes on the ground, but . . .

"You'll never get to them before I kill you. I'm guessing solid projectiles won't disappear in your little spike's range, and you'll have to deactivate it to try another, won't you? How about we talk instead?" Kallon suggests. I glare at him. Lily doesn't have time for this. But I don't have a good move here. "So you are Edward Endings, I presume? I hear your sister killed my father."

I gulp, open my mouth to answer, and then Lily's voice booms outside, loud enough to make my bones ache.

Lillith

My eyes fly open. There are four men looking down at me. Or there were, before all of them jump back and one of them shrieks in fear. The throbbing pain persists, but at least the hacking has ended. And . . . I don't know how, but my cancer has again receded. I don't understand it, but who am I to question it? At least I'm alive. I am down one arm. One leg. Oh fuck, he got my left foot too, didn't he? Why did he fucking leave?

Well. I'm glad he did. I have blood and a fresh scar on my gut too. Darian's bloodied sword is on the ground next to me. Ugh, I shouldn't have survived all that. What am I, a shonen hero? I guess I did get my ass isekai'd somehow. Maybe it comes with the territory. Fuck, what am I even thinking about right now? Did these guys heal me? Did I get on good terms with the church somehow? I try to speak and a pained half growl, half muffled scream escapes instead.

"She . . . she's alive? Shit, she's alive!" one of them howls. You got the wrong girl, folks. Frankenstein's monster is my girlfriend, not me. I try to speak again, this time prepared to respond to the pain.

"You were literally the ones watching *me* sleep. Why are *you* acting creeped out?" I ask.

"Contact King Darian immediately," another orders. Fuck. These chuds are with him after all, huh? I want to move, but the pain assaults me. Just as one of the priests is about to call their boss back to continue his casual torturing, I hear glass shattering. The area immediately fills with . . . green mist? Are these guys trying to get high right now? I mean, I get it, anxiety, but still. Now? The last thing I need is to get . . . Actually. Actually, you know fucking what? That actually sounds amazing. I take in a deep breath through my nose and let the mist out through my mouth. Two things happen.

While the pain doesn't dull, my focus shifts. Whenever I think about the pain, my mind drifts to something else. I also immediately recognize the batch of mist. It's Henry's. Stronger, safer, and more laced with poison from my blood than anything else on the streets. I smile. I can't get up on my own, but I have mana. It feels a bit like trying to pee while being watched, stubborn and resistant, but the mana comes and takes on the force aspect I have been using for so long. I feel it flicker and realize I need to get my artifacts back on soon. But first, I have to stop them from bringing Darian back before I am ready.

I pick myself up with force mana, literally carrying myself like some kind of mutilated ghost. I don't hesitate—I throw myself at each priest and just . . . slap them in the face. I have been sweating so much I don't have to worry about producing more. None of them have the strength that Baldwin had, so the first quickly realizes his divine magic is failing him and screams as the others flee. But I throw myself like a rag doll at each, ensuring I make contact at least once. None seem to be particularly powerful mages, and each is quickly writhing on the ground. My poison is a slow and painful death with divine magic impeding its progress. So I create four steel pellets and propel them into each of the priests' heads, ending their suffering.

I pant, looking around for my arm, when I see Henry and Autumn hesitantly making their way inside. "Jesus, Lil, are you all right? We thought you were dead! How aren't you dead? Can we help you?" Henry asks insistently as I sigh in relief. Then I raise an eyebrow at him.

"Jesus?" I ask. "Are you picking up my speech habits? How cute." I cough.

"I heard it somewhere else," he grumbles, blushing.

"God, I hope that's a lie," I say.

Again Autumn looks at us like we are insane. "Lillith . . . just tell us . . . what happened to you?"

"Ran into an asshole, that's all. Someone find my arm," I reply.

"Your arm? Lillith . . . I don't think we can fix . . . this . . ." Henry says, and I roll my eyes.

"The jewelry, jackass. I need the artifacts for my cancer."

He and Autumn jump into action.

"Right, shit, sorry, we are . . . a little off," Henry apologizes. He runs to the center of the room and picks up my arm. Then pauses, leans forward, and vomits.

"Fuck, did you just vomit on me?" I ask. He looks up at me with a sickly pallor.

"What? No, I puked on . . . Oh, shit, I guess I did," he says before hurling again. Autumn goes to join him. She chokes back some vomit herself, but manages to start pulling the bracelet and rings off. She repeatedly has to look away, but she does eventually get them all, wiping my brother's puke off the affected articles with her blouse.

Both of them, still looking sick, approach me to put them on my left hand. "Oh, Collector, you can drop that now, Henry!" Autumn insists as Henry literally forgets to drop my arm.

"Shit, I'm sorry, I'm not used to this stuff!" Henry says, literally throwing it back across the room. The two finally make it to me and begin sliding the artifacts in place.

"Wouldn't kill you to show a little respect. That was my good arm, you know," I complain. Again both have to choke back their bile. I am actually feeling pretty good. But, well, I am a little high. "Do you have your riot spikes?" I ask, and they both nod. "Great, I need one. Either one. You keep one on you, just in case."

"You're not seriously going to try to fight still, are you?" Autumn asks in horror. I try to shrug, but the act brings the pain to the forefront again, which elicits a muffled grunt from me before I can respond.

"I have to," I finally answer. "If I don't, he will kill . . . everyone. He's . . . He will kill everyone. I have to." They share a concerned look, but eventually, Henry pulls out a riot spike.

"Be careful," he says. "Promise you will be careful. Lil, you look like a butchered animal. If there was anything I could do, I'd fight in your stead. I have half a mind to try. If I didn't know how damn strong you are, I would. Shit, I don't even know how you plan to fight inside a riot sphere. You are literally carrying yourself with mana!"

"I'll figure something out," I reply. "I'm clever that way. Besides, I got a good hit in. The priests will have to work overtime to keep him alive with my poison running through him."

Henry sighs as I take the spike. "Stay safe." With that, I launch myself from the building. I have to be careful as I fly from the city. Not every anti-Lillith circle is horizontal, and the vertical ones will kill me if I fly through them. But I am angry, and I can breathe in the grief in the air. I make it to the field with the giant wave of ice, which I sit down on top of. I gotta make the little prick angry enough to come here, where I can fight without worrying about collateral damage. Where I can actually have a damn spike prepared.

I start summoning steel mana, making an extremely rudimentary foot for my left leg as well as a crutch. Finally, I gather sound mana and shout, amplifying my voice across the city.

"You didn't finish the fucking job, Darian. Darian the False King. Darian the Coward King. Darian the Weak King, who had to beg a girl for help and still failed. If you have the balls to fight me, a woman with one working limb and a fraction of your magic, well . . . I am waiting on the ice wall. If you are a king, come and fucking prove it."

CHAPTER FIFTY

Make Them Grieve

My sound mana dissipates and the world goes silent. I start working on something for my right leg. So long as I can stand, I can fight. I try a simple blade prosthetic, a brace with curved steel to create a little tension as I rest on it. It's not much. But I shakily lift myself with force mana and try to stand . . . only to immediately slip. Shit. Obviously, this is a giant block of ice. For all the help with pain the green mist is providing, my mind is too muddy. I aspect more steel, my skin vibrating and itching as I do. The mana, usually smooth like water in a river, flows a bit more like infected piss at the moment. But it works. I am able to add sharp, thin spikes to maintain my footing.

Lowering myself again, I manage to stand. Holy fuck does it hurt, but I can stand. It's enough. If I can get Darian into a riot spike's sphere of effect, I will actually have the advantage. And with all this very meltable ice around, I have a few tricks up my sleeve. But as I make my preparations for the fight, the world remains silent. My heart hasn't beat in years, but I still feel that familiar anxiety of aimless adrenaline. Maybe he is still working with the priests? My poison is not easy to flush from the system, but he did go to the church. He should be angry. He should be furious. He should still want me to call off the riots in all the other cities.

I am half dead. He must have left me on the brink and left the priests behind to heal me. So he could hurt me more. Because he still needs me. I look like a half-butchered calf. I have loose flesh hanging from a poorly closed stump of a shoulder. I already lost to him badly. If anything, the poison should mean he needs me more. He knows about the riot spikes, but . . . he is so powerful. So arrogant. He should know he can win. I sure as hell don't know if I can, and that should be encouraging for him. He fucking heard me, I am sure of that. He should be coming here to kill me by now.

And then I feel it. The pressure of his aura, exploding from the city. It makes me dizzy just to feel it. It must be fucking painful for any mages inside the city; is he insane? It's not a terrible idea for avoiding a riot spike, filling the area with mana. But surely waiting until he was out of the city would be better. Then I spot him. He is too far to see his face, but he is surrounded by five other men, and a deep red mana radiates off him as all six rise into the air above the city. Why is he aspecting it already? He pauses and an ominous chill peppers my body with gooseflesh. They start to rise higher. Then higher. Then higher still. Not toward me, just high above the city.

What is he doing? What does he hope to . . . I stop short, catching a quick breath as something hits me. Something I never would have considered in a fight against a man like this. He already handily beat me. I have a single working limb and a gut wound. I should no longer register as a major threat, just something he needs. Something that makes him angry. But not something he needs to fear, as far as he knows. But he is not coming to meet me as I'd hoped. A terrifying worry crawls up my spine like a centipede. He is too far to make out his facial expression, and he is not responding to my taunt.

It feels like I can read him, in a way. And he can read me. Our intentions travel across the distance without words and we are both unmoving. *Come here.* We both need the other to come to us. It's not something we want or prefer. We both need it. Because there is something I didn't consider when I adapted my plan to provocation instead of a trap. I failed to lure Darian out of the city the first time. He knows that's what I wanted to do. I thought he might come anyway, confident in his power and my injuries, but . . . I hit him hard enough to kill him while he had the advantage before. Without the priests, I may have won there. I poisoned him and forced him to run mid-interrogation to seek more healers. He likely hasn't beaten the poison yet. It is potent and attacks the nervous system, which his priests don't understand.

All this to say, he can't be confident about killing me. He has become aware of the danger of a small mistake. Maybe before he even met me, based on his own missing limb. But even more so now. He lacks the confidence I need him to have. He is afraid of me. He is too afraid to fight me when I have the advantage. The difference in our abilities is so wide, and his victory in our last fight was so complete, I didn't consider it seriously. But it's the smart move on his part. Out here, all I have to do is handle his priests, and he knows I can do that now. He may not know how, but he knows I can. It would be idiotic to come to me, however angry he may be. I have grown too comfortable relying on the arrogance of the powerful.

His entourage continues to ascend. I throw myself from the ice. This was a mistake. I propel myself with force mana to return to the city as quickly as I can. Shit. Shit shit shit. I can't beat him without a riot spike. I can't guarantee everyone's safety in the city. But this asshole knows that. He knows why I am here. He knows I fucking care about collateral damage. This means that while we both need the other to come to us, he has the means to force my hand. He proved it two weeks ago. He doesn't care if he loses a city. He cares if he gets what he wants. And what he wants is my cooperation. To stop the riots. To acquire my circle. To help get all the slaves back. I don't know. Two tones of red mana swirl through the air as I reenter the city at breakneck speeds. I don't have a choice. He's fucking insane.

There should be too many powerful nobles in this city for him to do this. To even threaten this! Visenar should have been the one city that was too dangerous to destroy. But I suppose for the same reason it is the most advantageous to eliminate. If he pulls it off, no other city in the country has anyone who can oppose him. Fuck, maybe he doesn't even care that much if I survive. He sure wasn't that careful about it the first time. Maybe he's cutting his losses and trying to drive the point home that fighting back means death for everyone, whether they were involved in the fight or not. Maybe he can't beat the poison after all and wants to punish me for it. I don't know. Maybe he really is just absolutely batshit. But his intent is clear. He is going to kill everyone in this city.

His mana feels like a storm as I fly through it, trying to reach him. I still have a riot spike. I can still stop him. We'll just have to fall together. I can accept that. I feel like I'm practically dead already anyway. I just . . . I just wish I could have saved Sarafyna first. But Ed will do it. Henry will help too. They don't need me. This mistake was my fault anyway. Believing my own goddamn legend. No one can stop Lillith: great woman of history. Fucking right. I was a spark, sure. But I've done my job. Now I just need to make it to Darian, activate this spike, and hold him in place until we hit the ground. But his mana, even spread over such a wide area, wants to devour me.

So I push harder. My artifacts feed spare mana back to me and help me push through. It's like swimming upriver in the middle of rapids. I consider using light and sound mana to obscure my approach, but it would take too much focus. I'm barely keeping my force mana stable as it is. I have almost no chance of reaching him successfully. I already saw how a blind charge will end. But I have no time to strategize. No time for clever plans. No tricks to level the playing field. I was supposed to be the distraction. Not the entire city. I owe them this Hail Mary.

The shades of red around me are all-encompassing and I can barely make out the figures above as I ascend to them. I push myself harder and feel my injuries protest the speed with which I fly through the air. I get closer, and closer, until I can finally see Darian's face through the red tint of the world. And he sees me as well. In an instant, his mana collapses around me and I am restrained again. I grip the spike in my hand. I just need him close enough. The red mana keeping everyone elevated comes from him exclusively. If I can dissipate it, we all die, and everyone below us lives.

He descends, just a little, and the obscuring mana around me parts. It rages in the sky everywhere else but creates a narrow gap where I am. He has everything he wants. I knew it was a desperate move. But I just need him a little closer. Just a little, and I can save everyone. "There you are. My little revolutionary." His drawl, as always, is mocking. "It was certainly an admirable attempt. Trying to goad me out like that. And I'll admit, whatever you did to me, the priests are struggling to keep it from killing me. Impressive, killing the ones I left with you, by the way. If a little ungrateful." I glare up at him silently. Come a little closer. Just a little closer, and this will all be over.

"You've shown your whole hand now," he remarks. As he descends, I can make out the bulging, discolored veins from my poison. Appearing and disappearing as the priests sweat above him, expending all their divine magic to fight it off. He may be in a position of power, but this move makes sense. He is just as fucking desperate as I am. I was overthinking it. He's not confident the priests can fix this at all. Maybe they can't. But he thinks I can. He tortured me privately to save the rest of the country. But he will kill everyone in the capital to save himself. I wish I could at least enjoy this small victory. But as it so often is for people in power, they will always make sure everyone below them suffers more than they do.

"You've shown your hand and I know exactly how to get what I want. I am done hurting you. I've done that enough. No. You will do what I say, or every single person in this city dies. Everyone but you, the palace, and the temple, of course. I have a feeling that loss will hit you harder than a limb or two. So what'll it be? Tell me what you did to me and call off your revolution, or watch another city die below you?"

I look up at him with defeat.

". . . All right. Give me a whisper sphere, I'll call them off," I promise. He examines me with suspicion, then looks at my hand, casually hidden behind my left leg. He scoffs and stops descending. Suddenly, the brighter mana all around me manifests. The sky over Visenar fills with burning magma in an instant. I can feel its heat drawing sweat from me. It hovers there, flowing into itself but failing to fall.

"I am holding this up with my mana. Would you care to take a guess what will happen if I lose control over my mana?" he prods, and my face falls. There goes plan A. My stomach begins to roil and nausea insists I lie down somewhere. Instead, I give Darian a cold stare. Those fluctuations in his veins remain. The fight against my poison. I am almost dizzy with the illness that assaults me now.

"The sphere," I say again. He nods and descends farther, until we are floating about a foot apart, eye to eye, then digs a sphere out with his hand. I tuck the spike into my belt and accept it. I hold the sphere up to my face and will it to call . . . everyone. Anyone with a whisper sphere. I don't know how many people will answer, but I want everyone to hear what I have to say. To witness what is about to happen. I give it a few moments while I glare at Darian.

"You're wrong, you know," I say. My voice carries to anyone who has picked up, more people with every moment.

"How is that?"

"They aren't revolutionaries. They are insurrectionists," I answer.

"What difference does that make?" he spits impatiently. I respond in two ways. First, I take advantage of my colorless grief mana to cast a covert sound spell, like I did on my execution day. This time, I want to be loud, but only down in the city. Throwing my voice is the first spell I learned, after all. Second, I take a deep breath as I speak into the sphere.

"Everyone in the city below, in Visenar. You need to run," I warn.

Darian sighs. "It will do them no good. I'll just expand the range. Do what you said you would do. There is no running from this."

"If the torches around you are fed by fuel, run to where they are magic stones instead. You will be safe under the light of stone, but you may die by firelight. So run," I warn again. This only colors Darian's face with confusion.

"I told you. There is no running from this. What does it matter what torches they use?"

I would have preferred to simply fall with him. But if this is the option I have, it is the one I will use.

"Because you made a fucking mistake, Your Highness. There are thousands of families beneath us. You are planning to kill thousands of families. Innocent or otherwise. Noble or otherwise. Slaves, and workers, and lords. All of them know you murdered a city before, and all of them can see death in the sky now," I explain. I do this more for the sake of anyone listening through their whisper sphere. So they will know what is happening in the city. So they will hear how to escape, and so even the nobles in other cities will know what is at stake. And so they will hear what happens next.

"Do you think telling people how dangerous I am will undermine my rule?" Darian scoffs. "Is this your last desperate attempt to buy time? Telling them how many people I am willing to kill? Go ahead. You're only cementing my rule. And so long as your little rev—sorry, insurrectionists hear me end you, it will have the same effect. Because"—he leans in to speak into the sphere himself—"if any other cities defy me, I will do the same to them. If only one city is left at the end of this, I will still be its ruler. And you will all be dead. So surrender. Tell them, Lillith of Endings. Tell them what you look like. Tell them what your desperate flailing resulted in. For you, and for all the innocent people around you. Or tell them to surrender. Your choice. Either way, your clever little call ends the same way. You think I would have given you that if I were afraid of what you were going to say to them?"

"No," I reply, "I am not trying to undermine your rule. You are right, everyone is already afraid of you. Everyone is already terrified of the man who ends cities down to the last noble, baker, and fucking child. So terrified, many will only lose heart when you do it again. That would have the same effect. That would stop the people from fighting back. But you missed the fucking point. I am not pleading with them in an act of desperation. I want them to know even you can be killed, and so can everyone who has ever used overwhelming power to oppress them. I want them to hear the execution of the last king of Potestia.

"You made a mistake, Darian," I practically spit. I feel so fucking sick. "You showed all those people below us their end. Their death. You announced that it is inescapable. You took hope from them. You gave them terror and took their hope. Do you know what that is doing to them? To the thousands of people looking up and seeing hell in the skies above them?"

"What?" he asks with irritation. "Tell me what it's doing and stop fucking stalling for a hopeless evacuation. I told you, I will only increase the range of the destruction. So get on with it. What is it doing to them?"

I feel as sick as I ever have, but it's an illness I have grown used to. Because it is an illness I have felt a thousand times before. Every single time I enter the Radiant Woods. I lock my eyes on his. "It is making them fucking grieve." At this, my force mana explodes from me, knocking Darian and his priests back like gnats and catching most of the molten rock over the city before it can fall. This isn't the same fight as before. Because now, I have the advantage. My invisible mana expands farther than the red, saturating the sky as the magma presses against it and I press back.

Darian isn't done yet though. He presses against my force with his gravity. I cool his magma by stealing his heat. But I am winning. Almost everywhere. Everywhere but the tall pillars of mana that fall in the only places I can't defend: columns where the vertical circles designed to disperse my grief mana point toward the sky. I try to cool the edges fast enough so they don't spread. But people are dying. I can feel people dying. It makes me more powerful. It makes me more sick. I fucking hate it. I would rather have died with him. But at least it means Darian is only more fucked.

I still hold the sphere, speaking so everyone who cares to listen can hear. "Today is the last day we suffer a king in Potestia."

CHAPTER FIFTY-ONE

The Last Kings of Potestia

Hugh

Lillith of Endings. The Mage of Mourning. The serial killer hunting nobles. Her fiancé died in Satusmor, but I thought nothing of it. Lord Godfrey claimed his head, after all, and he was treated as a hero for it. Then the campus incident happened. And who should be arrested for it but Lillith of Endings? The woman found to be responsible for hundreds of noble deaths all across the country. I don't know how she did it. All anyone knows is she somehow lives in the Radiant Woods. The only thing that matters to me is the reality.

Which I understood as soon as everything came out. She was always an uppity bitch. She hasn't known her place since I first met her. She has never known her responsibility. She would never have married Lord Baldwin. It's a short leap to realize that Godfrey would have killed him years earlier if he could have. Godfrey didn't kill Baldwin. Lillith did. The monster wearing a woman's skin. I don't know how, but if she could kill the king, she could kill a city lord. And she could kill my father.

I spent years hating the Manticorps. Thugs my father hired who supposedly turned on him. But they were innocent. They were always innocent. Victims of the same bloodthirsty whore as my father. My life was upended. I was barely able to gather the mana I needed to attend Facinley University, and what happened? I wasn't able to graduate. Because of Lillith's massacre. Of course, no one believed I'd had a relationship with her when I first made the claim. But once she was revealed for her bloodthirst? Everyone believed it then. Any reason to torment me.

And it all goes back to the death of my father. The murder of my father. The cold-blooded slaughter of the man who raised me. The man I so desperately wanted to be. The man I wanted to make proud. Murdered by a local guardsman's daughter. I am certain of this now. And I won't let it stand. I don't care about anything else. I just want to ruin her. Hurt her. Make her feel like I do. I don't know how I'll beat her, but I will, somehow. I have been one of the only people willing to leave their home more than necessary for weeks. All to catch a hint about Lillith. I knew she would come back, even if I haven't had much luck finding her. But finally, here she is, causing chaos, what with King Darian and almost a dozen priests sending their mana out everywhere.

She is broken. She is bloodied. She can't even stand without her mana anymore.

She is an abomination. And she is still. Fucking. Joking. Still arrogant. Still not hurting like I am.

I kneel just under a window, only daring the occasional peek at the group inside the building.

"Wouldn't kill you to show a little respect. That was my good arm, you know," she quips at her older brother. Henry, I think. She is being flippant about her own dismembered arm even as she bleeds from her stump of a shoulder. She seems more concerned with some kind of spike artifact than her own body.

"You're not seriously going to try to fight still, are you?" Autumn protests. She's the little twin bitch who always hung on Lillith's arm. I hold back a growl. That means she is still in fighting shape somehow. I suppose with enough mana, granted by a Collector-damned duke, anyone can. I want to try to ambush her somehow. To take advantage of her wounds to finally fucking kill her. But my breath catches. My legs won't move. My body knows what my mind wants to deny. Even in her current state, I will die if I try to fight her. I close my eyes and wait as they debate. It's not long before I hear a loud *clang*, open my eyes, and see Lillith escaping me again. I failed my father again. I never had the chance to make him proud, but maybe that's for the best. The man I became would never make him proud.

She is gone, and it's too late. "Well, shit," Henry says inside. "What do we do now?"

My breath catches. Maybe . . . maybe it's not too late after all.

Godfrey

There is fire in the sky. My grandson is a slave to Kallon. And I am near death. It's wrong. It's all so wrong. Ansel betrayed me. He actually stabbed me in the back the moment Dominic left. I barely managed to stop the bleeding after I escaped. I creep through the palace, nursing my wounds. If it weren't for my space magic, I would be dead now. My chambers are quiet as I turn the lock. The case waits on my bed. Ready to be used. I laughed when it was offered to me, but . . .

I am not fit to be king. I never was. I am a failure. A little commoner girl who organized my books is the only reason my home is anything more than ash and rubble. I glance at the book on my bedside table. *Court the Court: Wenches Unsheathed* Vol. 69. I'm only halfway through. It was the deluxe edition, almost impossible to find. It had the foldout . . . Well, it doesn't matter. I'd been so looking forward to finding out how Adeline avoided discovery by the prince. I suppose I'll never finish it now.

It was a silly thing to indulge in anyway. Unbefitting of a king. But I suppose that falls in line with my short rule very well. Unbefitting. Too weak for the crown on my head. I open the case and retrieve the elegant staff. I can feel the power radiating off it. Nothing like mana. Real, tangible divine magic. More than any priest I have ever met. If I give it an order, the world will comply. All it will cost is my life.

Dominic will be a better king than me. I have always known that. He is the kind of man I always told myself I was—lied to myself about being. I wrap the staff in my tattered, bloody cloak, and surround myself in space mana. They said I needed to go somewhere high up. It's not too late. I can still save this country.

Edward

"Today is the last day we suffer a king in Potestia," Lily's voice announces over the sphere in Kallon's hand. A red glow shines through the shattered window as our stalemate holds. Kallon glares at me.

"Drop the spike and let me through. I will let you live, for now, since it seems I am needed elsewhere," Kallon demands. He will let me live, if I let him hurt my sister. A traitorous part of me is tempted. I am afraid. I am so afraid. Part of me is in that alley with Henry, with an easy way to safety. I loathe that part of me. I hoped to kill what was left of it when I killed . . . the other man. Apparently, I didn't, not all the way. Maybe I never will. But I don't have to listen to him either. I look over my shoulder to where I can see Lillith, in the sky over the city. Everywhere but here shadowed by the burning sky.

She is pushing back. She is pushing hard. The fire above the city is slowly turning to stone, being crushed between Darian's red mana and Lillith's invisible mana. Lighter red mana continuously regenerates magma as swirls of Lily's bluish mana take its burn away. She is winning. I can't make out Darian, but I can hear her speaking over the whisper sphere. I set my jaw and grip the spike. "You're not going anywhere," I reply to Kallon. I am not the boy who left his brother behind. I will show Lily. And someday, I'll show Henry too. Kallon rolls his eyes.

"Then I will walk around, you absolute moron. Ansel, kill him. Do your very best not to fuck this one up." He sighs before standing. He looks at his captive in thought for a moment. Then toward the door, then back at the chained man. He groans. "Well, I see we have a problem. I have to kill one of you, don't I? I obviously can't take this to battle with your sister, not if she is capable of . . . that. And I can't leave him with you. Ansel just . . . doesn't have the history of follow-through I'd like. Well, I suppose he would be easier." He shrugs and begins to summon pink mana. I don't know what it is, but I know I don't have much time. I have to act. Whoever that man is, I am going to gamble on him.

I throw the spike as hard as I can toward Kallon, who immediately reacts with an actual explosion of mana in my direction. It dissipates the second it reaches the spike's sphere of influence, or rather, the second the spike reaches it. The stone shrapnel propelled by the explosion keeps flying, however, and cracks against the thick glass wall I summoned the moment I moved. "Ansel, kill him!" Kallon commands. His subordinate moves to obey immediately, fire rushing toward me as I dive for another of the scattered spikes. I don't get a chance to examine its size as I pour mana into it, creating another bubble of safety. Another smaller bubble. Shit.

But I did manage to grab a couple of larger ones. I just have to deactivate this one to use it. "You are starting to get on my nerves," Kallon growls.

"Well, if there is one single thing I have always been good at . . ." I reply. The thrown spike lies a few paces from him, but he is defenseless for the moment. Unable to attack. That still makes this two-on-one, however, as Ansel and Kallon both eye me—and the spike. Kallon dives for it and I lunge to close the distance, but Ansel tackles me to the ground. I hear Lillith's voice over the still-connected sphere.

"We are not revolutionaries. We are insurrectionists. Every petty tyrant in Potestia has so much more to fear than a revolution. Because you will never kill one of us and defeat the rest. You can kill me. You can destroy this city. You can kill a thousand of us, and you will still never feel safe again. It's already too late. Potestia has already passed the point of no return."

I swing an elbow back into Ansel's side. He grabs my hair and forces my head back, preparing to slam it into the marble floor. I release the energy in the spike and drill wind and glass shards into his side, forcing him off me. I scramble to my feet and activate the spike again, only for stone shrapnel to tear into my side. I'd moved enough to avoid most of the targeted blast, but my injuries are accruing. My mouth is starting to taste like copper. At least I got a good hit in on that Ansel creep. A deep, sharp throbbing in my side complains of my need for rest and healing. A sharper voice reminds me why I can't.

"How many more trades like that do you think you can survive?" Kallon asks.

"One more than you," I quip, fighting back a cough of blood. Lillith's voice keeps talking, motivating me to win.

"We already know it is possible to fight back. Even if we lose ten times and win once, we still fucking won once. And the surface cracks. Your mask of invulnerability falls. You bleed, just a little. It was too late for all of you the moment the first one bled. Because everyone—every single person in the country—has seen you bleed. Has seen you learn to fear. Even if you kill me, and every person by my side, they will still have seen you bleed. That scar is proof you can be fought. And once people know they can fight you? It's too late."

She is right. I just have to make Kallon bleed. I grit my teeth. His pink mana explodes again, firing sharp stones at me, and I am forced to both drop and deactivate the spike so I can defend myself. I successfully block the attack again, but it seems it wasn't his primary focus, as stone walls have surrounded the room when I get my bearings again, trapping us all inside. Fine with me. It will only slow him down if he decides to leave. I look around for Ansel, expecting him to come down on me at any time. All I see is a bloody pool where we previously fought. Again my sister's voice rings through the room.

"We know you can bleed. We know you can die. We know you can fall from your towers and crawl through the mud with the rest of us. And that's the thing, Darian. Any noble listening to this, actually. You don't have your mind control anymore. You don't have your infallible and uncracked armor. You are no longer pristine and untouchable. And a new world? A better world? That is a dream that has been fostered in minds across Potestia since long before I was born. Long before I ever drew blood. It is the sweetest, kindest, and most pervasive dream in the world. It's like honey and warm milk. Ambrosia of the heart. People have always wanted to fight for a better world."

Kallon's tactic becomes clear as the room fills with water. He plans to drown me. I continue to look around for Ansel. The water reaches my ankles. It's at the chained man's knees. I run. I fill the room with glass walls to defend myself as I propel myself with wind. After a burst of wind throws me forward, I fill a spike with mana and drop it in the water. His explosions propel projectiles. I escape the sphere, propel myself, and fill another spike. Again I drop it in the water. I have one left. The water is up to my knees when I land, and up to the chained man's waist. Lillith continues her speech.

"The problem was, they couldn't. They had no hope. They didn't have control of their own minds, and when they did, all they saw was an ivory wall they could never surmount. That's not true anymore. The wall is cracked. It can be climbed, breached, and brought low. Everyone who has ever dreamed of a better world can now see its light shining through your little wall. And it's worth it. It is so worth it. All the pain and fear and death you threaten them with. It has always been fucking worth it! They have always been willing to face it, the moment they had any hope that it would lead somewhere."

Ansel descends on me. I have no idea where he came from. He wraps his arms around my throat. He has one arm around my neck, gripping it with his other arm, which he uses to holds my head as I fill my final spike with mana. He squeezes, and I struggle to breathe. Water fills the room even faster. Kallon, standing unconcerned in a pillar of air, untouched by his own water, gathers a huge amount of earth and pink mana. I realize he plans to kill us both and panic, releasing the spike's effect and allowing my legs to give out beneath me. Ansel and I both fall into the water, where I press against the ground, rolling and forcing his body between me and Kallon. Meanwhile, I try to build even thicker glass to protect us, and send wind mana out into the water around me. Lily's voice grows more and more passionate, more and more angry as she continues to speak.

"Well, there is hope now. So even if any of you manage to survive without surrendering power, all you'll have won is a few decades. A few years. Weeks. Hours. Breaths. Even if you kill or enslave every rioter in the country. Even if you get your foot back on our throats and grind your heel. It will be too late. Because this is not revolution; this is insurrection. If ten people still want a better world, they will fight for it, and you won't be safe. If five people still want a better world, you won't be safe. If one person is willing to fight. You. Will. Not. Be. Safe. Don't you understand? Everyone knows they can hurt you, and everyone is one cruelty away from deciding it is worth it. And you should be afraid. You should all be afraid.

Because it will only take one wrong move, one mistake, and you will burn with all your wealth and power and little thrones in your little mountains. One false move, and you are dead."

Kallon's spell goes off. Glass shatters and fills the water. Stone cuts into Ansel, and into me once it tears through him. My wind mana starts to create whirlpools. The water around me is filled with misty red. The pain is almost muted by the water, like my skin is asleep as the stone ravages my body. It still hurts. As the whirlpools grow in strength, my own glass begins to shred my flesh as well. Ansel releases me and drifts away. And then . . . the plan works. The powerful swirling water catches the activated spikes and glass, momentum carrying the water as the wind mana dissipates. One of them gets just close enough. Kallon's perfect sanctuary collapses around him.

He was only watching me. Only watching my spike. Now water, glass, and blood close in on him, a perfectly mortal man. He killed his own ally. And I can still move. I grip the spike as I swim through the glass and the pain, letting the water's current carry me to my target. He is still reacting to the water, now up to his chest and cutting him with the moving shards of glass, when I make it to him and stab my remaining spike into his back, activating it as well. The next few moments are pain and confusion as the whirlpools tangle us together, assault us, and separate us. Finally, I gain my feet as the water slows, no longer fed by mana.

I don't hesitate. I move. I move to my new target before Kallon can recover. The chained man. I fill the keyhole at his neck with glass and turn, freeing him just as a massive explosion knocks me off my feet.

"I'll fucking kill you! No more of this shit! I am not playing your fucking game! This whole palace is fucking going down!" Kallon shouts. There is screaming from another source. I guess he got the spike out more quickly than I thought. But it's too late. The man I freed has a royal aura, and his mana is already surrounding Kallon. The water around Kallon freezes in an instant, holding him in place as heavy wood spears materialize and impale him from all directions. Just like that. He is dead. I look back at the man I freed to see he is still screaming. Still summoning spears. Still impaling the corpse of our enemy.

I reach one hand out cautiously, when a loud crack of thunder draws both our attention to the shattered window. The man grimaces, then sends a razor-sharp blade of wind to decapitate the already dead prince. Then we hear the *smack* of thunder again and are compelled to wade through the remaining water to the window. The man easily dismantles the stone wall in our way with more wind blades, and the water begins to drain like a fall. Thunder claps again, and again, and again. As we look outside, it becomes clear why. The sky is black and gray with crumbling stone, held up with thick, oppressive, invisible mana. The stone ceiling is marred with holes and scorch marks, leaving red wounds that still glow with dwindling heat.

In the center of it all is a woman. I can barely make her out, but she is an icon of fury, and terror, and grief. Lightning explodes from her at a rapid-fire pace as her mana disassembles the ominous stone above her. Again and again, angry bolts of electricity light the city, tearing through the stone at enemies beyond it. Counterattacks of red mana and lava rain down on her, but she bats them away like flies, all the while tearing at the destructive cover around her. She is like an artist, painting the sky with carnage. It should be death and horror, but as it flows across the sky like a brushstroke, lit with flashes of red and white light, it is beautiful.

One strike of lightning catches a body and it falls, hits the stone in the sky, gets caught, and joins the flow. Then another, and another, and another. Five in total. Corpses, swimming in a river of fire and grief in the heavens. The attacks from above slow, and Lily directs the stones out of the city, slowly revealing the clouds above and her final opponent. The remaining man seems to be struggling. All his mana concentrates to one point and he begins a desperate charge. But the dark red compresses around him and finally collapses. Then both descend slowly until I can't see them anymore.

Lillith's voice, which I had stopped listening to, speaks again, this time more quietly. "But you are not going to kill us all. You are going to lose. Today. You are never going to crush a city under your heel again. And I am going to show the entire city what happens to men who rule with fear."

The sky illuminates again, this time with a show of light mana. Two people slowly take shape in a massive replication of a scene happening on the ground. Darian. Beaten. Burned. Convulsing with blood running out of his mouth. And my little sister. She is . . . a horror. Strips of loose flesh hang from her right shoulder. The blood has mixed with enough dirt to look solid. Her right calf has been replaced with twisted, spiked steel in a strange curve. Even her left foot seems to be summoned steel. Thick blood leaks around the brace that holds it in place. Her shirt is a bloody rag, pierced right over her magic circle. I wonder if it has been permanently damaged. Her face, on the other hand . . . her face is cold rage. She has tear streaks through the dirt on her cheeks. That old scar that always reminds me of my failures can be seen by the entire city. Darian is on the ground, twitching and writhing. Lillith grabs his hair and drags him. Her makeshift feet scrape silently against the stone as she marches toward a fountain that comes into view. The whisper sphere floats behind her. As she reaches the fountain, she throws Darian against it, summoning steel to hold his hands and head in an elevated position against the stone.

"No king will ever rule over us again. No king will crush us beneath his arrogance. No kings. The people grieve under the weight of your crowns, and we will do it no longer." She summons a heavy steel crown and catches it in her remaining hand before fixing it on Darian's head. Finally, she creates a massive ax, one any man would need two hands to wield. She raises it over her head in just one as she stands to Darian's side.

"All hail the last king of Potestia." She swings, and the country is finally free. The man next to me falls to his knees with no care for the glass that he lands in. He simply starts sobbing as the vision in the sky fades.

CHAPTER FIFTY-TWO

Insurrection

Emeric

I'm not certain who I am anymore. Who I ever was. My faith mana has been shattered. I can't access it anymore, and I'm not the only acolyte with this problem. I was so certain of everything, growing up. Of the Collector. Of the future he had for me, and of the service I had for him. Then the truth about Lord Baldwin came out. His . . . divine magic. What he did to so many people's minds. And supposedly with the power of the Collector behind him. It didn't make sense, didn't line up with the Collector I had grown up worshipping.

But I pushed my doubts down. I endured. I was doing good work. Protecting children. I believed I was, anyway. For the last few years, faith has been dwindling. The temples have been emptying out, with fewer faithful every day. But this wasn't a mere crisis of faith like the average noble might have. No, it was far more like the day after Baldwin's death. People didn't just question the Collector; they didn't remember ever really believing in him in the first place. Like they came out of a fog and left their faith inside. At first, I had the horrifying belief that there were more nobles like him, controlling people with what should be the Collector's divine magic.

It lined up at first glance. Nobles were being hunted by some serial killer. Some said a monster. Others believed it was an agent of the church. But as more nobles died, more commoners lost faith. It was a clear correlation. But so too was there a correlation between the missing slaves and the loss of faith. And neither made sense, really. If nobles were controlling commoners, it wouldn't be to instill a love of the Collector. I couldn't make sense of it. That is, until the murder of Father Medici. A murder committed by one of Baldwin's victims, and one of my friends, apparently. It's hard to imagine. I still picture Lily as the child I cared for all those years ago. But she killed the head of the church. The church was the first to spread the news among themselves. But what I found really remarkable was . . . people lost faith even faster afterward.

The church is a mess now. Too many secrets were held by one man. Too much power. We were like a tapestry with a loose thread, unraveling all around the country. Too many secrets stopped being secret. Too many ranking priests, without order or direction, got too careless or too angry. It was confession. All along, it was confession. The Collector never had any common believers. Just slaves to the priests' divine magic. Divine. The magic of the Collector. I couldn't stomach it. Most of the acolytes couldn't. Most of us left. Many of us lost faith in the Collector altogether. And with it, we lost our endoaspect, and protection from the priests.

And of course, our kings. Our kings, in their disputes, massacred Tumult. Now the liberated slaves are returning. And with them, they bring a way to dissipate all mana in an area. Without a pre-drawn circle. They are angry. They want change. And the warmth of the Collector was nothing more than a brand the entire time. The priests are the only ones left who can fight them now. The knights are useless without mana. The guards were overwhelmed as soon as the former slaves met up with detractors in the city. The nobles are mostly too terrified to fight. They hide in their safe rooms, or surrender, or occasionally fight and die.

The priests would be the only ones who could stop them, if the temple wasn't burning down before their eyes. If I hadn't lost my faith. I flare the fire mana around my hand as my former home lights up the city. I think I want to meet Lillith again. I want to thank her.

Jean

The Chapman family has stood strong for a hundred years. It will not end with me. I am the lord of this city, and a few upstart commoners too proud of their magic will not be stopping me. I don't care how many nobles have died. I don't care what this "Mage of Mourning" can do. The rabble has grown too bold. Gathering outside my manor with their pitchforks, and torches, and . . . maces and spears, apparently. Well, they are a well-armed mob, I'll give them that. My whisper sphere starts gently vibrating, but I ignore it.

"L-Lord Jean, what do we do? They've made it past the gate!" reports a frightened, sniveling little man as I fiddle with a chunk of magical ice.

"Worry not, worry not, it's all in hand. I swear, you guards are truly useless, aren't you?" I mutter. So what if recruitment fell when the Mage of Morning was active in the city? So what if a few meaningless pawns died? Does that mean you all stop doing your jobs? It should not be the duty of the city lord to personally silence dissent. I'll have to see to it that their pay is docked even further. Why are we wasting money on a cowardly guard core? They haven't even managed to replenish our slave labor, and now this? Look at the fear on this man's face! "What have the other nobles been doing, anyway? A half dozen barons should have ended this hours ago!"

"Th-they've been captured! Or fled, or surrendered, or . . ." He trails off and I roll my eyes.

"Your men can't even report properly now? Perhaps we've been losing slaves because we are too sparing with the whip—on the product and on the guards. There are nobles in the city with multiple generations of mana accumulation. You expect me to believe a muddle of common slaves with their own makeshift magic circle managed to cow them? Speak some sense, you coward!" I release a deep sigh as my whisper sphere continues to vibrate. "Answer that for me, and tell whoever it is I am busy. I will see to this myself."

I can smell smoke now. I can hear cries and chanting. These fools are actually out there setting fires and calling for my head. As I approach my front door, a brick flies through the window beside me. I frown slightly. I am going to have to find who did that and make them eat the glass they broke. Perhaps that will help these serfs understand their place a little better. I casually open the door and step outside. There are dozens, maybe over a hundred rioters outside my front door.

"All of you surrender now and submit yourselves to slavery," I order. "Or you, your wives . . . Actually, you seem to have brought your wives with you. How quaint. Your children, then, all of them will die. It will be slow. It will be painful. So surrender now."

A stone flies from the crowd and strikes my head, causing the world to spin a little. "I fucking warned you, you little shits!" I snarl, summoning all my ice mana to crush them in a freezing death. Or . . . I try to summon it. It doesn't come. I can't feel any mana at all. The rioters advance.

I take a step back, then another. What did these cowards do? Too afraid to fight fairly, are they? Another rock flies and hits me in the chest. Then another in the leg. "Stop this! Stop this now! Do you have any idea what you are doing?" I demand.

A voice comes from behind me as if in answer, and I look to see my terrified guard holding the whisper sphere.

"You. Will. Not. Be. Safe," the voice threatens. I look back at the crowd, and my eyes widen.

"No . . ."

Jax

We don't have the numbers that some of the other cities have. Lord Anscom has been particularly cruel. Particularly brutal. Quick with punishment and twice as severe. Only eight of us volunteered to return to our home and fight for it. Only three joined us when we arrived. No riots in the streets here. The people are too afraid. Too wounded. But if the Mage of Mourning taught us anything, it's that we don't need any more than that. We can't make a big scene. But we can still end the suffering here.

We grip our riot spikes as we creep through the lord's estate. Lillith is right. The biggest mistake the lords and ladies of Potestia have ever made is arrogance. Pride. Building massive, luxurious monuments to their names and wealth. Everyone in a city knows where their lord lives. Everyone. They won't let us forget it. They smear it across our faces as they tell us to live in the dirt and pretend to be happy and grateful. They hire and enslave us to maintain the beauty of their homes. They tell us all where they live. And now? They have no way to defend themselves from us.

I worked in this mansion when I was a slave. I lived every day in fear. Terrified when I passed the ornate doors leading to Anscom's office. When the doors opened, one of us always felt the whip or the cane. It never mattered what we did. Someone would be made an example of each day. As we round a corner, a patrolling guard startles, but we are on him in a moment. We have been practicing for this, and my sword bites into his neck and Andrew's hand covers his mouth. We lower him slowly to the ground and let the blood pool. No one needs to speak a word.

And there it is. The dreaded office. The beautifully carved doors that always opened to pain. They will again, one more time. I flex my trembling fingers around the hilt of my sword. Just a little farther, and this city will know hope again. As we approach, a voice echoes through the door. My breath catches, but I remain calm. We were prepared for this possibility. If another guard comes, we will deal with it. For now, we just need to know how many bodies we are dealing with inside. I steady my breath and listen. The voice is muffled, but feminine. I hold my breath completely as we creep closer to the door, until I can finally make out the woman's words.

"A few years. Weeks. Hours. Breaths. Even if you kill or enslave every rioter in the country. Even if you get your foot back on our throats and grind your heel. It will be too late. Because this is not revolution; this is insurrection. If ten people still want a better world, they will fight for it, and you won't be safe. If five people still want a better world, you won't be safe. If one person is willing to fight. You. Will. Not. Be. Safe."

I haven't interacted directly with the Mage of Mourning many times. But I still remember when she pulled me out of this city. When she killed the man who bought me from Anscom like cattle. I know her voice. The lord is on a whisper sphere with Lillith of Endings. I don't know why, but it means he is alone. It is his turn to fear the opening of this door. I don't need to kick it in. I don't need to tear through the building. So I calmly approach the door and drive a riot spike into the wall. Slowly, like I'm hanging a painting. I activate it and turn the doorknob. Inside, Anscom sits at his desk and looks at us with surprise. He thrusts a hand out at us and . . . nothing happens.

"Hello, *master*," I greet him.

Troy

"Do not fear these common slaves. These terrorists. Do not fear what they will do. They are weak. Emboldened by the Mage of Mourning. Pushed beyond their means by a single brash woman. But do you know why we don't have to fear them?" I ask, addressing the soldiers under my command. "Do you know why they will flee from us? Why we will have them back in chains where they belong without a single casualty on our side? Why I know they are nothing more than bluster?"

My assistant tries to get my attention, but I ignore him. Now is not the time.

The rank and file are nervous. We have never had an uprising like this before. Hopefully, we never will again. But they are listening.

"Because the man our new king sent to help set our city straight is a hero. The mage they sent to heal the wounds caused by the Mage of Mourning is fearsome and terrible. He is not just a noble, worthy of respect. He is not a simple mage, fresh from the academy though he may be. He is a warrior. A man to be feared. And he is. Feared by all his opponents. To include Lillith of Endings, or as you may know her, the Mage of Mourning. He is, in fact, the only man she ever fled from. The only mage she was too afraid to fight. And he is here with us today," I announce to cheers.

Again my assistant waves at me, moving toward me to try to whisper in my ear, but I wave him off, eager to finish rallying the troops. "And soon, soon he will join us, and help us put these far-too-brave children back in their chains!" No longer willing to be waved off, the man I have been ignoring finally just announces his news out loud.

"No, Captain Troy. He is not. That is what I have been trying to tell you. Lord Ralf has fled the city."

CHAPTER FIFTY-THREE

The King and the Demon

I let out an exhausted breath. I feel like a dried out can of paint. Darian is dead. Victory cost an arm and a leg, but it was still victory, and the whole country knows it. I am so tired, and in so much pain. If it weren't for the blood of the headless corpse next to me, I'd be tempted to take a catnap on this damn fountain. I'd love to pack it up and go home for the day, but there is still so much work to do. So many people must have died in the areas of Visenar I couldn't protect. I warned as many people as I could. But my sound mana wouldn't have reached everywhere, especially not the centers of the dispersal circles.

There are people who need help. And, unfortunately, there are still dangerous elements in the city. I don't know where Godfrey or Kallon is. Or any other mage who might decide what they just witnessed was a job opening up. Godfrey was king last I checked, so it's possible he is dead. Kallon too, for all I know. But . . . I have to find out for sure. I also don't know if Edward is alive, or what happened to my father. I take a step and let out an agonized grunt as the poorly constructed prosthetic bites into barely healed skin at the new end of my leg. Fuck. Just call me Lillith of Endings a little too early. Yeah, I think floating around with force mana may be the way to go for a bit.

Accordingly, I lift myself from the ground with mana and release the tension on my legs. The pain doesn't fade, nor does the migraine it is bringing with it. In fact, as the green mist fades from my system, the pain is presenting itself more urgently, like a child desperate for attention. It's growing more difficult to focus on anything else. But focus I must because life isn't fair and God is dead. Or maybe because I give a shit. One of the two. Either way, I have to ignore the protests of my abused body and move as quickly as I can. I decide to head toward the palace, considering it the most likely place to find any remnants of royalty on either side and, I hope, Edward.

I still feel sick. The city is filled with pillars of igneous rock anywhere a circle was drawn on the ground instead of a wall. From up here, I can see them for miles, surrounding the great tree of the Radiant Woods. The tree that is probably, finally, unguarded. I could sure use a path to Sara's hat shop from there. I know not enough people escaped. This was too large a price. This was not what I planned. I may have won, but it was a heavy victory, one with thousands of casualties. I can feel they didn't escape. My grief mana is still being fed far more than it should. The death in the sky is gone. The man who was threatening them is dead. But they are still grieving.

And I still feel like a corpse. Any sense of accomplishment is strangled by the cost. All I can feel is miserable. My girlfriend is literally locked up in a dungeon. My brother is in danger. I am surrounded by the pained wailing of the families of the dead. And I am missing a few pieces. The shreds of loose flesh hanging from my wounds still sting somehow. I am starting to suspect Darian was unqualified to be performing amputations. I keep moving anyway, focusing on the palace in the distance. I feel like I am traveling urgently—I am halfway across the city only a few moments after killing Darian—but I'm not. Not enough. A bright, furious light shines from the highest tower of the palace. At the same time, the world grows muddy around me, like the air itself is made of wet sand.

Everything seems to blur and I feel a sense of . . . rejection. Like I have become unwelcome in my body. I mean, I can't blame it, considering what my choices have done to it. Still, it's *my* body. I can't be unwelcome in *my own body*. My skin begins to vibrate like the city around me has turned into some kind of shady carnival ride. I fix my eyes on the light. It's not mana. I can feel that in an instant. That feeling of too much blood being drawn starts in my fingers and crawls up my arm. Divine magic. Or Nexus energy. Whatever you want to call it, I recognize the feeling instantly. It brings me back to a bedroom, years ago, where a now-dead man tried to hurt me with it.

Now I truly move. I hadn't realized how much I was letting the pain and misery distract me before. I owe Ed an apology for that when I see him. Because I don't know what is happening, but it is some of the most powerful divine magic I have ever felt. And I can feel that I do not want whatever it is trying to do to me. I have something of a Spider-Sense for that sort of entitled ill intent trying to control me. I call it *being a woman*. I increase the power of the force mana propelling me and increase my elevation so I can easily avoid any of the horizontal circles still trying to limit my abilities. The vertical ones are easy to avoid now, at least. Even if the reason makes me sick to my stomach.

I need to use air mana to prevent air resistance as the speed I travel threatens to send me back to unconsciousness. I feel phantom limbs curl in pain as the excruciating protests of my injuries try to slow me down. The light grows brighter as I approach, and the world swims into itself, like I'm looking at it from underwater. I see visions of similarly confused allies across the country. Volunteers, staggering. I see Autumn, my mother, and even Ed, who I am pleased to see alive, if heavily injured. The images flash before my eyes at light speed. It feels like ages, but it is only a few seconds before I arrive at the source, on top of an open watchtower.

It's Godfrey. Of course it is Godfrey. This was always coming. I kind of hoped it wouldn't, but I knew it would. He is tightly gripping a tall staff, the source of the bright light. I slow and hover over the tower, catching his desperate, pained eyes.

He sees me as well and falters, the light dissipating for a moment. The world rights itself as he does, and I can see tears running down his cheeks, sparkling in his beard.

"Nice walking stick, Gandalf. Whatcha doing with it?" I ask.

He sighs. "As usual, I have no idea what in the three planes you are talking about," he replies. "What . . . happened to you? Lillith . . . you look worse than I do."

I look down at my right shoulder. "Fell down the stairs," I answer glibly. "Come on, man. What is that? I don't remember you being a divine mage. If you had the kind of power I just felt, Baldwin never would have given me any trouble. Hell, I'd never have met you at all. What are you doing?"

He looks down, weariness evident in his shoulders and head. He seems to be favoring his left side as well.

"Does it matter?" he asks. "I can just go somewhere else, you know. With my space mana. I'll be gone in an instant. You can't stop this, no matter what it is."

I raise an eyebrow at him. "Well, see, I don't think that's true."

"And why is that?"

"Well, old man," I begin, "if that were true, you wouldn't have started here in the first place. I'm fairly certain you saw my own light show a moment ago. Yet you still chose this spot for your own. Why start here if you had no reason to? It just drew my attention."

Godfrey sighs again, leaning against the side of the stone tower. "Perhaps I didn't know it would be so visible," he suggests.

I laugh, then lower myself to sit on the same stone lip he is leaning against. "That would honestly be hilarious, and I kind of hope it's the case. But it wouldn't matter. Because, well, that's not how space works, I'm afraid," I inform him. He looks at me with a furrowed brow.

"What do you mean by that?"

"Space." I shrug. "You said it was space mana, right? Well, space doesn't allow physical matter to move instantaneously. Only information, really. And the aspects you would need to make that work, never mind the mana quantity, are beyond even you. Basically, you can't go anywhere because your space aspect is bullshit."

He laughs humorlessly. "Lillith, I have been using space mana for longer than you've been alive. I know how space works," he replies.

"You thought you knew how space works," I correct him. "Now you know you were wrong. Even if you can get it to work, it's going to take a lot more out of you."

He shakes his head. "You think I will just take your word for it? How would you even know that? An apprentice telling me my aspect is wrong isn't going to break it, Lillith," he retorts.

"Yeah. Yeah, it will. Maybe not entirely, but doubt and mana aspects don't mix well. And here's the thing. You and I share a fatal weakness. A weakness a lot of people have paid for in blood, I think," I reply, gesturing to the ruined city behind me. Godfrey looks down toward the palace with some trouble of his own on his mind.

"We are friends, of a sort. We respect each other. We want to believe in each other on some level," he guesses. "We will gamble on what the other does. Is that what you mean?"

I nod, then grimace and hazard my own guess. "You tried to get the circle to work, didn't you?" He looks down in guilt. "Well. Did you?" He shakes his head.

"I managed to fake it. To fool the other nobles. By using it on a stone tablet, and enlisting priests to stop it from destroying itself. It made for a good show. But no. It never truly worked," he answers honestly. "How did you get it to work for you?"

I shrug. "I'm not sure. I kind of didn't. It's sort of been killing me lately. Just a delayed reaction for some reason."

He rubs the back of his head. "So it really was hopeless all along," he responds. "I've been a fool. A coward. As terrible a king as all who came before me."

"Kings always are," I say. It breaks my heart to know he actually did what I thought he might. So reckless. So . . . evil. He's always had a little of that noble entitlement, just under the surface. I remember the anger that used to bubble up at the wrong joke. But I still wanted to believe in him. He was my friend. But now . . . now he is just another king who needs to die. Still. Ed is still alive, it seems. We have a moment. "I don't suppose you have another wineskin on you?" I ask.

He laughs, pulling just that out of his robe, and tosses it to me. I catch it easily, only slightly aided by force mana, and open it to take a drink.

"I don't suppose you have a Danish?" he counters. I chuckle.

"Sorry, had it in my other hand," I reply before tossing the skin back to him for his own drink. "So. What's it do?"

He looks wearily at the staff, which is still standing upright entirely on its own. "It sets things right. Or so I'm told. Grants a deeply held desire. A wish, if you will. I remember your fondness for fairy tales. It has a century's worth of divine magic stored in it. All to set things straight. To bring my people back to Potestia. To make it whole again. It will cost me my life. But it will make my country whole again. And leave Dominic in charge to heal it," he answers.

I sniff. "We never should have been friends, should we?" I ask. "Look what it's left us with. What it's done to the people around us. Both of us, so desperate to convince the other to change something they never will. And here we are. You know I can't let you do this, right?"

He nods as he moves close to me, this time handing me the wine instead of tossing it. I take another drink. "But I still have to do it, you understand. You're right. I can't flee. But it doesn't matter. It's already started. It will protect me from you until it's done. That's what they told me anyway. I'm sorry. I know you believed you were helping. But look out there. You are as dangerous as I am. This country is better off whole, and without either of us in it." He finishes by holding a hand out, and I return his wine.

"So why did you stop when I showed up?" I question.

He smiles at me. "We have a weakness, you and I," he echoes.

I nod. "So it will stop me from harming you, will it? And what if I try to use it instead?" I ask.

"I . . . don't know." His eyebrows try to reach his hairline. "But I won't stop what I am doing, even if you do. And it will kill us both," he replies uncertainly.

I look up at the sky for a moment. There are specks of ash in the air from my last fight. Then I look over my shoulder at the ruined city. Finally, I shrug and hop down, landing painfully on my makeshift legs. I look skeptically at Godfrey for a moment, then try to pick him up with force mana. Light flickers from the staff, dissipating my mana before it reaches him.

"Well, fuck. Had to try," I lament. Then I wrap my one hand around the staff. "I guess we are going to see what happens." Godfrey looks at me with glassy eyes before hobbling over and placing his hand just above mine.

"Goodbye, Lillith," he says. "Thank you for giving me my life back, for a while. I'm sorry I was a disappointment afterward."

"Goodbye, Godfrey," I reply. "I wish . . . different choices had been made. Maybe in another life, we can be a different kind of friend. People who have any right caring about each other."

"Do you think there are other lives, after this one? Doesn't seem like the sort of thing you would believe."

"Yeah, well. I have a good feeling about this one."

We both begin to pour our wills into the relic. The light returns, divine magic enveloping us both. I feel the discomfort of his will, but also the familiarity of my own. I immediately know the answer to my question. I can feel it, and so can Godfrey. Only one "wish" will be granted. It's not like a genie either. It won't bring back the dead or grant eternal life. But it will allow one of us, whoever wins this battle of wills, to bend the world a little.

The vision Godfrey pours into it is ambitious. All the refugees from Potestia returned. Healthy. Safe. But here, and under the rule of Dominic. And me, gone. I suppose he doesn't need that bit anymore. I don't think either of us is likely to walk away from this alive. But the magic responds to the intent. I feel it all around me like a thousand leeches. Again I see flashes of the changes he tries to make in the world. Kallon is dead, I see that with my own intent. I need a counter wish. Something to direct my will toward.

I can't bring back the dead. I don't need the buildings back. No. Kallon and Darian are dead. Dominic . . . Dominic seems to be with Ed. Something tells me I don't want him gone. I'd like to help save the injured, but as I try to push that will, I realize my chances of winning dwindle. I need something smaller. Something easier to focus on than Godfrey's vision. Otherwise, it will be too close a call, too large a gambit.

There is one thing I want. One thing that fits. Someone. Godfrey's intent has to span the entire globe. It has to take the will away from thousands of people. Mine is far simpler. Mine is focused on a single woman, in a single town. He pushes, and

I push back. I watch him age before my eyes and wonder if I am doing the same. I don't feel like I am. I wonder if that means I am winning or losing.

I see the life draining from him, when suddenly the hatch leading to this tower opens and Ed pops out. Godfrey and I both look at him, neither of us able to stop what we are doing. Once Ed makes it up, probably responding to the same spectacle and feeling I did, he turns and waits. A moment later, Dominic appears, propelled by wind magic. He, too, is missing an arm. Is there something in the fucking water or what?

"Grandfather," he immediately calls. "Grandfather, stop this. Stop this now!" Godfrey turns to look at him, but his will remains just as strong. "I won't be king, and I think you know you can't be either. Grandf—Grandpa, it's over. Please. I . . . I saw how you fought in that battle. I know what you did to make it happen. We've already failed our dreams for the future. We have to let this go." That's all it takes. My will starts rapidly overtaking Godfrey's. The vision Godfrey was projecting starts to go dark with a few words from his grandson.

Godfrey looks over at Dominic with a weary, hopeful smile. "I know. I know I can't be king. I know I am a disappointment. I am so, so sorry, Dominic. But you . . . you can be. You can be better than me. You *are* better than me. When I'm gone . . . when the people are back, you can be the king I failed to be. You can heal the damage Darian and I have done," he pleads. His vision of the future grows a little brighter, until tears run down Dominic's cheeks and he shakes his head.

"No," he replies. "No, I can't either. Don't you see? I wasn't any better than you out there. I let people get hurt because of my overconfidence. Because of my lack of attention. Because of my failures. I killed a man, same as you. A man on my side, who trusted me. Maybe the reason was different. But that makes no difference to him. He is still dead, because he counted on my power to keep him alive and I got overwhelmed too easily."

Godfrey begins to look more desperate. "But ruling the kingdom won't be a battle, and you are a good man. Every man makes mistakes. Every woman. That doesn't mean we should give up!" His control over the future begins to waver and I keep pushing. I can see in Dominic's eyes that he is not going to be king. I don't need to say a word. Godfrey and I are having our own silent conversation via the Nexus.

"But that's the problem. I would rule the same way I fought. I haven't lived the lives of our people. That's what I was missing in that fight. I am still a child. I didn't understand the fear everyone else felt. I didn't even understand Kallon's anger. Your apprentice is right. We will never win a better future from a richly decorated throne. People in the streets count on our understanding of their lives to survive. They count on our empathy. On our decisions, so clouded by the insulation of our own safety. One bad day, and a life can end because of my decree. Another man on the end of my spear because I got overwhelmed. A kingdom can't sit on the foundation of a single man. And if *I'm* the best option they have? When it was my turn to stop the end of a city, I couldn't do it. Let it go. Maybe it's time to give this woman's vision a chance." Dominic gestures toward me. "Maybe the people should build their own better future."

Godfrey's tears flow more freely. His wrinkles deepen as the reality he is trying to create crumbles into dust and only my will remains on the relic. He fixes his eyes on his grandson and smiles. "Thank you, Dominic," he says. "I am glad you are safe. I love you."

It's as easy as that. Dominic doesn't want to be king, and Godfrey's vision for the future collapses. I feel his life draining out of him as he resigns himself to failure. I can see it in his eyes. It's not a sorrowful resignation. With his grandson's change of heart, Godfrey's regrets die, and he slumps against the staff before letting it go and crumpling to the ground in a weary heap. He looks between me and Dominic. He looks like he has one final thing to say, but his lip quivers, unable to vocalize whatever it is, until his last breath leaves his chest and the quivering stops. He is dead. It hurts, but it's a relief as well. Because, well. I would have had to kill him. He started as my friend, but he became something too dark to leave alone. He needed to die. And I needed to kill him. It sucks that it hurts anyway. I hate when I love people who hurt other people. I have to try not to think about it.

I try to withdraw my own will, but it's too late. It's already working. I look over at my brother and my friend's grandson. Then I shrug, just before I feel myself fall into the world like the ground is water. There is nothing but bright color and confusion for several moments . . . but I don't die. Instead, I find myself exactly where I have wanted to be for a long time. No longer in Visenar. Instead, I am in the Kingdom of Endings.

CHAPTER FIFTY-FOUR

Sapphic Murder Power Couple

April

I hurry toward the prison where Sarafyna is being held. Something is very wrong. Finally, *finally*, Rune has left. The sage breathing down our necks is gone. He seemed irritated and resigned when he left. Whatever he wanted from our prisoner, he clearly didn't get it. Considering the child is supposedly some sort of government higher-up, he waited here far longer than I would have thought reasonable. Far longer than I had expected. I was growing to worry he actually would get through to the girl.

Even when he did leave, I could feel his reluctance. Well, it's no surprise he failed. The girl lived alone in the Radiant Woods for years, I'm told. She is a stubborn one, nearly as stubborn as Lillith herself. It makes sense the two would form an unnatural relationship with each other. We needed Rune's help to capture her, but once that was done . . . he became a danger to us. Rune leaving was a weight off my shoulders . . . for an hour, anyway. Until the guards on the woman's cell failed to check in at an appropriate time. It's not impossible one of them fell asleep. But the timing. The timing is too suspect.

I can't help but worry Rune has somehow taken her with him. I don't understand how his magic works, other than it being similar to that of the Collector's priests. I've been growing more and more worried about this the longer he insisted upon staying in the kingdom. I knew he would have to leave eventually, but the more obvious his interest in Sarafyna became, the likelier it was he would try to take her with him. His interest certainly helps explain the extent to which they were willing to help us. But we need her. We need her to help us travel to Potestia and back. To truly be a kingdom. I am in no hurry, which is my greatest advantage over Lillith and Rune. But I need her to still be here if I want to persuade her over time.

As I turn the last corner between buildings, I can hear some commotion in the direction of the center of town. Two guards nearly knock into me as they rush by. I consider changing course to follow them, but . . . Rebecca knows where I am going; she will deal with this. Besides, as much as I hate to admit it, Lillith, the damn child, got in my head. Every time I have visited Sarafyna for a month, the hairs on the back of my neck have risen. A nameless anxiety grips me when I am alone in the room with her. Lillith's talk was all just bluster, I know that. But . . . "time to scream" is what she said Sara would offer. I just can't get it out of my head. I jump at shadows. I wake up covered in sweat. I feel so foolish. But I do, nevertheless, feel compelled to make sure she hasn't escaped.

Inside the prison, I descend the stairs to the underground cell and gasp as I reach the bottom. I was worried Rune had taken her with him. Now . . . now I am forced to hope he has. The door has been . . . shredded like paper. The steel door. Even worse, whatever tore through it seems to have caught one of the guards as well. His body is now in three separate pieces, discarded in a pool of blood and twisted metal. "Time to scream," she said. *Time to scream.* I have to hope Rune did this before leaving. I spend a long moment deciding whether to flee now or check if the cell is empty. I know someone has to, but all my instincts tell me to turn and run as far as I can.

But I have to. I have to know. I don't know what is going on upstairs, but I have to check. If it is something serious, having Sarafyna loose will only make it worse. But we have been increasing her poison dosage steadily. She should be incapacitated. I have to trust she has been incapacitated. I have to look. I take one step forward, then another. I grimace as I take my first step in the blood. There is dirt and gristle floating in it and I am soon to lose my lunch. But I do eventually make it to the door and peer inside.

It looks empty. Completely black and cold. No sign of movement whatsoever. I sigh in relief. Rune took her. He killed that guard. She is probably long gone by now. I am safe. It's fine. I am safe. *Time to scream.* The words echo in my head and my heart beats faster. The hall around me goes black as well, and I take a sharp breath. There is a flicker of white in the corner of my eyes and I jerk to look in the direction I came from. I can't see anything; the entire hall is now pitch-black. That doesn't make sense. The stairs aren't far, and it is daylight outside. Some light should be making it down here, even if all the torches went out at once.

Then I see it. A smile. It is wide, brilliantly white, and it stands out against the dark background. Like it is the only source of light. My breathing speeds up. There is another smile, this one with too many teeth. Another appears a moment later with razor-sharp, pointed teeth. And another, and another. One even has mandibles like a massive spider. All of them seem to glow in a way I don't understand. Until they all start speaking at once. As they open, I can see the light and the stairs on the other side, through the mouths. As the light reaches me, I see what I am facing. It is like a wall of flesh, covered with strange seams where I think it may open in some way. The speaking mouths are the only vaguely human feature about it. Well, them and the auburn hairs dispersed throughout.

I take a step back and trip, falling into the pool of blood, and retch as I panic and attempt to crawl away. As I desperately try to think of a way to escape this . . . horror, "She will give you time to scream" is all that fills my mind.

Lillith

I am in the Kingdom of Endings. I have somehow manifested in the town center, and there are shocked, horrified, and mildly disgusted faces all around me. I'm a bit surprised myself. For one, I am, notably, not dead. I'm fairly certain you staff was supposed to kill me. It killed Godfrey, and my man's wish went decidedly unanswered. That thought reignites a confusing cocktail of emotions, and I decide catching up on my current situation is more important. It didn't kill me like it was supposed to. Well, either that or I am an incredibly lively corpse. All right, a slightly more lively corpse than average. It's been a long day. Either way, my money is on *I'm not dead*, which is usually a safe bet for anyone capable of making it.

So the staff is apparently not always so deadly. Perhaps it is the relative size of my wish when compared to Godfrey's. He was trying to steal thousands of people from their homes, all across the continent. I just wanted a girlfriend. A specific girlfriend, and a pretty fucking amazing one, but still. It wasn't a big ask. Although, I suppose an argument could be made that since mine was . . . sort of granted and his wasn't, I had the greater *outcome*.

But not dying wasn't the only surprising result. I didn't want to come to the Kingdom of Endings. I was sacrificing my life in a battle of wills with an old friend and powerful enemy. I needed a strong but focused desire to push against his. Actually visiting the Kingdom of Endings? I'm a pretty persuasive bitch sometimes, but I don't think I could sell that as desirable, even to myself.

No, I wanted to bring Sara home. The wish I was pushing with everything I had was for Sara to be brought to safety. I mean, I guess firing me at the Kingdom of Endings like a particularly attractive torpedo might count in a way, but . . . I don't know. This is like the IKEA of genies. Wish granted, some assembly required. I guess I have to hope someone sets the relic aside for when I'm back. I will either study it or give it a stern talking-to about this "quiet quitting" attitude. For now, people are responding to my presence.

About a dozen guards, some in uniform and others only holding weapons and armor over civilian clothes, circle around me. Spears, pikes, bows, and of course mana threaten me from all directions. I, on the other hand, am three-fifths the woman I once was and am standing on painful slabs of steel held in place by blood-greased braces. The guards part so one of the stewards can approach me. Rebecca gapes at me with wide eyes. They all have whisper spheres here, although I am not certain if my call made it through or not. I willed it to call every sphere in Potestia, and this may not count. Either way, she is clearly surprised to see me.

"Q-Queen Lillith, I see you have finally returned to us," she says, and I smirk.

"Happy to see me, I'm certain. Where is your friend?" I ask. The guards shift uncomfortably, mumbling to each other. I give them a glance but keep my focus on Rebecca.

"April is . . . seeing to a guest," she answers timidly. I tilt my head at her. "You don't look well, Queen Lillith. Are you certain you are in any shape for the, uh, conversation we were planning to have when you finally made it here? You look like you could use more than a little medical attention. Sarafyna is in good health, I trust? As long as you have her, you will be all right. Right?" She is trying to hide a threat in that, which is pretty clear. But it worked a whole lot better from an unpassable distance.

"Thank you for your concern, Rebecca. I am feeling a little under the weather, but don't worry at all. I remain perfectly capable. If I might offer a bit of a suggestion of my own, I do think you should probably suck my dick," I respond with a saccharine smile. I turn to address the guards, all of whom seem confused about whether they should be pointing weapons at me or not. "Good news, everyone," I announce. "I have no way of knowing to what extent you were all involved in abducting, imprisoning, and hurting Sarafyna. The woman I am in love with. Rebecca here was involved directly, I know that much. And so Rebecca here is about to die. The good news is, while she tried to threaten someone I love very much, she tried to do it with subtlety. Which at least implies innocence on your part. In other words, I will allow everyone but her to run the fuck away from me while I end her."

The group does falter, but no one runs right away. "You abandoned them, Lillith," Rebecca announces proudly. Or . . . proudly on the surface, anyway. A tremor in her voice reveals she is less confident than she is pretending. "I have been caring for them in your absence. Providing them the leadership you denied them. They won't abandon me now because of the wild claims of a delirious woman in need of medical attention. Queen or not."

I give her another sweet look, like a Southern housewife offering a home-cooked meal.

"I'm so sorry, I am actually talking to everyone else here right now. I'll kill you in a minute, don't worry. In the meantime, you really can just go ahead and suck my dick." Again I address the guards. "I have had a pretty shitty day. I feel like I've been through a garbage disposal. I had to watch someone I love die and felt relief about it. My mom thinks I'm a changeling, my dad tried to kill me, and you know what? I wasn't going to mention this, but fuck it. I am currently in year eleven of my longest dry spell ever, which only makes me crankier every day, and my girlfriend is chained up in a dungeon somewhere at this woman's command. The reason this woman is not already dead is because I am tired and I don't want any accidental collateral damage. So I am saying one more time: run while I kill your fucking boss."

"Lil—" Rebecca starts, but she is interrupted by a woman's agonized screaming. It cuts deep to the bone and instills a fear in everyone, even me, that abandons most after childhood. The shrieking continues until the woman creating it literally runs out of breath, her articulation of pain threatening to suffocate her. That might be a relief if it frees her from whatever is causing her to make that noise. Rebecca looks at me with unadulterated terror and I sigh. I was hoping to spare Sara from this temptation.

"Well," I finally say, "it sounds like my girlfriend is free now. And I bet you are next on her list. You have two choices. You can wait here and use these men as shields until she gets to you, or you can let them go and I will handle it. But if you want my advice? Well, I kill quickly." At this, more than half the men around us turn, then run. Only a few remain, uncertainly holding their weapons in quivering hands and crowding around my target. I keep my eyes locked on hers. As the scream picks up again, Sara apparently having allowed her victim to catch her breath, Rebecca breaks and nods.

"G-go," she says. "It's all right, you can all go." That's all it takes. The remaining guards immediately flee. "All right, they are gone. But please, before you do it, let me—"

I crush her head with force mana and lift myself up to rush in the direction of the screaming.

Sarafyna

Rune is gone. Rune is finally gone. I felt his presence fade. And I am finally strong enough to control my body again. It is time to return to Annie. To help her heal. To heal alongside her. Escaping the cell was easy enough without Rune watching and with my abilities back. They are more than back, actually. I am stronger than ever. More ready to fight than ever. I feel like I felt before Annie found me in the Radiant Woods. Angry. Tired. And I miss my home. My home with Annie I never managed to move into. I want to make these stewards pay like I want to make the priests pay.

So after I tear my way out of the cell, killing one guard with two claws and grabbing the other with a fleshy tentacle, dissolving him like a stone in acid, I wait. I wait and I watch. As I wait, I feel Annie. Fighting reality all on her own. I don't understand it, but I have to lend her my power. I wonder if she is fighting priests, Nexus mages trying to kill her. It's no matter. She can draw life from me. I give her everything she needs, and it almost feels like she is tugging on me, trying to pull me to her, but it feels dangerous. So I pull back instead, until the tension disappears and I can feel she is safe. I sigh in relief. I wish she would stop doing that, but I will see her soon.

It is maybe half an hour before a worried April comes storming down the stairs. I watch her through a dozen eyes as I slither across the ceiling; I watch as she debates whether to check on me or flee. I watch as she worries about her dirty shoes. I watch as she sighs in relief when she fails to find me. And I move. I drip from the ceiling like grease and make a curtain of flesh across the exit, throwing her into complete darkness. I am so furious. And I feel sick. Sick because I am angry and . . . sick because I am excited. I am looking forward to making her pay.

I can't help but smile. And smile again, and again, and again. Different mouths form across my body, all grinning at the woman before me. The woman who hurt me. The woman who left Annie without me. I can't help but smile with everything

I am as she cowers before me. I open my mouths to speak. Only some of them are capable, but all of them move. They let the light behind me through and cast shadows of a thousand teeth on April's terrified face. She falls into the blood she was so reluctant to step in.

"I hate this about myself, you know?" I say. "I don't want to want to hurt you. I don't want to picture what I am about to do to you as I try to sleep. I don't want to wonder if it is simply too far. But you . . . you locked me up again. I hate being trapped. I hate being alone. The terror that I'll never see my loved ones again. The taunting and the smirks from the people who took me from a time when I was happy. I can't bear it. I couldn't bear it once, and I can't bear it twice. The cruelty. The manipulation. The sickness. And you knew. You knew I had been through this before. That I was only able to cope with it because of the tools Annie taught me. You knew. You knew I relied on a feeling of absolute safety just to sleep. Just to avoid visiting that lonely hopelessness with every waking moment."

She is begging me for something. Pleading. Apologizing. She doesn't even see the blood anymore. She doesn't care. She just wants to be spared. Well. So did I.

"And then there is Annie. Or, I'm sorry, Lillith," I continue. As I do, tendrils of flesh creep along the ground and wrap around her ankles, forcing a terrified whimper from her.

"I'm sorry, I just . . . I'm sorry, please . . ."

"Lillith. A woman you knew I was in love with. Who needed me. That was the line you really shouldn't have crossed. She was in pain. She was dying. She was desperate, and she needed me. Over and over again she went to bed suffering. Over and over again she died. And she didn't have to. But you wanted to use me. You wanted to own me. You wanted me to help you like she was helping you. Because you wanted to be a little queen of a little kingdom." I drag her across the floor, and she rolls over, desperately trying to crawl away from me. I keep dragging. Teeth, nails, talons, and claws all sprout from the same place at the bottom of my curtain. Right where I am dragging her. They begin to click against each other and gnash with a wet squelching sound.

"I am going to make you hurt like you let her hurt," I growl as I drag her. She starts to scream. I haven't even started and she screams like she is in more agony than I have ever been in. How dare she? How dare she act like this fear is anything like what she put me through? What she put Lillith through? As I slowly pull her, she continues to struggle, screaming all the while. She screams until her voice goes hoarse and she flails so much she slams her own head against the cement floor. I pause for a moment, something itching at the back of my mind. No. She deserves this. She deserves it. She hurt Annie and me so much. And she did it for nothing.

I begin to pull again, and she finds her breath, continuing her desperate scream as she gets closer, and closer, and closer to an agonizing death. But it doesn't feel satisfying. It doesn't feel vindicating. Then she looks back at me, and I see blood running down her face, over her left eye. I pull a little more, until she is so close to the death I have prepared for her. The death that will make this whole kingdom regret hurting us.

But the cut . . . I let out a frustrated scream, my voice joining hers . . . and I stop. I return to my actual body, filling out the dress I have been dragging along inside me. April is sobbing in front of me and I want to cry with frustration. Instead, I extend one arm toward her in the shape of a massive crab claw, and I sever her head in a single move.

Finally, I turn to ascend the stairs and find Annie at the top, staring down at me with watering eyes. And I feel so relieved I didn't follow through, at least all the way, with what I was going to do. I don't want Annie to see me like that. Enjoying someone's death.

She looks like she is in so much pain. She looks so weary. So used up. So . . . beautiful. I run to her and wrap my arms around her, then pull her into a deep kiss. It tastes of blood, but I don't care. I am just happy to hold her again. To be free. She tries to hug me back, with her single remaining arm. Finding this lacking, she instead runs her fingers through my hair and kisses me back.

It is . . . sweaty. It's bloody. It should be disgusting. It's the happiest I have ever been. "I love you, Annie. I love you so much. I missed you so much," I finally gush as soon as we come up for air.

"I love you too," she replies with the warmth of the sun after months underground. "Let's go home."

I am about to agree when a dark worry clouds my mind.

"How . . . how did you get here? Did you meet . . . anyone strange?" I ask. I have half a feeling I know. That strange feeling from before. Like a rival Nexus mage was trying to spend life Lillith didn't have. The way I pulled her toward me when I felt it, and the rival mage seemed to agree with my intent. She looks at me with slightly narrowed eyes before deciding to take the question at face value and answer.

"No one in particular. It's a long story, and one I don't even understand. I'll tell you when we get back," she says, and I nod. It's the answer I needed. She didn't meet Rune. She didn't hear anything she shouldn't need to worry about.

"All right. Let's go home."

CHAPTER FIFTY-FIVE

One Mistake

Leo

The world shifts around us as Charlotte and I stumble to the ground together. We entered the woods through a tree line, but we land in a field of chrysanthemums. The pink, yellow, and orange flowers expand in all directions before any taller foliage presents itself again. Immediately, everything Lily has ever told me about the Radiant Woods collapses like an inescapable wave over my mind. No. I can't be here. I can't be here. Anywhere but here. My entire body tenses with the fear of being hit, my skin aching with the anticipation of pain. It will take my mind. It will take me from me. I can't be here!

"Where are they?"

My body aches and I can feel my heart pulsing in my head. My skin itches. Every fear I have ever had is contained in this field, and I can feel its breath hot on my neck. I wait to lose control. I wait to lose everything.

"Where are they, no no no no, where are they?"

I wait, and I wait, and I wait. And . . . nothing happens. No one takes my body from me. Nothing happens at all, until Charlotte's hands grasp my shoulders and pull me back into reality. "Leo, where are they?" she pleads, and I look around, still shaken.

"Where are what?" I respond, my heart still beating from the curiously missing control of the woods. I can barely process my environment, much less the question.

"The others!" she insists. "Where are the others who fell in here with us?" This immediately forces my mind to focus and scan the environment. Only Charlotte and I are here. Charlotte, me, and the flowers.

"We have to find them," I agree immediately. Questions about Charlotte's choices can wait. I don't know why the woods aren't hurting me. The woods aren't controlling me, but we have allies here who don't deserve what will happen to them if we don't find them. I do what I have been forced to do my entire life, what Charlotte has been forced to do her entire life: I push the fear down. I strangle it. And we begin to move. To make sure everyone else is safe and comfortable. To prioritize them over ourselves. As soon as Charlotte points out their disappearance, we no longer have to communicate before we begin to search together.

We have no way to know where we came from, much less where anyone else might have gone. We don't even know how long we will have the freedom to search. But one thing is certain. Charlotte can protect these people better than they can protect themselves. I don't question why she wants to. I can't process why she has done what she's done, but I still know her. She is still the only mother I have ever wanted. And she doesn't want them trapped in the Radiant Woods any more than she wants me here. Any more than she wants to be here herself. So we run. We shout. We call out for them.

No matter how far we go, we never escape the field of flowers. As I look around, I realize we haven't even escaped the center of the meadow. One look at Charlotte and I can see in her eyes she has realized the same. We can't leave the spot we are in. It feels sickly familiar. This field. This spot that was chosen for us, that we can't escape no matter what we do. Something inside me rejects this. Calls it a lie. A perversion of reality to be dismantled. I press back against that feeling. It won't serve me here. My skin itches. "What do we do?" I ask in desperation. But Charlotte's eyes are wide, afraid, heartbroken. She covers her face with her hands.

"I . . . It wasn't supposed to happen like this. It wasn't supposed to . . ." She trails off. She doesn't have an answer any more than I do. But . . . maybe she never has. I've always known Charlotte has struggled with everything I have. The walls, constantly closing in on both of us. But . . . I've always had her. Since we first met, I have had somewhere to look for a solution. For safety. Just somewhere to look . . . up. But she made the wrong choice, so . . . where do I look now? I look into her panicked eyes and realize there is nothing I can do. I scratch my face, grip my head, and sit down in the flowers. That resistance inside me bends again, like thin wood under too much weight. I scratch my face again.

Charlotte sits down next to me, silent but for her heavy breathing. We are probably never leaving the Radiant Woods. We aren't saving the others. We aren't going anywhere. We aren't going anywhere, ever. The only people who can get us out are either chained in some cellar somewhere or walking into a trap. I want to sob. I want to puke. The wood bends in my soul. My skin itches. The only thing we can do now is talk.

"Why?" I ask quietly. I hear Charlotte's breath catch. "Please. It doesn't matter now. But still, I need to know."

She is silent for a long time. That bending feeling is back. My skin itches. I push it down. I scratch my face.

"One mistake," Charlotte finally answers. "You know what I mean. You know exactly what I mean. One mistake. That is one mistake more than we are allowed to make. Back in Potestia. Back with Lillith's friends. Anywhere we go, no matter how we are treated, we will always live one mistake away from rejection. From disgust. From hatred, and from being disposed of. I have known many people, in power and otherwise, who make mistakes. Major ones. Minor ones. They will do it day after day, and laugh with those affected in the next breath.

"Because most people are allowed to make mistakes. Most people don't live lives of borrowed tolerance. Waiting until their friends, families, and allies turn on them. Waiting until something goes wrong and everyone in the room looks to them as the easiest target to blame. The easiest to reject and cast out. Waiting until everyone who despises them finally finds an excuse. But you and I do. And this is true no matter where we go. No matter what we do. Leo, we have to do what it takes to survive."

I sit in that for a moment. That bending feeling increases under the pressure of her words.

"I know that. But . . . I can't accept it," I respond. "Because it's wrong. It's so sick, and twisted, that people should be allowed to do this to us. To make us fear . . . everything. That's why I was willing to fight. To fight alongside the people who see us as people. As who we are. For a new, better world where people don't have to feel that way anymore. I thought maybe, just maybe, we could earn one mistake. We could take it. I want so, so badly for the mistake that *they* made to be putting that weight on us. Turning on us should have been their one mistake. That tears them down from their thrones. And we had a chance, Mom. We had a chance. People willing to make that happen. To stand side by side with us. I wanted it so badly." Already I've accepted the failure of that plan. It's too late now. The pressure builds. The wood bends. My skin itches.

"Lillith was going to fail," Charlotte responds. "I've been alive a long time, Leo. I've fought with everything I have to be everything I am for a long time. It's a miracle I was born with enough mana to justify my existence to the people around me. But I know what we are up against. I have been up against it my entire life. She was going to fail, whether I did something or not. And she was going to drag so, so many people down with her. All of them were going to die. Her family. Her friends. My son. All of you were going to die fighting for a world that will still reject us. That will still be waiting for that one mistake.

"I saw what was coming. I knew how it would end. I love Lillith. I love Sara," she says earnestly. "I love what they tried to do for me. I don't want to see them hurt, abandoned, or dead. I don't want to see you dead alongside them. So I made a friend. Someone who could stop this without bloodshed. Who could, and would, forgive them for everything, so long as the country stands. Because *Lillith* is allowed one mistake. And you are not. Lillith is allowed revenge for the wrongs done to her, and you are not. And Lillith started all of this by taking revenge. For you. And that's the thing about our one mistake, Leo. We don't have to be the ones to make it. If it happens near us, we will still be the ones who pay the most. She was—is—going to lose. I'm sorry; I wish it wasn't the case. But it is. And they were going to kill you for it."

She struggles to continue despite a trembling jaw. "So I made a friend, to buy your life. To buy everyone's lives. You. Lillith. And everyone who comes after us. Godfrey wants change too. Not enough. Never enough. But he's been putting the pieces together for a new world for a long time. A world that we can actually win.

A world where you and I have the power to make one mistake. One where *everyone* has the power to make one mistake. The power to defend themselves when the world tries to punish them for stepping out of line. I believe in that world, Leo. And I think Lillith would too, if she could just *see* it. And she will. Because Godfrey loves her, and he needs her people. No one has to die. No one has to get hurt. No one has to pay for a mistake their friends made for them."

As her words wash over me, things slide into place. Charlotte's desperation to turn everyone around. To prevent today's plan from happening. The way she tried to use Ed as an excuse, and the way she failed to show relief when the truth came to light. She wanted to stop the violence and buy a peaceful end to things. But it still wasn't right. I understand what she is saying, but . . . "I heard what he called you. Your friend. The one who will let us make mistakes. The one you report to so we can have that future. It wasn't your name, Mom. It wasn't a name anyone who cares about you would ever speak," I say.

Charlotte winces. "That was only Ansel, Godfrey's aide. Godfrey would never speak that name. I trust him, Leo."

"But that's the thing. Godfrey's aide. It tells the whole story. Godfrey would never do that to you. Never. But the person closest to him feels perfectly comfortable doing it, doesn't he? That's the entire trade. A world where we have the power to defend ourselves. Most of the time. But we still don't get to be welcome. We still don't get to be loved. Our great benevolent leader would never hurt us; he will only allow his friends to do it without consequence," I throw back.

"That will always be the case," Charlotte counters. "Even here. I was called *he* the very moment I stepped out of line! It will always be there, just under the surface, no matter where we build our homes. There will always be sneers behind our backs. And if we can't change that . . . the power to defend ourselves from more than sneers is more important than ever."

The world bends. My skin itches.

"Yes. There will always be sneers," I say. "People who hate us. If we change our bodies. If we change our clothes. If we change our names. There will always be someone who hates us. Who wants us gone. Who will take their mask off and snarl the moment we make that one mistake. But it makes a difference whether or not those people are welcome! It makes a difference what kind of mistake we are allowed to make. Because I don't want turning the wrong corner on the wrong night to be my mistake ever again. I don't want trusting the noble who promised me safety to be my mistake ever again. And if a man who calls you by a name you discarded is welcome? If he is welcome, then we will never be," I cry.

"I know!" Charlotte agrees. "I know that! I hate it. I hate him. It hurts me, Leo. It hurts me every single time. It's like bathing in sewage! Every time I hear it, it's like a sliver of flesh is torn from me. But I have carried this pain all my life, and I will carry it for the rest of it if I have to! I will let them call me by old, dead names. I will let them tear that skin bit by bit and call me whatever foul things they need to, so long as I can build my way to a world where they call you Leo! And they will never give us that world. We have to take it. We have to have the power to take it. Lillith's ideas are lovely, they are. And I wish we lived in a world where they would work. But they are too dangerous. Too much of a gamble. They only offer a *chance* at a world where my son can be himself and use his name safely. I need certainty. I need you to be safe, and I will suffer through anything to make that happen." She buries her face in her hands. And I believe her.

The world bends. My skin itches. I scratch at my face. I turn to look at her, but she keeps her face hidden. "I love you, Mom. I love that you care for me so much. But . . . you already know where that falls apart. Even if you can keep me safe, even if you can keep every wolf and all their teeth out of my throat, I still won't be safe. No safer than you have been. I've seen it in your eyes. You always push through, but . . . these boxes they try to force us into . . . they're dark. They are oppressive. They close in on you. If you behave exactly as they want, they change the rules. I could go to school as a man, so long as I kept to myself. I could call myself Leo, but I had to stay in the women's dorms. I could wear whatever I wanted, but I had to call myself a woman. I played along, and they changed the rules.

"I followed the new rules, and they changed them again. Until they were tired of warning me and I ended up broken and bloody in the dirt. Because they never really changed the rules. The rule was always *Be who and what we demand or we will hate you. We will hurt you. Stop living as who you are, or stop living.* You may be able to build a world where they can't safely beat me. But this method will never build a world where I am safe. Because the walls will always close in.

"And you know what it's like, standing on that precipice." I reach a tentative hand toward her knee. "Giving those concessions. It will kill me, Mom. You know what I mean. Living in the world you chose will kill me. And maybe you're right. Maybe what I want to fight for with Lillith will be the same. But it carries the hope that it won't be. And I need that hope, or I will die," I say, nearly losing my breath as I try to force the words out.

Charlotte looks up at me with red eyes.

"I know. I know. I know. But what else can I do? She's going to lose, Leo! She is going to die and they are going to punish you for it! Unless I can buy your lives. I know it's not enough! I know I can never do enough to make you safe! It feels like ice under my skin, but I had to do what little I could anyway! Don't you understand? Don't you see? I have done all of this before! I have known Lilliths before. I have had friends, and allies, and loved ones, and I have fought! I have fought and fought and fought. I have tried and pushed. It ends the same way. It always ends the same way. With a beaten girl, taken from her family. With fathers hurting their daughters. With death, Leo. With so much death. I have seen too many hopeful corpses. I have been forced into the ground too many times," she sobs.

Charlotte has never shared any of this with me before. She has never spoken of her past like this. I always knew she must have struggled, but the fear in her words is so . . . visceral. The loss. "I thought . . . I thought I was the first . . ." I respond weakly.

She shakes her head. "No. All my life they have been taking. Every time I stick my head out too far. I have seen it again, and again, and again. They will always win. They will always be just a little more brutal than we can be. Just a little more powerful. And everyone who fights it dies. Everyone but me. And Lillith . . . Lillith is bringing so many people into it. Do you know how terrifying that is? Seeing so many people heading toward a bloody end, knowing they are all going to die? I had to save them, Leo. I had to save you. And I had to save Lillith. I just want everyone to be okay. I just want them to be okay. I can't see one more hopeful corpse, much less thousands. I know why you all want to do it this way. But you are going to die if you do! That's just how the world is built! That's reality!" She weeps. I can't accept it. The world bends. My face itches.

"Thank you, Mom. I know you are kind. I know you hurt whenever any of us hurt. I . . . I didn't know about the rest. I can feel what it must have done to you, and I want to learn more. If you didn't feel this, down in the deepest reaches of your soul, you would never have given up on what Sara and Lily could help you with. Or maybe you still would. Because that is who you are. Someone who will hurt for her entire life so the people you love don't have to. Lily reminds me of you, in that way. I do understand how we got here. I even admire you for it. I love you. I do.

"But no. No. That's not reality. That's a lie. A lie they built and call reality. It's no more real than the words they nail to our bodies when we are born, and it's no more real than the names they force us to carry. That's *their* reality and it is a lie! It's like this forest. A distortion. A perversion. Reality as it looks to people who have grown sick with their own love of control. Lily isn't going to lose. Even now. And a world where we are just treated as people is real. It's real. It is reality, because we are real!" I shout.

And the pressure grows too much. The bending wood in my soul breaks, and in an instant, the flowers around me wilt, dissolve, and disappear. My face itches.

If the Radiant Woods are the manifestation of people who control reality, I will be their opposite. I will scrub their will from every corner of the map. I touch my face. It has a roughness to it as tiny hairs have started to grow. My skin itches like rain in a drought.

CHAPTER FIFTY-SIX

Equivalent Exchange

I groan as I wake up in a familiar bed. The world is blurred around me as I try to get my bearings. The last thing I remember is speaking with Sara. She was expanding the roads to her hat shop and we were discussing what it should be called. Nothing fancy like *the Radiant Woods*, just *the hat shop*. That's how she thinks of it. Not as an impossible extradimensional space entirely in her control, just as her hat shop. This is incredibly cute, truth be told. In fact, the last thing I remember is considering how furiously attractive that was, and . . . I must have passed out. I suppose the moment of relaxation was the opportunity my body needed to force rest. Sara must have princess carried my ass back here.

But . . . I wasn't done. There were so many people all across the country I could still have helped. My brothers, for one. Visenar needed more than a little attention. Yeah, I managed the violent bits, but there is a lot more work to do than that. I suppose I was in no shape for it. Sara made the right call.

I rub my bleary eyes with both hands as the world starts to take shape. The hats Sara has given me, hanging all on one wall. The black-and-purple comforter. My desk with unfinished enchantment designs. I am home. Moonlight fills my room, and I feel well rested for the first time in a long time. To my left, Ed is asleep in a chair while Clarrise writes in a notebook to my right.

"Evening," I say, and she smiles without looking at me.

"Glad to see they are working for you. Dominic said the new circle interfered with his control, but I had a feeling you'd be all right. You have a tendency to break the rules with these things," she replies.

"Huh?" I ask, rubbing the back of my neck as I sit up. "What do you mean? No, never mind that, what happened in Potestia? How many people made it back safely? I need to go back."

She shakes her head. "One thing at a time. We need to see how your body responds to the prosthetics first. Your body was in pretty bad shape when you got back, and you are remarkably resistant to Sarafyna's healing. Now, wiggle your toes for me. Can you feel them?" she asks, stopping me from climbing out of bed. I pause for a moment and pull my hand from behind my head, giving it a proper look for the first time since waking up. It is . . . not my arm. At least, not my original. I mean, I guess the last one wasn't either. I am fitted with a prosthetic like the boy I saw a couple of months ago. It's . . . amazing. I channel mana through it as easily as my own flesh, and it moves with zero latency. I didn't even realize it wasn't my real arm.

I feel it, under the surface. A complex arrangement of thin metal fibers and cables simulating muscle. The top has some sort of very slightly opaque material that feels almost exactly like skin. It doesn't look like skin, but it feels like it. I lack fingernails, and I look a bit like a half-finished Terminator, but the feedback I get from it is indiscernible from my left side. "This is . . . amazing," I say.

Clarrise looks over her glasses at me.

"Toes," she reminds me. "Wiggle them."

Oh right, she did tell me to do that. As I do, I can see the slight movement under the blanket. With them covered I almost have a hard time believing they aren't real. Well. This is a slight upgrade from the little steel self-torture devices I was trying to use. The woman really was wasted teaching basic math to a bunch of kids. Magic itself has been wasted for generations. This is incredible. My prosthetics seem to run entirely off mana, and they somehow feel like they have grown into my flesh. It is not seamless, but they're legitimately part of my body now. Nice of her to bother giving me toes.

"Wiggling away," I reply, and she smiles.

"Amazing. You know, the arm we gave Dominic only worked once we removed the circle, but all of yours work perfectly. Fascinating," she muses.

That's right, she mentioned Dominic. And a circle.

"Dominic is here?" I ask. "Also, what circle?"

She begins writing furiously in her journal again as she answers. "Yes, he and your brother came back together. Seems he has decided to defect to our side entirely. The last nail in the coffin of Potestia, I suppose. The most powerful mage left alive is now standing in opposition to the monarchy. Truly amazing. As for the circle, can't you feel it?" she questions, nodding to my arm. I examine it a little but fail to see anything. Then I probe it with my mana. My arm is . . . it is gathering mana, like it is inside a circle. My right leg and left foot seem to be doing the same, just like my body. Wait . . . no, my body isn't anymore. That is strange. "Finally noticed, did you? Yes, it seems you took a severe injury to your former circle, despite the apparent thickness of your skin there. Clever doing that, but it wasn't foolproof. Your original circle has officially broken. But . . ."

"But my new . . . pieces aren't made of blood and bone," I finish. "They have never entered a circle before now. So you adapted my old circle to this new material, and are using it to gather mana where my body has stopped. That's . . . brilliant. But it shouldn't work, right? Don't you need a unique design to enchant this to work as an arm at all? How are you using it for two things at once like this?"

"Three things, actually. Ember worked with me on it. They work like your bracelets as well, balancing and gathering excess mana in your body and preventing the spread of cancer. And yes, you are right. It shouldn't work. We tried a less complex version on Dominic, and his arm simply didn't move. You are something of an anomaly. A mystery in all things. Just as we still haven't confirmed our theory of why your cancer took so long to manifest, we only have theories about why this works. I believe—and this is why I bothered to try—that it has something to do with your body remaining something of a mana space itself. We'll want to study it for a long while before you do anything dangerous," she explains.

I flex my fingers and turn my new hand around.

"A lot of guesswork for something you attached to my body while I was sleeping," I muse. "Actually, how did I sleep through all that?"

Clarrise shrugs. "Talk to Sarafyna about it on both counts. She is the one who assured Victor, Ember, and me that it was safe to do. As far as your continued sleep and consent, that is."

I want to contest this. I do love Sara, but unless I'm actually dying, she can't make that decision for me. On the other hand, I have to pause. She did answer exactly how I would have, which isn't enough on its own, but . . . I somehow managed to visit her in my sleep before. I'll ask her about it later, but maybe she did ask me somehow. It worked out this time, so I will worry about whether a boundary was crossed or not later. Right now, I need more information.

I manage to rush Clarrise through the rest of the conversation about my new prosthetics. It is interesting to learn they are actually considerably physically weaker than my organic arm while being stronger magically. But what I really want to know is what happened in Potestia.

Finally, after what feels like an hour, I get Clarrise to give me the rundown. Apparently, all things considered, we won. Visenar was the bloodiest battlefield by far, and almost every city in the country has ousted their former lord. It is only a matter of time now. The kings are gone. The support. The magic. The volunteer fighters have been relieved by people distributing food, rebuilding shelter, and establishing communication.

Visenar, however, had a death toll in the thousands. Everywhere people lived where a dispersal circle aimed at me existed, people died. It makes me sick to my stomach. So many things could have prevented this. If just a couple of them had fallen into place, I could have stopped this. But Potestia is free now. It will never be ruled by a king again.

"Where is my family? And Sara?" I finally ask. I know Ed is still sleeping a few feet from me, but I'd love to see Henry and Mom soon. And Sarafyna. The time I spent with her was far too short. I don't want to spend the next month just admiring her and giving her back rubs. Clarrise flinches.

"You've been asleep for over a day now. Unfortunately, we all had work to do in that time. Sarafyna is in the woods. The traitor . . . the traitor was Charlotte. I don't know why. But . . . Leo found out, which is the only reason you found out. There was a struggle and . . . they fell into the woods with a couple of the others. Sara is looking for them."

My heart is ice. Charlotte? Why would she . . . ? The woods? Fuck, no wonder

Sara didn't wait around. I hate the thought of her on her own again, but she would never leave them there. Not if she could get them out. I just wish I had been awake to go with her.

"Fuck" is all I can come up with.

"Lily . . ." Ed says, nearly startling my new limbs off my body. When did he wake up? "Lily, you're awake."

"Hey, Ed." I smile weakly at him. "Everything all right?"

He looks at me with a funeral in his eyes. "No," he replies coldly. "Everything is not all right. After you disappeared . . . After you disappeared, there was a lot left to do. A lot of people who still needed help. Dominic stood by me, and we both did what we could. We found as many survivors as we could, but . . . but then we found Autumn."

Autumn

The sky is on fire. Lillith is up there, fighting a man who is willing to kill us all, and I have never been more terrified.

"What does she mean about the torches?" I ask Henry nervously. "How is she going to stop this? What do the torches have to do with anything?" I am breathing heavily as we walk through the city. Henry ponders as he listens to Lillith's voice through the whisper sphere.

"Well, I don't know how she is planning on doing it, but . . . I think she is going to try to catch all of that"—he motions upward toward the swirling, red threat over the city—"before it hurts anyone. I believe she mentioned the torches using magic normally, and fire where mana was dispersed. Or rather, where the circles Godfrey put in place to catch her are drawn. If I know my psycho sister, she is considering a contest of mana up there. Come on, let's go," he says.

I look around. "But . . . the torches here use mana stones. Shouldn't we be safe?" I ask. I don't like this. Something about this feels wrong. Like bugs burrowing under my skin. I have to fight back tears I don't understand. Not the tears of my fear. Not the tears of despair. Something else.

"Yes," he agrees, "but lots of places aren't, and not everyone will hear this message. We need to warn people before it's too late." He is right. Of course he is right. I don't know what I was thinking. I look up again. I can feel the heat from here. Liquid fire, ready to kill everyone in the city, and my twin brother's hopeless crush is floating in the sky trying to catch it. It's too much. I know what this feeling is. I didn't a moment ago, but as I look up, as I feel the heat of death sear into my skin, I know exactly what it is.

"How . . . how long do you think it took Godfrey to draw these circles?" I ask.

Henry shrugs. "He used to do nothing but sit around reading romance novels and making Lillith sell his books for him. After that, he just did the same, but . . . with more money, I guess? He's had a lot of time on his hands. Still. There are a lot of them. He must have known he was going to need to capture or kill Lily for years now. Maybe as soon as he got to the capital. No other way it gets this extensive in time. Guess Lily slipped up somewhere," he says.

My heart sinks. "And all these people . . . all these people are going to die because he did it, right?" I ask. He pauses, a dark look on his face.

". . . Yeah. People are going to die because of him. But you and I can save a few. Think about that. And hey, at least we aren't being sent to collect my sister's limbs anymore," he jokes, trying to lighten my mood. It doesn't work. *People are going to die because of him. People are going to die because of him. People are going to die because of me.* I break into a sprint.

"Come on, we have to warn as many people as possible!" I scream, running ahead of him. He catches up easily, and I begin screaming through the streets as we finally reach a border where the torches change from stone to oil. "Run! Run to where the lamps are stone! It will be safe there! It will be safe!" I cry. That's all it takes for most. Everyone can feel the heat. Everyone can see the sky. It may seem like an empty promise, but many were already reluctantly wandering from their homes. Many, but not all. Lillith sent sound mana all throughout the city, but some people won't hear the warning or won't take it seriously. That is where we come in.

More and more people, farther into what must be a dispersal circle, begin to flee toward us. People are desperate for any hope at all, even one they don't understand. A mother runs toward us from too far away, holding a child in one arm and dragging another behind her with her free hand. Then it happens. The sky of fire begins to fall. I can see it. Only in the circle above us, it starts to fall. I look at the mother and her children, and my eyes bulge, but Henry is faster than me. He runs before I can even process it, into the falling death. The woman moves too slowly, held back by her struggling son.

Henry meets them halfway, scoops the second child up, and runs alongside the frantic mother. Sped up by his aid, they approach us faster, faster. The fire descends upon us; I can feel its heat trying to push me into the ground. I look back at Henry and time slows. He is practically dragging the woman now. The sky falls. Henry runs. My heart beats. Then, finally, he passes into safety a breath before the liquid fire collides with the ground. I am worried it will splash, but it cools immediately into some kind of strange stone wall. Henry is safe. So is the family. They are alive. Henry grins at me.

"Sorry to scare you!" He beams, putting the boy down as the woman next to him falls to her knees, pulling both her kids into an embrace.

"Thank you, thank you so much, thank you thank you thank you," she practically chants.

"I'm happy to help. I'm just glad you all made it. And hey, I have drugs too, if you need to relax now. I know I do," he offers. The mother is too frantic to care about his stupid jokes. I sigh. He and his sister both. Never serious enough. But . . . I appreciate it, and he knows it. I love him so much. I'm glad I met Lillith if only because I met her brother. For a moment of inappropriate silliness, I forget about all the other deaths. For a moment. The weight of it may crush me if I look back at it. For now, I just sigh and admire the man I love.

Sharp stones fly past me and Henry both, colliding with the strange wall behind him. Piercing it. Cracking it. I freeze and the entire world slows. A man I vaguely recognize runs past me. I had a class with him, I think? My mind fails to process what is happening as the boy tackles Henry into the now-cracked wall. I can't process it as it shatters behind them. Time crawls and the two men seem to swim through the air like it's molasses. Henry looks directly at me before his eyes clench shut and a lifetime of grief strangles his expression. It only lasts a moment, then his eyes are open again and he is offering me a shattered smile. *"I'm sorry,"* he mouths. Before I can even think about what he means, both disappear into the still-boiling fire beyond. I am standing still, thinking about my love for Henry, as the hot liquid again cools when it reaches the boundary of the circle.

I stare at the cold wall. Why did everything go quiet? I can't hear anything. What is going on? Where did Henry go? Why? Why is he gone now? What happened? I fall to my knees before I know why. No. No no no no no. I don't understand. I am speaking, I think. "It's my fault. It's my fault. It's my fault. It's my fault."

CHAPTER FIFTY-SEVEN

I Am Not Me

That's all she could say when I found her," Ed finishes, after recounting Autumn's story to me. "'It's my fault. It's my fault.' She was just on her knees, repeating it again and again while I was trying to find out where . . . what happened. Lily . . . Lily, I don't . . ." He fails to finish his sentence, choking through each word with labored breathing. He didn't mention Henry's name once, unable to get the word out each time he needed to. I feel like I am standing in front of a great, impassable wall. Or maybe a dam. There is a flood on the other side. Grief that will violently drown me and leave behind only a washed-up husk. And I am holding my hand up against the stone. I can feel the pressure it is holding back.

It is a monument, sturdy and impassable. It is razor-thin glass, and it will shatter with a tap of my fingernail. Ed is on the other side. Broken. Snot and tears running down his face. He's like a fish in the water, vibrant scales shimmering in the moonlight and demanding my attention, but he is insulated. Separated. The wall will not be denied. Or . . . I will not deny the wall. I am a stone staring through it. Waiting for it to break on its own. Nothing reaches me. No one. I am vaguely aware that Edward is wrapping his arms around me. Vaguely conscious of Clarrise looking guiltily away from the scene. They are both so far away. I want to pound on the glass dam. I want to feel its shards cut through me as the water carries me away. I *need* to feel the pressure and pain it promises.

I am too afraid. I am too cold. I can physically feel the grief. Boiling around me. I don't know how I missed it when I woke up. It is thick in the air like steam. Only the oceans I left behind before sleeping could disguise the lake around me now. Henry. Not Henry. A tap of a single finger would break the glass, but I watch Edward on the other side instead. I let the scene happen to me. He is reaching out to me with more than his arms, but I can't reach back. I am not here. I am not me. For some reason, I can't help but fixate on his snot, smearing against the shoulder of my nightshirt. It doesn't bother me in the way it usually would. It just . . . doesn't make sense. He is too far away.

At some point, I pull myself away limply, dig through a drawer for a new shirt, and change it. I am again clean. It makes sense again. But the dam is still there. And the water is too fast. How is it not overflowing? How could so much water be held back like this? How is it not crashing down on me? A single tap.

I don't know why. Maybe I just want to distance myself from the temptation to tap the glass. Maybe my new feet have minds of their own. Maybe I just can't breathe in this room anymore. But before I can say a word to my grieving brother, I feel myself walking toward the door, pausing, and opening it. Mom is there, standing with a tray of food in her hands. We are both motionless for a moment. I see it coming, as the tray falls to the ground. I could avoid it if she weren't on the other side of the dam. As her slap connects, I fail to register it. It too is distant. Beyond me.

She claps her hand over her mouth and watches me with glassy eyes. She speaks to me with the distorted sounds of a creature underwater. Her fists grasp onto me and pull me to her, where she begins crying into my new shirt. Ed's hand lands on my shoulder. The glass begins to crack. Just a little, right in the middle. I can't be here. I can't. I begin to walk away. Toward the quiet. Toward safety. Toward the cold. I hear voices calling after me. Feel hands trying to hold me back. But they aren't here. Not really. I am not here. I am not me.

Their hands were never really on me. They were never really speaking to me. How could they? They are on the other side. I don't notice when I pull away from them. I don't know when they stop following me. I am alone now, finally. But I haven't escaped. The wall has followed me. But the crack is no longer webbing. I wander up the stairs to the next floor, then the next, until I have reached the unused part of the building. Finally, I sit down and try to breathe. I put my hand up against the glass again. Rapids rage on the other side. I am in there with it. But I am not me. I need to feel it. I need to feel it to be me. I am grief. I have always been grief. I need to feel my own.

Steps. Soft, quiet steps. These are the only sounds I can hear. Mom's voice. Ed's sorrow. These washed over me like waves in a dream. But these footsteps. They are real. Maybe the only real thing left in the world. And they are above me. I am on an upper floor; there should be no one above me. I grasp onto this like driftwood in the middle of the ocean. I am not sure why. But following them doesn't hurt, so I do. I continue to climb. So do the steps above me. We continue our quiet chase until I emerge onto the roof. The mountains tower over us, challenging our audacity to ascend so high. Autumn isn't looking at them, however. Autumn stands on the precipice, looking down at the ground so far below.

I hear each and every breath she takes. They echo through me in a way that makes my bones ache. She is on this side of the wall with me. She is not her. The crack begins to spread as I walk up and stand beside her.

"How . . . how did you know?" she whispers.

"I didn't" is the only response I give her. "But . . . here I am."

"I'm glad you are all right," she offers after a moment of silence. I don't respond. I don't look at her. I just follow her gaze to the distant stone below. I let the silence drag until she speaks again. "Are you going to stop me?" she asks. I nod. "And if I come back to try again?"

I take a deep breath. "I suppose I'll stop you then too," I respond.

She bites her lip. "Why? Why?"

The crack spreads.

I don't know. I just know it's right. "Henry" is the only answer I have.

"It's my fault," she replies. "He is gone because of me. You couldn't protect him because of *me*. It's my fault. Do you understand that? He is dead because of me."

The crack spreads. I can hear it, in the air. *Criiick.*

"No. It's mine. You both went because you trusted me. You trusted me to protect you. To keep you safe. I failed. It's not your fault," I say. Hot water runs down her cheeks. The crack begins to leak, and I feel a trickle washing through my hair. She shakes her head and takes a half step closer to the edge.

"No, Lily. It's my fault. It's all been my fault. Henry, and everyone else who died in Visenar. It was me. I told Godfrey about you, all those years ago. After the first time we fought. I told him . . . everything. Everything you planned to do. Exactly how dangerous you were. The dispersal circles were drawn because of *me*. Because I was too scared. Because I turned on you. And because, even after I changed my mind, I didn't tell you. Do you get it? It was because of *me*. He died because of *me*. They *all* died because of *me*. You would have saved them all if not for *me*! Do you understand now, Lillith? I killed them all! Your brother is dead because of *me*!" she confesses.

My blood freezes.

More cracks appear, water bursting through holes in the dam. It pools around my feet. My hands tremble. All this time. All this time and she knew. She knew. She knew she knew she knew. I don't . . . I don't know how to process. I am not me. One hand reaches out, presses against her back, and pushes. I watch as she falls, branches of the trees shredding her skin as she passes them. She doesn't even scream. She just falls, and falls, and finally . . .

"I thought so—even you know I would be better off . . ." she finally says, pulling me from the intrusive thought. I jerk back to reality. The glass cracks, the water rises, I swallow my words. "It was me. And Henry . . ." She doesn't finish her thought, simply taking one more step, over open air. I reach out and grab her.

"No . . ." I say. "No. This . . . this is wrong, Autumn."

She looks back at me.

"I'm a murderer, Lily. I . . ." She sighs, putting her foot back for a moment. "Do you think . . . do you think he has a new life somewhere? Like you? Do you think he got to start over too?"

I pause at this, still holding her arm.

"I don't know. Maybe. I hope" is the best I can do. *Criiiick.* Henry is dead. The water is up to my waist. Henry is dead. And I'm afraid. I am terrified. I can't see the way forward and Autumn . . . Autumn is on the edge. It's her fault. It's her fault. It's her fault. I clench my fists.

"Do you think . . . I'll end up in the same place?" she asks. "Do you think I could start over and meet him again?" *No. No, you don't deserve to meet him again. You put him in danger. You let him die. You killed him.* I want her to jump.

"I don't know," I answer. "But I knew Henry. I loved Henry. This . . . this isn't what he would want. This isn't what anyone wants. You'll be leaving so many people behind. What about August? What about me? What about everyone who loves you? Are you just going to abandon them?" I plead. The glass cracks. She looks at me with pain. *Criiiick.* I will drown soon, if the water keeps rising. She leans almost imperceptibly forward. A little closer to jumping. Of course she does. Of *course* she does. You can't guilt someone out of this. I know that. So why did I . . . ? I want her to jump.

No. The glass cracks. The tides are furious and chaotic. The dam is coming apart. Autumn takes a deep breath. A preparatory breath. "Well. There are far more people I won't be letting down. Tell them, when I am gone. Tell them the one responsible for their family's death is gone. Tell them I did the right thing," she says, closing her eyes and leaning forward, almost letting herself go. I hesitate to catch her. *Criiiiick.* There are so many holes in the dam now. Torrential rain falls from the water above. Then finally, finally it breaks.

I am surrounded by rapids. I am drowning. Splinters of glass tear into me. Everything I am trying to distance myself from engulfs me at once. This is wrong. This is so wrong, what am I doing? The woman Henry loved is about to fall. She is about to die. I am me. I try to wrap my mana around her, to pull her up. But . . . it dissipates as it reaches her. I can't use it against the intent of her grief. I leap forward and wrap my arms around her instead, and she drowns with me.

"No, Autumn. No, it's not your fault. You don't deserve this. I'm sorry. I'm so sorry, I don't know what I . . . No. It doesn't matter. It is not your fault. Henry had a murderer, and I killed him. I killed the man who murdered all of them. It was no more your fault than mine. Please . . . I . . . I don't know what to say, I don't . . . I love you, Autumn. I love you like a sister. And . . . and I am you. I pushed him. I pushed him and I pushed everyone. I understand the loathing. I understand the hate. I tried to lock myself away from it, but . . . no. You tried to stop this the best way you knew how. So did I.

"But there are monsters in the world, Autumn. There are monsters in every dark corner, and we don't always know how to fight them. How to hide. Sometimes we try and we make the wrong call. Sometimes we fuck up. Sometimes we fuck up again, and again, and again. And nothing will make it better. Nothing will heal the wounds of our mistakes. Of our false turns. Of our secrets. Henry isn't coming back, and we can't go to him. You know we can't. But you and I . . . you and I care. We just want to stop the teeth and the claws under our beds. We just want the world to feel safe, and neither of us . . . neither of us saw every false step around every corner." She is still in my arms. She doesn't fight. Not exactly. But she doesn't hold me back. She lets her legs slide off the edge so only I hold her up.

"Everyone in that city who is alive is alive because of your mistakes," she challenges me. "And everyone who is dead is dead because of mine." I squeeze her tighter. That same intrusive thought invades my mind again, of squeezing her until

I crush her. Throwing her over the edge. But this time, as she falls, she is me. I don't want to die. But I know her. Letting her die on Henry's behalf would be no different than jumping myself.

"No," I sob. "No, that's not true, Autumn. I know. I know because I am grieving. I am grieving for my brother. I am grieving for myself. I have lived my life grieving. Weeping for everyone else. Ed held me and I couldn't grieve. My mother hit me and I couldn't grieve. I couldn't do it. I knew it was a simple push away, but I couldn't grieve. But you . . . I confronted you, I heard the truth from you, and I could grieve. I hold you and I can weep. I can feel it. I can hurt. I can hurt, because you. You know. You know. You know."

She remains limp, but I can feel her body shaking in weak sobs. "How do I move forward?" she asks. "How do I keep doing this?"

"Please," I beg. "Give me one more day. Give me one more day, and weep with me. Let me weep with you. Say goodbye to my brother with me. And after that, let me ask again. And again, and again, and again, until I don't need to ask for one more day anymore. Please. Please. Please."

The next moment is eternal. The world storms around me. The tsunami of my own grief tries to throw me to the ground. It bites into me. It is agony and aimlessness. I drink it all in. I feel it, and I loathe it, and I am me. It's weak, but she wraps her arms around me. It is the closest thing to assent I am going to get. She is her. I am me.

"Finally awake, huh?" Ember asks outside my room. She looks irritated but I don't care. I finally got Autumn to bed. I ran into Clarrise and asked her to keep an eye on Autumn as well. Now I need to face the family I left behind.

"I'll talk about our deal tomorrow," I say. "I haven't forgotten it, but all right. Just . . . go to sleep."

"We don't have forever to—"

I walk up and flick her on the chin. "I said we'd talk about it. You'll be all right, sport. Let me take a night off, yeah?"

"Fine, but I will be knocking on your door in the morning," she says. I roll my eyes. Honestly, fuck her. I don't have the energy to spend on this, and she is really expending it. The facade isn't for her. I need to present it to Ed and Mom. I need to be the strong one. I failed earlier, but I need to make up for it. I don't know if I can. But I need to. I blow Ember off and take a deep breath. Finally, I open my door.

Ed is gone. My mom is gone. Instead, Sarafyna is inside, holding one of her hats and running her hand along the workshop bench Autumn and I made for her. Again I feel guilt well up. But as she looks over her shoulder at me, the overwhelming emotion I feel is relief. The facade melts immediately as she rushes over to me, and in her arms, I allow myself to sob. I let it all catch up to me. The pain. The failure. The injuries. The truth about Autumn. The time away from Sara. Mom.

Henry.

She holds my head against her sternum and I cry all of it into her. I let it all out, and months of exhaustion finally catch up to me. She accepts it all.

I feel so, so selfish. These last few months have been torture for her. She has known nothing but fear and desperation and pain. But I can't stop. She pulls it out of me with a single touch. She accepts it. I don't need to be strong for her. I can be me.

When we moved in here, we had separate rooms. But when I finally lie down for the night, rolled onto my right side, she is behind me, holding me. Letting me know it's okay to sleep. It's okay to hurt. I am safe.

CHAPTER FIFTY-EIGHT

Promises

Rune

This trip has been a massive headache. Traveling halfway across the planet just to visit some backwater village calling itself a kingdom . . . There was no direct route here. It is on the wrong side of the barrier, and the only way to get through it without approaching the Nexus took months. I am exhausted. And now that I get here, it's even worse than I imagined. The buildings are fairly impressive, considering how the residents of . . . what was it again? Potestia? I have a hard time tracking all the minor little playgrounds in the third plane. This one has clearly been abandoned for far too long if the residents are escaping and trying to form new settlements.

They are doing all right, I suppose. Although there are startlingly few children about. There is little about at all, in fact, excepting the busy fumbling of people recently in distress. The most I am likely to find to entertain myself here are a couple of books based on their dull culture and a few people to admire my Nexus magic. I wave down a man in something that looks like a makeshift uniform. I prepare for the tired song and dance I always go through as they assume I am a child. Asking where my parents are. Refusing to take me seriously. I already have a massive water spell brewing, not with mana but with the Nexus, just to skip that bit.

He sees me and I roll my eyes, prepared to be brushed off by the very people I am here to help. "Lord Rune!" he exclaims instead. "You have returned! Thank the Collector, we need the help. Please, my lord, it's the stewards. They've been murdered. It's the former queen . . . She . . . Please, we need your help," he begs.

I look at him in bafflement.

"What do you mean 'returned'?" I ask. "I've only just arrived."

Leo

Charlotte and I stare in shock. We escaped the field easily once my abilities manifested. But . . . the whisper sphere broke at the same time. The Radiant Woods wilt and recede anywhere I walk. The world reestablishes reality, rejecting whatever warped atrocities have been done to it. I leave a trail behind me where the Radiant Woods cannot exist. But we are trapped now. We don't know where we are. We don't know how to get home. We can't call Lily. We don't even know who won or if Lily is alive.

All we can do is wander, and survive. That much has been easy enough. The sky over us is normal again. As we walk, we discover rivers that heal as I approach. Charlotte's magic keeps us safe. The itching on my face is unquestionable now. I have a beard growing in. Without Lily. Without Sara. Just me. Charlotte's body is changing too. Slowly. In little ways. It is everything. It's slow, but every morning, we both wake up a little more ourselves. More validated. Like river water leaving dirt and impurity behind as it flows ever forward.

But now, we both gape. Because we have found our first monster. Our first victim of the woods. They were sleeping as we approached. And once we got close enough, they began to change too. Teeth receding into their face. Extra joints and a hard carapace contorting and dissolving as a human man emerges. Weary, and wrinkled, and human. And I feel it. Going back . . . that's not what I want to do. I scratch my face as it becomes clearer. Charlotte and I don't just need to find the other two people who fell into the woods with us. I want to find every single victim. I want to give them what I now feel. The body they belong in. The freedom that has been denied them. The future they deserve.

Lillith

I take a deep breath. Then another. My heart is as still as ever, so why does it feel so heavy? My fist hovers in front of the door. I helped bring down a country, but knocking on this door is far more terrifying. But I made two promises. I was reminded of the first this morning as my catty neighbor pounded on my door like she was trying to knock it down. The sound wasn't the worst thing waiting for me with consciousness, but it wasn't the best.

The cold of a world I wanted to deny tried to freeze me to the bed. So many things reminded me of the reality I had left behind as I slept. Each one burned my skin like ice. The cruelty in it felt more real than ever. More unavoidable. More constant.

There was also the warmth of a woman, reminding me I still had a reason to accept it. I woke up with my arm around her waist and my head on her shoulder. Something in her bleary eyes at the sound of the banging door still sent butterflies through my stomach. Even now.

Ember would not be dismissed again. I promised to help her fight the sages, if they were what she said they were. I wanted the morning to catch up with Sara. To hear about what she went through. How she communicated with me. How she took part of the Radiant Woods back. But . . . I made two promises, and the first was at my door. I shared a look with Sarafyna, the mist of sleep still in her eyes. A thousand words passed between us, and I nodded. Then I forced myself from the bed. I had one night. One night to be vulnerable. But the world is still waiting for me. And there is more left to burn.

Ember was irritated but quickly appeased when I agreed to begin planning to leave right away. She was easy. She was the first promise. She was the promise I could still fulfill. But I made two promises. Before I do anything else, I have to face the one I broke. What had I said? Something about keeping her real kids safe? It seemed so clever, so biting at the time. But it wasn't supposed to bleed like this. I didn't feel the sting when she first slapped me. I brushed her off. I ran away. I can feel it now.

I have finally worked up the courage to knock when the door opens. Again we find ourselves in a doorway, sharing a terrified look. My breath catches and my knuckles stay frozen in the air, ready to rap against a door that is no longer there. My mother and I share more than grief in that moment. More than loss. She feels as terrified of me as I am of her. As her hand rises to my face a second time, I flinch, and she freezes. A heavy moment passes, both our hands waiting awkwardly in the air. I feel that unique tension that always precedes oncoming pain, but instead, her hand rests on my cheek. Her fingers are as cold as ice. Her gentle touch as warm as the sun.

I have to present a strong face for her. Same as I always have. Same as I did when she shut down the first time we lost Henry. Same as I always have, for everyone but Sara and Henry. Now . . . for everyone but Sara. I steel my expression. I need to apologize. But I need her to know I am still strong. Still able to fight. I broke my promise to her, but I can still keep her safe. I can still keep everything she has left safe. I need to be the pillar holding a roof over her head. I need to be Lillith. I believe I can. I can take any biting words she has. Any condemnations. I can be her pillar and take her rage. Until she says a single word.

"Lily," she whispers, and I am undone. I always feel taller than my mother, but I am not. It just feels that way. Lily. She called me Lily. Not Annie. Not even Lillith. Lily. She towers over me with a single, barely audible name. "Lily, I . . . I'm sorry. I meant to bring you dinner. All of you. I don't know . . . No, that's a lie. I know what I was thinking. I shouldn't have hit you. I just . . . Lily. I know you tried. I know. I know. I do, and I know Henry, he . . ."

She is speaking to herself as much as me. All my attempts to present a strong front have dissolved. I can taste the tears running past my lips. I can't find the words. She speaks again in my stead. "I spent yesterday wondering if I was going to lose two of my children. My *real* children. I don't know how I questioned that. When I saw you . . . when Sarafyna brought you back, I knew. I knew who you were. I know who you are. I'm sorry. I am so sorry. I love you, Lily. Thank you—for being alive. Thank you for coming back. Thank you for protecting my children."

"I . . . I didn't," I finally answer. "Henry . . ." I feel her hand tense, the tips of her fingernails just barely pressing against my cheeks. Her face grows tight for a moment, and I see it. I really am her daughter. She is shredded inside. But she . . . wants to be strong for me. She wants to put on the brave face I failed to present to her. It breaks my heart. But . . . I need it. I can feel it. It's my turn. I failed her. I broke my promise. I let her son die. But she remembered I am her daughter, and she loves me just as much. And she is telling me it's my turn. This only makes me cry more.

"You protected two of my children, in a city where thousands died. So . . . thank you, Lily," she says. My hand, no longer furled for a knock but still awkwardly running through my own hair, finally falls. I rest my head on my mother's shoulder. We don't embrace. We still feel too much pain. My turn or not, this is a brave face she is putting on. The tension of my broken promise remains. Still. I can't help being the broken one for a moment. I can't talk about this anymore.

"I . . . I have to go again, Mom," I say. I feel her tense up further, but she doesn't speak yet. "I have more to do. More . . . promises. I have to leave. I have to help Ember. And Sara couldn't find Leo and the others, and . . ." I pause. She knows all of this. "But . . . I'm not taking Ed. I want a few people to come with me. But Ed and Gil . . . they'll be here. With you. Safe," I promise.

"I know," she finally responds. "I know. But . . . promise me. Promise me you will come back again? I want all th-three of my children safe. I want you safe too. Please . . . promise to come back?"

I wrap my arms around her and bite my lip. I can't. I can't promise her that. Not after breaking my last one. It makes me feel sick when I open my mouth to try.

"I'll do my best," I answer weakly. She doesn't respond for a long moment, then pulls herself back, away from me. Leaving me empty again. She gives me a terse nod.

"Well. You had better begin making arrangements, then," she says. She quickly retreats back into her room, apparently forgetting why she opened the door in the first place. A glistening on her cheek explains why. The mask is going to crumble. I sigh and my shoulders slump as I leave her alone. When I reach the corner at the end of the hall, Sara's warm hand runs over my shoulder.

"How is she?" she asks. I walk alongside her for a moment before answering.

"She is in pain. And she is wonderful," I say, failing to elaborate any further. Sara doesn't push and we walk in silence for a while. I don't know where I am going, so I just approach a window, breathing in the fresh smell of the fruit and the foliage growing along the outer wall.

"Who are we going to take with us?" she asks, answering my request before I can make it.

"You assume I'm bringing you?" I joke half-heartedly. She hears the question behind the quip and gently bumps her shoulder against mine.

"I am never leaving your side again, my love," she whispers in my ear. I close my eyes and let the clean air blow across my face.

"Nor I yours," I murmur. I need her to help search the Radiant Woods anyway. Something strange is going on there; she should have been able to sense our friends the moment she entered. But they were nowhere to be found.

"So. Who are we bringing with us?" she asks again.

I ponder for a moment. Maybe I think it will distract her. Maybe I think it will give her purpose. Maybe she really does need me, day after day after day. Maybe I am just selfish, and *I* need her to remind me to feel. To remind me that, even with my mistakes, I am human.

"Autumn," I reply. She is one of our weakest mages. But . . . if she'll come, I want her with me. "And August, I suppose. Then just Ember."

Sara nods. It's a small group. And the twins may not agree. But I'd prefer a small group. Fewer people to protect.

"The old team, back together again," she says.

"Everyone but Pete," I say with a smile.

She looks down. "Everyone but Pete," she agrees. She hasn't spoken to me about her family yet. Her father and her son. She must have seen them, as I slept. But we have time. We have time to talk about everything. Because we are never going to be apart again. We remain quiet for a long time before she finally changes the subject. "I met a sage, you know."

I look at her curiously. "And?" I prod.

"A real asshole. I think Ember may be onto something. But . . . he said something to me. About my . . . scars." Of course. Sara is wonderful. Sara is amazing. Sara is beautiful. And she has been leaving so much space for me, but she has her own trauma and grief to unpack. The very scars she mentions are fading and returning to her face like a holographic card. "He said that . . . anyone who acted like they didn't see them was lying." She leaves the question unasked. I nod.

"I see your scars, Sara," I answer. "Of course I see them. Just as you see mine. Just as you have seen mine all morning. Just as you saw mine when I came home last night and needed nothing more than you. Your scars are you. They are a part of you. I see them, and I think of them constantly. They are one of the sharpest aspects of your beauty." As I say this, they lock into place, covering her face again, exactly as they should. She takes a deep breath through her nose and smiles.

"Hey, Annie," she says. "In your world . . . did they let women marry each other?"

I give her a genuine, full-lipped smile. The world is so dark. So hopeless. I hurt so, so much. I still can't reconcile the fact of Henry's . . . absence with reality. I can't. But I do have a sweet woman by my side. A woman who loves me, and a woman who hurts when I hurt.

We look out the window together, toward the east. There is a new world in front of us, and a newer one behind us. There are more chains left to break. I can move forward, if she can. I hold her hand in mine, and remember there is still hope, even when everything hurts the most.

About the Author

Dreamer's Riot is the author of the Otherworldly Anarchist series as well as a computer scientist and indie video game developer. Based on his experiences in the US Air Force and later as a student, his stories aim to tackle themes of power and autonomy.

JOIN THE FELLOWSHIP

follow us on our socials

 podiumentertainment.com

 @podiumentertainment

 /podiumentertainment

 @podium_ent

 @podiumentertainment